OVEREXPOSED

K. EVAN COLES

K. EVAN COLES

WRITING DIVERSE STORIES
FROM THE HEART

Overexposed

Copyright 2022 K. Evan Coles

For information contact:

http://www.kevancoles.com

Book and Cover design by K. Evan Coles

Edited by Rebecca Baker Fairfax

OVEREXPOSED

An unexpected chapter in a vampire's guide to staying alive.

As the only vampire employed by the NYPD, forensic photographer Noah Green isn't exactly popular. He's worked alongside humans for decades and avoids attachments with the bleeders around him ... but hasn't done much to avoid a certain West Village baker, who has no idea what Noah really is.

Danny Kaes is done hooking up, at least when it comes to fangers. He's too busy running his Filipino bakery, Nice Buns, to dwell on the dramas of dating, and if he misses the thrill of sharp teeth on his throat, he knows he's better off with his own kind ... like the CSU hottie who stops by before sunrise.

While working a string of suspicious deaths, Noah finds Danny at a crime scene, traumatized after discovering a body, and now in in the killer's crosshairs. Surprising even himself, Noah offers Danny his couch, knowing he'll have to come clean about his blood eater identity.

Days bleed into nights as the killer closes in, leading Noah and the cops in a mad scramble to protect Danny from dangers he never imagined. What Noah can't protect *himself* from are his feelings for Danny and how they've made him question every-thing he thought he knew about his own vampire life.

Overexposed is a 92+K paranormal mystery MM romance. It features a crime scene photographer who thinks he's got the whole vampire thing figured out, a bakery owner who's sworn off inter-species dating, an unfortunate number of murders, more mayhem than anyone asked for, and a hard-won, deeply satisfying HEA.

For my son, who makes me laugh every single day and puts up with all of my yammering.

Enormous thanks to Randall Jussaume and Barb Payne Ingram who generously donated their time to help fix my words, as well as Helena Stone and Shelli Pate, and to Rebecca Baker, the editor ninja.

And a major shout-out to Tanya Chris, who organized the Working Stiffs anthology that spawned this story in its fledgling form (and a big bunch of characters who just wouldn't shut up).

The Devil whispered in my ear: 'You are not strong enough to withstand the storm.'

I whispered back: 'I *am* the storm.'

— unknown

PROLOGUE

October 30, 1919
7:05 P.M.

Fire licked through Noah Green's lungs. He kept running anyway, ignoring the stitch in his side. Growing up, he'd always been fast, the tall kid everyone picked for games, knowing his speed came with endurance. Once Noah had possession of the ball, he could be counted on to keep driving toward the goal.

Noah was doing that now. Pressing forward, legs aching and his breaths loud to his own ears. He'd keep running for as long as he could. Had to, though his chances of 'winning' anything were slim.

He wasn't playing a game tonight. He'd made a mistake. And now he was running for his life.

Taking a corner, he searched for another burst of speed, the slap of his boots on the pavement echoing off the buildings around him. Lighter footfalls followed behind, so different from Noah's desperate pounding. They'd matched his perfectly from the very beginning of this race, no matter how fast he ran, and he'd known after only a few blocks that the vampire tailing him was enjoying the chase. And that maybe the only reason he wasn't already dead was because the fanger wanted to exhaust its prey before pouncing.

Noah didn't know this neighborhood—he'd taken a wrong turn somewhere several blocks back. The streets and sidewalks were empty and the lights over every doorway dark. A citywide dusk-till-dawn curfew had been in place for weeks, barring humans who didn't work nights from being outside and, even then, only at their own risk. New Yorkers complained bitterly about the restrictions during daylight hours, but were quick to disappear after sunset, locking themselves in their homes and drawing the blinds to keep the night out. Staying outdoors after dusk was dangerous now that the supernatural beings who'd always lived among them were walking around in plain sight, and every human knew it.

Noah would be inside too if this were a typical evening, either in his own Chelsea flat or his parents' place in Midtown. He dined there several times a week after work and always stayed overnight. His mother was so certain her unmarried son was languishing alone in his set of rooms, helpless at keeping house or feeding himself. Noah didn't mind indulging her imaginings. Not when sitting down to eat corned beef hash and listen to her thoughts on finding him a wife made her happy.

He'd been prepared for more of the same tonight. Dinner and talk about Noah needing to be married. But Niels and Marion Green had started in on a far more serious topic during dinner, namely the rash of inter-species crime that had thrown the city into turmoil.

"A young man who lived two doors down was killed this week!" Noah's father exclaimed. *"Meanwhile, we all live in fear, hiding inside our homes every night because it's not safe to go out. I don't understand why the mayor doesn't do something."*

"Like what?" Noah set down his glass. *"He can't just order the fangers to vacate New York, Dad. Most have probably lived here longer than you've been alive."*

"*And? That's hardly a reason to let them and the shifters run roughshod over the rest of us.*" Niels made a face. "*Supernaturals are dangerous, Noah, especially the vampires. The gangs are ruthless, killing people and worse every day.*"

"*I know.*" Noah frowned. *He'd heard the stories of humans being taken and changed; they all had. He still knew better than to assume that every person who died or disappeared did so at the hands of a supernatural.* "*But we can't pin the gangs' behaviors on any vamp as if they were all cut from the same cloth.*"

"*They are cut from the same cloth, and it's entirely unnatural.*" Niels shot a grim look at his wife. "*Those things may live among us, but they are not welcome in the human world. Vampires and shifters have their own places to go in this city. They've practically taken over Five Points, and there are blood bars popping up all over downtown.*"

Marion's face was haunted as she met Noah's gaze. "*I've heard those awful places are full every night, even with the curfew. But ... I just don't understand why any decent human goes near them. Mixing with fangers. Offering themselves up as if they enjoy it.*" She shuddered, her voice dropping to a near whisper. "*Those poor souls are damned.*"

Noah ground his teeth and took another corner. He and his friends talked about visiting the blood bars all the time, just for a thrill. Hearing his parents speak like that, though—understanding how profoundly they hated beings they'd never even met—had been painful. He'd stood his ground anyway, firm in his belief that a world where humans and supernaturals were equal was better for everyone, while his mother and father raged back at him, their hurt and confusion plain.

None of it mattered now. Because Noah was so, so screwed.

He'd opted to go home to Chelsea after dinner instead of staying overnight with his parents, hopeful that some time apart would help cool their tempers. But he'd forgotten to heed the time and the darkness falling over the streets, and he'd only traveled a block or two before the fanger had started tailing him. Now Noah was lost with nowhere to hide, and knew that if he died out here tonight, losing him would hurt his family far more than any dinnertime argument.

Voices nearby caught his attention and Noah's heart leapt, hope nearly choking him. He pulled up short as two figures appeared in his path and almost knocked him off balance.

"Jesus." Chest heaving, he swung his arms in wild pinwheels, fighting to stay upright as a young girl and boy stared up at him like Noah had lost his mind. "What the *hell* are you doing out here?"

The boy's eyes narrowed in his pale face. Though he and the girl looked barely past childhood, he gave a mighty scowl. "Could ask you the same," he said, voice hard. "Ain't none of your business."

The girl sniffed in seeming agreement. "Anyone with eyes can see y' don't belong here," she said to Noah.

"Maybe not," he started, "but you don't understand—"

"And I don't wanna, Mister." The girl frowned at him. "You oughta go if you don't want no trouble."

She jerked her head at a nearby alley and Noah spied what he thought might be a brewery at its end, doors standing open and a broad-shouldered figure just beyond the threshold. But before he could speak again, a hand settled on Noah's shoulder and the air in his lungs rushed out of him in a single whoosh.

"Off you go, young miss," said a silky-smooth voice, "before I show you what trouble really looks like."

Noah stood, unable to move as a figure fitted itself against his back. He heard the kids run off, boots clattering over the cobblestones as they hustled toward safety, but he knew better than to expect they'd send any help. No one was coming. The workers inside the brewery would bolt the doors, and even if they'd had some way to contact the cops, the NYPD weren't going to risk their own skins for some fool who'd broken curfew. Even if said fool was a tender-age kid working for pennies under the table like the boy who'd run off, or a young man like Noah who just wanted to get home.

Noah's breath split the silence that followed, and the hand on his shoulder moved, gently cupping his jaw. A second hand took hold of his waist, the light touches guiding Noah around until he was face to face with the vampire who'd chased him. He—it?—was shorter than Noah and slim, with a shock of light hair and ordinary features that belonged to a man. The vampire's eyes were beautiful, however, shining and so dark. They grabbed hold of Noah more tightly than the hands on his body.

"Oh."

Noah knew he'd spoken, but it felt like a dream. He'd read plenty about vamps and other supernaturals and learned from a young age to stick with his own kind if he wanted to be safe. That the species shouldn't mix. And he should be afraid of this being before him, despite his gentle voice and eyes.

Noah didn't feel any fear, however. And nothing could have moved him from that spot.

He forgot his aching lungs and legs, and the hammering of his heart sounded distant. He'd never been this close to a vampire, at least not that he'd ever known, and saw immediately that they were nothing like he might have expected. His touch wasn't cold at all but warm, and he was vital, so shockingly alive. Pink lips curved in a smile, while the eyes fixed on Noah saw inside him. Captivated him so totally, he hardly knew how he was still standing. Noah was enthralled. And didn't mind one bit.

"What's your name, sweetheart?"

The vampire's tone was wonderfully easy, words like caresses over Noah's skin while a spicy, luscious scent filled his senses. He closed his eyes against the heat buzzing through him, and it warmed his blood in a rush.

"Noah."

"A name that suits you well." The vampire was still smiling when Noah opened his eyes, and he moved his hand gently over Noah's cheek, stroking skin that burned hot. "Look at that blush. And those eyes, mmm. You really are enticing."

Noah leaned into the touch with no idea what to say. He was probably being rude. But the vampire didn't seem to mind at all and took another step closer.

"My name is Morgan," he said. "Would you like to have a drink with me?"

"Have to ... I have to work tomorrow. But yes."

God, Noah wanted. The drink. To hear this Morgan speak. Noah didn't give a damn, so long as he could have more of that electric touch. He wanted it. More. It didn't matter that he wasn't sure what 'more' even meant. Nothing *could* matter when Morgan swept him close and everything else fell away.

Lips too soft to be real brushed against his throat.

The following sting was fleeting.

And it made Noah fly.

CHAPTER 1

November 10, present day
Wednesday, 12:30 A.M.

"Hey, bloodsucker!"

Noah quelled a sigh. Nothing like some name-calling to spice up his evening, especially from one of his least favorite humans. Not that he had many favorites to begin with. Framing a shot, he pressed the shutter button on his camera, then lowered the Nikon enough to meet the gaze of the homicide detective before him.

"Evening, Detective Callahan. Can I help you with something?"

"I have no idea." Callahan stared at Noah with undisguised disdain. He exhaled a cloud of blue tobacco smoke, then shifted his attention to the crime scene and frowned, his deep brown skin shining under the glare of the portable floodlights. "What a fucking mess. Though I don't suppose 'mess' really fits with this scene, considering the guy's as dry as a bone."

Noah didn't respond. He hadn't been surprised when the medical examiner had declared massive blood loss as the cause of death; the victim's extreme pallor was an obvious indicator.

The utter lack of blood at the scene was more unusual, however. As was the neat wound in the victim's throat.

Stepping around the body, Noah tilted his head, considering the angle at which he'd been shooting. He went still when an unexpected flash near the guy's wrist caught his eye.

"What is it?" Callahan's tone held an edge. "Scene bringing back fond memories for you?"

Noah didn't look up. "No. I make an effort to keep things from getting to this point."

"Bullshit. I've never met a fanger who didn't get dewy-eyed the second blood is spilled."

"Not every vampire is wired the same way."

"Says who?"

"The handbook," Noah said, voice as flat as he could make it, and looked over at Callahan. "You get one right after you're turned and there's a chapter on avoiding killing your prey."

Callahan stared at him a moment. "There's a handbook for vampires?" His voice rose at the tail end of the sentence and, for just a second, Noah wanted to laugh.

"No," he said instead. "I made it up."

Callahan sneered but still looked a bit queasy. Knowing you worked with a vampire was one thing; hearing him talk about eating people was another. But Noah was more interested in tracing the flash he'd caught than Callahan's moaning, and he called out to the lead CSI on the scene.

"Hey, Cho? Can I get a UV light over here?"

"You bet." Detective Cho Min-jun was immediately by his side, flashlight in hand. "What did you find?"

"Not sure. Could be something on the victim's inside left wrist." Noah dipped his head at the body. "A smudge or writing, maybe a pattern. I'm thinking tattoo."

Kneeling, Cho took hold of the victim's forearm with one gloved hand, then shone a blue-black light over it so a ghostly image swam into view.

"Nice catch. Not a tattoo, though." Cho squinted at the marking. "I'd say it's a stamp, like from a bar or club. Judging from the lack of fade and smearing, I'd say it was made within the last couple of hours."

Callahan squatted beside him. "There are at least a dozen bars and clubs nearby, so that's not exactly helpful." He cocked his head and leaned in further, peering at the stamp. "Is that a snake?"

"Ouroboros," Noah replied to which Callahan gave him a hard look.

"Yoo-row-what now?"

"Ouroboros. A serpent or dragon devouring its own tail." Noah drew a circle in the air with his finger. "It's an ancient symbol of renewal."

"From the Greek for 'tail' and 'eating.'" Cho stood. "Life, death, rebirth. Sounds like an old rock song I know. How did you catch it without the light?" he asked Noah.

"Good question," Callahan said. "And I've got another one for you, Green. Where do you recognize it from?"

Noah let a beat pass before answering. "I've seen it used at a blood bar over on Morton. It's called The Last Drop."

"A blood bar you've been in," Callahan guessed. "Can't say I'm surprised. This scene has fanger all over it."

Cho cocked a brow at him. "It's a club stamp, Bert, not a smoking gun. You might want to slow your roll."

Noah hid a smile. Cho *was* among his favorite humans and despite the strange, often terrible nature of their jobs, Noah liked working with him. Before his employment with the NYPD, he'd never even picked up a camera without intending to capture something beautiful. He'd had no experience with policing or forensic science, and had said so to his recruiter at Monster-Board, an agency that specialized in placing supernaturals in jobs among the human workforce. The recruiter had coaxed Noah into taking the job anyway, and he was glad he'd listened to their advice. Cho had proved an excellent teacher with a real talent for looking past the anxiety that came from working alongside Nosferatu. They'd formed a real friendship during the course of Noah's training, and he'd become a highly competent crime scene photographer who won the respect of his peers in the police lab.

Noah's relationships with cops outside of the Crime Scene Unit, however, remained tense, if not outright hostile.

"Cho, come on." Callahan glowered at Cho. "There's a hole in that guy's throat and he's literally emptied of blood. Of course I'm looking at the leeches. If that hurts Green's feelings, he's got more human left in him than I thought."

Noah managed not to roll his eyes. The more things changed, the more they stayed the same. "Green is right here," he said. "And he's going to get back to his job."

"No one's standing in your way." Callahan pocketed his e-cig. "I do need a favor, though, and I'm fairly sure you're the only one I can ask."

Cho whistled quietly. "That had to hurt."

"You have no idea. This involves both of you, though." Callahan sighed. "Last week, the 10th Precinct took a call from West Greenwich Health about one Aaron Josephs, a patient who some believed passed under less than natural circumstances."

"What do you mean by 'less than natural'?" Noah asked.

"Josephs was barely conscious when he was brought into the ED and died shortly after treatment began—cardiac arrest brought on by hypovolemic shock. The doc who treated him estimated he'd lost forty percent of his total blood volume."

Cho's expression was grave. "Man. He was likely already dying by the time he was brought in—I'm surprised he was conscious at all. Do we know what caused the blood loss?"

"Nope. That's where the less than natural part comes in," Callahan replied. "Because the ED doc had no idea what to make of the small, circular wound on Josephs' throat either, located directly over the jugular."

Ah.

Noah looked down at the victim. "Just like our John Doe. That's quite a coincidence."

A tight laugh came out of Callahan. "This is too weird for coincidence. Josephs died before he could tell the doc anything and the neighbor who brought him in didn't know jack. So, the cops at the 10th checked Josephs out and found him squeaky clean with one notable exception—he was a regular donor at a blood bar over on Morton Street called The Last Drop. When was the last time you were in that bar, Green?"

Noah regarded him steadily. "Early summer. The week after Memorial Day. Definitely not anytime tonight."

"He's been with me since the start of shift, which you know, Bert," Cho said. "So, how about you put us out of our misery and tell us why you came over here?"

Callahan studied them both for several seconds before answering. "I want you to check out Josephs' apartment. Together. Use the vampire whammy or whatever and see if anything pops."

Noah stared at him. "Vampire whammy?"

"You know what I mean."

"I assure you, I don't."

Callahan made a sound like the weight of the world was upon him. "C'mon, Green. The detectives at the 10th found no evidence of foul play, but maybe your freaky leech senses will turn something up and we can figure out how two seemingly random guys are connected to each other and a bunch of fang-bangers who haunt The Last Drop."

"There might not be any connection to the bar," Noah reasoned. "Not every human who spends time around blood eaters is a donor, Detective."

"Okay, but Aaron Josephs was and, so far, I'd say the odds are good this guy tonight was too." Callahan rubbed a hand over his mouth. "Personally, I think a person who lets a vamp chew on them is fucked in the head, but there are no laws against it in the state of New York provided everyone's a consenting adult and walks away happy."

Noah said nothing. While Callahan acted like the world's biggest pain in the ass, he was also right. Donors were supposed to have fun spilling blood, not end up dead in a park or hospital. *If* that had even happened to Aaron Josephs *or* their John Doe.

"Give us the address," Cho said to Callahan. "Noah and I are almost done here, and we can head to Josephs' on our way back to the lab. And just so you know, Bert, we didn't find much of anything. The body and everything surrounding are basically immaculate."

Callahan worried his lip with his teeth. "Yeah, I kind of got that just from watching. I'll text you the address. The building super is a shifter and told the cops he's up all night—he should answer when you ring his bell." Pausing, he fixed Noah with a stare. "I'll want to talk more about the blood bar on Morton, specifically your membership."

Unease crept up Noah's spine. Inviting this man into his personal life held no appeal at all. But he wouldn't feel right not cooperating if there was even a small chance he might be of some help. "I don't know how much I can say that you won't already know. The Last Drop is like any other bar in the city."

Callahan snorted. "I don't hang out with the fangers, man, but I know a blood bar is *nothing* like other places in this town. I'll be in touch," he said, then headed off into the night.

The dark promise pricked at Noah, but he put his focus on his work. After Cho signed off with the medical examiner, they packed up their gear and started loading it onto the van.

"I hate to tell you this, but Aaron Josephs' apartment is in Alphabet City," Cho said over his shoulder, a set of floodlights in each hand. "We need to move it if you want to be out of there before dawn."

"Okay." Noah followed him aboard with the remaining sets of lights and waited while Cho set his burden inside a storage bin. "Hey, back there, you asked how I'd spotted the stamp on that kid's arm."

"Yeah. Did you use the vampire whammy?" Cho grinned, but there was real interest in his eyes.

"Not purposely. But my pupils do open wider than yours, and some light must have caught an edge of the ink at exactly the right angle for me to see it."

"That was lucky. Pretty fucking fascinating, too. But the ME would have found it on autopsy, so don't let Callahan get in your head."

"Too late." Noah grunted. "Especially now that we're doing him a favor. I'd be fine with him going back to ignoring me."

"Sorry, homeboy. Don't sweat it for now and let's talk about Nice Buns instead." Stripping off his latex gloves, Cho moved aside so Noah could get at the storage bin too. "Not yours, of course, but the ones over on Bleecker."

"Of course," Noah said.

Cho rubbed his hands together with a grin. Nice Buns, a Filipino bakery located several blocks south, sold the best bread in the world according to Cho's daughter, Kage, who loved everything the place sold with a four-year-old's passion: pure and fierce. Noah's own interest in Nice Buns had nothing to do with baked goods, but it was nearly on par with Kage's, and how that had happened he wasn't quite sure.

"Are you sure you want to go to the bakery?" he felt bound to ask. "You know it's in the opposite direction of where we need to go."

"I am aware. Unfortunately, the bread we've been bringing back from Jersey this week hasn't been cutting it and my kid is about to rebel." Cho sighed. "She'll give me the sad puppy eyes that haunt my sleep and say, 'So disappointed, Papa' in her softest voice." He looked askance at Noah. "I blame you, you know. She'd never have known the place existed if it hadn't been for you."

"You act like I dragged you in there kicking and screaming."

Cho pulled the van's keys from his pocket. "Kicking and screaming are what happen when I go home these days without a box of rolls for my child."

Twenty minutes later, he parked the van across the street from Nice Buns and turned off the ignition, cutting off the old-school hip-hop track they'd been listening to. "Let's say a half dozen," Cho said. "There's one with cheese—"

"*Ensaymada.*"

"Yeah, and Spanish bread too, so three of each, please. Plus something extra I can stuff in my face right now, doesn't matter what."

"And a coffee."

"Duh." Cho grabbed an insulated coffee mug from the cup holder in the van's dash and handed it to Noah. "You know my habits way too well for a guy who doesn't eat. Something you know you ought to explain to your baker friend, Danny."

Friend.

Noah wanted to wrinkle his nose at the word. He didn't keep human friends. Outside of Cho, of course, and Kage by extension. "I don't know why he'd need to know."

"Because he'll catch on at some point, Noah, and explaining yourself will be awkward."

Noah ran a hand over the front of his blue tac shirt. He'd never tasted the bread he bought from Danny Kaes, the gregarious, totally attractive, and thoroughly human man who co-owned Nice Buns. But Noah'd never told Danny he was a supernatural either, and that would be even more awkward to explain. The funny thing was that Noah had always been open about being Nosferatu. Sure, he'd learned to downplay some things about himself to keep humans from running away screaming. He'd never actively hidden them in the hundred years since he'd stopped being Homo sapiens though and wasn't sure why he'd started doing around Danny.

"I'm a vampire who's paid to photograph crime scenes," he said to Cho. "Awkward is my jelly."

"I think you mean jam, big guy." Cho smiled. "It doesn't have to be if you leave out the level of gore and body count, and stuff that might scare the average being on the street. Most people I date are cool with my single-dad status, but they're either uber grossed out by my job or *way* too fascinated, which is almost worse."

"Danny and I are not dating."

"You could be. *If* you forget those rules you have about buddying up with the meat. But go, get moving," Cho said with a nod. "I'm hungry and the doors lock at two, which gives you fourteen minutes to get your awkward on right."

Inside the bakery, the air was thick with sweet, malty aromas, and music was audible from the kitchen located behind the storefront. Humans were clustered around the counters in groups, the tourists, students, and young people mixing with a few working girls and rent boys, all looking for pre-dawn snacks. A familiar figure behind the glass display counter stood straighter as Noah closed the door behind him, but Danny's smile was a smaller version of the one he typically showed his customers.

"Hey, Noah." He fiddled with the edge of the white bandana tied around his head, biceps bunching under the sleeves of his Nice Buns t-shirt. "You here to raid my supply of bread?"

"I am. *Ensaymada* and Spanish Bread, if you have it—Cho wants three of each." Noah stepped up to the counter and set the travel mug on its top. "Also, coffee and one of anything else you think he might like. He's fine with the pre-made joe since you're about to close."

"Sure." Danny toyed with the bandana again, brown eyes losing focus for a second as he thought before snapping back. "How about *asado*? It's the round bun stuffed with shredded meat, and we have pork and chicken tonight."

"Sounds great. Better make it one of each, though, or he'll wonder what he missed."

"Heh. I'll pack a couple of both and that way you can share."

"Thanks." Noah's smile felt stiff. He didn't like lying. Or not knowing how welcome he'd be here if he owned up to his true nature.

With practiced movements, Danny constructed a bakery box from brown paperboard, then lined it with wax paper. Swapping places with Merlin, a member of the baking crew, he balanced the box on his palm and bent behind the case, plucking rolls from the trays. He sounded almost tentative when he spoke again, and kept his gaze lowered.

"Been a while since we saw you. Thought maybe you'd found someplace new to buy bread."

Time to get awkward. But at least this was a work-related weird. Noah and Cho had been in a hangar at a New Jersey airport for the last several nights, cataloging the remains of a crashed plane and its passengers. Noah could be up-front about that while leaving out the gore and body count just as Cho had suggested. Or edit out even more of the details and hope Danny didn't put the pieces together.

"Cho and I were in Jersey all week," Noah said, then shrugged when Danny's eyes met his. "With a ... thing at one of the airports. It took us a few days to work through it."

"Oh, *right*. The plane crash in Newark?" Danny winced. Because of course, he'd put things together. "That looked bad on the news. Was it horrible?"

"Ah ... yes." Noah frowned. "I don't think you want to hear about it, though."

Danny scrunched up his nose again. "Heck, you're right. I'm sorry. It's none of my business and I shouldn't have pushed." Closing the box, he set it on the counter, then took Cho's mug to the coffee area, a flush tinting his cheeks.

Noah loved that uniquely human trait. The discomfort written across Danny's face not so much.

"It's fine," he said, then paused. He sounded like a creep-tastic ghoul. Which he literally was and couldn't help. "You didn't push. But I don't know how to talk about my job that isn't weird in a dozen different ways, and you really don't want that stuff in your head."

Danny carried the filled mug back, looking thoughtful. "I get it, I think. What about you?"

"What about me?"

"Does it bother *you* having that stuff in your head?"

"Sometimes, yes. I talk to Cho when that happens."

"Cool. So, how about this—I won't ask you about work again." Danny gave him a wry smile. "But I'd be happy to listen if you ever did want to talk about it."

Noah smiled back. "That works. We can not talk about my job anytime I come in here and pretend the CSU on my jacket stands for Chicago State University."

"Is that where you went to school?"

"No. I went to NYU."

"You are bananas." Danny was chuckling, but then his expression changed, growing more sober. "I meant it, though. I've watched enough true crime TV to understand that ignorance is bliss. But if you ever *need* a friendly ear, Noah, I can be that guy. Even if it means I won't sleep for a while."

A warm feeling rose in Noah's chest. Most humans he met went out of their way to avoid discomfort. Knowing Danny would put himself through something he clearly dreaded just to make someone feel better struck him as oddly nice.

"Thank you."

"No problem." Danny totaled up the coffee and rolls, then gave the bakery box a pat. "You're good to go. Unless I can tempt you with a sweet little extra?"

Oh, if only you knew.

Noah did his best not to smirk as he handed over Cho's money. "I'll remember to save room for next time."

CHAPTER 2

Danny Kaes considered himself a patient man. Had to be in his field, as baking was not a craft meant for those desiring immediate gratification. He was used to plotting out recipes and measuring ingredients with precision and confidence. Waiting for doughs to rise, then working them with his hands, cutting and shaping the pieces only to set them aside to proof again. The baker in Danny knew some things couldn't be rushed. But he wasn't surprised by the disappointment welling inside him as the bakery door closed behind the tall figure in the CSU windbreaker, nor the following flare of impatience.

Impatience was an emotion he experienced regularly around Noah Green. The guy had been coming into Nice Buns for months and friendly from the start. They still hadn't gotten beyond small talk and bread selling, however, and Danny could blame only himself.

"What's with the face?"

"I was born with it." Danny aimed a long-suffering look at his apprentice Merlin, who sighed noisily in response.

Walking out from behind the counter, Merlin went to the door. He flipped the cardboard sign to CLOSED, signaling to the customers in the shop that it was time they made their choices and paid, then stood sentry while Danny rang them up. Once the store had emptied, he turned the locks with a flourish.

"Your tall boy came back, huh? Just like I said he would," he called out to Danny.

"Yes, you're very smart."

"I know this. What did he have to say for himself? Because I hope it started with 'Sorry I ghosted you, Heavy D. I'll never do it again.'"

"Please don't call me that."

"Please don't change the subject. Did Noah apologize or what?"

"You were there." Danny walked out from behind the counter himself. "You really going to tell me you didn't eavesdrop?"

"I tried, but it was too goddamned noisy in here."

Danny couldn't help laughing. He sometimes envied Merlin's lack of shame. Punching a code into a keypad on the wall by the entrance, he watched as metal shutters slowly dropped in front of the bakery windows and door.

"Noah didn't have to apologize because it turns out he didn't ghost me," he said, his cheeks going hot. "He was out at a crime scene in Jersey all week."

"Oh, wow. The plane crash?"

"Yeah."

"Dude. And here you were all pining and angst."

"I didn't pine. Or angst. I was kind of a jackass tonight, though." And a dopey hot mess who needed to get a grip.

"How so?"

Danny bit back a sigh. "Noah tried to explain where he'd been *without* explaining where he'd been, and I think I came off kind of pushy. He was nice about it, though. Told me it was better not knowing all the gory details and I think he was right. I can't imagine doing his job."

"Me neither." Merlin made a face. "I mean, this is New York

—we both know it gets wild out there. It's probably not all murders and mayhem every night but I'd steer clear of talking about crime scenes when you finally ask the guy out."

"I … who said I wanted to ask the guy out?"

"Me, just now. Are you having a stroke?"

Danny pinned him with a look. "Cut it out. I don't even know if Noah's into guys."

"You never will if you don't get to know him better. Which, seriously, should happen soon." Stepping closer, Merlin took Danny's face between his hands. "You'll get frown lines from all this pouting and then you'll need Botox."

Chuckling, Danny freed himself. "I'm not pouting. Noah's cute and I enjoy chatting with him, but that's all there is to it."

"Mmm, no. You were majorly bummed this week while he was gone. And I get it. You like the boy, Danny. And you should ask him out." Merlin beamed at him. "It doesn't have to be a *date*-date. Just meet him for breakfast some morning after you both get off work. And, for the record, I think he's into guys. I see the way he eyeballs you when you're not looking and, son, he is *look*-ing at more than the buns you bake."

Danny belted out a laugh. "Oh, my God. What if you're wrong?"

"Then I'm wrong and my gaydar is busted! At least then you'd know if the angst has been worth it." Merlin's smile gentled. "You can't keep shutting guys out, dude."

"Ugh. But yeah, okay. Asking a guy to grab breakfast isn't a big deal, right?"

"As long as he can stay awake past sunrise, sure. And stay out, if you know what I mean."

"Hah. I do and that's not funny. You know I have rules about vamps. As in never again, no thank you, no way."

Merlin rolled his eyes. "You need to work on your trust issues, man."

Wouldn't be the first time.

Danny shook off the thought. "Probably. Still done messing with vampires." He made his voice firm and meant every word.

He wasn't wired to be with a fanger. He'd learned that lesson with Galen, his former friend and suck buddy, who was one-hundred-percent Homo Nosferatu and a total asshole. In his head, Danny knew his ex's bad behavior had nothing to do with his species—the guy was just a jerk. Danny's psyche had still been bruised by their time together, and he had no desire for a repeat. Not when it was so much simpler to put his energy toward finding an actual living man in this city instead and forget about the complications of interspecies dating.

Gently, he nudged Merlin's ribs with his elbow. "Let's clean. The dough for *monay* will be ready in thirty and we're making a triple batch tonight because the cafe orders from around town are way, way up. We have four hundred buns to get ready for six."

"Aww, yeah." Merlin raised his arms and flexed both biceps. "I'll take lead on that so you can work on getting the rest of the morning bake on. You have to promise you're gonna ask your tall boy out, though."

"Merlin."

"The next time he comes in," he pressed. "No dragging it out like I'm gonna forget."

"*Fine.*" Danny fiddled with the bandana covering his hair. "If we're not slammed and I can get him sort of alone for a minute, I will ask Noah if he'd like to grab breakfast. Or coffee. Or maybe share a stick of gum."

"Christ, you're a pain." Merlin laughed. "But I'll take it, Heavy D, and I'll hold you to it."

Danny felt lighter as he worked his way downtown later that morning, despite his back aching along with his knees and his feet, and most of the muscles in his body being sore. An eleven-hour shift spent mostly standing and in constant motion would do that to a person. The bread he and Merlin had baked had been gorgeous, however, from the *monay* to the *asado* to his long-time favorite of pillowy *pandesal*, each recipe turning out exactly as he liked it. They'd even made *kahilim*, a whimsical confection comprised of bread stuffed with sweet puddings they'd tinted vibrant shades with beet root and ube.

Red and purple puddings did not put that dopey smile on your face.

Yeah, that was true. Seeing Noah again was the reason behind Danny's good mood, though they'd only had a few minutes to talk. That was the norm for them. Quick conversations when Noah dropped in if Danny had a few minutes between tasks. Noah was chatty in an easy way that made him fun to talk to. And look at because the guy was a total biscuit and hot as fuck. But *nice*, too. Courteous even, and gentlemanly in a way that never got weird or too heavy. Danny liked that a lot.

He enjoyed their exchanges and prized the small, close-lipped smiles that made Noah's eyes glow over the plain navy uniforms. And Danny sort of loved hearing the names of the breads he'd baked rolling off Noah's tongue in that deep voice, buns and rolls he wanted to feed the tall, rangy guy and put some roses into his pale cheeks.

Danny was no fool. He'd recognized his growing infatuation after only a few weeks. But he hadn't realized just how much he looked forward to seeing Noah walk through his door every few nights until the visits had stopped cold. The more time that had passed, the lower Danny's mood had sunk, until finally, the thought crossed his mind that Noah might not come back at all.

A strange sense of loss had filled him, and he'd almost laughed at himself—talk about over the top. Danny didn't *know* Noah, not really. The total time they'd spent around each other probably amounted to just a few hours. There were places in every neighborhood of the city where a CSU guy could grab late-night eats too, and Danny didn't doubt Noah and Cho often stopped at the places closest to them when they needed a break. So, the relief that had slammed into Danny at seeing Noah again tonight had baffled him and did again now.

Sighing, he pushed his sunglasses higher onto the bridge of his nose. This wasn't good. Worse, it felt familiar. While he wanted to think otherwise, his reactions today proved he needed to work at keeping his heart from getting a jump on his head. And that maybe he wasn't as ready as he'd thought for anything deeper than an after-work breakfast with anyone, including— and maybe especially—Noah.

The sun had just peeked over the buildings as Danny stepped onto his block, but the neighborhood was already humming. He greeted people he knew and waved at vendors setting up shop, then knocked on the window at Charon's, his favorite West Village diner, smiling when the shifter server behind the counter blew him a kiss.

Danny's energy had mellowed by the time he let himself into the tiny studio he called home. Stifling a yawn, he hung his bag and jacket on the back of the door, then quickly peeled off his clothes. Clad just in his boxers, he left his clogs behind and carried the rest to the bathroom where he slid the armful into the hamper and started the shower. He didn't wait for the water to fully warm, instead shucking his underwear and stepping under the tepid spray. He groaned and leaned into it, the water so wonderfully cool after a night of heat from the bakery's ovens, only rousing himself from a near stupor when his stomach reminded him to eat.

Danny had a towel around his waist when his phone started chiming but he didn't rush to answer. He recognized his sister's ringtone and knew she'd call again. He'd gotten as far as sleep pants when the phone started up again, and this time he answered, smiling when Dorothy's face appeared in the chat app. She squished her eyes closed the second she saw Danny.

"Bro! Are you naked?"

"Of course not." Danny laughed. "Totally wearing pants, Thea."

"Thank God. I know we need to talk, but biz can wait for clothes." Thea peeled open one eyelid and smiled. "And no fair showing off when I have to work out twice as hard to keep from looking like I'm made out of dough."

"Meh. My skin *is* the color of dough, and you know you'd hate that."

Thea giggled. "I would. You need some sun, honey."

Like Danny didn't already know. He and Thea shared the same dark brown eyes and hair color, but her complexion had always been a golden tan that bronzed deeper if she spent time outdoors, even wearing sunscreen. Danny's skin was much lighter in comparison and overly prone to blushing, and the years he'd spent working nights meant he typically verged on pasty. He thought he looked okay with or without clothes and ran five miles several times a week, but he relied more on wrestling dough to keep him in shape than any gym or fitness routine.

"Did I catch you at a bad time?" Thea asked.

"Nah. I was about to start on food." He maneuvered a brown paper bag of bread from his tote bag and held it up to the screen.

"Nice. I've got some of your fancy purple pudding bread here and it is *delicious*. Oh, hey, I found your water bottle in the kitchen—do you want me to have someone drop it by?"

Danny swallowed a grunt. What kind of day would it be if he didn't leave a thing he needed behind? "That's okay. Just stick it over in the coffee station and I'll pick it up tonight when I come in."

He set the phone and bread bag on the counter as they chatted, then fixed a simple meal of bread, cheese, and chamomile tea, accompanied by some hardboiled eggs he'd made the day before. He and Thea normally met up in person when she arrived to open the bakery, but after she'd been waylaid by a puppy with a cranky belly that morning, they'd been forced to resort to apps and screens.

"I know you hate hearing this," she said, "but we need to get on board the holiday baking train."

Danny sat on a bar stool at the tiny butcher block cart he liked to use as a table and sandwiched a wedge of cheddar inside a roll. "Yeah, agreed. Thanks for letting me put it off for a while. I hate that official goodbye to fall."

"I know you do. But with October behind us—"

"We need to dive into the winter season. I'm ready. I tweaked a bunch of recipes from last year that I know you'll love. Brown sugar fillings and ginger-chai glazes. I'm even willing to make gingerbread *shakoy*."

His sister's eyes went wide. "You hate making doughnuts."

"I do. They're messy as fuck and a huge pain in the ass. They're the first thing to sell out every night, though, so whatever."

"You're such a good guy." Thea stared at the pudding-stuffed bread in her hand, brow furrowed. "We should do this with cranberry. And pear."

"Yes, girl. Cinnamon flan. Oh, *silvanas* with maple buttercream. You know how people love a sandwich cookie with frosting."

"Guh, I swear I could cry right now. And Dad will really dig them."

Danny had no trouble imagining their father's enthusiasm for buttercream frosting. "You're right. He'd eat more than he'd frost!"

"Come over and make them for him once you've got it mapped out." Glancing off camera, Thea held up a finger, then quickly refocused on Danny. "Gotta go. Things are getting hectic out front, and you need sleep anyway. Send me your notes when you're ready?"

"Absolutely." Danny gave her a wave. "Later, sistah."

He finished his meal while making notes on his tablet, planning out recipes with an eye toward seasonal flavors. Nice Buns prided itself on turning out authentic Filipino breads and pastries, but Danny and Thea weren't shy about riffing on recipes to keep up with the marketplace. As long as the *panaderia* stayed true to its mission of celebrating their ethnic roots and sticking to locally sourced ingredients whenever possible, the siblings were happy to flex their creative muscles and win additional business.

Fatigue weighed on Danny after he'd brushed his teeth though, and he sighed as he drew the blackout curtains over his windows. He'd keep plotting after he'd had some sleep. He pulled a Murphy bed from its hiding spot in the wall behind the couch, then lay on the mattress and stayed still for a while, simply absorbing the relative peace of an early morning in the city while his limbs grew heavier with each breath. But Thea's comments about the cookies and their dad kept surfacing, persistent enough that Danny rolled up onto one elbow. He stared at a small, framed photograph on the side table, a soft melancholy falling over him as a trio of faces beamed out of an image he'd taken just before his sixteenth birthday.

The snap had caught Thea and his parents in the golden sunlight of an autumn afternoon, during a day trip to Vermont to admire the fall foliage. Thea had a to-go cup of hot cider in one hand, and the whole family was grinning widely at the camera, wholly unaware of the coming drama that would blow their picture-perfect existence to pieces. Thanks to Danny's big gay coming out, of course, an event that had fucked his relationships with his parents and sister all to hell and thrown everything into chaos.

The chaos was Reba's fault. She was the one who ruined it all.

Danny rubbed the bridge of his nose. His mother *had* turned her back on them. Walked out on her marriage and motherhood and left the rest of the family reeling from wounds so profound they'd hardly known how to process. Especially Danny. Whom Reba Kaes had publicly disowned before declaring he had no place in her house, actions her husband Keoni had refused to accept.

He'd gone on loving his son, gay, straight, or whatever he chose to be, and kept Danny from falling apart. Keoni made sure his children healed, even as he'd struggled with healing himself, and he'd insisted from the start that Danny wasn't to blame for the family's implosion. Most days, Danny believed it. He still had trouble not blaming himself anyway, sure his coming out had been the catalyst. A tiny, hateful part of him liked to play an awful game of 'what if' where Danny didn't come out and maybe his family stayed whole. Where maybe he just went away because that would be better for everyone.

Thea would hate that. And Dad would be so fucking mad. Christ, you didn't like it when Noah disappeared on you, and you barely know the guy.

Sighing, Danny picked up his phone. Between work and life, he hadn't spoken with his father in almost a week and that just wasn't cool. So, he put off rest for a while longer and tapped his dad's number, unsurprised when the call went through after just one ring and a familiar, much-loved face appeared on the screen.

Keoni Kaes gave his son a big grin. "Danilo! What's cookin', good lookin'?"

"Hey, Dad." Danny laughed at the goofy refrain. "I've got cookies on the brain and, of course, I thought of you."

CHAPTER 3

Despite the pre-dawn hour, the building superintendent at 329 East 6th Street was indeed awake when Cho rang his bell. Miles Cleggett's pale yellow eyes spoke of wolf-shifter genes, and though his sweatpants and hoodie were somewhat rumpled, he didn't appear put out by the request to enter Aaron Josephs' apartment.

"I needed a break anyway," he said as he led Noah and Cho down a long hallway. "I've got an exam tomorrow and been studying since one—my brain feels like it's gonna leak out of my ears." He paused outside unit 708. "Here we go."

"And no one's been in or out since Mr. Josephs was taken to the hospital?" Cho asked.

"Not through me." Cleggett shrugged. "His family should be here in a few days to pack up his things, but there haven't been any other requests to get in. Outside of the cops who were here last week, I mean." He withdrew a keyring from his pocket. "I still can't be totally certain the place has stayed empty. Mr. Josephs could have given copies of his keys to friends, and I know for sure he gave a set to his neighbor in case of emergency."

Brow furrowed, Noah drew on a pair of latex gloves. The

door to Aaron Josephs' apartment was wholly unremarkable, painted the same boring brown as the other doors along the hall. "Are you sure this is the right unit?"

"Yeah." Cleggett pushed several thick locs off his shoulder and frowned at him. "Mr. Josephs was a tenant in this building for three years—it's not like I'd forget the unit number just because the guy died."

Cho's lips quirked upward. "CSI Green is just being thorough, Mr. Cleggett. How about we step back a bit so he can get some shots of the door?"

Noah captured images of the hallway and door while Cho and Cleggett chatted about the degree he was earning in information security. They exchanged cards before Cleggett unlocked the apartment, and he was whistling as he headed off back to his books. Noah shot a smile at his handler.

Cho returned it with an arch look. "What?"

"CSI Green? Did I get a promotion no one bothered to tell me about?"

"No, but you *could*. You're good at this job, Noah. There's no reason you couldn't be certified if you wanted to do more than use the camera."

"Except that the CSU Training Program doesn't accept supernaturals."

"True. But the unit also didn't hire civilians before you came along and look at how great that's been going. If you want a career in forensics, I think it could happen. I just need to figure out how. Okay." Cho pulled on a pair of gloves too. "You get everything you need out here?"

"All good. I was expecting some sign of police activity, though. Like crime scene tape or dusting powder."

"According to the notes from the cops at the 10th, there wasn't a crime scene to process. Josephs didn't die here. No signs of struggle or evidence of foul play were found and, outside of the thermostat being turned way down, the place seemed ordinary enough." A thoughtful look crossed Cho's face as they

walked into the apartment. "The thing about the heat is interesting though, and it is cool in here, at least to me. Do you feel
that?"

"Yes." Noah wasn't sensitive to temperature changes in the
same way as humans, but he was aware of the chill. He glanced
around the open plan space. "Do you see a thermostat
anywhere?"

"There." Cho gestured toward Noah's left, and they crossed
the floor together to a panel set in the wall beside a door Noah
assumed opened into the bedroom. "Fifty-five," Cho read from
the screen. "It's possible Josephs wanted the place cold. Like
maybe he ran hot or wanted to save money on his bill."

"Okay. Why do I sense a 'but' coming?"

"Because decreased blood volume makes a person suscep-
tible to hypothermia. If Josephs was already a couple of pints
low ..." Cho gave a sharp nod. "Could be why he went downhill
so fast even after treatment had started. I'll request his hospital
records from the ME."

"We could talk to his neighbor," Noah suggested. "Cleggett
said the guy had a spare set of keys, so it sounds like they were
friendlier than saying hi in the hallway. Maybe he'd know if
Josephs kept his heat low."

"Yeah, that's good." Cho checked his notes again, then his
watch. "Said neighbor is a Peter Del Sol who lives two doors
down. Del Sol works for an ad agency in midtown so I'm
guessing he'll be up in an hour or so. We can finish up here in
the meantime and see if anything jumps out."

They got to work, each taking one end of the space and
moving toward the room's center, crossing paths as they back-
tracked each other. Just as the cops from the 10th had noted,
nothing about the place even whispered atypical. Noah flagged
the contents of Josephs' desk anyway, then found Cho had done
the same for a collection of business cards and flyers stuck to the
refrigerator with magnets. His stomach sank slightly as he noted
most of them advertised events at various blood bars around the

city, including one held at The Last Drop only two days before Josephs had died.

Noah'd made up his mind to call Cho over when a compact smart speaker on Josephs' desk let out a peal.

"Good morning, Aaron," it said in a buttery tone. "It's time to make breakfast and watch the sun rise. I hope you have a pleasant day."

Cho's expression fell. "Well, that's just depressing. At least the robot can't miss him." Returning to the desk, he ran a hand over a neat stack of paperwork. "Lots of bills here, most overdue. Maybe not surprising considering the rent on this place can't be cheap. Find anything interesting in the stuff stuck on the fridge?"

"Information we already had. Josephs was active in the vampire/donor community and interested in blood exchange. Do we know if the ME found a club stamp during his autopsy?"

"Not yet."

Cho crossed the room to Noah's side and together they started bagging the cards and flyers from the refrigerator. "Exactly what goes down at a bloodex event?" he asked. "Outside of the painfully obvious, I mean. Wait, is this covered in the vampire handbook too?"

"You heard that, huh?" Noah grunted at Cho's laughter. "Bloodex events are mostly geared to help humans who are curious about becoming donors meet others in the community."

"So … like human-vamp hookup parties? Or am I just missing the mark completely?"

"You're close. The events are more about networking and sharing information, but humans and vamps do make connections. Those tend to happen *after* the events though, especially if you happen to be at a venue like a The Last Drop which is set up to make an exchange easy." Noah followed Cho to the far end of the apartment. "You've really never been in a blood bar?"

"Oh, I have, but I was just there for cocktails and staring, if you know what I mean. I should read up on the vampire/donor community though, because Callahan is dying to check out The Last Drop and I'm two-hundred-percent sure he'll want us there when he does."

Noah suspected the same. He didn't like thinking about a visit to his favorite bar while in the company of the NYPD and opened his mouth to say so. But then Cho swung the bedroom door open, and a large part of Noah's rational brain checked out.

There.

His skin prickled in the wash of stale air. An earthy aroma hit him, plush with a vegetal spice. Sweet and velvety, it wrapped around him and clung, making his nostrils flare. He went still, mindful that Cho had stopped moving too, and wasn't surprised to find his eyes wide when Noah looked his way.

"Uh. You okay, Noah?" Cho's voice was far quieter than usual. "You look kind of ... intense right now."

Noah shoved down an urge to laugh. He imagined he did look intense. Eyes glittering, too hard to be ignored, and his body tense, like a snake about to strike. Which wasn't a typical look for Noah when he was around humans.

He didn't often meet other blood eaters while working. He smelled them and other supernaturals all the time out in the field, but mostly in passing since the vast majority of crimes investigated by the CSU involved and were perpetrated by humans. And while he was sometimes forced to hide in strange places to avoid sunlight, Noah worked hard at appearing 'human' during working hours. Some of his coworkers had been skittish in the beginning, but he'd never sensed true fear, and he thought he did a fair job of maintaining a certain veneer if they didn't look closely. Everything about Cho in that moment told Noah he'd caught a glimpse of something different just now, because not once in the year they'd been working together had Cho looked so wary of anything, never mind the unarmed civilian he worked with most nights.

He's never seen you show your teeth before.

Noah exhaled with care. He wasn't showing his teeth, of

course. But his vampire instincts *were* pinging hard. He hadn't expected to find traces of his own kind in this human's apartment or to have to clamp down on the side of himself few humans saw outside of the blood bars. Foolish assumptions given what they knew about Josephs. And now Noah had to work to keep his voice even.

"I'm good. There's a smell in here that belongs to someone like me."

Cho's eyebrows rose almost comically high, and he cast a stricken glance at the open door. "Meaning another vampire? Are they here now?"

"No."

"Fuck, man. You scared the snot out of me." Exasperation replaced the alarm in Cho's expression. "I thought we were about to bust in on God knows what kind of *private* moments your species gets up to."

Noah fought not to bristle at those words. Cho didn't mean to be an ass—that was the adrenaline talking.

"It's faint enough I didn't notice it until you opened the door," he said, then stepped into the room and glanced around, gaze landing on the closet. "Maybe on something Josephs wore."

He located the source within seconds on a black pullover and pair of jeans that lay on top of a clothes hamper, their fibers exuding a tantalizing mixture that teased as Noah breathed them in. Ordinary scents of detergent, body wash, and cologne completely undercut by the seductive note of human sweat and a woody warmth unmistakable to Noah and any of his kind.

"We should bag these." He held the pullover and jeans out. "The scent is recent. Maybe a week since he was near the vampire who left it."

Cho nodded, but it seemed a very long time before he stepped forward and took the bundle from Noah. He held it away from himself as if fearing the clothes would burst into flames and Noah would have thought it funny if his handler's eyes weren't so watchful, lingering on Noah for an extra beat before Cho turned away. The unease in his posture made Noah's spine stiffen too. He knew Cho didn't trust him right now, and it pained him more than he would have imagined. He also couldn't blame the guy.

Human instincts to hunt grew dull with disuse. Their instinct for self-preservation, however, needed only the lightest touch to flare bright.

"Nothing else unusual, right?" Cho asked on his way to the kit they'd left by the door.

"No. No blood or bodily fluids beyond what I'd call normal amounts of perspiration."

"Really? I thought there'd have to be since you picked up a vamp."

"Josephs was physically close to a vampire for a time, and we can guess that contact happened at his favorite bar. Doesn't mean he hooked up with a blood eater." Noah walked to Cho's side. "Even if he did, Josephs probably removed at least the sweater before any kind of exchange went down."

"Okay, I'll bite." Stopping short, Cho looked up and smiled. "Heh. Sorry. Dad jokes are part of my DNA but that was unintentional."

Noah smiled too. Cho cracking crappy jokes was a good sign, especially now that he seemed far less freaked out and instead simply curious.

"Something you want to ask me, Cho?"

"Oh, so many things." Cho's grin broadened. "But let's start with what you meant about Josephs removing the sweater before the exchange."

Squatting, Noah withdrew a pair of evidence bags from the kit. "There are different ways to conduct an exchange. The donor and vampire agree how it occurs—from the donor's wrist or neck or back of the knee, whatever spot on their body they've decided they want to share. The neck and wrists on Josephs' sweater are too tight to get comfortably close to a vamp, and he might have wanted more skin-on-skin contact regardless. Touch can play a big part in a bloodex."

Cho fixed his eyes on the clothes as Noah stood. "Okay, that makes sense. The literature I've read doesn't go into bloodex at that level, you know."

"Because it's geared toward helping you understand the physicality of the act instead of the personal dynamics that might play a bigger role. An exchange is an intimate act. Personal, maybe even emotional in the moment, even if the vampire and donor have never met before. Participants feel ... connected, like I said earlier. Joined, if only for a short time. The donor may be the only one spilling blood, but they get something out of it too, and that's what makes it an exchange." Tucking one bag under his arm, Noah held the other out so Cho could put the folded sweater inside it.

"Is that true for you? You've said a hundred times that you're not into humans, so now I have to wonder."

"Yes, it's true for me. The act can be just as good with a stranger as it might with someone I know."

"So it's like good sex, right, plus a little extra? Everyone's blissed out and feeling awesome?"

"Feelings like that can happen, but a bloodex isn't about sex, at least not in the way you're thinking," Noah said.

Much more than feel-good hormones passed between vampire and donor in the moments that followed blood being spilled and a donor's life hanging in the balance. Noah did his best to explain it while they worked but wasn't sure what to make of the doubt he continued to see in Cho's eyes.

"Are you really saying you don't get off when you're doing your vampy thing? I shouldn't be asking you any of this," Cho said then, almost to himself, "but whatever."

Noah smiled. Humans always thought the vampire had all the power during a blood exchange. Certainly, they were stronger and far more naturally lethal than the human donors who offered themselves. Blood exchanges operated at the donor's discretion however, starting and stopping when they gave the word, and those acts gave them far more control than the uninitiated might gather.

"I definitely feel good. Getting off isn't the point, though, at least not for me. It's about the blood and controlling the exchange. That's why the bars are so successful. They make it easy to hook up and stay safe at the same time. Everyone knows the rules when they walk into a place like The Last Drop."

"But exchanges happen away from the bars, too."

"Of course. And I can't tell you anything about them."

"But … if a bloodex happened outside of a bar, there could be a greater chance of things going wrong, right? Like somebody going too far." Cho's gaze had grown knowing. "Maybe that's what happened to Josephs and the kid in Jackson Square. They got in over their heads with someone who either ignored the rules or didn't have any in the first place. What do you think?"

Noah looked at the bed. "I really don't know. But my instinct tells me that blood eaters weren't involved in the deaths of Josephs or our John Doe. The wound in the vic's neck tonight wasn't made with teeth—I could tell just from its appearance. And even with the vampire scent here on Josephs' clothes, we already know he was a donor and went to the bars to network."

"True." Cho glanced at his watch when it chimed, then turned toward the windows. "It's half-past four, Noah—you should head out before it gets too bright. I'll finish up here."

Noah scoffed. "No way. We both know you could use my help today. I have more knowledge on this topic than even you, mighty science guy, *and* I have the whammy."

"Hah, okay. You're gonna end up lying on the floor in the back of the van because the fucking sun is too bright, though, and that'll be the second time this week."

"Yes, and it won't be the last." Noah sighed. "Just don't tell Callahan and we'll be good."

CHAPTER 4

November 12
Friday, 8:30 P.M.

"Are you not a coffee drinker?" Danny raised an eyebrow at Noah. "It's just occurred to me that you've never once bought one for yourself in all the times you've come in."

Noah gave him a crooked little smile. "I quit a while back."

"Ugh. I could never." Grabbing another box from the stack under the counter, Danny started folding. "I *need* caffeine to get me going after I wake up. I've been working nights a long time now and I'm used to it, but I'm not sure I could ever give up caffeine completely. Especially coffee."

"Cho's the same way."

"He's a single dad—he's probably been living on the stuff since Kage was born."

"True. And he's in good company. Every shift of the NYPD runs on caffeine and sugar, and the guys at the police lab will be excited to see some Nice Buns."

"Wanky," Merlin murmured on his way past, and Danny rolled his eyes.

"Shut it." He wasn't sure how he felt about baked goods in a crime lab, but still had to smile. "I was just thinking it's been a while since you came in here before the witching hour," he said to Noah.

"Some of the techs complained about missing out on the bakery runs, so Cho wants to bring the Nice Buns to them."

Noah glanced at a foursome of young women who had clustered beside him, presumably to examine the bread in the display case he was leaning against. They got all up in his dance space though, grinning and making goo-goo eyes at him, and the look he turned Danny's way next held a silent 'help me.'

Stepping closer, Danny set his hands on his hips. "Anything I can get for you, girls?" He laid the Brooklyn accent on thick and grinned when they turned his way, happy to play up the flirty neighborhood baker routine. He'd never been interested in women but knew that charm paired with free samples was always good for business. "We've got a bomb cake tonight with *pandan* buttercream if any of you are interested."

A pretty redhead with big eyes cocked her head. "I'm not sure I know what that is."

"*Pandan* is a green plant," Danny said. "It tastes like vanilla with a hit of coconut, and I know you're gonna love it because this guy—" he waved Merlin over "—is magic. Merle makes the best frosting in the city."

The young women around Noah simpered as they got an eyeful of Merlin's brown curls and dimples, and he was delighted to field their questions, banter flying fast as he led them away.

Chuckling, Danny shot a look at Noah who appeared much more relaxed. "Sorry about that. Fridays are always busy, what with tourists and people being in a party kind of mood. I know you've got somewhere to be though, so give me two seconds and I'll get this squared away."

"It's fine." Noah smiled at him. "Cho and I've worked more

overtime than usual this week and the unit chief ordered me to start late and end early tonight."

Well, wasn't that lucky? The CSU guys had been by the night before, but again on the heels of the bakery closing. Danny'd had no time to work up the courage to ask Noah about breakfast, but clearly that opportunity was right the heck now if he could just get the freaking words to come out of his mouth.

"I'm trying to leave early tonight too," he said, aiming for casual. "Merlin's training a new apprentice. He knows how the overnight shift works by now and I think it'll be good for him."

Noah pulled his wallet from his pocket. "How early is early? If the bakery closes by two ..."

"I'm hoping to be out before four." Danny's pulse quickened. Noah wanting more details was a good thing, right? "Thought I'd grab a meal that would count as a late-late dinner instead of breakfast since it's been way too long I had even a small piece of a Friday night to myself."

"Technically, it'll be Saturday morning, but for me it never truly feels like the night is over until the sun comes up."

"Yeah, same. I'm not on again until Sunday which gives me more time than usual for catching up on projects I've been putting off."

Like finding out if those lips of yours taste as good as they look.

Certain his cheeks were red yet again, Danny silently cursed his traitorous brain. He slipped several of the maple *silvanas* cookies into the bakery box and tied it off with a length of twine, but before he could say anything else, Noah's phone chimed, and Danny knew what was coming before the guy had it out of his pocket.

Because the universe was an asshole and tonight it had Danny's number.

Noah's smile faded as he read his phone's screen. "Cho's about ten minutes out and wants to meet on the other side of the park."

"Got it. Let's get you over there." Swallowing a sigh, Danny turned to the payment station but paused with his fingers poised over the touch screen. "Anything else you want to throw in? Like maybe something you don't have to share with the rest of the lab?"

"I almost forgot." Noah's eyes lit up. "There is something else. Would you put two Spanish bread in a separate bag, along with a catering menu if you have one? Cho and his mom are planning a birthday party for Kage, and they want Nice Buns for everyone."

"Heck yeah! How old will Kage be?"

"Five."

"That's all kinds of awesome. I'll have to dream up some kind of special birthday cookie. Anyway, our website is up to date, but the paper menu will give them any info they need, too. Is the Spanish Bread for Cho's mom?"

"Ah, no—it's for him. He didn't get any this morning because Kage had friends over for breakfast and every Nice Bun in the place got eaten, including Cho's private stash."

"He has a private stash of bread?"

"Apparently."

Noah's chuckle made Danny do the same. Grabbing several pieces of the coveted sugared bread, he slipped them into a paper bag and set it beside the box. "There's plenty for both of you in there and don't let Cho tell you otherwise." He reached for one of the tri-fold menus he kept in a holder on the counter but noticed only then the stack he'd put out earlier in the evening was gone. "Huh. That's weird. I didn't even notice people taking them. I'll run out back for more if you can wait another minute?"

Noah shook his head. "I really shouldn't. Cho and I are meeting someone, and we can't be late. I'll grab one the next time I come in."

"How about I send you one instead? Happy to shoot a file over the next time I get a break if you have a card with your email address or number." Danny's insides went a bit gooey at Noah's quick smile.

"Perfect." Plucking a card from his wallet, Noah set it on the counter along with several bills, then gathered up the box and bag. "Message when you can, and I'll forward it on to Cho."

Oh, I'm gonna.

But Danny's internal victory dance ground to a halt as Noah started backing toward the door. "Wait, hold up. You need change, Noah, because this is—"

"Money for the tip jar," Noah called back. He smiled bigger when Merlin threw him an air high-five, and the corners of his eyes crinkled. "Thanks again, Danny. I'll keep an eye out for your message."

Nearly five hours later, Danny swore he still felt the warmth of that smile, and he wanted to barf at his own cheeseball brain. He closed the shutters on the bakery's doors, then made his way behind the counter, working quickly at shutting down the sales system while the crew wiped down counters and mopped floors. They headed for the kitchen once the bulk of the cleaning was done, leaving Danny alone to box up the few leftover buns and pastries remaining on the display trays, a task he looked forward to every night. The simple act of taking physical stock helped mellow his energy and put him in just the right frame of mind to work with dough.

His crew was buzzing with extra vigor, however, and he chuckled as their giggling and a burst of salsa music floated out from the kitchen behind him. Clearly, they were in the mood to dance. He knew as much from the occasional sneaker squeak against the tiled floors and Merlin's patient counts of "front-two-three and back-two-three" over more rounds of giggling.

Danny felt no urge to join in tonight. His back ached more than usual and the thought of settling down in a booth at Charon's with a beer and a plate of steak and eggs sounded a hell of a lot more appealing, particularly if he had company for that late-late-dinner.

A smile played about his lips as he thought back to his conversation with Noah and the catering menu he had yet to send. His plans for flirty texting had faded after the bakery had gotten slammed harder than usual, and outside of the occasional hurried bio break, he hadn't had time to fool around with his phone.

He slid the empty trays onto a rolling rack, then set the box of leftovers on top and wheeled it all toward the door, pausing a moment to flip off the store's overhead lights. He was humming along with the music as he pushed into the kitchen and only just managed to pull up short as the new apprentice darted past with a tray in each hand.

"Sorry, boss!" Tina met Danny's raised eyebrows with a sheepish grin. She was a cheetah shifter and stupid quick on her feet. "Merle and I got a head start on the *monay*, so we'd have time to go over the new recipes with you."

"Excellent, thanks. I also want to double the amount of rice desserts and rice flour cakes because we've run out of gluten-free offerings for three nights running and I'd like to see how they sell during the day. Merle, can you start a batch of plain *pandesal* in the meantime?"

"You bet." Merlin hauled a bag of flour to one of the big mixers. "The seasonal flavored bread batches are smaller, and we always make one plain," he said to Tina. "Not everyone likes a flavor twist in their roll unless we're talking doughnuts. Because we could make triple-sized batches every night and they'd sell out, no matter what the glazes taste like." He laughed at Danny's groan.

"We are *not* making *shakoy* in triple-sized batches. Frying them up in a regular-sized batch is torture enough."

Tina looked aghast. "Wait, you don't like doughnuts?"

"Oh, I like them just fine, if I'm the one eating and someone else is making."

Merlin made a face. "You're such a poop."

"Please don't say poop in my bakery," Danny replied, then

cut a couple of dance moves of his own before he got back to work.

O

Because he had the best crew in the world, Danny was out the door at ten minutes past three and felt nothing but confident everything would go smoothly in his absence. He couldn't help feeling a little dejected too because he'd failed yet again to suggest Noah share a cup of coffee or breakfast or even that stick of fucking gum with him, despite the prime opportunities he'd had tonight.

A night that's not really over until the sun comes up, he thought out of the blue.

Biting his lip against a grin, Danny crossed the street toward Bleecker Playground, then stopped under a streetlight so he could pull his phone from his pocket. He tapped out and revised until he found words he thought struck the right mix of casual-friendly and low-key flirt.

Late-late dinner? Snagged a catering menu—can hand deliver if you're free.

He hit Send and set off, stuffing the phone back in his jeans pocket and intent on getting home to shower. He wouldn't turn down the opportunity to feel and look more human after a shift, even if the only beings he'd see tonight were inside the Charon diner and couldn't care less how he dressed.

Danny'd just entered the playground when a solid wall of ... *someone* materialized out of nowhere, moving so fast he had no chance of getting out of the way. They crashed into him with bone-jolting force, flinging Danny backward so his arms flailed, and his tote bag went flying off to the left. Danny's breath left him in a big whoosh when his ass hit the ground, and he had just a second to register how much falling on pavement fucking hurt before someone was on him, pressing Danny backward and down.

"Get off," Danny gasped, still winded, alarm flooding his body when the figure hovering over him *laughed*, their voice lower than Danny's and raspy. A sharp, antiseptic odor filled his nose, strong enough it was choking.

"Relax. I don't have time to play with you right now." The guy lowered his head enough that Danny caught a smudgy glimpse of fair skin and a square jaw in the streetlight's glow, though the rest of the face was obscured by a sweatshirt's hood. "Kind of a shame, though, because you feel like a lot of fun."

He nuzzled at Danny's cheek, breath hot and tinged with more of that ominous laughter, and the sheer *weirdness* made Danny's insides draw tight. He thrashed hard, shouting at the guy to get the fuck off, his voice louder now. Someone yelled back from the sidewalk beyond the park's iron fence, and Danny's already pounding heart thundered into overdrive. He wasn't alone with this creepy fucking fuck, thank God, who didn't seem bothered one bit. Moving easily, the guy rolled away, on his feet in an instant while Danny was still struggling to get vertical. He stared with mounting outrage as the guy walked over to where his bag had landed and plucked it up from the ground.

What the actual fuck?

"Hey!" he had time to yell before the guy took off, leaving Danny scrambling up and sprinting after him, fury burning his insides. He heard footsteps pounding against the sidewalk on the other side of the park's perimeter, but whoever the good Samaritan was, they were too far away to help him right now, their movements restricted by the park's tall iron fence.

Danny had just chased the guy past a play structure when he had to lurch left to avoid tripping over a bundle—a someone?—lying lengthwise across the middle of the path. The unexpected motion made his lower back scream, and the deep ache hobbled him, slowing Danny's steps just enough that he quickly lost sight of the guy and his stolen bag.

"Fuck!"

Knowing it was too late, Danny kept after him anyway, lungs burning as he burst out through the park's exit and onto the sidewalk. He rounded on a pair of young men running toward him, his fists clenched before Danny recognized them. He knew these guys, Mekhai and Luther, neighborhood kids just past their teens. They came into the bakery regularly, often to buy bread for their families but sometimes for the occasional treat for themselves.

"You okay, Danny?" Mekhai asked, his brow knit under his beanie as he scanned the sidewalks and streets around them, all empty of the man in the dark hooded sweatshirt and Danny's goddamned bag. "We heard yelling and saw someone hassling you through the fence. Couldn't get past the gate, though."

"We should've doubled back," Luther muttered, still looking around. "Who was that guy? Did you see where he went?"

"I have no idea and no." Leaning forward, Danny braced his hands on his knees with a groan that sounded pained even to his own ears. Holy shit, he hated running in clogs. "Asshole got my bag, but he only ran off because of you two, so thank you a lot. The next time you come into the bakery, I'm gonna load you up with so much stuff you won't be able to carry it all."

"Awesome." Mekhai grinned at him. "Sorry about your stuff, though. You got a phone to call the cops?"

Danny straightened with a grunt. "Yeah, I do. I think I saw someone lying in the path back there so I'll ... I dunno, make sure they're at least awake before the cops show and write them up for vagrancy."

"You'll be doing them a favor." Luther huffed through his nose. "It's supposed to get real cold later and guy won't be happy if they wake up half-frozen to the ground."

"True. Thanks again, guys, really." Danny gave the boys a tired smile. "You did me a huge favor tonight."

Moving much more slowly, he walked back into the park, feeling every one of his twenty-seven years. The figure was where he'd left it, and yeah, it was a person, fair skinned with light hair visible under the edge of their coat's hood. A young man, Danny saw, curled on his side on the path, maybe blitzed out on booze or drugs or both.

"Hey, man," Danny said. "You can't sleep here. I have to call the cops because some dickface stole my stuff, and they'll probably arrest you if you don't get your shit together and go on home."

He'd gotten close before he understood something was off. Frowning, Danny slowly squatted, gaze moving over features slack with what looked like sleep. Except ... this guy wasn't sleeping. Couldn't be, with skin bleached so white it practically glowed in the light coming off of the old-fashioned lamp post nearby. This guy wasn't moving at all either, his utter stillness so alien that Danny's insides froze.

Oh, fuck. I don't think he's breathing.

He spotted the opening in the guy's neck then, and a small smudge just below it that he knew could be only one thing. It put Danny on his ass for the second time that night, a lump in his throat so big he didn't trust himself to speak.

CHAPTER 5

November 13
Saturday, 3:40 A.M.

"Look at this crowd," Cho muttered. "People in this town take the 'city that never sleeps' thing way too literally."

He steered the van along Hudson Street, its flashing lights cutting across the onlookers who'd gathered. Though it was almost four in the morning, people stood in clumps on the sidewalks surrounding Bleecker Playground, drawn by the police cars and activity.

Pulling up to the curb not far from an ambulance, Cho cut the ignition. "This can't be good. Five cruisers plus medical, and an unmarked car or three. Jesus. We're going to be here past the end of shift."

Noah didn't doubt him. After meeting with the doctor who'd treated Aaron Josephs at West Greenwich Health, they'd gone back to the police lab in Queens. They'd hardly had a chance to set down the box of Nice Buns before being called back out again and had spent the hours since crisscrossing the city answering additional calls. Now, whatever was going on in that playground would likely keep them until dawn, despite the orders they'd been given not to work any overtime. Noah knew it was for the best.

He'd seen the hope in Danny's eyes when they'd talked about ending their respective shifts early. Read it in the text Danny'd sent suggesting they meet up. Noah could guess Danny was interested in more than sharing plates of food that Noah would only pretend to eat, and he'd known better than to say yes. Of course he had. However fun Danny was to talk to, or curious Noah might be to know how those plush lips of his tasted, it was better for them both if he kept his distance.

Still, something'd held him back from messaging a firm 'thanks, but no thanks'. Noah hadn't liked the idea of disappointing Danny, but the idea Danny *wouldn't* be bothered appealed even less. Both arguments were ridiculous, given Noah'd been so busy he'd had no choice but to let the opportunity slip by. He only hoped that whatever Danny was up to tonight, he didn't find out until tomorrow about the body discovered across the street from his bakery.

Armed with the camera bag and field kit, Noah and Cho grabbed sets of floodlights before heading out of the van. A peculiar heaviness hung over the park as they walked to its center, growing thicker the deeper they went, and Noah thought the faces of the uniformed officers they passed appeared extra grim. He understood why when he got an eyeful of a man laid out under the glare of the playground's lights, bloodless and still in an all too familiar manner.

It's not him.

Noah knew it wasn't Danny without looking hard, because this vic was blond, fair hair shining in the light that came from the park's lamp posts. He scanned the young man's features anyway, hardly daring to breathe as he took in the ashen face. He quickly came up blank but still glanced in the direction of the bakery, just visible through the trees in the park. He knew from Cho's low oath that he'd had the same thought.

"Does this guy work over there?"

"I don't believe so." Noah glanced back to the body. "They had new staff working tonight but unless something changed, they're locked inside the bakery and probably don't even know we're out here."

They set up the lights and a ScanStation that would capture a 3D digital image of the scene while Cho spoke with the uniformed officers who'd responded to the 9-1-1 call. After he'd done a walkthrough of the area, Cho sketched out a plan for processing the scene, then turned to Noah, his attitude more serious than usual.

"Don't hold back."

Noah cocked his head. "I'm not sure what you mean."

"I know. Let me try and explain." Cho frowned at the body once more. "Obviously, we have work to do but I think we both know what we'll find here tonight."

"Similarities to the scene at Jackson Square Park."

"Yup. If that's the case, there won't be much in the way of physical evidence or even footage from the traffic and street cams. Whoever this perp is, they're meticulously clean and good at avoiding people's attention. If we're going to get ahead of them, we need to leverage any advantage we have, even if it takes us into unfamiliar territory. That's where I think you can help.

"I had no idea, you know." Cho sighed. "That when you're around me—around humans in general, I guess—you're playing a part. Playing human for lack of a better word. Purposely holding yourself back so you fit in."

What could Noah say? Moving among bleeders demanded control, particularly when he was out in the field, and he was long accustomed to tamping down senses that went beyond the range of 'natural.' He used a friendly, bland front so resolutely non-threatening that it put humans at ease.

Cho waved at the scene in front of them now. "If being more

... *yourself* helps you pick up on things the rest of us might miss —stains, scents, whatever—I want you to do it."

Now it was Noah's turn to frown. "That's not a good idea."

"Why not?"

"Because I have good reasons for not acting more 'like myself' and doing a lot of mouth breathing in general."

Cho winced a little. "Uh. Yeah. I get it."

"No, you don't. I don't expect you to. I'm good at appearing human because I used to be one. Memories from that life inform the way I act when I'm with you but I'm *not* like you, Cho. Haven't been for a long time." Noah pursed his lips. "Honestly, I'd expect you to understand that after what happened in Aaron Josephs' apartment the other night."

Eyes flashing in the glare from the floodlights, Cho held Noah's gaze. "I do understand. And I haven't forgotten anything about what happened the other night."

He's afraid of you.

Understanding hit Noah like a slap of cold water. Between a solid wall of calls and diving deeper into Aaron Josephs' life, they'd been constantly on the move the last couple of nights. Cho had been as professional as always and continued piping the hip-hop tracks on his endless playlists through the van's speakers, yet he'd seemed distracted too, and his typical joking manner had been absent. Noah'd put it down to being over-worked, but clearly, he'd been wrong. Cho was scared to be around him and probably would be for a while.

Noah slipped his hands in his pockets. "Cho—"

"Whatever you're gonna say, we need to table it until later. I need help, Noah." The anger in Cho's face turned almost pleading and he tipped his head toward the man on the ground. "*He* does. And I know it's not fair, but I'm asking you to do whatever you can to help us find the person who's doing this."

The urgency in those words stayed with Noah as he turned to his work. There were distinct similarities between this young man and the one found in Jackson Square Park, including the club stamp on the inside of the wrist and a hole in the throat, along with thoroughly empty pockets and veins. Though the medical examiner still had to make a ruling, it seemed obvious the police now had two suspicious deaths on their hands with a similar M.O., each possibly connected through The Last Drop to what could be a third victim, Aaron Josephs.

After capturing long-range images of the immediate surroundings, Noah moved in closer to the body for mid-range and close-up shots, and he was squatting by the victim photographing the wound in his throat when a shadow fell over them both.

"We've got to stop meeting like this."

Callahan's distinctive growl raised the hairs on the back of Noah's neck and poked at his predatory instinct. It took effort to keep his face straight when he looked over his shoulder at the detective because Christ, he could not lose his grip again. Standing, he cupped the Nikon in his right hand.

"For the record, I'd be fine with that. Don't read into this too much, Detective, but I'm sorry to see you again."

"Same. You can read as much into that as you like." Callahan sucked on his e-cig and exhaled the smoke noisily. "I find myself in an unusual position, Green, in that I need your help for the second time this week."

"With the vic, you mean? Obviously, I'll do my best."

"Yeah, I know. But no, not with this kid. With a witness. A guy on his way home from work tonight was assaulted by a man who may have been the perp. The plot twist is that the witness knows you—or says he does—and how do you like those odds?"

Noah frowned. What the hell? "I live three blocks from here. I suppose the odds are better than average. What is the witness's name?"

"Danilo Kaes, twenty-seven, born and raised in Brooklyn," Callahan read from the tiny pad of paper he used for notes, seemingly unaware Noah had gone still. "Says he goes by Danny and asked if you and Cho were working tonight when he heard

CSU was on scene." He glanced back up. "Do you know him or not?"

"I do." Noah let the camera hang from its strap and dropped his hands to his sides. "Danny Kaes owns Nice Buns, a bakery across the street."

Tucking the e-cig away, Callahan rolled his eyes skyward. "Yeah, he told me the shop's name. Cute as fuck."

"Buns are what they sell, Detective. I'm in there a couple of times a week."

"What the hell for? It's not like you can eat anything they sell."

"I'm usually buying for Cho and Kage, and sometimes I grab boxes for the lab."

Callahan's lips tilted in a humorless smile that made Noah want to punch him. "I see. And those are your only interactions with Kaes? Buying food you can't eat? Because he told me he lives in this neighborhood too, so maybe he does more than bake you nice buns. The guy even had your card."

What an ass.

Noah blew a breath out through his nose. Getting snappy with a homicide detective—and Callahan in particular—would do him no favors, not when all he wanted was to see Danny and make sure he was okay. The sooner that happened, the better.

"I gave Danny my card so he could send me a catering menu," he said. "We chat when I stop in at the bakery, but I've never seen him outside of it."

If we'd met tonight like he'd wanted, he wouldn't have been in this park at all.

Cho appeared without warning. "I know Danny Kaes too, and Noah asked for the catering info at my request. Kage's birthday is coming up and she'll want as many nice buns as she can grab hold of." He flicked a look at Noah, his eyes alight with sudden mischief. "I've never appreciated that bakery's name more than right now."

Noah allowed himself a smile, then returned his focus to Callahan. "Is Danny all right?"

"Mr. Kaes is being treated for signs of shock."

"What? Why?" Noah glanced toward the ambulance parked up the street. He'd assumed it had been called for the victim. "What happened?"

"The guy saw a dead body, that's what happened." Callahan shrugged. "He kept it mostly together until officers arrived at the scene, but he's been falling apart since. And, like I said, asking for you." He paused then, features set in grim lines, and the short silence told Noah how deeply it pained the detective to seek out his help again.

"I want you to talk the guy down," Callahan said at last. "I need Kaes focused when he answers questions, and I figured a friendly face might help chill him out. As long as you don't, you know, try to eat him or anything."

"I already ate, so he should be safe." Satisfaction surged through Noah at Callahan's wince, because screw this guy and his shit attitude. "And sure, I can do that, if Cho says it's okay."

Cho held out a hand for the Nikon. "Go. As we expected, we haven't found a damn thing and I can finish up here. Give me a heads-up when you know how the rest of your night's going to play out."

"Thank you. I was in the middle of close-ups, and we need more long- and mid-range shots with the evidence markers."

"No problem, Noah. Tell Danny I said to hang in there."

Despite his earlier posturing, Callahan fell silent as they made their way toward the ambulance, his brow furrowed deep. Normally, Noah wouldn't have cared—the less he heard from the man, the better. He needed to know what he might face in the next several minutes if he wanted to keep his head, however, whether or not Callahan understood the reasons why.

"Hold up," Noah said, a hand poised over Callahan's forearm without touching.

Callahan paused and turned, then took a step back, clearly wary. "What now?"

"How is Danny really? Stressed, obviously, but what else do I need to know?"

"Kaes is more than stressed, Green, he's agitated. Like panic-attack kind of agitated. The EMTs are talking about a transport to the nearest ED."

"So let them."

"I'd rather not have to wait for the guy to come down off a Xanax before I can question him. It's better he talks now rather than later—the possibility he'll forget some of the finer details increases every minute."

Noah knew as much. Didn't mean he enjoyed the idea of Danny suffering just so he'd be more useful. "Earlier, you said he was assaulted."

"He'll have a black eye in the morning, and he's a little banged up, but outside of some scuffs on his palms, there wasn't a scratch on him that I could see." Callahan narrowed his eyes. "Wait. You said you'd be okay," he bit out, voice charged. "You said you weren't fucking *hungry*."

"I'm not. I still need to go in there knowing what to expect. Is that so hard to understand?"

"Hard? No. Fucked up? Yes. I don't like wondering if the guy I've asked to handle a witness is going to lose his shit and kill them." Callahan set his hands on his hips and glared. "Fuckery aside, Green, are you okay to do this? Because if you feel even a little shaky or moody or *whatever*, I'm not taking you over there. Kaes has been through some shit tonight and he doesn't need to be worrying about how a stupid fucking virus re-wired your DNA to eat him."

Noah's frustration evaporated. Callahan was right. This moment wasn't about their crappy interpersonal dynamics—it was about Danny. Who needed support and a friend, something Noah could try to be for as long as he was needed. And which probably meant that hiding his true nature from Danny would soon become impossible.

"I'm good," he said, but shook his head when Callahan made to start walking again. "Danny doesn't know I'm a blood eater."

Callahan's eyebrows went up. "For real?"

"For very real. I told you, I don't know him well. We chat when I drop by the bakery, but ..."

"You never bothered mentioning your supernatural status."

Ugh. The truth was more complicated than Callahan knew but, again, he wasn't wrong. Noah hated the smug look on the cop's face though.

"That's the first thing about you that's ever made sense, Green. I sure as hell wouldn't want anyone to know I was a vampire if I could help it. Anyway." Callahan jerked his head toward the ambulance. "Let's get this shit-show over with."

Within a few steps, Noah heard voices coming from the ambulance and knew Callahan had been right—Danny wasn't handling finding a dead body well at all. His shallow breaths were too fast, despite coaching from the EMTs who told Danny in low, even voices to relax and breathe slower.

Rounding the back of the rig, Noah spotted the baker half-reclined on a gurney, wrapped in a silver space blanket with a plastic oxygen mask over his nose and mouth. Danny's face was chalky in the harsh light pouring out of the ambulance's open doors, his eyelids moving sluggishly with each blink. Genuine sympathy ran through Noah as he took in the scene, followed a heartbeat later by a surge of pure want.

God, Danny smelled *good*. Sweat and adrenaline and the sweet-sour tang of yeast rolled off him, mixing together in exactly the kind of fear stink any vampire craved. Especially one like Noah, who sometimes liked to do more with a bleeder than simply feed.

In that instant, Noah liked the idea of doing everything with Danny.

And knew that he couldn't.

Keenly aware of Callahan's eyes on him, he shoved his instincts down hard. He approached the rig, keeping his motions slow, and nodded at the EMTs, who were already shifting around in an effort to make room for them.

"Hey, Danny. It's Noah Green. Detective Callahan said you asked for me?"

Danny swung his gaze Noah's way, his eyes going slightly wider. "H-hey." The word came on a small gasp muffled by the mask. "Can't ... catch my ... b-breath."

"You're going to be fine," Noah said. "Is it okay if I sit down?"

He waited for Danny's jerky nod before settling onto the rig's bench, but then Danny grabbed at him, his fingers clammy against Noah's skin. He groaned softly as the pulse oximeter attached to his index finger came loose.

One of the EMTs plucked it back up. "Let's move this onto your other hand," she said, then repositioned the sensor, the machine beeping loudly all the while. Danny's panicked eyes stayed locked on Noah.

"Breathe with me," Noah said.

As the EMTs had done, he led Danny through the motions of exhaling before inhaling deep, then holding the breath for a count of four before starting again. He kept his hold on Danny's fingers light while Danny worked at calming himself, a thin whine coming out of him when the technique didn't immediately work. But as the minutes passed, his breathing slowly improved and the wildness in his eyes eased.

"Thanks," he said at last, voice scratchy through the mask. Some of his color had returned, though a bruise stood out on his right cheekbone and his skin was shiny with sweat. His hold on Noah didn't loosen at all. "That's never happened to me before."

"I'm sure you could say the same about a lot of things tonight, Mr. Kaes." Callahan's tone was gentler than Noah had ever heard. "I'd like to ask you some questions about what happened, if that's all right?"

"Sure." Danny went silent for a moment, then met Noah's eyes once more. "Will you … is this okay?" He squeezed Noah's fingers with his own. "It's helping."

"Of course," Noah said. "I can hang out for as long as you need."

Danny sat back against the gurney, his eyelids sliding closed. "Thanks. I know you're working right now."

Noah could almost feel Callahan's stare. "Cho knows where I am. Probably badly in need of a coffee, too, considering the night we've been having."

"Hah." A ghost of a smile curved Danny's mouth, though it didn't quite happen. "I can call over there and have Merlin bring out some stuff? It's not like hearing from me at this point would make his night any weirder."

Callahan broke in before Noah could turn Danny down. "Unfortunately, everything has the potential to get weirder tonight, Mr. Kaes. If you feel able, I'd like to start with what you were doing in the park at three o'clock in the morning."

CHAPTER 6

Fatigue wrapped itself around Danny like a wet blanket as he spoke with the detective named Callahan. But he worked hard at staying clear-headed, determined he'd help the police figure out what had happened to that poor guy in the park because fuck, he'd never seen anything so terrible.

Just thinking about it made his guts clench. The nausea lessened each time Noah squeezed his hand though, the touch soothing against Danny's damp fingers. And out of nowhere, he found himself caught between a laugh and a sob. The first chance he got to spend time around Noah Green away from Nice Buns and it just happened to be at a goddamned crime scene with Danny playing the role of near witness to what sounded like a murder.

Goddamn but the universe really *was* an asshole.

"Walk me through what happened just before you called 9-1-1," Callahan said.

Danny nodded tiredly. He'd already given those details to some cops wearing uniforms, but it wasn't like he could go anywhere right now.

"I was on my way home from work. I live six blocks from

here on Grove Street," he added. "I usually cut across the play-ground and walk down Hudson."

"In the middle of the night?"

"Well, I left the bakery early today. Normally, the crew on the overnight shift clock out between four and six depending on their job, but I had an extra baker on tonight which meant I was free a lot earlier."

Callahan hummed. "You cut through the playground, you said?"

"Yes. Or I started to." Swallowing hard, Danny forced himself to stay chill. "The park is small and there's plenty of light on the paths and people around, so it always seems safe enough. I ran into someone tonight, though. Crashed, really. I didn't see them coming until they were on top of me."

"Did you recognize them?"

"No. Like I told the other cops, I didn't get a good look at their face. They were white and I think they were male."

"You *think* they were male? What makes you say that?"

"His voice. He was strong. Pinned me down so I couldn't get up."

"Strong like a human or more than?"

"Uh." Danny blinked. "Strong like a human." Again, he described the figure he'd seen only in flashes, someone around his height but slimmer, features obscured by a sweatshirt's hood.

Callahan moved his pen over his little pad. "Did he threaten you?"

"I'm not sure. He said he didn't have time to play with me. But I don't know what that means. Sorry, I—"

"Those were the suspect's words?" Callahan's tone wasn't hard, despite having cut Danny off. "He didn't have time to play with you?"

"Yeah. And something like wasn't it a shame because I seemed like fun." A shudder shook Danny's frame. "He laughed. There was a smell. Like … almost like band-aids?" He raised a hand to his cheek. "He put his face here. Like he was going to kiss me."

"*Did* he kiss you?"

Struck by the urgent note in Noah's voice, Danny looked his way. "I think ... He rubbed his lips against my cheeks, so sort of?"

"He needs an exam," Noah said to Callahan. "A skin swab and fingernail scrapings and—"

"But I don't want to go to the hospital." Another wave of fatigue hit Danny, thicker than before. Fuck, he was a mess, voice going shaky and thin as he tried to make Noah understand. "I just want to go home. I'm a little banged up but it's nothing. Not like the guy in the park. The, uh—"

"The victim," Noah said, voice so gentle that Danny's eyes stung.

"Yeah." The victim. Not a guy who'd been sleeping or injured or partied out after a fun Friday night. A dead person, who would never, ever wake up again. Danny tasted metal and shivered, though he didn't feel cold at all. "I'm gonna be sick."

The others carried on talking while he emptied his stomach into a bag that one of the EMTs handed him, and the actual words faded in and out. Noah's hand stayed on Danny's back though, pressed firm between his shoulder blades, and the meaning behind the conversations came through. Detective Callahan wanted more information and he'd stay with Danny until he got it. If Noah didn't like it, no one was stopping him from leaving except Noah himself, because Noah made it clear he wasn't going anywhere, thank you very much.

"M'okay." Danny slumped back against the gurney at last. "Sorry about that."

The EMT closest to him patted his shoulder. She had the long eyes of a cat shifter with haunting, vertical pupils, and her friendly attitude put him at ease. "Don't worry about it. I know you'd rather go home, but we'd better get you strapped in for the ride over to Chelsea Med."

"Fine." Danny cut his eyes at Noah and grumbled some more. "I blame you for this."

Noah gave him a very small smile. He rode with Danny during the short trip, and while Danny wanted to stay aggravated, having Noah there helped so much. He explained there could be evidence on Danny's person they'd need to collect, and that he would have a shit-ton of paperwork to fill out. The conversation flowed so easily, Danny started to feel more like himself, and it was an ugly shock to his system when the ambulance doors popped open again and the full scope of just how fucked up his evening had gotten hit him like dough slapping a board.

He'd been mugged. And found a body. Then freaked out and barfed in front of the guy he'd been crushing on for weeks. Quelling a sigh, Danny pulled the space blanket tighter around his shoulders. He wouldn't be surprised if Noah disappeared after tonight. And his internal fretting must have shown on his face then because Noah looked at him askance.

"What's the matter?"

"I'm not sure where to start," Danny replied. "This wasn't what I had in mind when I asked if you wanted to meet up for a late-late dinner."

Before Noah could reply, the EMTs were climbing aboard, and the weirdness level of his night increased yet again.

"I wish I could tell you more." Shifting, Danny swung his legs over the edge of the exam table and grimaced at the twinge in his lower back. The doctor on call had hardly finished her exam—so strange with the added skin swabs and fingernail scrapings—when Detective Callahan had shown up again. "Some guys from the neighborhood passing by heard me yelling. They tried to scare off the guy who jumped me, but it was like he didn't care. He let me go and grabbed my bag, and then just ran off like it was no big deal he was stealing my stuff."

"What about those neighborhood guys? Think they could ID him?"

"I don't know. They were on the other side of the fence."

"I'll talk to them anyway." Callahan made note of Mekhai's and Luther's names. "And you're certain you didn't recognize the victim?" He cocked his head at Danny. "Sometimes, details about an incident of this kind will come back to a person after they've had a chance to process what's happened."

Danny shook his head. He had no idea how to process what he'd been through. He didn't know the guy from the park, though, of that he was sure. Thank God, too. It was bad enough someone had died almost on the bakery's doorstep without it being someone he'd known. "I don't recognize the man who died."

"All right. Thank you, Mr. Kaes. You've been very helpful." Callahan pulled a business card from his jacket pocket and handed it over, then pointed at the numbers printed across the bottom. "That's my mobile. You call me anytime something comes to mind, no matter how small."

Palming the card, Danny shoved it into his jacket pocket alongside the bottle of ibuprofen he'd scored for his bruises and sore back. He fell silent as they walked to the exit, so tired he felt like his head and body weren't really attached.

"What happens next?" he asked, once they were outside, glancing from the detective to Noah.

"We may ask you to come into the precinct as the case develops or so you can make an ID," Callahan replied. "You'll also need to file a report for the items you had stolen."

"Yeah, Noah mentioned paperwork."

Shit. Danny had almost forgotten about the stuff he'd lost. He carried his wallet and phone in his jeans pockets out of habit, but there'd been things in the bag he wanted back. His tablet and sunglasses, not to mention the stupid, expensive water bottle he kept leaving in the wrong places but had somehow remembered to pack up tonight. Pulse picking up once more, Danny patted himself down, heart sinking when he didn't immediately find his keys. He knew without asking that nothing good would come of that.

Noah's gaze was sharp when Danny turned his way. "What's wrong?"

"My keys. For the apartment and bakery." Danny hated the grim look Noah exchanged with Callahan. "They were in my bag, along with some mail I picked up on my way out last night. That means he's got my address, right?"

Callahan reached for his phone. "We have to assume so. It's possible he saw you leave the bakery as well, which means he'd know where you work. I'll send a squad car over to your apartment. I think it's unlikely anyone will try to break in but from what you've told me, this perp is brazen and might show up anyway. Your building super will have to rekey your locks and I'd advise you do the same for your bakery." He paused at Danny's pained noise. "In the meantime, stay away from your apartment. Do you live alone, Mr. Kaes?"

"Uh, yes?"

"No partner in the picture?"

What the fuck? Danny didn't dare look at Noah. "No. Why does that matter?"

"Because, like you, they'd need to stay away from your apartment for the next couple of days."

"Shit. I don't have a boyfriend. But I really can't go home for a couple of *days*?"

"I strongly advise you don't. Do you have friends or family in the city who can put you up?"

"Um. Sure. My sister lives in Harlem and I have friends I can buzz once … once it gets lighter, I guess?" Danny grimaced. All he wanted was to forget this hideous, very long night had ever happened. "Goddamn it, I'm tired."

"Why don't you come back to my place?"

Danny turned his head so fast in Noah's direction he swore his neck creaked. "Say what now?"

"I've got a couch that pulls out into a bed." Noah seemed impossibly relaxed in the face of Danny's goggling. "And I live on West 12th, not far from the bakery, so you'll be close once your locks have been rekeyed."

Detective Callahan's words ran into Danny's when they spoke at the same time.

"Green, what are you doing?"

"I can't ask you to do that."

"Why not?" Noah spoke only to Danny. "I have plenty of room and there's a security desk downstairs. I'll keep you safe, I promise."

Danny swore he heard humor in his voice, almost as if Noah were teasing. His gaze was deadly serious, however, and steady in a way that cut through the noise in Danny's head.

I'll keep you safe.

The knots that had been twisting Danny's insides loosened for the first time in hours. Maybe he'd get a late-late dinner with Noah someday after all.

"Are you sure it's okay?" he asked. "I don't even have a change of clothes."

Noah shrugged. "We'll figure it out. You can call your super on the way over and get him started on rekeying your locks."

"Yeah, about that. Unless there's water involved, it usually takes a couple of requests before Mr. Tyler shows up for repairs. I could be on your couch for more than one night."

"I can handle it if you can."

Callahan held up a hand, his features marred by a mighty frown. "Hold the fucking phone, okay? I didn't say either of you could go anywhere."

What the hell did that mean? Danny chewed the inside of his cheek, but Noah folded his arms over his chest and shot an unreadable look in Callahan's direction.

"My apologies, Detective. I assumed you were done." Again,

his tone was light, and Danny watched a muscle in Callahan's cheek jump.

"I suppose I am for the moment," the detective ground out. "*But* given it's already past five in the morning and everything Mr. Kaes has been through, I think a ride back to your apartment is in order, wouldn't you agree, Green?"

Callahan glanced up, and Danny followed his line of sight, unsure of what he was meant to be seeing besides a gray sky that was starting to turn pink. But Noah and Callahan were staring at each other when Danny looked back to them, their silence charged with an energy he couldn't interpret. They were on the move a second later though, Noah's hand on Danny's elbow as they walked, and Danny didn't bother holding back his sigh.

Something weird was going on with these guys. Danny just didn't have the brain power to figure it out.

Time passed in a literal blur during the ride to Noah's and Danny fought his body's slow slide toward sleep. He called Thea and broke the news about needing to rekey the locks on the bakery's doors, then spent the rest of the journey reassuring her that he was okay aside from some bruises. His eyelids were like stone by the time he climbed out of Callahan's Ford Taurus, and his head swam as he followed Noah into a stately brownstone building. A friendly-faced man in a black suit nodded at them from behind a desk in the foyer.

"Good evening, Mr. Green."

Mr. Green? Wait. Noah had mentioned a security desk in his building, but this guy looked more like a concierge.

Noah greeted the man with a nod of his own. "Hello, Jasper. I'm expecting a colleague from the police department shortly by the name of Bert Callahan."

"Very good," Jasper replied politely. "I'll send him up."

Danny frowned as they moved away from the desk and toward the elevators. How did Noah afford to live in a building with a freaking concierge? And who the heck named their kid Jasper?

"What kind of salary do you make at the NYPD?" Heat flooded Danny's cheeks and he quickly slapped a hand over his mouth. "Shit," he mumbled through his fingers. "I'm sorry. That was rude."

Leaning forward, Noah tapped the elevator call button, and he sounded amused more than anything else. "It's all right."

"No, it's not." Sighing, Danny dropped his hand. "I didn't mean to say that."

"Out loud, you mean. Because you obviously meant to think it."

Danny fought an urge to squirm. "I ... yeah. This is a nice building."

"It is."

Good Lord. Awkward much? Danny grimaced to himself as they boarded the elevator, but quickly found himself talking yet *again* as the car zipped toward the eighth floor. Apparently, being this tired meant losing his filters.

"My building is nice too, but nothing like this. *Mr.* Green," he added, then smirked at Noah's knowing glance.

"I've asked Jasper to use my given name, but he has some old-fashioned ideas about how to do his job and I don't expect him to change. Speaking of names, Callahan told me the one on your license is Danilo," he said then. "Am I saying that right?"

"Almost. Emphasis on the second syllable and make the vowel like a long 'e'. Dah-NEE-low."

"Got it. Is it a Filipino name?"

Danny stifled a yawn. "By association, yes. The Spanish occupation left a lot of culture crossover in the Philippines, including names like Danilo. Why?"

"I assumed there was a reason you'd opened a Filipino bakery, but never put the pieces together until tonight."

"Oh, right. My dad's roots are German and Filipino." He smiled. "My grandmother is the one who got my sister Thea and me baking, and she gave us her family's recipes. Dad came up with the bakery's name. I was going for artisan and pretentious, but he said it'd be better to go with a pun that'd make people smile but also be memorable. He's pretty much the only person who calls me Danilo. To everyone else I'm just Danny."

He yawned outright then, his eyes watering as they exited the elevator and approached Noah's door. "Ugh, I'm sorry. I dunno why I'm crashing so hard."

Noah pulled keys from his pocket. "Fight or flight instinct is a real thing. Your body needs time to recover."

"Guess that's why everything hurts, even after the ibuprofen. Well, that and I got knocked on my ass."

Noah waved him inside. "Have a seat. Can I get you some water? I don't have much in the way of food right now, but Jasper could find you some takeout if you're hungry."

"I'm not." Danny crossed the room to the couch and sat down, grunting at his body's aches. "Water would be great though, thanks. If you need to eat or whatever, Noah, don't mind me."

"I already ate. Are you sure you're not hungry?"

"So sure. Too tired to chew. And I swear I can still taste the juice bag the EMTs gave me, but I suppose that's better than tasting barf."

The surprise in Noah's face made Danny chuckle, but he felt awful a second later. What the hell was wrong with him? Someone had *died* tonight. Someone who still didn't have a name.

"Don't do that."

"Do what?"

"Beat yourself up for laughing."

Danny's jaw went slack. "How did you ...?"

"I can see it in your expression." Noah set a glass on the low table in front of Danny. "People cope with horror in different ways, and there's nothing wrong with using whatever means you have to get through it."

"Certainly feels wrong." Slugging several gulps of water,

Danny stared at the glass in his hands. "The guy in the park was so young, Noah."

"I know." Noah settled on the couch beside him. "I documented the scene."

"God, that's right. I don't ... Why would someone do that?"

"We don't know yet."

Would knowing make it better? Danny set the glass back on the table and leaned his elbows on his knees.

"Detective Callahan said I need time to process what I saw, but how? How do I reconcile finding someone dead in the playground without thinking about how it could have been me or someone who works on my crew? Fuck. I didn't recognize that guy, but he could have come in to Nice Buns."

"Maybe it's wrong of me to say, but I'm grateful it wasn't someone on your crew. Or you, Danny. You had a close call tonight." There was a world of sorrow in Noah's voice.

For a second, Danny couldn't breathe. Squeezing his eyes shut, he wrapped his arms around himself and held on, desperately fighting off what was shaping up to be the second panic attack of his life. His chest twisted when Noah once again set a hand between his shoulders, but that small contact helped immeasurably. Danny rocked himself as the tension in his body gradually ebbed, Noah's quiet, encouraging words grounding him enough to keep him from floating completely away.

"I'm sorry I missed your message," Noah said. "Cho and I were on another call, and I couldn't get away. Maybe this wouldn't have happened if I'd been able to meet up."

"Maybe. But that guy in the park would still be dead." Danny winced at his own croaky voice. "And you're here now. I need ..." Goosebumps rose on his arms as Noah shifted so their shoulders made contact.

"What? What do you need, Danny?"

"This." Danny opened his eyes. He glanced up into Noah's face and fell headlong into ocean-blue eyes.

Oh.

He'd never been this close to Noah before. Until tonight, the bakery's counters had always stood between them, and even in the ambulance, Noah'd been an arm's length away. Mere inches separated them now, with Noah watching Danny closely, his eyes framed by the longest lashes Danny had ever seen on a man. He frowned slightly when Danny didn't answer, his lips turning down at the corners just so. But they were still gorgeous and full, and shaped exactly the way Danny liked.

"Danny."

Holy shit. That murmur sent a wave of heat straight to Danny's groin and he waited, breathless as Noah raised a hand and brushed his knuckles over Danny's cheek, lingering over the bruise. The room around Danny blurred and fell away, and he sank further into the couch cushions, lips parting when Noah's gaze fell to his mouth.

A buzz ran through Danny. He watched Noah's eyes, tracking their movement over Danny's neck, shoulders, and chest, and his blood warmed even more. A soft gasp left him when Noah met his eyes again, the compassion in his face replaced with heat. Noah spread his fingers over Danny's jaw, and Danny couldn't help his groan. Fuck, he was hard. Aching, in fact, though Noah had barely touched him. And Danny wanted to kiss him more than he'd wanted anything in his whole life.

A loud ringing cut the air, so sudden Danny almost screamed.

"Shh. It's all right." Noah's voice was oddly tender. His expression shifted again, gentle now as he ran his thumb over Danny's lips in a slow, sensual drag that had Danny reeling. "You should sleep."

Dazed, Danny could only stare as Noah got to his feet. The ringing came again, this time accompanied by several loud bangs, and Noah cut a look across the room before he walked away. Danny's heart lurched into his throat.

No.

He tried to follow; he really did. But his bones were jelly and the weight of the exhaustion he'd carried since the mugging—since finding the body—dragged him down too far to return. He heard voices and wanted to get up. Help if he could. Make sure Noah was okay. Touch him again, God yes. But Danny couldn't do it. Couldn't do anything at all, actually, except close his eyes and sink.

CHAPTER 7

"Christ, Green. I was only gone for twenty minutes. What the hell did you do to him?"

"Nothing. How about you keep your voice down?" Noah held the door open for Detective Callahan but glanced over his shoulder at Danny, who'd passed out at last.

"Why?" Callahan shoved an armful of paper bags at Noah before stalking past him. "Kaes is clearly past caring. And white as a sheet!"

"Because he's exhausted." Moving to the kitchen island, Noah set the bags down, then scowled when Callahan bent and set his fingers against Danny's neck, clearly checking his pulse. "Hey, I told you already—I didn't lay a hand on him."

Which was not strictly true. Like any vampire, Noah could easily enthrall a bleeder if he wanted to and, once he got close enough, it'd been easy to knock Danny for a loop. Except … Noah hadn't truly meant to stun him. He'd just wanted to be close. Once he got there, nothing else in the world had mattered.

The air between them had crackled as they'd sat on the couch, and Noah's attraction for the sweet-faced baker had transformed into a hunger he hadn't bothered hiding. That need had further scrambled Danny's senses, which were already muddled by fatigue, leaving him dazed and loose limbed, staring up at Noah with blown pupils and his palms turned up and open on either side of his thighs. Setting the back of his head against the couch, he'd lifted his chin and exposed the long, pale column of his throat, every inch of him begging for touch.

Thunder filled Callahan's brow. "Do me a favor and shut up. You're talking like we didn't find a body emptied of blood tonight. Like you're not capable of doing the same thing to Kaes. Maybe even thought about doing it before I rang the goddamned doorbell."

Noah couldn't help bristling. "I didn't."

That wasn't a lie. Of course, Noah wanted to know how Danny's blood tasted. Thirst wasn't the only thing driving his desire, however, and the fact remained he wouldn't act on any of it. Not with Danny terrified and strung out. He wasn't about to explain himself to an asshole like Callahan either, who'd made up his mind about Noah and his species years before they'd ever met.

Scrubbing a hand over his head, Noah fought to keep his tone neutral. "Believe what you want, but I'm not going to hurt him. I'd also have to be monumentally stupid to even think about it given half the NYPD knows Danny is in my apartment."

"That's part of the problem, Green. You're not stupid— anyone who cares to pay attention can see it."

"Thank you?"

"It wasn't a compliment. I've seen the way you fuckers can charm people and you're smoother than most. Don't think I didn't notice the way you were eyeballing Kaes while I questioned him, and this was after you told me you hardly knew him."

"I *don't* know him outside of his bakery."

"Yeah, the place you go to buy bread you can't eat, which makes you a bigger creep than I thought, something I didn't think possible." Callahan sneered at him, then shifted his focus back to Danny. "You're lucky he hasn't already guessed what you are."

"I know." Noah thought about the last conversation he'd had with Cho on this topic and winced internally. Things really were going to get awkward now and he had no way around it. "Thank you for not outing me."

"I didn't do it for you. Fuck, Kaes needs to get himself some safer friends."

"We're not really friends. And he is safe with me."

The furrow was back on Callahan's forehead. "It's funny—I almost believe you mean that. The problem, Green, is that you wouldn't be able to help yourself if it came down to it. My cat watches birds through the windows with the same kind of attention you do Kaes and, like it or not, you *are* what you eat. Kaes could be your next meal and pretending otherwise doesn't make it less true."

Regret trickled through Noah. Callahan's prejudices against vampires weren't wholly unjustified. In most humans' eyes, Noah's species was a barely contained threat; even the most mild-mannered fanger could be compared to a grenade with a loose pin. While Noah hadn't meant to stun Danny, he clearly had, and oh, how easy it would have been to go much, much further, especially with Danny's defenses already weakened.

Yet, he hadn't. Yes, Noah was dangerous. Lethal, in fact. But he wouldn't take Danny simply because he could.

"I won't hurt him, Detective." He waited until he had Callahan's full attention before he continued. "I understand why you'd have trouble believing me. Why anyone would. But I've worked around humans a long time and I'm practiced at keeping my instincts under control, far more than you realize. Just like the blood eater behind the desk in the foyer and more than half the residents in this building." He watched Callahan flinch. "Vampires are more than stereotypes, Detective, and I know what I'm talking about when I say Danny is safe with me."

"God." Callahan made a face like he'd tasted something

bitter. "This is such a fucked-up conversation. You see that, right?"

Slowly, Noah shook his head. "No, I don't. I've been this way long enough that it's all I know. Whatever you think about vampires or me, we both know Danny's in less danger from the man who attacked him *here* than he would be at a hotel on his own or even surrounded by friends."

"If you say so. Not sure anyone's ever truly out of danger around someone like you."

Noah managed not to roll his eyes. He didn't feel much in the mood for yet another circular conversation with this man. "Trust me, *you're* out of danger. You're not my type, for one, and the nicotine high I'd get off your blood might finally kill me."

Callahan's bark of laughter seemed to surprise him as much as it did Noah, but the shadows in his dark eyes lightened. "You're sick. Glad to know my filthy habit has been good for one thing."

Pulling a throw blanket from the back of the couch, he tucked it around Danny's sleeping form, and when he stood straight again, seemed to truly take in the apartment around him for the first time.

"Nice place. More homey than I'd have expected."

"Because you expected boarded-up windows and a coffin on the floor?"

"Maybe." Callahan raised a brow. "Being a cop, I can't help wondering how a guy who works for the city can afford this neighborhood."

Noah huffed a dry laugh. "I don't think that has anything to do with your job or mine. And since you've asked without really asking, the apartment was a gift."

"Like ... from family?"

"Something like that. The blood eater who made me gave me this place."

Callahan's attitude turned wary. "Do they also live here?"

"No, they do not."

"Okay, good. I don't think I can handle more than one of you freaky fuckers at a time. No offense to your ... offspring, or whatever."

"I don't have any of those either, Detective. It's just me."

"Even better. Well, at least you don't have to worry about rent."

Noah shrugged. "Co-op fees are forever. I've had nearly a hundred years to save up my pennies and that helps." He wanted to smile at Callahan's obvious bewilderment.

"Jesus. How old were you when—" Callahan waved at him.

"Twenty-two," Noah replied.

Callahan didn't respond right away, and it was obvious he'd been taken off guard. Then again, Noah doubted he'd ever truly considered that vampires were made and not born.

"So young," Callahan said at last, in a much quieter voice. "Bet a handbook would have come in handy, huh?"

Noah snorted. "It wouldn't have hurt. But I've done okay. I've mostly lived and worked around humans since the change. Without issue," he added.

"So it seems." Callahan stared at him a moment longer before giving himself a good shake. He gestured to the brown paper bags Noah had set on the island. "I brought a few things from the bodega on the corner."

"Surely not for me?"

"Hah, no. There are eggs, milk, and bread in there and some prepared foods and fruits. You might want to have some more stuff delivered." He glanced around at the stainless-steel appliances in the kitchen. "This place looks functional enough but, there are things Kaes needs to be comfortable. Like plates and glasses, and things to help get food into his mouth so he doesn't have to eat with his hands."

"Yes, I recall the function of flatware."

"Good for you. But unless you have human guests on the regular, you'll have none of that stuff, and I'd remedy the situation now."

Huh. Noah peered over the edge of one of the bags. This was the strangest evening he'd had in quite some time. In the year he'd worked for the NYPD, Bert Callahan had asked Noah about his personal life exactly once, just six days ago and in relation to police work. Yet here they were, in Noah's home, discussing things he rarely spoke of to anyone, and the man did seem to want to help.

"Thank you. I appreciate your advice and the groceries."

"Yeah, well. Pretty soon you'll be stuck here until sunset." Callahan waved at the sky beyond the windows, which had brightened to a rosy gold. "Not sure if you need to crash but Kaes can at least feed himself while you do whatever the fuck you do during daylight hours."

"I mostly catch up on paperwork for the lab."

"That is surprisingly boring."

"Sorry to disappoint." Noah smirked. "I don't have much need for sleep anymore."

"Right. Don't forget—Kaes needs to file a report for the assault and the things that were stolen from him."

"I'll make sure it happens." Noah frowned. "I haven't had time to log into the lab yet and read up on whatever Cho processed at the scene, but I'd guess it wasn't much."

"You'd be right." Callahan met Noah's gaze. "He said the scene was squeaky fucking clean even after Kaes literally ran into the perp. There was a stamp of a tail-eating snake on the inside of the victim's left wrist though, which ties him to the kid in Jackson Square Park and probably Aaron Josephs. We both know what that means."

"That you'll be checking out The Last Drop."

"Actually no, though I do want to talk to you more about the bar," Callahan said. "What I meant was that we're going to ask the public for help ID'ing the victims. There's a press conference happening in a couple of hours. We'll get calls from every fanger conspiracy theory nut in the five boroughs since that's par for the course, but maybe we'll also get something we can use."

Noah nodded. Asking the city's citizens for help meant sifting through thousands of useless tips; he knew as much from his work with the CSU. Circulating information about the victims probably also meant that the name of his local blood bar was about to be known by a lot more people.

"What do you want to know about The Last Drop?" he asked.

Callahan's smile was thin. "What it'll take to get in. I tried myself yesterday and didn't get far. I had an extremely civilized conversation with Dominika Ludmilla though, the nice old lady who owns the place. She advised me to get a warrant if I planned to do more than grab a cocktail at her blood bar or any other in the city."

Noah knew Dominika Ludmilla by sight, having glimpsed her in The Last Drop on occasion and couldn't help feeling charmed by the idea of the tiny silver-haired lady ordering around this gruff cop. Still, he could tell where this conversation was headed. "My guess is that you don't have a warrant."

"You are correct. Which means I need your help again."

Noah pursed his lips. "This is turning into a habit."

"If it makes you feel better, I'm not happy about it either. But I need to get into that bar so I can start figuring out how The Last Drop is connected to three DBs."

"I think you mean 'if.'"

"No, I really don't." Callahan said, and Noah thought he looked very tired. "Green, I know you want to tell me to fuck off and die, and I get it. But the fact is, I have three suspicious deaths on my hands and, whether the killer is a vampire or not, they're still out there. I want that fucker off the streets before he kills anyone else, and I'll do whatever it takes to make sure it happens."

O

After seeing Callahan out, Noah drew the window shades and distracted himself with efforts to make his place more habitable for a bleeder. He stowed the contents of the grocery bags in the cupboards and refrigerator, carefully moving his own food supply to the very back of the bottom shelf, then arranged for Jasper to procure more human-based creature comforts, like throwaway plates and flatware and toiletries for the bathroom.

Though Noah took pains to be quiet as he moved around the place, he found it didn't matter. Danny slumbered on, hardly moving as the morning hours passed. Noah had just finished changing the sheets on his bed when a soft, choked noise reached his ears.

Striding back out to the main room, he found Danny sitting up, the blanket pooled around his waist and his eyes open. The bandana he'd been wearing on his head was balled in one fist and his short dark brown hair stood up in tufts.

"Okay, Danny?"

Danny's eyelids moved in a heavy blink. Noah moved closer, carefully keeping his movements slow as he took the seat beside him. Danny didn't appear to notice, his stare unfocused over the purpling bruise on his face, as if he were caught somewhere between slumber and true wakefulness.

"Danny?" Noah made his voice low. "Are you awake?"

Danny blinked again. "He's cold."

"Who is? Are you cold?"

"No. I'm okay." Slowly, he rubbed a hand over his head, further mussing his hair. "I can't ..." Brow furrowing slightly, he turned toward Noah, his expression going from blank to searching. "Am I home?"

Noah decided he'd keep things simple. "You're at my place. We agreed you could stay here, remember?" He frowned when Danny's face fell. "What's wrong?"

"Thought I was." Danny sighed, the sound so forlorn, Noah set a hand on the back of his neck. At the touch, Danny closed his eyes and hummed. "Is this okay?"

"Yes, it is," Noah replied.

He knew the words were right, but he wasn't truly prepared for Danny to shift closer and lean into his side. What the hell? Without thinking, he slid his arm around Danny's shoulders, then held his breath as Danny set his head on Noah's shoulder.

"Danny?"

The answer that came took the form of a soft puff of breath against Noah's neck. Because Danny had slipped back under into sleep in just the few seconds, his arms linked around Noah's waist and his body beautifully warm and solid. Noah held still. He knew he shouldn't like this. Holding this human. How easily —*perfectly*—Danny fit against him. Still, satisfaction settled over him in a warm wave that he didn't fight. He closed his eyes instead and sat, relaxed in a way he rarely felt, ears attuned to city's sounds while he breathed in the sweet, salty scent of the body beside him.

Hours passed before a light shiver shook Danny's frame, and it took no effort at all for Noah to lift him in his arms and stand. Danny slept on as Noah carried him to the bedroom and settled him on the bed. His eyelids fluttered as if he might wake, but he burrowed deeper into the pillows instead, pulling one into his arms. He snored softly as Noah pulled the clogs from his feet and the crumpled bandana from his hand, then drew the bedding up over him.

Straightening, Noah studied the slumbering form in his bed. Despite the beard stubble on his cheeks and chin, Danny looked terribly young in sleep. His eyelashes were dark against his fair skin and his strong brow relaxed, but it was the steady rise and fall of his ribs Noah watched most closely, those quiet breaths reassuring him in ways he didn't bother to examine. Particularly since Danny would likely be gone in a day or two.

His phone's buzz cut through Noah's musings and he quickly checked the screen.

10-10 reported in Kaes's building.

He frowned at Callahan's use of the police code for 'possible crime.' That was a bit vague from someone who was so often painfully blunt. Noah stepped out of the bedroom, then headed for his workstation on the other side of the apartment, tapping out a reply as he moved.

When?

06:00, Callahan replied. *Don't let that guy out of your sight.*

Noah hit the call button, sure now something was off and baffled Callahan didn't just come out and say so.

"What aren't you telling me?" he asked when the call had connected. "You almost had an embolism when I offered Danny a place to stay, and now you're telling me to keep him here?"

"A neighbor reported someone she didn't recognize leaving Kaes's apartment, Green, and we both know he hasn't been home."

Noah went still. "Damn it."

"Yeah." Callahan sounded distracted. "We've got a sketch artist with the neighbor now but, like Kaes, she said the perp's face was mostly obscured by a hood."

"Was there any damage to the apartment?"

"No, but that's hardly the point. The perp gained access to the building in broad daylight—"

"Which means we're not dealing with blood eaters."

"More like there's at least one human involved in these crimes."

Noah rolled his eyes. "Are you being serious right now?"

"I can't be anything but, Green," Callahan shot back. "Whoever gained access to Kaes's building showed no concern about being seen. That tells me he's not done looking for Kaes, and we now have a *second* person who can provide a partial ID."

Noah ran a hand over his mouth. "You think the neighbor is in danger?"

"We can't rule it out."

"Danny's going to freak."

Callahan made a noise like he agreed. "Keep him in your apartment until we get a better idea of what's going on. I know we talked about him filing a report at the precinct but given the circumstances, I'll bring everything to him instead."

"Fine. He's still out but I'll call as soon as he wakes."

"You do that. I'm gonna grab some sleep in the crib while I can, but I've stationed cars outside Kaes's building and across the street from his bakery." It sounded to Noah like Callahan was smothering a yawn. "I'll send a car to your place, too."

"Don't bother." Noah eyed the short hallway that led to his room and something fierce rose in his chest. *He* would keep Danny safe. The perp from the park wasn't getting anywhere near either of them. If Noah found him first ... He swallowed a growl. "I'll keep an eye on Danny, Detective. You just work on nailing this guy."

CHAPTER 8

Where the hell am I?

Danny stared up at an unfamiliar ceiling. He had no idea whose bed he was in or why he was still clad in jeans and a t-shirt, and definitely not why he smelled like the world's sweatiest loaf of bread. But a deep, familiar voice teased the edges of his hearing and—somehow—it kept him from freaking out.

Head swimming, he levered himself up and winced as his body ached. Memories crashed over him in a flood.

The playground. Being jumped. Chasing someone along the asphalt paths until he'd nearly tripped over a figure curled up on the ground. And Noah, voice soothing while Danny lost his shit.

Fuck.

Danny put his face in his hands and ow, his eye.

Noah had talked him down. Twice. Held Danny's hand and kept him sane, then offered up his sofa for as long as Danny needed. Which meant this was Noah's apartment. No doubt his bed too, but how the hell had Danny come to be in it?

"You started out on the couch."

Danny jumped a mile, a loud squawk tearing out of him, and dropped his hands to his lap. "Jesus!"

Noah winced. "Sorry. I thought you heard my knock."

"Not your fault."

Sighing, Danny pulled his knees toward his chest and wrapped his arms around them, and he tried not to stare. Because of course, Noah looked … fucking fantastic in civilian clothes, the neat jeans and gray jersey so unlike the endless navy uniforms Danny usually saw him in. Still not *entirely* casual, what with the clean shave and every strand of his golden-brown hair perfectly styled. The guy was immaculate. But then he hadn't slept in sweaty, yeast-smelly clothes he'd worked in the night before. And Danny was gawking at him like an absolute idiot.

Danny scrubbed his hands over his head. "So. I started out on the couch?"

"Yes." Hands clasped in front of him, Noah leaned against the doorframe. "You woke up after a while and seemed out of it, sort of half in and out of sleep. We talked for a bit, and I figured you'd rest better in a proper bed, so I brought you in here."

Well, that's fun.

Heat flashed over Danny's face. Trust him to cap off a truly awful night with a lucid dream in front of a guy who'd already seen him at his worst. Danny knew he was far from lucid during those episodes—he'd heard as much from friends and family and lovers over the years. He suspected he'd said or done something silly too, but then that was hardly surprising given humiliating himself in front of Noah Green was his letter of the day.

"Shit. I'm sorry. Sometimes, I sleepwalk when I'm overtired. Or sleeptalk, rather. Pretty sure I've never gotten up or walked around."

"You've been through a lot in the last twelve hours."

"Yeah, well. Panic attacks and puking take a lot out of a guy." Danny frowned then. "Wait. Did you say twelve hours?"

"More or less. It's one-thirty now, so—"

"Okay, good. I still have time before my shift at the bakery." Letting go of his knees, Danny drew the sheets aside. "Is it all right for me to go back home? I mean, I know that detective will probably read me the riot act if I do."

Noah's face was solemn. "I'd bet on it, yes. I told him I'd call as soon as you woke up. You have to file a complaint today and I'm sure you're hungry and want a shower." He paused at Danny's heartfelt groan.

"God, yes, I want a shower."

Smiling faintly, Noah waved at a bundle of clothes stacked on the foot of the bed. "There's a bathrobe there and a few other things you can wear until we get you something more suitable."

"Thank you." Danny snickered. "Not sure I'll be able to go anywhere in them, though. You're a lot taller than me."

"A few inches at most." The twinkle in Noah's eyes made Danny's stomach flip in a pleasant way. "But as I said, those are just temporary."

"Well that's good. I don't want to sound ungrateful, but the last thing I need is to flash a bunch of cops after the sweats you loaned me fall down. Am I going to the station on West 10th or somewhere else?" Danny tried to recall where he'd put the business card he'd been given. "I can't remember which precinct Detective Callahan works in."

"Don't worry about it. Callahan said he'd bring everything to you." Noah stood straight again but this time didn't meet Danny's eye. "I'll call him now and let him know you're awake."

"Okay."

Danny watched him walk off. Weird. He'd never seen Noah close down like that. Granted, Danny didn't know the guy well, but his gut told him something was off. Sitting there obsessing wouldn't get him anywhere though, so, with a groan, he swung his legs over the side of the bed, unsure which pained him more, his body's aches or the smell coming off him.

The shower made a world of difference though, and he felt so much better by the time he emerged from the bedroom dressed in the too-big sweats and carrying the sheets and his discarded clothes in his arms. The space beyond the bedroom was a single large area, which made it easy to immediately spot Detective Callahan at the kitchen island. The scene was almost homey. Danny smelled coffee and sweet, bready things, and jazz music played at a low volume on the computer workstation in the corner. But Callahan wasn't wearing a coat or suit jacket, and the gun in the cross-draw holster resting snug against his left ribs appeared *extra*-large and shiny and not at all homey to a city-dwelling, bread-baking nerd like Danny. He swallowed hard.

"Hi, Detective Callahan."

"Hello, Mr. Kaes." The detective wiped his mouth with a napkin, and it was then Danny noticed the food spread on the counter along with several large to-go cups of what he desperately hoped was coffee. "Nice shiner," Callahan added.

"Hah, thanks. And it's Danny, please." Danny scanned the room and nope, no sign of Noah. "Where'd he go?" he asked Callahan.

"Down to the concierge to pick up a delivery. Said not to wait on him to eat." Callahan nodded at the chair beside him. "Not that I ever would."

O...kay?

Danny frowned. What the heck did that mean? Setting the laundry in a pile on the floor, he seated himself and stared at the different rolls arranged across the platter. *Pan de coco* and Spanish Bread, as well as *asado* he could tell were filled with spicy-sweet chicken, just from the smell.

He gave the cop a smile. "Are these from my place?"

"Mmm-hmm. I dropped by Nice Buns so I could talk to your crew," Callahan said, "and your sister loaded me up with enough food and coffee to feed an army. She put your favorite rolls in a separate bag." He tipped his chin toward a small paper sack by Danny's elbow. "You need to call her, by the way, or she's going to come over here and kick your ass into next week. Thea's words, not mine."

Danny picked up the bag. "Sounds like her. How do you like our bread?"

"I get why there's a line out the door and Cho Min-jun goes back every chance he gets—everything I've put in my mouth is delicious." Callahan glanced at the half-eaten bun in his hand, then took another generous bite. "I'm not sure what it all is, and I don't even care. I had meat a minute ago and now this one's sweet."

"That's *pan de coco* in your hand. The filling is grated coconut, butter, and sugar, and it is dangerously delicious. Can I have one of those coffees?"

"Help yourself. I also have a stack of paperwork for you." Drawing a manila folder over the counter, Callahan flicked it open. "Obviously, we're aware of what happened to you yesterday, but the report is still important."

Danny worked his way through his meal and answered more questions, and though the food made him feel steadier, he didn't truly relax until the apartment door opened and Noah stepped back inside.

"Hi." Noah set a pair of cloth shopping bags beside the pile of laundry. "Those are for you. I ordered a few things you could wear while the rest of your clothes are in the washer."

Danny's insides swooped a little. "Shit, Noah, you didn't have to do that. You definitely don't need to do my laundry."

"It's no trouble." Noah shrugged. "You seemed concerned about the sweats falling down, so I figured you'd appreciate not having to worry about it for longer than necessary."

"Thank you." Despite the heat in his cheeks, Danny couldn't help grinning. He was such a sap. "Do you want coffee? I think Detective Callahan brought enough for everyone."

Noah shook his head. "I'm good, thanks. I already ate."

"If you're sure." Glancing back to Callahan, Danny was surprised to find him watching them. "Uh, can I go back to my apartment, Detective? My super hasn't called yet, but I already told you he's kind of a slacker and I'm guessing the locks haven't been rekeyed. If you want me to stay out of my place for longer I can, but I'd love to grab a few things before I start my shift tonight."

"About that." Callahan set his pen down and folded his hands, attitude more serious than it had been only moments ago. "You can't go back to your apartment just yet. Or work."

"What? Why not?" A chill worked its way through Danny as the detective and Noah traded another look. For two guys who didn't seem to like each other, they sure did a lot of talking with their eyes. "Did something happen?"

"Someone was in your apartment this morning," Callahan said. "Your neighbor saw them exit the unit as she was on her way out, and when she couldn't identify the person, she entered your apartment and realized you weren't at home."

Danny blinked. "Someone broke into my place?"

"No. Someone let themselves in," Callahan clarified. "They used your keys to enter the building and your unit, Mr. Kaes. They also may have gone through your things, so we have to assume they were searching for information about your location. Someone is trying to find you and the most obvious conclusion is that it's the same man who assaulted you in Bleecker Playground."

"But … I don't understand. Why would he be trying to find *me*?" The knot forming in Danny's chest pulled his voice thin. "It's not like I saw him do anything. I'm not even sure what he looks like."

"The suspect doesn't know that, Danny." Noah's voice was quiet. "For all he knows, you could ID him in a police lineup."

"Well, fuck."

"Now it's possible the guy may just have been trying to scare you," Callahan added, "but until we know the locks in your building have been changed, we need you to limit your movements and stay away from the places you'd usually go."

Danny closed his eyes and pulled in as much air as he could.

"Okay. But if my neighbor saw this guy too, can't you make my super do the thing I asked him to?"

"I've spoken with Mr. Tyler," Callahan said dryly. "He's been made aware of the urgency of this matter."

"Great." Danny opened his eyes again only to roll them. "He'll maybe get to it before the weekend is over, but I shouldn't get my hopes up." He grimaced at Noah. "I'm sorry about this."

"Don't be."

Danny turned back to Callahan. "What do I do now?"

"You stay here with Green. We've asked the public for help and we're tracking as many leads as we can find. There are also officers stationed at your apartment and Nice Buns in case this guy makes himself more visible."

Shit. Please, don't let anyone else have been hurt.

"Is everyone at the bakery okay? What about those locks? And my sister? My dad and stepmom live on the other side of her duplex." The lump in Danny's throat made it hard to speak, but Callahan held up a hand in a 'take it easy' kind of motion.

"Your sister had the bakery locks rekeyed this morning and no one's reported any kind of disturbance. Wherever the suspect is hiding, we don't believe your workplace or your family are on his radar."

Danny forced himself to meet Noah's eyes. "But then I shouldn't be *here*, right? Because this guy might try to hurt you and I don't want that."

"We believe the chances of anyone outside of the NYPD figuring out you're here are low. Not even Thea knows my address." Noah set his hand on Danny's shoulder. "If the man who hassled you does show his face, I can handle it."

"But …"

"Seriously, it'll be okay."

Noah's smile tied Danny's tongue. Made his head swimmy and his body thrum and Danny nearly got lost in those sensations. He bit back a gasp when Noah stepped away.

What the fuck had just happened?

"Don't worry about Green," Callahan was saying. "He's got skills."

It was a struggle for Danny to shift his attention back to the cop, and when he did, Callahan appeared oddly amused. Were all of Noah's working relationships with the NYPD this weird?

Blinking, Danny watched Noah pick up the pile of laundry from the floor. "I know I can't go back to my place—"

"Not for a few days."

"—and I get it, I really do." Danny ran a hand over his still damp hair. "But I need clothes and, like, my *stuff*, you know? I'll need to go *outside*. I can't stay here cooped up like a bird. Not to mention it's not right taking advantage of Noah like that."

"You're not taking advantage of anything." Noah sounded both calm and determined, two things Danny didn't feel at all. "I'm sure Detective Callahan and I can work something out to get you some of your things. Just give us a rough idea of what you need, and we'll work on making it happen."

"Okay, but—"

Callahan spoke over Danny. "I know you don't like this, kid, but we're trying to keep you safe."

"Yea-a-a-h but I'm not a kid." Danny knew he was bristling but found it hard to give a damn. "This is my *life*, Detective Callahan, and I've been taking care of myself for a long time."

Callahan made the calming gesture with his hands again but Noah's smooth voice soothed Danny far quicker.

"There's a private roof deck upstairs. It's not always warm at this time of year but there's a functioning fire pit and you can spend as much time up there as you need if you want a break from me."

A break from you is not what I want, Danny had time to think before Callahan stood, brow furrowed once again.

"How private is private?"

"The only access is through this apartment." Noah inclined his head toward a heavy-looking door set into a wall in the kitchen area. "This building is two stories taller than the ones surrounding it as well, which prevents an average person from getting up there via another roof."

"Huh. I'm starting to understand why you've lived here so long." Callahan looked almost impressed. "What about the non-average person? How hard would it be for someone like that to get into this unit from the roof?"

For a split-second, Danny was sure Noah hesitated, but he recovered almost instantly.

"Difficult but not impossible," he said. "I can show you, if you like."

Noah hadn't said so, but Danny took the invitation to include him as well as the cop and didn't hesitate to grab his jacket from the back of the couch where he'd left it. He followed Callahan around the kitchen island to the door, which he now saw bore three separate deadbolts. Noah slid them back and opened the door, revealing a narrow stairwell beyond. At its top, a second, equally heavy door was unbolted before Noah gestured Danny and the detective out past the bulkhead.

"Take as much time as you want," he said to Danny. "I've got a few things to do downstairs."

Danny bit his tongue against an urge to ask Noah to stay. He'd never been the needy guy who constantly wanted his hand held. So, he focused on his surroundings, which were, in a word, stunning, and found himself wondering again how Noah could afford this place. At the roof's center, a sheltered seating area beckoned with low couches and chairs arranged about the firepit, and the skyline unfolded around them in a gorgeous 360-degree view.

"Damn." The admiration in Callahan's voice was plain. "Every time I think I've got this guy figured out, he messes with my head."

Yeah. That cut close to home. Danny'd thought he'd been getting to know Noah too, at least a little. But this place, this view … they spoke of money that a guy who worked for the city probably didn't have. And the way Noah and Callahan spoke to each other, like there was something going on in the background neither of them wanted to share ... all of it made Danny wonder who the hell Noah Green really was.

"What about a non-average person? How hard would it be for them to get up there?"

He stared at the skyline until it blurred, replaying the question in his head and bouncing it against some of his own. How could anyone get up to the roof *or* windows of an eight-story building without using the elevator or fire escape? What the fuck was a non-average person? And why had Noah stayed inside instead of coming out here with them?

Heading for the stairs, Danny was back in the now empty kitchen within seconds. He glanced at his surroundings, unsure of what he was searching for but certain it was critical if only he could ... Wait. Danny's gaze fell on the remains of his meal, and, without conscious thought, he turned toward the refrigerator.

"I already ate."

That was Noah's standard response any time he was offered coffee or baked goods at the bakery. But he'd said it here too, in his own apartment—last night when they'd come in and again today after he'd been offered coffee. Now that he thought about it, Danny'd never seen Noah eat or drink. Not once. Sure, maybe the guy wasn't hungry. Maybe he'd refused food out of politeness or because he was watching his weight. Fuck, Noah could be diabetic for all Danny knew. But something told him none of those options fit.

He opened the refrigerator door. Saw food on the shelves though not much, which made it easy to shift things around until he found the tall glass bottles arranged in a row at the back of the bottom shelf.

"Danny."

Straightening, he turned around, the image burned into his vision: bottles filled with a deep red liquid more vivid than anything else on the shelves. Until Danny blinked and the image faded, leaving behind an ordinary kitchen and faces he knew, one of which now belonged to a stranger.

Noah stood silent as Danny stared him down. His gaze never wavered despite his solemn, almost sad expression, and he didn't flinch at all when the refrigerator door shut with a muffled *fwump*.

"What the fuck, Noah?" Danny was proud his voice didn't waver. "When were you going to tell me you're a goddamned fanger?"

CHAPTER 9

This wasn't going to plan. Noah sighed. Not that he'd *had* a plan, which was the reason this day had gone straight to hell in a handbasket and Danny was incandescently pissed off. That was all squarely on Noah. He'd seen this moment coming when he'd offered Danny a place to stay. And still said nothing in some misguided attempt to protect him from … what exactly?

Danny had said it himself; he wasn't a child. He didn't need anyone making decisions for him about what he could or could not handle in his own life, regardless of anyone's good intentions.

"There never seemed to be a good time," Noah said, and fell silent again when Danny looked even angrier.

"Really? You don't think today would have been a good time? Or maybe this morning when you told me that I could stay here? What about all those times you came into Nice Buns and picked up food I know you never ate? Wouldn't those have been good times to tell me, Noah?" Twin spots of color burned high on his cheeks. "Why the hell do you even buy the stuff I bake?"

"The lab geeks love it. And you *know* how much Min and his daughter like your bread." Frowning, Noah glanced from Danny to Callahan and back. "Is that really so hard to understand? That I'd buy food for other people?"

"It's ... surprising, maybe," Callahan offered in a measured tone. He made a vague gesture with one hand toward Noah, almost like a wave. "Supernaturals aren't exactly known for their generosity, Green."

"How would you know?" Noah demanded. "Outside of giving me a hard time, how many of us do you have regular contact with?"

"Not many. Supernaturals tend to be law-abiding, or at least adept at keeping their crimes under wraps."

Ugh. Callahan's tone rubbed Noah exactly the wrong way, even more than the bullshit comment. He knew how to handle Callahan being an ass, but this weirdly sympathetic side was throwing him.

He turned back to Danny. "I wanted to tell you. Went back and forth a dozen times in my head about whether you needed to know what I am. And yes, I know I should have said something, especially if you were going to stay here. But I've learned over time that not everyone *wants* to know the truth, Danny, even when they say they do."

"And you decided I was one of those people?" The anger on Danny's face faded, turning softer and sadder, and Noah felt even worse.

"Yes. I shouldn't have."

"You're right. You should have respected me enough to make up my own mind. I hate being lied to and I really hate being judged."

"I didn't—"

"You did," Danny insisted. "You made up your mind about how I'd react, then decided it wasn't worth finding out if any of it was true. That *I* wasn't worth it."

Noah's stomach tumbled. He didn't understand the depth of the pain he glimpsed in Danny's eyes, but it was clear someone had hurt him even before Noah had added fuel to the fire. "I'm sorry."

But Danny fixed his eyes on the floor. "I don't want to talk to you right now. I'm ... I need to check in with Thea," he muttered, shoulders rigid as he headed for the stairs leading to the roof.

Neither Noah nor Callahan spoke as his footfalls on the steps echoed back to them, but once it was clear Danny was on the roof, Noah looked at the detective once more.

"I'll keep an eye on him."

Callahan licked his lips. "All right. You were right about the roof—it's definitely secure. But you do realize it's still light out, correct?"

"Yes. I can hear him from here."

"For real?"

Noah gave a small shrug. "Sure, if I listen closely. Not that I think I'll have to, but if there's a reason I need to step outside, I'm fast enough to keep from damaging myself much."

"Yeesh. You really are a creepy motherfanger." A gentler grimace passed over Callahan's face. "I can ask Kaes to come back down, if—"

"No, leave him be. He needs some space right now and the least I can do is give it to him." Noah made himself ignore the murmur of Danny's voice, easily audible to him. "Is there anything else you need from me, Detective?"

"Not right now." Callahan walked to the kitchen island and collected his things. "Not sure I mentioned it, but the ME didn't get much from the body Kaes found in the playground. She confirmed the guy was hypothermic in addition to missing way too much blood, but we may get something from the traffic and street cams in the area. A few caught a figure in a hooded sweatshirt moving away from the park, though he slipped them after about a half a block, either by blending in with other pedestrians or using an alley. Cho wants to widen the search by a few blocks and see if the same figure pops anywhere else." Callahan grunted. "Also, it's been determined the wounds on the neck are inconsistent with bites. That's true of Josephs and the John Doe from Jackson Square as well."

Noah nodded slowly. "The perpetrator is likely human."

"Yes. And we still have no idea what method was used to extract the blood from the bodies. I'd keep your mouth shut about this with Kaes."

"I'm sorry, but did you miss the part where he said he doesn't like things being kept from him?"

"That's fine when it comes to your personal life, Green, but this is police business." Callahan waved a hand at the ceiling and roof beyond. "We don't have anything to give Kaes right now that'll make him feel any better about this situation and until we do, I say we keep his level of freak-out as low as possible." He frowned.

"I can't believe I'm saying this, but I would have preferred you worked the crime scene at Kaes's building. You might have picked up on stuff the rest of us would miss, what with you being … you."

Noah set the plates he was holding in the sink. First Cho and now Callahan. How strange that, for the first time since he'd been brought into the supernatural life, the humans around him actually wanted him to act like a vampire.

"I could go over there."

"Sure. Go on over after sunset, let me know what you find."

"No, I mean now. Take me in the trunk of your car." Noah ignored Callahan's wide eyes. "It wouldn't be the first time. Cho and I were at Jacobson's apartment until almost eight in the morning on Wednesday and I ended up in the back of the van under mylar while he drove me home."

"Don't take this the wrong way, but I'd have paid to see that."

"Not sure there is a right way I could take it, Detective."

"Fair." Callahan's lips were pursed, and Noah could tell he was trying not to smile. "But while I genuinely appreciate your dedication to the job, the answer is no, I will not take you over there in the trunk of my car. Stay here and keep an eye on Kaes. My chief has already been in touch with yours to let her know you'd be out for a day or two." His voice became less strident. "For the record, I don't blame you for holding back telling Kaes about the vamp thing. I'd have done the same in your shoes."

Noah laughed quietly, the taste bitter in his mouth. "That's no surprise. Everyone in the NYPD knows how you feel about working with me."

"Yeah." The two watched each other in silence for a moment before Callahan walked to the front door. "I'm sure Kaes will come around," he called back. "The guy needs your help, whether he's ready to admit it or not."

The parting shot did nothing to ease Noah's conflict. Going to his desk, he logged in to the CSU's portal, his mood growing more gloomy every minute. He should have been at the crime scene, regardless of what time of day the suspect had entered Danny's building. Should be at the lab right now, poring over the photos and evidence the unit had collected and using his unique perspective in a way that, for once, might be constructive.

He'd reviewed roughly half of the crime scene photos taken at Bleecker Playground when Danny's voice cut off above him. Noah stayed seated, unsure of what he wanted to happen next. What if Danny picked another fight? Or refused to speak at all? Noah dreaded hearing sharp words, but the idea he might be shut out completely was much more sobering, no matter how determined he was to do the right thing.

But why? It's not like you wanted to be Danny's friend.

Except maybe Noah did. Which was stupid right now, no matter which way he looked at it. Danny's safety was more important than whether he forgave Noah for having lied to him, and his well-being a greater priority than banter they might yet have over bread. The idea of not having those friendly conversations with Danny—probably not seeing him anymore—still made Noah … sad. More so than he would have expected. Which was no doubt a sign he badly needed distance from the bleeder on his roof.

Noah'd gotten comfortable around Danny Kaes and hadn't even noticed.

The silence stretched, five seconds, then ten, as Noah waited for another sign of movement. It thickened, growing choking in an instant, and the hairs on the back of Noah's neck rose. Without a second thought, he stood and called Danny's name, even knowing there was no way for a human on the roof to hear him at this distance. Noah pricked his ears, listening harder on his way across the room, now hyper-aware of traffic humming on the streets and birds crying out overhead, sounds he didn't give a damn about when they had nothing to do with the man he'd let go up to the roof alone.

At the stairwell door, he called again, then pressed his lips into a hard line at the awful quiet. And then he was climbing, his strides a shade too fast, taking him to the bulkhead's outer door. He peered beyond it to the deck, which stood stark in the harsh afternoon light.

"Danny?" Noah stepped forward, stopping just inside the threshold, and strained to catch a heartbeat or breath over the city's ambient noise. "I need you to answer me, Kaes, or I'm coming out!"

The silence that met the warning set Noah's body in motion without his having to think at all. And in the seconds that followed, he burned.

Sprinting to the shelter, he whipped around, heat instantly building under his skin despite the canopy above him. There was no cloud cover, and the sunlight was too strong at this hour, even late in the afternoon with an autumnal chill in the air. Eyes squinted almost closed, he brought an arm up to shield his eyes and scanned the rest of the roof, his breath catching as he spotted a flurry of movement behind the stair bulkhead he'd just left. Noah went on full alert, teeth bared and muscles tensed to spring, and only the sight of Danny's face, slack with shock, snapped him back to reality.

What the hell? Did this guy think they were playing a game?

Danny ran toward him, shouting for Noah to get back inside, but Noah was already moving. He had the presence of mind to hope no one was watching from taller buildings nearby as he made another mad dash for the bulkhead door, his very cells screaming for dark and cool and quiet. The shade slipped over him, door thumping shut, and though Noah tried to stay silent, a whine came out of him anyway and he couldn't find the energy to give a damn who heard it.

Fuck, he hurt.

"Jesus, Noah! Are you okay?" Danny's voice trembled, as did the hand he set on Noah's shoulder.

Noah's nerves bristled under the touch. He'd been outside ten seconds at most but every part of him felt desiccated. Oh, *God* he was thirsty. And he hardly dared breathe, because if he caught even the barest scent of human meat right now, he had no idea what he'd do.

All right, yes he did. He'd eat the guy standing behind him.

Eyes clenched closed, Noah pressed his forehead against the stairwell wall. "Give me a minute," he muttered, marshaling control as best he could, aware Danny sounded terrified through his babbling.

"I'm sorry. I just needed a couple of minutes to myself. But I didn't think you'd come outside! Why did you do that, Noah?"

"You didn't answer."

"I know." Danny's voice sounded thick. "I know I didn't and I'm so sorry. It was stupid. I just … I didn't realize you'd worry. Let's go downstairs where there's less light, okay? I can help you."

Less light sounded great. They descended to the door below, and Noah opened his eyes. He didn't really need Danny's help. Already, the pain from being exposed was manageable. He could feel where his skin had been scorched but with some blood and rest he'd recover. Noah didn't say as much, though. Partly because he liked Danny's hands on him and didn't want to think too hard about why. But more so because he could almost feel how much Danny *needed* to help.

Guilt was a funny emotion. Far more powerful than people liked to admit. Noah had been a blood eater far longer than he'd been a human and still knew what it felt like being sucked under by its heavy tide.

Back in the kitchen, he gently shook Danny off and went to the refrigerator. The blast of frigid air when he opened the door made him sigh and the sensation of icy glass on his palm and fingers was so, so good. Normally, Noah liked his blood warmed. He didn't give a damn about anything right now though, so long as the blood was in him. Having Danny so close
…

"I need to feed," he got out, eyes stinging just from the refrigerator's tiny light. "You don't want to see this."

"It's okay." Danny sounded calmer now. "Feeding is nothing new to me. You're not my first vamp."

Noah's whole body tingled at those words, but he didn't turn around. Uncapping the bottle in his hand, he lifted it to his lips, and everything around him receded under the roar filling his ears.

Yes.

Even cold, the blood was luscious. Salty. Meaty. Everything.

All.

It slaked Noah's thirst and warmed him, and soothed the final remnants of the pain that came with burning.

Pleasure swept through him in a devastating wave. Eyes screwed shut, he emptied the bottle and gasped, head lolling back in the following shock of arousal. Noah couldn't stop the low sound that filled his chest, bliss coursing through him head to toe. Then someone made a soft gasp behind him, and the tiny sound pulled Noah back and forced him to reach deep for control.

Recapping the bottle, he set it on top of the refrigerator and slowly turned around. He found Danny staring, eyes still too wide, but though he appeared shaken by the scene on the roof, there was more than fear in his expression. Longing and need flashed in his eyes, making them glow as Danny moved closer. Noah knew that look. And liked it.

"Not your first vamp, huh?" He licked his lips. "I don't know how to feel about that." The surprise in Danny's laugh made him smile, and it only grew wider as a flush stained Danny's cheeks.

Mmm, gorgeous.

"I wouldn't blame you for being pissed," Danny said. "Not after the way I acted. You're not the only one who's been keeping secrets. Should have told you I've been with a vamp before."

"I don't know how it would have come up. Besides, the level of secret between yours and mine aren't exactly in the same ballpark."

Danny took another step toward him. "You're sunburned," he murmured, then slowly raised his hand. Touch light, he traced his finger over the bridge of Noah's nose, then cupped his cheek so gently, as if Noah were made of glass. "Does it hurt?"

"Not anymore."

"What's going to happen? Will it fade or turn to freckles?"

"Both."

"I can't wait to see it."

The heat from his fingers was intoxicating. "Danny," Noah started but shut his mouth again when Danny shook his head and moved closer yet.

"I know what you're going to say. That I'm not in my right head."

"You're not." Neither was Noah because *damn*, it was hard staying still with a bleeder so close. *This* bleeder, Danny, who was touching Noah and scrambling his senses completely. Who needed truth right now more than anything. "Not after everything you've been through," Noah made himself say. "And me lying. You just watched me drink a pint of cow's blood, for Christ's sake. You ought to be trying to get as far away from me as you can."

Danny shook his head slowly. "I don't care about that."

"You should."

"Why? So, you're a vampire and I wish I'd known sooner. I'd still have been interested in you the first night you came into the bakery." A scant inch separated them now. "I just wish I knew how much of what I feel when I look at you may not be strictly natural."

Noah held Danny's stare. "I don't know the answer. But I'm interested in you, too. Have been for a while."

"Why didn't you do anything about it? You've been coming to the bakery for months."

"I know. But I didn't want you to know what I am. And, honestly, it's been a while since I met a bleeder in the wild."

"I have no idea what that means. But I also don't care." Looping his arms around Noah's neck, Danny's eyes shone. "I only care about now, and I'll be damned if anything else matters."

Noah had just enough time to smile before Danny rose onto his toes and kissed it right off his mouth.

CHAPTER 10

Electricity jolted through Danny, so intense his knees wobbled. The kiss was every bit as devastating as he could have imagined, wild and consuming, like a fire burning out of control. He squeezed his eyes shut as the copper tang of blood hit his tongue and he groaned, rapture rolling through him in a wave that had him panting and hard in seconds. But then the thought he'd given voice to only moments ago flashed through his mind and everything inside him went rigid.

Danny didn't know *what* he was feeling. And couldn't trust himself around Noah.

Around any vampire, really, because all one had to do was get close enough and turn on the thrall even a tiny bit and Danny's brain turned to mush. Just like it had early that morning when he'd been an utter wreck and simply looking into Noah's eyes had rendered him weak. As if his body had recognized the fanger beside him though his brain still hadn't caught up.

It took everything Danny had to break the kiss. And his heart sank further when he understood the only reason he was able was because Noah let him. He backed away, moving until his ass hit the kitchen island and stopped him going any further.

Danny's body was chilled, and the cold inside him intensified as the surprise on Noah's face shifted to apology then wariness, though he didn't say a word.

Danny's throat went tight.

They could have died up on that roof. Noah had been burning for God's sake, pain evident in every line of his body as he'd shuddered against the stairwell wall. Danny'd gotten up in his space too, something he'd *known* not to do. But instead of draining Danny dry, Noah'd battled his instincts and together they'd helped each other regain control. Danny could hardly wrap his head around how close they'd come to losing … everything. Or how fucking good touching Noah made him feel.

The problem was, he still had no way of knowing if any of it was real.

"You … damnit, Noah, you should have told me!" His voice broke. "I thought I was just exhausted and strung out this morning. That the panic attack was messing with my head. But it was *you* messing me up, wasn't it? Making me all dopey and compliant so I'd do what you wanted."

Noah was shaking his head even before Danny'd finished talking. "No. That isn't what happened at all. I wasn't trying to make you do anything."

Danny wanted to laugh. Noah sounded offended, and how fucking dare he? "I told you—I've been around vamps before. I know what you're capable of."

"Exactly." A muscle jumped in Noah's jaw. "You know what I am. What I could have done to you this morning when we were sitting on that couch. But I didn't. I didn't want to with you."

Danny had to look away. He wasn't sure what was worse— Noah screwing with his head or stopping himself because he didn't want Danny at all. And if that didn't speak to how messed up Danny's whole life had become, he wasn't sure what would.

"What a disaster," he muttered. "Well. At least I know why I swooned like a babe in a bodice ripper."

"Don't."

"No, *you* don't." Danny bit out the words, his voice gruff as he turned to Noah again. "I don't want your apologies. I want you to be straight with me and stop acting like I can't handle hearing the truth. And I really, *really* want you to stay away from me so I can think."

The pain on Noah's face took Danny off guard, but he was all out of fucks to give. Stupid vampire and those damned blue eyes, turning his thoughts inside out. How long had Danny been under his sway? From the first time Noah'd walked into the bakery? God. That probably explained why he felt so unsettled if more than a couple of days passed without a visit from Noah. Danny scrubbed his face with his hands.

"Why did you come into Nice Buns?"

Noah furrowed his brow. "What do you mean?"

"I mean why come into my store at all? We both know the draw wasn't bread. Was this ... has this all been some kind of game for you?"

Fresh anger washed through him as he thought about all the evenings he'd talked to Noah about his rolls, coaxing him with extra pieces in the contents of boxes he bought for Cho or the guys at the police lab. Noah hadn't tried them; he couldn't have eaten the bread even if he'd wanted to. Which meant he'd knowingly let Danny talk out his ass over and over and smiled as he'd done it. That understanding zapped the fire in Danny and sent his stomach straight through the floor.

I'm such a fool.

He was across the room with a hand on the doorknob before his brain had truly formed the intention to move.

"Danny, wait!"

"Done talking," he said through lips that felt oddly numb. "I'm going home."

A big body caged him against the door from behind then, and Danny went still, barely able to breathe. Oh, man, this was bad.

A melting sensation crept over him, urging Danny to sink backward into Noah and stay there. Tears filled his eyes.

"Leave me alone, Noah."

"I can't."

The regret in Noah's voice was so clear. He sounded just as tired and sad and done with this day as Danny, but Danny gritted his teeth against the sudden urge toward leniency. He hated this. Hated Noah right now, in fact, and the oh-so-patient, let's-be-reasonable vibe he seemed intent on shoving down Danny's throat.

"Need space so I can think," he got out, every inch of him tensed for a fight.

"I know you do. I'll give it to you," Noah replied, "but you have to promise you'll stay here. You can't leave, Danny, not when that guy is still out there and has all the information he needs to find you."

Danny wanted to pound his fists against the door. "You're not making sense! I can't put my whole world on hold because some asshole has my address—he may never show his face again! I have a life I need to get back to, and it's like you and the cops are pretending I can camp out here forever because none of it matters." He bit back a whine as Noah shifted against him, pressing closer so his cheek rested on Danny's temple.

Why did this have to feel so good?

"Noah, please—"

"Of course your life matters." That low voice crawled right inside Danny's brain. "I know you're angry. A lot of terrible things have happened, none of them your fault, and I can't make any of it better. But I *can* help the police keep you safe. That's why we brought you here. The man who attacked you doesn't know you're here. Doesn't know you have cops and supernaturals standing in his way."

"Supernaturals? As in plural?"

"There are more in the building besides me. And that's

another thing we can use to protect you, which is what I'm going to do even if you come out of this hating me."

Danny almost growled. "I'd hate you a lot less right now if you'd back the fuck off of me so I can get my head on straight!"

"I will." Fuck, Noah sounded so infuriatingly calm. "I won't come near you again if you *promise* you won't bolt. I don't want to have to chase you down."

"So don't."

"Then it'd be up to Jasper and the concierge staff, or the cops parked outside, and I know you don't want that either."

Danny set his forehead against the door. He was being an ass and knew it. He was also totally out of options if he wanted to stay both safe and sane.

"I won't go anywhere," he said with a sigh. "I promise."

He kept still as Noah peeled himself away, waiting until the craving to touch and be touched receded enough he could trust himself to open his eyes. He heard water running as he turned himself around, and his gaze immediately went to Noah, who'd retreated to the kitchen sink and was keeping his eyes lowered.

Danny cleared his throat. "Why did you come into Nice Buns?"

"I'm not sure." Noah rinsed the glass bottle that had held the blood he'd drunk. "I try to avoid humans when they're eating. They'll ignore all kinds of things you'd think would be obvious, but they're quick to notice the person in their midst who doesn't put food or drink in their mouth." He shut off the water and reached for a dishtowel.

"At first, I thought that was one of the reasons you were always after me with food when I came into the bakery—maybe you'd noticed I didn't want any. But then I saw you were like that with everyone and understood it's part of who you are. You like taking care of the people around you."

Danny didn't reply. But he moved from the door toward the middle of the room and stood by Noah's sofa. He fought every second against an urge to be angry that Noah still wouldn't look at him.

"Anyway, I think you know the police lab is out in Queens, which means riding trains," Noah said. "I walk to the station on 14th from here, which takes me past Nice Buns." Pausing, he set the bottle he'd cleaned and dried on the counter, then frowned gently.

"I'm still not sure what caught my eye. The light from the windows. Maybe the crowd gathered outside because the line in the shop got too long. Something made me want to stop, though I knew it was foolish. What was I going to do in a bakery besides admire the food I couldn't eat?" He pursed his lips then, looking almost bashful and damnit but Danny liked that way too much.

"What is it?" he asked.

"I stood outside some nights so I could watch your crew at work. I'm sure that sounds strange."

"Yes and no." Danny's voice was quiet to his own ears. "There's a pizzeria in the neighborhood where I grew up. The guys who work there stand in the window and toss and spin the dough for the pies and put on a show. There are always people standing outside and watching."

Sighing, he settled his ass against the back of the sofa, then crossed his arms over his chest. He hadn't thought about Papa Fiore's in years. "When I was in middle school, my lola would meet me by the shop most days on my way home. Lola is like 'grandma' for a lot of Filipinos," he added. "She let me watch the pizza guys throw pies anytime I wanted. She always loved pizza. And I seriously thought those guys were the shit."

Noah laughed softly but still didn't look up, and Danny tried not to sound hurt when he asked his next question.

"Were you listening to us through the glass when you stood outside of the bakery?"

"Not purposely. I tune that kind of noise out as much as I can because it's constant and distracting. If I listened to every conversation happening around me, I'd be too overstimulated to stay upright. But I could hear that you and your team laughed a lot while you worked and sometimes there was dancing." Noah licked his lips. "I never intended to get any closer than the windows outside, but I'll admit I was curious after hearing Merlin say he'd teach you all to cha-cha."

Danny laughed then but it got stuck in his throat, and his choked noise finally drew Noah's gaze. Which only made Danny ache and, to his horror, find himself precariously close to tears. He'd been so busy being angry tonight. At Noah for not being truthful and himself for being absurdly oblivious. Because he could see now that he'd gone out of his way to be exactly that around Noah. Danny knew how to spot supernaturals, and vampires in particular. If a tiny part of him had ever wondered if the tall guy in the CSU windbreaker was something more than human, he'd squashed the idea because he hadn't wanted it to be true.

Which meant Danny might have been wrong about Noah.

He hadn't been trying to deceive Danny—he'd been trying to connect. He'd gotten used to standing on the outside looking in, exactly the way Danny sometimes felt. The difference was that Noah'd probably been doing it for such a long time, he might not know any other way.

"I've had all kinds of ideas in my head," Danny told him. "Imagined you've been fucking with me, just because you could. Toying with me."

Noah's expression fell. "I wouldn't."

"I want to believe you. I think I almost do. The problem is, I've experienced that kind of behavior with someone like you and I'm still figuring out how to get past it. Which is just one more reason I wish you'd told me the truth from the beginning."

"Would you have been okay with it?" Noah asked. "If I'd mentioned my vampirism the first time I walked into your place, then asked you about the breads you'd made anyway? Because I imagine the answer would have been 'no' after what you just said about 'someone like me'. You'd have kicked me out of Nice Buns and told me not to come back."

Danny raised his brows. "So this was better? Me finding a half-dozen pints of blood in your refrigerator and then yelling about it?"

"I'm sure we both could have done without the surprise reveal or the shouting." The gleam in Noah's eyes told Danny he was trying hard not to crack up. "But I liked talking with you in the evenings. I can't say the same about many humans, Danny, and now I'm hoping you'll want to keep talking to me even knowing what I am."

Danny fought not to roll his eyes. Vampires usually brought the drama; leave it to him to find one completely hell-bent on being logical.

"Sure, talking is cool. I'm still mad at you for lying but ..." He blew out a long breath. "I don't think I have the energy to stay that way. And if we're going to be stuck with each other for the foreseeable future, I say we make the best of it."

"All right, but—"

"But nothing. If I've learned anything in the last twenty-four hours, it's that all this could be gone tomorrow. After last night and today, can you think of a good reason not to just enjoy life? Because I can't. Unless your babysitting duties to the NYPD are going to get in the way."

"They might," Noah said. "But I hardly think it matters if you don't trust me to get closer than a room's length away."

Ugh, again with the logic. Danny still found himself nodding. "You're right. I'll work on that. And since we're being all truthful, this is probably a good time for me to say that you're not what I expected. At all. And I'm not one for surprises."

"You know, I got that." Noah's tone was dry as fresh flour. "I'll do my best not to let any more happen, but I won't make a promise I can't keep. Am I allowed to ask questions, too? Like the meaning behind 'you're not my first vamp' even though I can probably guess?"

His effort to mimic Danny's Brooklyn accent made him laugh.

"Oh man—you have to do that for Merlin sometime. And yeah, you can ask questions. If I can ask what you meant when you said it'd been a while since you'd met a bleeder in the wild." Danny chewed the inside of his cheek for a beat. "Or how this happened to you. How you were turned and when."

Noah didn't get a chance to reply before a chime from the workstation on his desk brought him out from behind the island. He gave Danny a wide berth as he moved and kept his hands up as if to prove he wasn't dangerous.

"I'm not a horse." Danny frowned at him. "You don't have to walk around on eggshells because you're afraid I'll be spooked."

Noah gave him a small smile as he picked up his phone, but it soon disappeared, and he turned his attention to the windows. Danny saw then that the sky beyond the open shades was shading rose and gold, a sign they were nearing sunset.

"What happened?" he asked.

"I have to go in."

"I thought Callahan wanted you to stay here?"

Noah simply nodded. "He did. But now he wants my help, and Cho's on his way to pick me up."

Danny narrowed his eyes. Despite the argument and his insistence on being given room, the idea of Noah being *anywhere* but here didn't sit well at all. They hadn't settled anything, plus it was too light, and what the hell else was Danny going to do here alone besides sit and stare at the walls? "Does wherever you're going have to do with the guy from Bleecker Playground?"

"Possibly." Noah moved his mouth like he was going to elaborate, then shook his head. "Cho didn't give me a lot of information, but even if he had, I wouldn't be free to discuss what I knew."

Dread pricked at Danny. He thought that non-answer was answer enough. "I'm really supposed to stay here?"

"Yes. Callahan's going to station some more uniforms here in the building."

"What, like out in the hall? Are you telling me I'm actually under armed guard?"

"They've been out in their car before now—this is just a lateral shift indoors." Noah sounded almost amused. "Nothing has changed about keeping you safe and away from places that might put you back on your attacker's radar."

"Attacker." A weird, squeaky laugh worked its way out of Danny. "We both know the guy is killing people, or at least working with the person who is. I don't see what point there is in my hiding when he's already been in my apartment."

"I'm sorry I don't have better news." Noah met Danny's eyes without flinching. "But staying away from the places you'd normally go is the safer option until the police have a better idea of what's going on, if not for you then the people in your life."

Danny hated this so goddamned much. "Fine, fine. But being stuck outside of my own life is killing me, Noah. It's like … I'm caught somewhere I don't belong. If I could go to work or get some of my things, or even do stuff that makes me feel *normal* instead of caged up, I'd probably be a lot less snappy."

"You have a right to be snappy. Feeling like you don't know which way is up is hard and I know sharing space with someone like me doesn't help. I'll try to figure something out." Noah gestured to the apartment around them. "For now, make yourself at home, okay? I'll send you the Wi-Fi password and there's plenty of human foods, and we can talk more when I get back."

Danny turned to the windows as Noah left the room, and there were goosebumps on his arms. He didn't want to be alone.

More like you don't want to be left.

Fuck everything if that wasn't true.

CHAPTER 11

Striding out of his building with a baseball cap jammed low over his eyes, Noah hurried toward the CSU van, skin stinging as the last of the daylight slipped over him. He still felt raw from the earlier sun exposure and being outside wasn't doing him any favors. Burning wasn't the only reason Noah was off balance, of course. Walking away from Danny had scraped like a raw nerve, especially with Danny still angry and so much between them uncertain. Noah had no real idea of where they stood or how he was going to make anything better.

Cho's eyebrow went up even before Noah had closed the passenger side door. "What's up with your face? You look like a white boy just back from Spring Break, all red and freckly and like you need to be dipped in aloe."

"Got some sun and shouldn't have. Kind of like a white boy just back from Spring Break who needs to be dipped in aloe. Here." He handed Cho a set of keys on a ring. "These will get you into the building and my apartment and the concierge staff already have your and Callahan's names."

"Why would I need to get into your apartment?"

"Maybe you won't. But if Danny needs help and I'm not around, I want you to be able to get in there."

Cho stared at the keys for several long moments before looking up. "What happened?"

"Nothing. Why?"

"I'm not sure. You're sunburned for one. And two, acting strange. Like … I don't even know what this is. But both are a weird look on you, Noah."

Noah laughed and pulled the cap from his head. "It's been a long, strange day, and I get the feeling it'll only get stranger."

"Oh, good!" Pocketing the keys and ring, Cho turned his attention to easing the van out into traffic. "How's Danny holding up? Keeping it together as much as he can?"

"Keeping it together sounds accurate," Noah agreed. "His injuries were superficial, but his emotions took a hit. He's still processing what happened."

"I'm sure being able to stay with a *friend* helps."

"I like how you make 'friend' sound X-rated." Noah shook his head at Cho's chuckling.

"I almost shit a brick when I heard you took him to your place."

"I'm pretty sure Callahan did. I thought his jaw was going to fall off his face."

Cho outright cackled. "Damn, I'm sorry I missed that." He was quiet a moment before speaking again. "Danny knows, right? About you?"

"Yeah. Callahan didn't tell you?"

"Tell me what?" Cho was frowning when Noah glanced his way. "He asked me to come get you but it's not like we talked."

"There was some drama and we're still working it out. But Danny was going to find out anyway, what with the stuff I keep in my refrigerator."

"Gross. It was about time, though. Watching you pretend you aren't into the guy is one of the best, most excruciating things I've ever witnessed."

Noah rolled his eyes. "I'm not talking about this with you."

"I'm not talking about it with you either. But he's really okay?"

"He's strong. More so than you'd guess just looking at him."

Danny's fiery side had surprised Noah after so many easy, late-night conversations over the bakery's counters. He'd liked that spark and sizzle and seeing Danny fierce. "He's not thrilled at being temporarily under house arrest, but he gets it. Cops in the hall maybe less so. And then there's Callahan with my number on speed-dial. The man has been in my apartment twice in under twenty-four hours and it's like my world has been turned upside down. Warren G. Harding was president the last time I had a human roommate."

Cho made a thoughtful noise. "Okay, you were right about this night getting stranger. But listen. The scene we're headed to is going to be like the others. The details I already have sound very goddamned familiar." The bleak note in his voice caught Noah's attention. "Three bodies in a week is a spree, but if you add Josephs in ... shit, Noah. We could be looking at a serial killer with almost no cooling-off period."

Neither spoke as they drove further downtown, Cho's music filling their silence. The tension at the scene once they arrived was palpable, hanging like a shroud over the stone-faced cops working it. As had been the case with the victims found earlier in the week, the body in James J. Walker Park was male, early-to-mid-twenties, with no ID, a small wound in his neck, a UV stamp on the inside of one wrist, and a shocking lack of blood in his body. Outside of the typical bits of trash one might find in a city park, the crime scene was bare of evidence and there had been no witnesses to the crime, which meant making an ID still rested squarely on the shoulders of Danny Kaes, a disquieting thought given how thoroughly the perp seemed to vanish into the night after each killing.

"You said you don't smell anything unusual right?" Cho asked Noah. "And by unusual, I mean vampy?"

"Not that's fresh, no."

"Once more proving this case is the weirdest shit ever."

Framing another shot, Noah frowned. Like the other men found, this victim was located nearly at the park's center and positioned on the ground, though close enough to a bench he might have been sitting on it shortly before death.

"Cho. Josephs' neighbor said he found him on the couch, as opposed to his bed, right?"

Cho looked at Noah. "That's right."

"The couch was located at the center of Josephs' apartment. Kind of like this spot is at the center of the park." He gestured to the bench by the body. "Why do you think the killer does that? Brings the vics further into the parks?"

"Instead of leaving them by an entrance, you mean?" Cho glanced at the trees and paths surrounding them. "Interesting question. The wounds on the victims' necks were fresh, indicating they were made roughly around the time of death or shortly before. So why kill this guy here? Why not do it closer to the entrance and make a getaway easier? We haven't found any blood at the scenes, so it seems likely he's carrying it out of the parks with him—lugging a half-gallon of it around has got to be awkward."

Noah nodded. "That's another weird thing. It's dark enough at this time of night to provide cover for all kinds of stuff, but the streets around these parks are rarely deserted, even late at night, and there are streetlights everywhere. We haven't had good luck so far finding witnesses, but all it takes is one person in the wrong place at the wrong time—"

"—and the whole thing is blown," Cho finished. "Like what happened with Danny. He shouldn't have been in Bleecker Playground at the same time as the perp, but he left work earlier than usual. He'd have missed the whole thing otherwise, and we'd have been in and out of there before he even knew what was happening."

Noah winced. "Maybe. Or, he'd have found the body later on that morning without being mugged."

"Good point. It does seem like he was destined to make the discovery, unfortunately. I know he took it hard, but at least there wasn't a ton of gore. Somehow. I'm still not sure how that happened given the perp literally knocked into Danny but somehow kept whatever blood he was carrying from spilling." Cho blinked then, clearly struck by his own words. "Unless he *wasn't* carrying blood. Because maybe … maybe the bloodletting happens somewhere else, and the parks are just where he's bringing the victims to die."

"Huh." Noah pondered that. "Meaning he walks them in here and waits for them to stop breathing? That's—"

"Sick as fuck." Cho ran a hand over his mouth. "And I hate that I can see it. Josephs still doesn't fit because he wasn't left in a park. But the hypothermia among all of the victims … that would help hasten their shock and decline."

"And could explain why the bodies have been positioned near benches. He leads them in, gets them settled, then lets biology take over."

"Would you do that, Green?" Callahan stepped into the glow cast by the spotlights, face oddly blank as he stared at Noah. "Drain a blood sack in one place and bring them someplace pretty to die?"

Noah let his camera hang from the strap around his neck. "No. I told you already that I make efforts to keep from killing them at all."

Something ugly flashed in Callahan's eyes. "Yeah, I remember. That's why you go to the blood bars. But you had to have made mistakes, right? Back in the day when you first got your fangs and probably snapped at every passing human? There's no way every human you latched on to walked away with a smile."

"None of which has anything to do with this crime scene tonight," Cho cut in. "Noah didn't kill *this* guy and giving him shit about a past you know nothing about gets us nowhere."

Callahan made a disgruntled noise, but the hardness in his eyes eased. "Is Kaes still pissed at you?" he asked Noah.

"Yes. We talked it out some, but he's angry about a lot of things."

Turning back to his work, Noah pretended the detectives weren't watching him and, within a few seconds, Callahan cleared his throat.

"Walk me through what you've got," he said, "approaching it from this idea you two cooked up where the vic is drained before they enter the park. You really think this guy walked in here voluntarily? And no one passing by noticed he was in a bad way?"

Cho squatted down beside the body and used his flashlight to further illuminate the small hole in the victim's neck. "Depending on size, age, and general health, an adult can lose close to fifteen percent of their blood without noticing any side effects. Once you pass fifteen percent, symptoms like confusion or disorientation may come on, and some people pass out. Supposing they stay conscious, a second person with reasonable strength probably wouldn't have much trouble steering them here."

"The low light would keep a passerby from seeing their faces." Noah cast another glance at the bench. "All the killer would need to do is sit beside the vic, maybe put an arm around his shoulder and they'd look like any other couple."

"A couple who hangs out late at night in the cold?" Callahan's gaze held a challenge when he met Noah's again, but Noah wasn't daunted.

"Not every couple feels welcome showing affection in a bar or restaurant, or even in their homes. Hanging out after hours in a quiet place like a park is sometimes the best option available."

Callahan rolled his eyes. "Fine. Let's say you're right and the killer brings the vic here. Does the blood loss make them easy to manage or does the perp need extra skills to be persuasive?"

Noah fought off an urge to scoff. Why did this guy have such a hard-on for vamps? Cho had no difficulty picking Callahan's idea apart.

"The blood loss is enough. The vics would be weakened and probably not fully aware of what was happening to them. Take Josephs at the ED. His chart said he was barely conscious, and I'll bet he was too out of it to understand where he was. The whole thing will go a lot faster if a body is hypothermic, which we already know is happening to these vics before they die."

"Josephs wasn't left outside in a park, though," Callahan said. "His neighbor found him on the couch in his apartment."

"True, but the heat in the apartment was turned way down. It was fifty-five degrees inside the rooms when Noah and I were there, so ..." Cho raised his eyebrows at Callahan. "The guy was inside a set of walls, but that was just geography. He might as well have been out here with the rest of the vics."

"Why wasn't he? What makes Josephs different from the rest of these guys?" Callahan asked. "The neighbor said he was single, right? That he dated around and hadn't been exclusive with any one guy for a couple of years."

"Correct," Cho said. "Outside of the one particular set of clothes, Noah didn't find any scent markers that were out of the ordinary."

"Yeah, don't get me started on how weird it is that you literally *sniffed* around for evidence," Callahan muttered, squatting beside the body. "Or that I'm the one who asked you to do it." He cast an uneasy glance at Noah. "Is there anything on this guy that smells in common with the others?"

Noah stared at him for what felt like forever. Despite his conversation with Cho about not holding back, the question—coming from Callahan of all people—rankled. Noah wasn't prepared to drop his human façade in front of someone who regularly derided him for something he couldn't control. He just hoped Cho backed him up.

"I haven't checked this vic for scent markers," he finally said.

"Why not?"

"I'm paid to photograph the scenes and stay out of the way as much as possible, and that's what I've done."

Callahan cocked an eyebrow at him. "You're telling me you shut off your sense of smell when you're walking around a crime scene?"

"I breathe through my mouth around bodies, especially when there's blood present."

"I ... God, you're weird."

Noah's voice came out flat. "I'm a blood eater, Detective, something you enjoy reminding me of often. But my job is documenting those crime scenes, not acting like some kind of dog-vampire mutant."

"Well, maybe it's time your job was changed. Think he could do it?" Callahan asked Cho. "Identify commonalities by smell?"

Noah's heart sank when Cho didn't answer right away, instead rubbing the back of his neck with one hand.

"If they exist? Yeah, I think he can," Cho finally said. "Doesn't mean it's not weird to ask him to do it, Bert. I'm not even sure we *can* ask without getting into a mess with HR."

"I know." Callahan held up a hand before either Noah or Cho could speak. "Believe me, I *know*. But we're still missing a real connection between these vics and Josephs and we keep coming up with nothing. No prints to match the ones from Kaes's apartment, no cigarette butts, or gum wrappers. Not even a single fucking sneaker print to run through the SoleMate database. So, for now, Josephs is the vic we know best. Maybe the killer knew him better than the others, too. Hooked up with him on the regular or was even his friend. If we can find *anything* to link these men together or to Danny Kaes's studio, maybe we can catch this fucking guy and I'll be able to really sleep the next time I try."

The apology in Cho's gaze when he looked Noah's way dashed any hopes he'd held of not being treated like a dog-vampire mutant.

O

"I know you don't want to do this." Cho set a series of bags on the table with a sigh. "And I can't imagine that evidence like scent markers will hold up in court, but we can worry about that if and when the time comes."

Arms folded over his chest, Noah leveled a glare at his handler. He'd always been good at keeping his moods from affecting his work but tonight ... well. Sulking might be an ugly word, but he felt justified doing it. He wanted to sneer at Cho's sheepish attitude too, because while he clearly felt bad for asking Noah to sniff a bunch of clothing, he'd been quick to arrange for the evidence to be brought out of storage.

Noah knew he wasn't being fair. Cho and Callahan were trying to solve crimes. Catching the man who'd been leaving bodies in the city's parks would be happy news for Danny, too. But Noah's inner crab refused to be quelled. He didn't *like* this at all. And was hardly aware he'd been muttering about all the favors he'd be collecting from the NYPD in the future until Cho's ears turned an unattractive shade of red.

He still met Noah's gaze calmly. "Do you want me to step out and give you some privacy?"

"We both know you can't." Uncrossing his arms, Noah moved the bag of clothes they'd collected at Aaron Josephs' apartment to the side. "You've been the lead tech at every scene, and you need to be here. Just promise me Callahan won't hear the recording because we both know he won't hesitate to rub it in my face."

Cho frowned. "I wouldn't do that to you or anyone, and neither would anyone in this lab. I'll make note of your observations, just like I do of my own when I'm examining evidence, and that should be plenty for anyone to work with."

"Fine."

Cho got the recording started while Noah examined the contents of a second bag.

"Clothing collected from Aaron Josephs at West Village Health," Noah said for the record. Unfolding the shirt and jeans, he brought them close to his face and inhaled, then held the breath for several seconds. The scents on these clothes were vastly different from those he'd singled out at Josephs' apartment.

"Something medicinal. Sharp. Like ... band-aids. *Peroxide*," he said, and yes, that piece was clear now. "This is a smell like hydrogen peroxide. I remember it from the spray bottles we keep in the van for disinfecting equipment. Danny said he caught something similar on the guy who mugged him, didn't he?"

"Yes, he did." Cho sounded tense.

"There's ... earth. Like garden soil."

"Which would make sense on the vics we found at the parks, but Josephs died at the ED so that doesn't track. Anything else?"

"Iron. No rust."

"Maybe from whatever was used to make the wound in his throat." There was excitement in Cho's voice now, but Noah was already reaching for the bag holding the clothes that had been on the body left in Jackson Square Park.

The same notes were present, all underscored by the sweet salt of human sweat. But that odor was more intense here, acrid and cloying in a way Noah knew very well.

"Earth, medicine, and iron again. But this man was scared." Noah glanced down at the flannel shirt in his hands. "He might have been too out of it to fight back, but he was afraid of what was happening to him. He knew something was wrong."

Cho blinked when Noah looked back up. "You can smell that?"

"Yes."

"And Josephs *wasn't* afraid?"

"No. There was nothing on any of Josephs' clothes even close to this."

"Shit, Noah."

Lips a tight line, Noah opened the bags of evidence collected from the remaining two victims and quickly found the same combination of notes: earth, metal, medicine, fear. His head spun at their potency, though, and he wondered almost dazedly why they seemed to increase with every second.

"They're the same," he got out, voice rough and deeper than it had been when he'd sat down. "I need ... this is too—"

A burst of fear stink hit him like a physical wall then, so thick the foundations of his control buckled. That was the moment Noah understood he was breathing in more than old scents on discarded clothes. The fear in the room with him was *alive* because it was pouring off the man seated across the table, no doubt staring at Noah in abject horror.

Noah stopped breathing entirely. If he looked up right now, Cho might run and that wasn't a thing Noah ever wanted to see. A large part of him would want to give chase. And if he did, his working relationships within the CSU—and his friendship with Cho—would never recover.

Eyes lowered, Noah pushed away from the table and got out of the room, moving faster than he knew was wise. He headed for the stairwell leading to the roof of the building that housed the police lab and waited until he was far from the bulkhead and surrounded by fresh air before he started to drop his guard. It was all he could do not to growl when the door behind him banged open.

"Noah!"

"I need a minute," he threw over his shoulder without fully turning around. "Just ... stay where you are until I say you can move."

"I'm *sorry*," Cho called back, his voice strained. "I didn't mean for any of that to happen."

Noah closed his eyes. "I know. Neither did I."

But he should have known better. His control was shaky tonight and his emotions all over the place. The burning he'd experienced earlier in the day could be to blame. But, in truth, he hadn't been himself since he'd walked off Bleecker Playground and seen Danny in the back of the ambulance.

Noah had no idea what to make of it.

Cho stayed quiet while he got himself together. Regret poured off him in big waves when Noah finally recrossed the roof to his side, and his eyes were troubled.

"We should talk about this," he started, then paused at Noah's headshake.

That didn't sound good. Noah didn't expect anything his handler had to say would. He and Cho had always worked well together, but this was the second time in a week Noah's control over himself had slipped, and there was no way Cho could let it slide. Or should. A heavy sensation filled Noah's chest.

He liked this job. Liked Cho. He'd screwed up badly enough that tonight could be his last with the CSU and the idea of moving on to something else felt … wrong. Which was a strange thought for Noah to have and very unlike him.

"What is there to say?" He sighed. "I started to lose it again. You reacted the way any bleeder would."

"You started to lose it because I put you in a position you couldn't have anticipated. That is on me." Cho frowned. "I'm your handler. I should have thought through what I was asking you to do more carefully."

"I suppose? But we both know it doesn't matter at this point." Noah squared his shoulders. "I understand if you want the MonsterBoard to transfer me out."

Cho's surprise would have been comical under any other circumstances. "Um, no? I don't want you to leave. I like working with you, Noah. And you gave us more information in fifteen minutes than we've been able to collect in a week. I told you, you're *good* at this. Like really good. As much as I appreciate your skills with a camera, I think you're being wasted acting only as a photographer."

Noah couldn't help smiling. "Thanks, I think."

"You're welcome." Cho smiled too. "And I mean it. You

should be doing more on top of shooting crime scenes and I'm going to talk to the brass about getting you certified. *If* you want me to."

"Not sure it matters what I want. Especially since they're going to laugh you right out of the room. Besides, you nearly wet your pants just looking at me back there."

"This is true. Because you were being scary as fuck." Cho's laugh sounded strained, but his gaze was deadly serious. "And again that was on me. Obviously, we'll need to figure out some new boundaries to keep each of us from driving the other over the edge, but I want you doing more. We'd never have gotten the details you've been able to pick up and now we can connect the victims, definitively."

"Because they smell the same." Noah grimaced. "You're right. I don't see how that evidence will stand up in court if we even get that far."

"Maybe it won't. But now I know we need to process the victims' clothes again and throw every test we have at them. Because if you *smelled* dirt and peroxide on them, maybe the nerds in the trace lab can find it." Glee filtered over Cho's face. "That, my friend, *will* stand up in court."

Noah didn't answer. He should have been celebrating. He'd wanted more from this job, almost from the beginning. To use the monstrous part of himself to do something good. Help victims like Danny feel safe again. And now maybe he could. The trouble was, Danny might not want Noah's help anymore. Because while the police were inching closer to identifying a killer, Noah could almost feel Danny slipping away.

CHAPTER 12

November 14
Sunday, 4:10 A.M.

"Damn, those smell amazing. Are they muffins?"

Officer Hadim, one of the cops keeping watch over Danny, leaned forward in his seat, eyeing the tray in Danny's hand. Danny gave him a smile.

"Cheese cupcakes," he replied. "Sweet vanilla sponge cake mixed with grated cheddar for a shot of salt, then topped with more cheese. So tasty you don't even need frosting."

"Who needs frosting when you can have more cheese?" That from the officer named Gaddy, a rookie and Hadim's trainee. She paced before the counter now, fanning herself with her uniform's hat, its badge gleaming under the lights. "I could have gone my whole life not knowing cupcakes with cheese existed," she said. "Now I'll be in your bakery every chance I get, discovering more things I don't need to eat."

"You're welcome." Danny set the muffin tin on a cooling rack and picked a baking sheet up next, this one filled with cookies. For the first time since his life had blown up, he felt relaxed. Or less like falling apart maybe. The air around him was hot, and he hummed along with the music coming from Noah's flatscreen TV as he headed for the oven. He'd been streaming old episodes of *Glee* for hours, because few things went better with marathon baking than McKinley High singing, dancing, and drama.

Hadim bit into a chocolate-stuffed roll and scanned the plates and trays covering the kitchen's counters. "Were you serious about us taking this stuff when our shift ends?" he asked around his chewing.

"Yep. As much as you can carry," Danny said. "There's only so much bread I can eat on my own."

He did his best not to dwell on the glance Hadim and Gaddy exchanged. Of course they knew about Noah—everyone in the NYPD would know a vamp worked among them, if only through word of mouth. Not that Danny was thinking about Noah's lying ass—much. His goal tonight was to ignore his super-fucked-up life, which he'd done quite well, thank you, by turning to the tools available to him and calling in a favor from his sister.

Thea'd come through for Danny, thank God. He'd been on his own for almost twelve hours now, with only his thoughts and the cops working the shifts in the hallway for company. The second-shift officers had brought in the bags Thea'd sent over from Nice Buns, then came back when Danny had asked, more than happy to sample the fruits of his labor. He'd sent them off with bags of baked goods after Hadim and Gaddy had arrived for the night shift, and Danny had gone right back to work and filled the kitchen back up.

He was at the sink washing bowls when Hadim's phone chimed, and he eavesdropped shamelessly as the officers checked in with command. Unfortunately, he didn't learn anything beyond what time yet another shift of officers could be expected, which meant he was still banned from places he'd normally go, a state of affairs that instantly tanked his mood.

Danny stared down at the water. He wanted to keep baking —the buzz in his head demanded it—but he'd been awake almost eighteen hours and was starting to feel the physical effects. He was considering brewing up another pot of espresso when a figure loomed over him, and Danny found himself confronted by Noah's frown.

"Yo." He hated the waver in his voice. "Where the hell did you come from?"

Noah stepped back so fast it was almost a leap. "I'm sorry. Why are you awake?"

"Because I am." Danny shrugged. "I needed something to do and figured I'd make myself useful. I know you can't eat this stuff, but the rest of the cops in the place can."

"And have been, according to Officers Hadim and Gaddy. You've made some new fans tonight." Cho Min-jun strolled up with an outstretched hand and Danny managed a smile as he quickly dried his own and took it. "Callahan's not sure whether to hug or strangle you since you messed with his whole guarding-the-door plan, but he'll want to eat the hell out of everything in sight anyway, same as me."

"Please, help yourself." Danny waved at the trays. "Take as much home to Kage as you think she'd eat."

"Oh, I will. If you sit down with a plate too, because you look about as whipped as I feel. Noah, you take over washing and Callahan can bring us all up to speed."

Danny considered complaining. He wasn't a dude in distress, and he didn't need coddling. But he found it hard to speak as Cho ushered him around the island while Noah backed away farther, giving them both a large berth. Clearly, he was trying to respect Danny's earlier demands for space. So why did the gesture make Danny want to flinch now?

Because you are a wreck and don't know what the fuck you are doing.

And yeah, Danny felt seconds away from losing it yet again, throat thick and eyes stinging. He kept his gaze lowered and didn't say much when a plate and cup of tea appeared in front of him, but he paid close attention to the voices around him. The snack worked like magic too, quickly smoothing out his snarly mood, and he felt a whole lot steadier by the time the uniformed officers headed out. That was when Callahan, Cho, and Noah started talking in earnest about, of all things, a West Village blood bar Danny knew well.

"I'd love to tag along," Cho said, "though it's been a while since I was in any kind of bar. I'm sure I could pull off a UC gig, though. Maybe fake some vampire whammy." He grinned at Callahan's narrow look. "What?"

"You're about as undercover as a car crash. And why would anyone want to walk in there at all? No offense, Green."

"None taken."

Cho, in the meantime, appeared skeptical. "You're so full of shit, Bert. You're dying to look around The Last Drop and it has nothing to do with police work."

"I already know what I'll find," Callahan replied. "A place humans go to meet fangers and hopefully not end up dead."

Noah raised a brow at him. "I've already told you—not every human who walks into a blood bar is there as a donor. Most just go for the cocktails and staring."

"I'm sure they enjoy a lot of both." Callahan's expression turned arch. "The only reason you don't think the bloodex scene is completely fucked, Green, is because you play for Team Fangbanger."

Danny knew his eyes were wide, though Noah looked almost amused.

"Maybe. But blood bars aren't the hellscapes you imagine, Detective. And no one walks out looking like someone used a hole punch on their throat."

"That's true." Oops. Danny swallowed as three sets of eyes swung his way. He hadn't meant to say the words out loud but the obvious interest in Noah's expression spurred him on. "If blood bars weren't subject to membership regulations and some of the weirdest zoning laws in the city, the average person wouldn't know there was anything special about them."

"Despite vampires roaming around freely and blood exchange events?" Callahan scoffed. "That'd ping my weird-o-meter, if not the average person's."

"Only because you've got the wrong idea about bloodex events. They're like social clubs—people meet up and talk about a thing they're drawn to, the same way sports fans or car buffs or comic book collectors do," Danny said. "An *actual* exchange almost never happens in public unless it's part of a demonstration or ceremony. As for vamps roaming around, they do that anyway, Detective Callahan, whether you're in a blood bar or not."

Understanding dawned on Callahan's face. "Are you a donor, Mr. Kaes?"

"With respect, that's none of your business."

"With equal respect, that's not a no. Can I assume you've been to The Last Drop?"

Danny sighed. "Sure. I haven't been there in a while, but it's kind of an institution for this neighborhood."

"Green's local watering hole, too. Funny you never ran into each other."

God, Danny's whole life might be different right now if he'd met Noah in the shadows of a blood bar instead of over the bakery's counter. But Noah merely shrugged.

"We might have if we didn't work nights," he said to Callahan. "But I'm already on duty when the bars open their doors and I know Danny is the same. That's probably the same reason the first time we met *outside* of Nice Buns was yesterday at Bleecker Playground."

Whoa.

Danny stared at him. "That was *yesterday*? I feel like I've been in this apartment for a week!"

"Probably because you made enough food to last that long."

Danny snorted on a laugh before he could stop it, which made Cho chuckle too, and then all three of them were snickering like fools. Callahan made a show of sneering at them.

"Mr. Kaes, I need a favor." He regarded Noah for several beats before meeting Danny's eyes again. "And I wouldn't ask if I didn't believe you're in a unique position to help me."

O

Danny felt drunk with fatigue by the time Callahan and Cho headed out. He weaved slightly as he stood up from his stool at the island, aware of how guarded Noah appeared, as if he expected another meltdown. Which was fair. Only a few hours ago, Danny absolutely might have lost his composure. He'd never been asked to work with the police before, and definitely not while posing as the donor half of an inter-species couple. *With* a guy he'd crushed on for weeks before that little slice of fun had been turned upside-down along with the rest of his life.

Danny thought he had a right to lash out. He just didn't want to. He was done being emo and resentful that Noah hadn't come out and told him about being supernatural. And since Danny's world was about as pleasant as a dumpster fire at the moment, patching up the friendship they'd been building seemed more important right now than taking a stand he wasn't sure he needed to.

"You're too quiet," he said to Noah. "I know you have an opinion about what Callahan's asking us to do. The vein pulsing in your forehead says so."

Noah's lips quirked into a near smile. "There's nothing pulsing in my forehead."

"True. But you do have an opinion."

"Yes. We can talk after you've slept, and Callahan isn't around to offer opinions I don't need."

"What is it with you two? You're like a divorced couple who are only polite because a judge ordered you to make nice for your kids."

"Does that make Cho and you the kids?" Noah walked around the island, then gestured in the direction of the bedroom.

"Callahan doesn't like me," he said. "Any supernatural, actually, but blood eaters in particular. He'd have had me fired by now if only he'd figured out how to get around department regulations."

Huh. Danny'd never gotten a vibe that Callahan had it out for Noah. True, they bickered and snapped, and there were times the detective edged into the mean zone. But it seemed the cop needed the vampire around far more than the other way around and knew it.

Nearing the bedroom, Danny paused outside the door and turned so he could face Noah. He frowned at the distance between them. "So why are you helping him? I get why Callahan asked me to walk into The Last Drop—he needs a human who understands the scene. But you ... You don't have to go with me, Noah."

"I want to." Noah slid his hands in his pockets. "Most days on the job, I'm not trained to do more than support Cho and the CSU. But this case is different. I know things the cops don't, purely because of what I am. And if something is off at the bar, we both know I'll see it before any bleeder with a badge." His face was so grave, Danny's fingers actually itched to touch him. "For the first time in ... maybe *ever*, I can really help someone. And I want to, Danny. I'd like to help get justice for you and guys like Marty Jensen, who died in Bleecker Playground not long before you found him."

Danny covered his mouth with one hand. Holy shit. "We know who he is?" he asked when he trusted his voice not to shake.

Noah gave him a tiny nod. "Jensen's partner filed a missing person's report when he didn't come home, and the police were able to match his description to the body you found." He blew a long breath through his nose. "I don't want anyone else going through that, Danny. To feel scared the way you have. So, I'll help where I can, despite Callahan being an ass. If we can prove a vampire wasn't involved in the murders while we get you back to your life, it'll be worth it."

The conviction rolling off him humbled Danny to his core. "Thank you," he said quietly. "I don't know what to say."

"You don't have to say anything. I know you find it hard to believe, but I am on your side."

Danny's throat went tight. He really needed sleep. But more, to make Noah understand that he did believe him. That he was grateful for more than the promise in Noah's words. And needed him terribly right now, though getting the words out stripped him bare.

So show him.

His heart beat so hard he wondered Noah couldn't hear it. Closing the distance between them, Danny took Noah's hands in his and instantly, his cells seemed to hum.

"I know you're on my side," he said, "and I'm sorry I was such a dick to you yesterday. The truth is, I'm afraid of the hold you have over me, Noah. The last time I let a vamp in my life, I didn't always make good decisions. But you … I know that you're different. Not everything I feel when I'm around you is because you're a vampire."

"Are you sure?" Noah looked almost weary. "We both know how easy it would be for me to convince you to do almost anything."

Danny nodded slowly. "I'm sure. You're not trying to sway me into doing things I don't want. You wouldn't do that."

Not to me.

That notion was too big and scary to voice. Regardless, Danny believed it, his certainty growing with each breath. And it seemed maybe Noah heard the unspoken words too, because he bent and kissed Danny, and the mere brush of his lips lit Danny up from head to toe.

Wrapping his arms around Noah, Danny deepened the kiss, his insides blazing with a buzz that went straight to his dick. Instantly, achingly hard, he gasped as Noah crowded him up against the wall and fought the urge to melt into him as the kisses grew rougher. But then Noah groaned, and the low, feral noise made Danny's knees wobble.

"Oh, shit. Need to touch you, Noah. Right the fuck now."

Noah's low laugh curled around him. "You're sure this is what you want?"

"Quit asking me, man—I know what I'm doing." Danny laughed along with him. He doubted he'd have been able to stop even if he'd wanted to—the simple act of keeping his eyes open was already nearing impossible. Danny wanted no part in stopping, however, because it had been far too long since someone had touched him like this. Galen had been all about the blood, wanting little else beyond the occasional kiss or embrace. But Noah genuinely seemed to enjoy touching Danny, and Danny soaked it up greedily. He loved being kissed and held and lying with a partner skin against skin for no other reason than to drown in feeling good. And right now he needed that as badly as he needed air.

"I want to feel something with you," he murmured. "My whole life is fucked right now, Noah. I can't go home or to work, or even outside without a babysitter. But I can do this, here and now with you, and I *want* it."

So goddamned much. To kiss and fuck and come so hard he forgot his name with this otherworldly man who made him feel alive, despite the specter of death that hovered so close.

Again, Noah seemed to understand what Danny didn't say. He kept an arm around him as they moved into the bedroom, then took a moment to turn on the bedside lamp. Eyes bright, he slid a hand under Danny's t-shirt, skimming his abs with his fingertips, the heat in the caress so delicious Danny hissed.

It felt good—right—to let go with Noah.

To surrender.

So, he did.

And though his body trembled, Danny's heart remained quiet, an eye in the storm of near overwhelming sensation. He sighed, head lolling gently as the strength in his limbs ebbed and Noah peeled the t-shirt and jeans from his body, the drag of the well-worn cotton over his limbs making Danny's skin prickle. He gasped, cock jerking hard as Noah palmed him through his boxers, and this time when Noah kissed him, he set a hand on the back of Danny's neck, the press of his fingers possessive and perfect.

Danny's lust soared to dizzying heights and he fell into it, uncaring of anything beyond the pleasure glutting him. He loved Noah's moan, a guttural sound more like a growl that made the hairs on Danny's arms stand, and he forced himself to move, driven by a need to touch every inch of Noah he could reach. Until he misjudged his own footing and crashed bodily into Noah with a not very subtle 'oof'.

"Sorry." Danny laughed. "I'm kind of a mess."

"Yes, you are," Noah agreed. "No wonder given you've been awake almost a full day."

Coasting on good feelings, Danny let himself be herded onto the bed where he stretched out, grateful for the mattress that rose up to hold him. Noah slid Danny's boxers down over his thighs and petted him for a bit, fingers painting soft fire over Danny's skin. Danny stayed quiet, unsure what to make of the clear admiration he glimpsed in Noah's eyes, and he felt thoroughly dazed by the time Noah stood straight again. His mouth went dry as Noah peeled off his shirt, revealing broad shoulders and a leanly muscled torso. Outside of the rosy sunburned cheeks, Noah was pale beyond being simply fair, the fine hairs on his chest gleaming gold in the lamplight. Danny thought the ethereal cast just made him all the more striking, and a sensation like drowning came over him.

Expression rapt, Noah climbed onto the bed beside him and rubbed slow circles into Danny's belly with his hand. "Gorgeous," he said, so Danny melted just that little bit more.

"Bet you lie like that to all the boys." Danny's voice was dreamy, and he smiled at Noah's cocked brow.

"I do not. There are no other boys right now, or girls, for that matter."

"Pfft. Of course you like both."

"It's more that I like everything." Noah gave him a sly look. "You can call me a slutty vamp, Danilo, but I had equal-opportunity appetites back when I was human."

Danny basked in their shared laughter. He wasn't sure he believed Noah's claim that there were no other boys or girls, but he'd worry about it later. Like when he wasn't about to lose his mind with a goddamned vampire who seemed focused on everything *but* feeding, because fuck yeah, did Danny love that.

He shuddered hard as Noah licked a hot stripe along his jaw. "God. Are you trying to kill me?"

Noah raised his head and smiled, and Danny swore his teeth were sharper. "That's not an option."

Danny had to stifle a groan. Equal parts lust and terror crashed through him, so intense his balls drew up tight. And yet his cock ached as he watched Noah's gaze drop back to Danny's throat, and the world around him blurred.

Please.

Noah lowered his head. He nuzzled the skin just above Danny's right collarbone, pressing deep, wet kisses there with a slow deliberation clearly aimed at driving Danny mad. Except Danny was already there, whole body throbbing as he arched into Noah, too far gone to be embarrassed by his own desperate noises.

"*Fuck.*"

"That's it," Noah crooned.

"I just—" Danny's chest clenched. Reaching blindly, he grabbed Noah's hand, pulling it down so, together, they could take him in hand. And that was all it took to make his body jolt before he shot so hard the first spurt hit his chin.

"Oh, Christ." Noah's voice was hoarse.

Danny could only gasp. The orgasm crashed through him in huge waves, leaving him boneless and floating for a time with a head too muzzy to think. He only managed to peel his eyes open when Noah shifted away and left an empty space between them that seemed to stretch for miles.

Don't.

Danny ached at the idea that Noah might not want him after all, but Noah didn't go far. He parked himself close and looked Danny up and down with a hot, greedy gaze, though he didn't move or speak, as if unsure that he should. Danny reached over and set a palm on his thigh. Noah's eyes slipped almost closed then, and a soft hum rose from him just as a shiver raced over his body. Pride swelled inside Danny. He'd never seen anything more erotic. And he'd done that. Made this gorgeous creature literally vibrate under his touch, head tipped back in a sigh that sounded so yearning.

"Danny—"

"Just get your ass over here."

Smiling now, Noah straddled him without hesitation, caging Danny's torso with those well-muscled thighs. He squeezed Danny's ribs with a steady, perfect pressure, so Danny's hands shook when he grasped Noah's waist.

"Tell me what you need," Danny murmured.

Noah didn't answer. He leaned forward instead, fingering the spot on Danny's throat where he'd lavished so much attention, and the change in his face made Danny's groin throb as if he hadn't just come. Hissing softly, he pressed his head back into the pillow, deliberately exposing the line of his neck so the fire in Noah's gaze blazed even brighter.

"Mine," Noah said, the single word slashing into Danny and burrowing deep.

Yours.

"Take it," Danny heard himself say, no fear in his heart as Noah bent forward and latched on to his throat with a snarl.

An instant of heat and sting before he flew so high he swore he left the earth. Time stretched, white noise rising inside him, and Danny was lost, forever or for now, he truly didn't care. He came—or maybe didn't—over and over, cells throbbing with a pleasure he'd never known outside of moments like this. Danny belonged here. Enraptured and gasping like this with Noah, and he didn't want it to end.

Yes.

Time snapped and restarted without warning, like a heart skipping a beat, and Danny dropped down and down and down, into the heavy weight of his flesh. Limbs weak, he stirred, his body streaked with sweat and cum. Sure he'd be lost if Noah walked away now.

But Noah didn't leave. He stayed where he was and wrapped Danny up, then held him tight without speaking. Exactly what Danny needed to keep him from falling apart while they waited together for his frantic breaths to slow.

CHAPTER 13

A noise from the bedroom drew Noah's attention to the clock on his computer's display. Danny'd quickly lost the battle against consciousness once down a pint of blood, not surprising given the literal all-nighter he'd pulled before their spur-of-the-moment and very unplanned bloodex. He'd slept for over eight hours, clinging to Noah through most of it, and Noah hadn't minded, held there as much by the human's tight grip as by the immense satisfaction that came from feeding on someone living for the first time in months.

Not that Danny was like the donors Noah met in the blood bars. They were fixated on the high that came from spilling blood, something Noah understood completely. After all, feeding brought him its own perfect bliss. Danny, though … he'd wanted more from Noah than simply to get high. It had been there in those searing, hungry kisses. The sounds he'd made, the awe in his face as Noah'd made him come. His surrender when Noah'd sunk his teeth home. The mere memory sent heat zipping under Noah's skin even now, making him want to growl and preen and indulge the beast inside him by falling on Danny again so they could do it all over.

But Noah shoved his need aside. He had a job to do and a donor to care for and he couldn't afford being distracted, even by a human as enticing as Danny Kaes.

Going to the kitchen, he withdrew a package of red plastic cups from a cabinet and quickly fished one out. Noah mixed cold water with juice in it while he didn't think about how beautiful Danny had been when he'd offered himself up. Brown eyes liquid with trust. Head tipped back, pale skin on his throat gleaming. Body shivering as Noah fed, his name like a prayer on Danny's lips. Writhing as he came in Noah's arms, every inch of him so wonderfully alive.

Pop.

The cup collapsed in Noah's grasp, sending watered-down juice splattering over the counter. Sighing, he carried the flattened, dripping remains to the trash, then spent a minute cleaning the mess, all the while counting backward from fifty. Noah wanted to be calm before he got close to a human again. Especially the one in the next room, who needed to keep all the blood inside his body.

Fresh cup in hand, Noah went to the bedroom, his hard-won reserve wavering the second he spied Danny sitting in the middle of the mattress, sheets in a pool around his waist. He yawned and stretched, eyes still firmly shut, body flexing as he brought his hands to his head and scrubbed at his hair. The bruises under his eye and on his neck had grown beguilingly livid, and the tiny punctures in his throat called to Noah as clearly as any words.

Awareness pulsed through him, raising his hackles just as it did his arousal. This impulse was new. Normally, he didn't expect anything from donors beyond the blood and pleasure. He didn't get to know them or make them his friends. He fed and made sure they got off, and then walked away because he didn't *do* friends with bleeders who were just going to die. Noah didn't want to learn the different ways they might laugh or tease out their secrets. Get close enough to know when they might need comfort. Hold them close while they slept, infinitely aware of blood and breath and scent.

The way he had been with Danny from the moment he'd approached the ambulance parked by Bleecker Playground.

Noah wanted all those things and more with Danny and honestly had no idea what to make of it. He couldn't forget, though, that the one thing Danny needed above anything else was shelter, and that Noah had promised to give it to him.

After counting backward from twenty this time, Noah tapped the door with his knuckles. "Hi."

Danny opened his eyes. "Well, hey." Though smiling, he appeared pale and somehow still tired, but his regard for Noah's black tailored shirt and trousers was frankly appreciative. "Have I told you already how much I like you in street clothes? Because I do. And did you bring me a beer?"

"Ah, no." Noah glanced down at the red plastic cup in his hand. "Juice and water since we both know you need the sugar."

"You're no fun."

"You're not the first person to say so."

Chuckling, Danny scooted back on the mattress so he could lean against the headboard, and Noah crossed the room toward him. Taking the cup, Danny drank deeply, eyes slipping closed again and throat working as a low groan rose from his chest.

Jesus.

Noah sat on the mattress and stared. The erotic power this human held was lethal, though Noah no longer knew who was more at risk, Danny or himself. He couldn't bring himself to care just then either, since fate had brought this bleeder into his life and, for now, was keeping him there. Gently, he tapped a finger against Danny's wrist in a wordless warning against guzzling too much drink in one go.

"Mmm, I'm okay." Danny sighed. "I've done this before, remember?"

Yes, Noah did. He still liked the teasing note in Danny's voice. The color rising in his cheeks and the way his lips shone with moisture once he'd lowered the cup. Noah's cock twitched when Danny reopened his eyes, and it took everything in him not to lean over for a drink of his own.

You're going to be counting backward all night in every language you know if you don't get your head back where it belongs.

"Your favorite detective's been messaging," he said, and hated the way Danny's face instantly became guarded. "He wants to talk as soon as you're able."

"Of course. I'll get cleaned up and meet you out there." Danny moved to set the cup on the nightstand but went still when Noah tapped his wrist again.

"Take as much time as you need," Noah urged quietly. "I meant it when I said 'as soon as you're able'. You don't have to talk to Callahan or me or anyone else until you feel ready."

Danny didn't answer right away. But then he exhaled, and the stone in his features melted into a mixture of worry and sadness. "Not sure I'll ever feel ready for anyone who isn't you," he murmured. "I know I need to be, though, so thank you. I appreciate that you'd run interference for me, considering Callahan isn't your favorite person." Amusement crossed his face. "Unless that's part of the appeal?"

"It's not a deterrent." Noah tried not to sound smug, but knew he'd failed when Danny snorted softly.

After Danny disappeared into the bathroom, Noah went back to work, losing himself so thoroughly in files and data he stopped paying attention to the passage of time. A gasp pulled him back to the present and he whirled in his chair, dismayed at finding Danny standing close behind him, phone pressed to his ear and wide-eyed at the images filling Noah's screens.

"Is that ... Noah, are those photos of my apartment?"

"Ah. Yes." Turning back to his keyboard, Noah locked the screens, then spun so he could face Danny again. "You weren't supposed to see those until after Callahan had a chance to explain."

"Danilo? Are you still there? What happened?"

The tinny voice coming from Danny's phone seemed to break through his shock, and his cheeks mottled as if he'd been slapped.

"Y-yeah, Dad, I'm still here," he said in reply. "It's, uh, nothing, but I have to go, okay? I'll call you back later. Tell Gina I said hi and I love you both."

Despite his easy words, Danny's hand was shaking as he slid the phone into his pocket, and Noah wanted to kick himself for his mistake.

"I'm sorry, Danny."

"You said there wasn't any damage to my place."

"There wasn't. After the first break-in."

"The *first* break-in?" Danny's brows rose. "There's been more than one?"

"Yes. Someone has been in your apartment at least twice between your assault and today. The police were called in when sounds of a disturbance were heard in your unit, but no one was found after they arrived."

Danny screwed his eyes shut and swore. "Aren't there cops parked right outside the building?"

"There are. Which means the perp has a means of entry the police haven't found."

"Well, that's fucking great. I'll bet there's fingerprint dust fucking everywhere."

"There is. But the prints that have been recovered aren't in the system, so we still don't have a name." Noah blew out a long breath. "And there's more."

Danny opened his eyes again. "Of course there is. Is it about wherever the hell you disappeared to last night or were you working another case altogether? And why did you wait to tell me about my apartment? You promised you wouldn't keep shit from me!"

Noah held up a hand. "I didn't keep anything from you, Danny. I wanted to wait until after you'd rested before we talked about what's been going on with the case. But I only found out about the second break-in at your apartment just before you woke up."

Danny's shoulders slumped. "Sorry. I shouldn't have yelled. But I'm awake now and I want to hear *everything* you think I need to know."

Noah walked him through the CSU's theory that the men who'd died in the West Village parks had been led there by the same person, but only after they were so weakened they were almost certain to die if they didn't get help. Though Danny stayed quiet, his eyes were flat as Noah spoke, and his complexion turned a sickly gray-green when he heard about the trace evidence Noah had scented on the victims' clothes.

"God." His voice was gruff when he spoke. "They didn't need to die, Noah. They might still be alive if he'd … Fuck, why did he leave them behind?"

Noah shook his head. "We don't have a motive yet."

"Like that would make it any better? Knowing they were scared. That you could still *smell* it on their clothes."

Noah licked his lips as Danny's face crumpled. "The police are working every avenue available to solve these cases, Danny. Including yours in case you thought otherwise."

"I didn't. I know how hard you've all been working. I'm just so fucking done with everything and—"

"I understand."

"Don't." Danny gave him a hard look. "I was being a dick, and you should have called me out on it."

Turning on his heel, he stalked off, but headed for the kitchen rather than the front door, which Noah counted as a win. He got up and followed anyway, knowing by now Danny would need to keep talking even if he didn't realize it just yet.

"Is everything all right with your dad?" Noah asked.

"Huh? Oh, yeah." Danny opened the refrigerator. "He just wanted to check in. He and my stepmom Gina live next door to Thea, so it's not like they don't know what's going on with me. Well, as much as I've told Thea, anyway, which isn't a lot."

"Because you don't want them worried?"

"No. They'll worry no matter what. But I don't want them scared. The way I am." Danny's eyes were stormy when he turned back to Noah. "Will you show me the photos of my apartment again?"

Noah watched him closely. They needed their wits about them when they went to The Last Drop tonight, and neither of them would be at their best if Danny was pissed off and emotional over possessions that, in the grand scheme of things, meant nothing. Noah still knew better than to say any such thing.

"Yes. But can I ask why you want to see them?"

"Maybe it'll help?" Danny bit his lip, expression uncertain again in a way that tugged at Noah's heart. "It's my home. I might spot something another person would miss."

Noah took that as proof that Danny was holding strong in spite of the chaos surrounding them. "All right. But I'd like to wait until after tonight. Callahan and Cho will be here soon with the tech unit, and we can't be distracted from whatever plan they've cooked up for the trip to the bar."

"Okay." Danny glanced down at his sweats. "I think my clothes are going to be a problem, though. I can't go in there looking like I just left the gym and the clothes I wore to work the other night ... no. We're not bringing the cops in the hall with us, are we? Because we are *not* going to blend in with the crowd if there's a matching set of police officers tailing us."

Noah doubted Danny would ever truly blend into the crowd at any blood bar in the world. He was far too memorable. "The uniforms will stay here. The tech team will be in the van with Cho and Callahan with us, so we'll have ample backup."

"Not that you really need it, I guess," Danny sounded thoughtful as he turned to the task of making himself something to eat. "Do you really go to The Last Drop on the regular?"

"I used to more often, but this job makes it hard to find time." Noah also hadn't been in much of a blood bar kind of mood during recent months, but no one needed to know that. "Why?"

"Just curious. I was thinking about what Callahan said—that it was kinda funny we never met there. Do you bring your donors back here a lot?"

"No. I've never brought any of them to this place," Noah said without thinking. "I go to the bars to feed—that's what they're for."

What donors are for. Blood and nothing else.

He stopped, suddenly aware how callous he must sound. "I didn't mean that the way it came out."

"I think you did." Danny cleared his throat. "I asked you to be honest with me and you were, so, that's cool." He shot a glance toward the bedroom. "So … what happened back there between us was, what? An anomaly?"

Despite his casual tone, Danny's mouth had turned down at the corners. And the guilt that flooded Noah made his brain buzz.

He had nothing to feel bad about. Noah made his donors feel good. He never took more than he needed, and he cared for them after the bloodex ended so they walked away smiling. He *knew* what the bleeders needed from him. So why did these pieces of life that had fit so well for over a century suddenly feel misshapen and wrong?

What the hell was wrong with him lately?

The silence stretched and hummed while Danny made his sandwich until Noah thought he'd choke.

"I could give you a dozen reasons why I don't get involved with bleeders," he said without truly meaning to.

Danny went still, gaze guarded when he looked up. "I'm sure

you can. And you fed on me because—" He stopped short when Noah held up a hand.

"Whatever you're thinking, I guarantee you're wrong."

"Yeah? Feel free to explain then because I'm kind of at a loss."

Noah knew the feeling. How he dreaded saying the wrong thing and hurting this human. Despite his strong will, Danny was fragile right now and badly in need of a friend. And though he was almost cosmically ill-suited for the part, Noah really did want to be that friend if only he could figure out how.

"I could give you a dozen reasons why I don't get involved with bleeders," he said again, "and every one comes back to the same thing. I'm not suited to be intimate with humans long term. I don't believe any blood eater is. We're wired up here"— Noah tapped a finger against his temple—"to see you as prey, even when we're not hunting. Things you do in your daily life like shaving or cooking or using sharp things are dangerous around someone like me. Even just falling down hard enough to draw blood ..." Noah pressed his lips into a thin line. "Moments like those have real potential to end badly. To end with you *dead*. That's not fair to you. The blood bars exist and thrive for exactly that purpose. To bring humans out of their everyday lives and into an environment that's as safe as we can make it."

"That's what you meant yesterday when you made that crack." Danny's voice sounded hollow. "About having met me in the wild. You don't meet donors outside of the bars."

"No, I don't. Outside of work and the bars, I try not to get close to bleeders—humans—at all."

The way I have with you.

Noah knew better than to put that thought into words. He couldn't give Danny hope of anything more than hookups between them, because this would all change after the man who'd attacked him was caught. Danny would go home then and back to his life, and Noah wouldn't see him unless one or both of them wanted to connect in ways that ensured Danny stayed safe. Exactly as things should be.

Chest tight, Noah eyed the bruising and puncture marks on Danny's throat. And then he calmly changed the subject so he could keep pretending he didn't already feel more connected to Danny Kaes than any human he'd ever known.

"Did you meet your ex at a blood bar?"

Danny rubbed the back of his neck with one hand. "No. I met him in the wild, actually." His half smile quickly died. "Galen came to work at Nice Buns, and we started going to the bars together after we figured out there was mutual interest. Most of the time we ended up at Death Becomes Her down in Tribeca but I'm not sure why. Galen always said The Last Drop was the dopest bar in the city."

"I don't disagree. The Last Drop is quite dope if memory serves."

"Cute. And work really keeps you from going there?"

"Yes. But I can be selfish with my free time. When I'm not working with the police, I like taking photos around the city."

A soft look passed over Danny's face. "That's a very human thing to say."

"Is it? I'm not sure I'd know anymore." Noah smiled to himself. "I worked with cameras before I was changed. Never with the police, until I got the job with the CSU through MonsterBoard. Maybe they sent your Galen to Nice Buns?"

"They did," Danny said dryly, "along with some other vamps and shifters who're still on the crews. But Galen would be the first one to tell you he was never *my* anything, even though we hooked up for almost a year."

With practiced movements, he held up his left hand, then slid his watch band down, exposing a thin, silvery scar on the inside of his wrist. "Galen liked it from here. Probably to keep me from getting too close."

Noah bit back a growl. He'd been the one to ask about the ex and, territorial pissings aside, had zero business expressing opinions about how any vampire treated his donor so long as the bleeder stayed safe. It just didn't feel like it now that he and Danny were becoming something like friends.

"Galen's not actually a baker," Danny said. "He writes stories about his life among humans for a news magazine. I didn't get to know much about that part of his life until we were about done, but everyone was aware that he'd come to Nice Buns to do research for his writing."

Noah wondered at the pain he saw so clearly in the lines of Danny's face. There was more there, bigger and deeper than the typical angst of a breakup. But Danny was already muttering about his appearance again, clearly distancing himself from the moment. Noah didn't stop him. Danny had enough on his mind without being pushed for details about his personal life that weren't Noah's business in the first place.

"Really wish there was something I could do about this." Danny gingerly fingered the bruising around his eye. "I'm gonna be a total schlub standing next to the vamp god."

Noah glanced down at himself. "That's ... so not what I am. But you're welcome to poke around my closet for something to wear."

A small smile lit Danny's face. "Really?"

"Of course. I think we're even close to the same size shoe. But I'll warn you now that there's a lot of CSU gear in there."

"Aw-w-wesome. I'm down for some roleplay if you are." Danny winked at him. "I just hope you've got something to cover my neck. Callahan may want us playing a couple tonight, but he will legit have a baby if he gets an idea of what we've been up to."

Noah laughed but there was a hard edge in it, and the urge to guard and protect rose in him, so fierce he had to ball his hands into fists. "Nothing I do when I'm off-duty is Callahan's business."

"You're right." In one smooth move, Danny stood in front of him, close enough that the heat from his body ghosted over

Noah's skin. "And maybe we should practice looking like a couple anyway," he murmured, "because I want people to believe it when I do this."

His lips were soft against Noah's and the kiss entirely chaste, lasting only a heartbeat before Danny pulled away. Noah still felt it head to toe, even after Danny had walked away, and it took everything in him not to follow and chase down many more.

CHAPTER 14

"I thought you were gonna tone down the cop vibe."

"I did. What do you call this?" Callahan gestured toward himself and Danny bit back a laugh.

"You looking like a cop wearing a civilian costume, dude. Your clothes might be street, but your face still says, 'I've come to chew gum and kick ass, and I'm all out of gum.'"

"What the hell are you talking about?"

Danny sighed at him. "It's a line from an old movie. What I'm saying is that you look like a cop dressed up in nice clothes."

The detective was definitely both of those things. Handsome in his black-on-black ensemble and sophisticated in ways Danny hadn't expected. He still carried a distinctly tense air, however, as if likely to punch you as buy you a cocktail. Danny wasn't sure that would do them any favors tonight when the whole idea behind walking into The Last Drop was to mine information from the patrons. Scaring them seemed like a terrible strategy. Then again, blood bars served all types including shifters in among the humans; maybe someone in the crowd would appreciate a well-dressed grouch whose attitude screamed 'I hate everything'.

"It'll be dark inside," Callahan said, as if he'd heard Danny's thoughts. "And no one is going to notice me. Not next to you and a six-foot-two vampire."

Danny hummed softly in agreement. He glanced overhead, unsure if the moon appeared so bright tonight because the skies were extra clear or because he was finally losing it. Being outside for the first time in days—as in feet moving over actual pavement and city noise up close and personal—had his head spinning. He'd used the roof deck at Noah's when he'd needed a change of scene, but the lack of stimulation was slowly turning his brain to mush, and he'd leapt at the chance to go to the club tonight, especially after scoring some sturdy boots and a sweet black leather jacket from the back of Noah's closet. Until the apartment door closed behind them and he'd instantly wanted to turn back.

God, he was fucked up.

Danny *needed* normal. Like sleeping in his apartment and eating dinner with his family, and definitely working at Nice Buns baking foods that made people happy. He wanted regular, boring old nights where no one got hurt or killed, and the guy who'd mugged him was locked safely away so he couldn't fuck with anyone else. The longer it took to get back there—to the mundane and easy and *safe*—the more adrift from reality Danny felt. He wanted his life back so much his insides danced just thinking about it.

Except …

Noah didn't have a place in those regular, boring, deeply human nights. Oh, he'd probably keep in touch when all this was over. Danny could easily imagine him keeping up with the banter over the baked goods he bought other people. He might even want to hang out beyond the confines of Nice Buns, because while Noah didn't do relationships with humans, he might make an exception. Maybe consent to sharing something with Danny that was slightly more than friendship. Danny would take that if it meant keeping Noah around. And that was funny, really, after what he'd gone through with Galen.

Blinking back to the present, Danny looked at The Last Drop's front door, now only half a block away. "Here we go, I guess."

"We can keep walking another two blocks and then double back," Noah said, "if you'd like some more time."

The 'so you can get your shit together' was implied yet Danny still shook his head. He reached to smooth the black silk scarf he'd wound around his neck with his fingers, but then Noah caught the hand in his and held it with such ease that Danny's stupid heart flopped around in his chest.

He was really, *really* fucked up.

Walking a dozen more blocks wasn't going to change his mood. The creep who'd already messed up too many peoples' lives would still be out there. And Danny would still be stuck on the perimeter of his own life. With no freaking clue how to handle a whole bunch of feelings he had for a guy who was just barely his friend.

"I'm good," was all he said, then braced himself because Callahan was looking them over, that sharp gaze lingering on their joined hands for what seemed like an eternity before it rose to meet Danny's.

"Right," Callahan said in an exceedingly measured tone. "You remember the safe word? And you're sure you don't want an earpiece?"

"The code word is Harlem. As in 'my sister lives in Harlem.' And no, I don't want anything in my ear. Wearing this thing is distracting enough." Reaching up, Danny took hold of a pendant hanging from his neck on a fine leather cord. Fashioned from a glossy black material that mimicked obsidian, the nickel-sized stone concealed a listening device so small Danny had trouble believing it worked. The stone was warm in his hand, however, despite the chilly air, and he swallowed over another bout of nerves. "I don't want a bunch of voices piped into my skull with no rhyme or reason," he said. "I honestly think it'd make me hurl."

"Well, then I'll listen for us both." Noah tapped a tiny black earbud in his right ear with one finger. "Cho and the team are parked over on Hudson. If we get separated or you think you're in trouble, drop the safe word and they'll get you out."

Danny licked his lips. "I know. And thanks. I'm just a little keyed up."

"Don't be." Noah squeezed his hand. "You know this place, Danny. You're going to do great."

Those words—coupled with Noah's smile—did a lot to zap Danny's jitters. So … maybe there was a touch of the thrall in that smile. Danny wouldn't have blamed Noah for using the vampire whammy on him just then, if only to keep him calm. Noah'd also had a point, though—Danny did know this place. Knew the crowd and the vibe and how to move around in it with ease. He was also with a freaking vampire and a cop, and he trusted them to do whatever they needed to keep him safe.

He felt almost easy as they presented their membership cards to the bouncer, a stern-looking woman named Astrid. She didn't smile, but her eyes were warm when she greeted them, and she gripped Noah's hand firmly, the way she might have a friend's. After checking Callahan's ID, she stamped their wrists with the club's tail-eating serpent and even after a year of having stayed away, a sensation like being at home fell over Danny.

He glanced around the vast room that made up the main part of the club, as charmed by the old-fashioned speakeasy decor as he had been the first night he'd seen it. Clusters of amber and garnet lamps cast a warm glow over the humans swarming the giant bar at the room's center, a legion of conversations flowing among them and mixing with the low, pulsing house music that was part of The Last Drop's trademark energy. A hum nestled behind Danny's ribs.

Damn. He'd really missed this.

Heads turned as he walked to the bar with Noah and Callahan, and he couldn't blame a single being for staring. The cop and vampire cut striking figures with their contrasting coloring and dashing good looks. Both were tall and athletic, Callahan burly while Noah was lean. But despite Callahan's rugged appeal, Noah outshone him with an exotic, diamond-like brilliance in that room's honeyed light.

And no wonder. The Last Drop was one of few spaces where someone like Noah was free to be himself without judgment. And though he'd proven over and over he was adept at control, his pupils were huge and strange when he looked Danny's way, the intent in them clear.

In that second, Danny truly knew what it was like to be stalked. He froze, conscious of Callahan's low oath behind him. Noah wasn't hiding the otherness that set him apart. The air of predator prowling in the midst of a herd, regal, strong, and terribly lethal. But unlike Callahan, Danny welcomed the idea of being taken down and mauled very much and didn't know whether to laugh or rage when the detective's grunt dragged him back to the here and now.

"Don't look so goddamned happy, Green. I get that these are your people, but your Vlad vibe is messing with my mojo."

Noah's wide smile was a tiny bit terrifying. "Sorry, not sorry. Maybe a drink will help. I'm sure we can find something you'll enjoy, even if you have to take a pass on the spirits."

"You know I do. I'd kill for a fucking smoke." Callahan shot him a withering glance, but Danny saw the sweat beading on his forehead. The big cop was nervous. Of *Noah*, for God's sake, and maybe it wasn't anything new, but Callahan had done a good job of hiding it until this moment. "I'll take anything in a bottle that might pass for booze," he said, "and make sure it's opened in front of you. You say I'm safe as houses in here, so I guess I'll try and find us a seat without getting killed."

He strode off toward some booths located some distance from the bar while Danny stared after him with a frown. "Should I go after him?"

"He knows what he's doing."

"You sure? He's never been in a blood bar before. I mean …

he just basically said he expects his drink to be spiked when he isn't watching."

"The scenario isn't entirely impossible."

Danny looked at Noah askance. "I think it's extremely unlikely in this place. Or any blood bar."

"Perhaps. But I suspect his bluster is all for show." Leaning in close, Noah set his palm over the pendant resting against Danny's chest and murmured, "Callahan lied about never having been in a blood bar before."

Danny closed his eyes. Moving so his cheek made contact with Noah's, he nuzzled in closer, his body thrilling when Noah mimicked the gesture. Danny was getting better at steeling himself against Noah's thrall, but it was a moment before he could shape his thoughts into words. "What makes you say that?"

"He knew to go for a booth. Bleeders sit at the bar when all they want is to check the place out or find a hookup that's just about sex."

Peeling his eyes open, Danny turned his head and got a good look at the busiest place in the room. Humans talking and laughing together, excitement obvious in their expressions and motions. The sight made him smile. He'd been just like them when he'd walked into this place with Galen. Starry-eyed by the crowd and the fancy oak bar with its colorful cocktails, but equal parts eager and frightened to know what might be happening in the shadows where figures moved and sometimes vanished entirely.

He'd definitely noticed Galen disappearing and how changed he'd appeared when he'd turned back up over an hour later. Galen's grin had been thoroughly electric, and his gaze so bewitching Danny had put aside all of his nerves and wanted to know who or what was responsible.

"I was like that too at first," Danny said, voice low. "Galen brought me here—I know I told you that already. We'd been flirting during shifts at the bakery and when he offered to bring me as his guest, I didn't hesitate. I'd never been in a blood bar, but I'd been curious for years."

"I'd like to have seen it." Noah's eyes traveled over Danny's face, trailing invisible fire along his skin. "You here on your first night, seeing this place."

"Yeah?"

"Oh, yes. Although, I doubt Galen would have appreciated my attention. Because I absolutely would have noticed you."

Danny's head swam at the words. "I'd have noticed you too," he whispered.

"Was your first bloodex the same evening?"

"No. We were just doing a casual hang out with some of the crew from Nice Buns. Or so I thought, anyway. Afterward—like, much later—Galen told me he'd brought me here to see how I'd react." Danny smiled down at his shoes, more amused than embarrassed. "Said he could tell I wanted it before we even walked in. Which I did. I'd just never done anything about it."

Leaning close, Noah ran the tip of his nose along Danny's cheek. "Why not?"

"Different reasons. Coming out to my family wasn't easy on me or them. Everyone's life changed a lot and things were never the same." Danny looked up, and the compassion he glimpsed in Noah's face took him off guard. "I didn't want to drag everyone into the drama of another coming out."

Or force them to decide whether they could still love me.

Danny already knew that sometimes the answer was 'no.'

Noah nodded slowly. "They don't know you're a donor."

"No. I never told them about Galen either, other than that he worked for me. To be fair, it was probably more because I knew I couldn't count on him to be there. For me. Us, whatever." Danny frowned. There'd never been an 'us' with Galen. And he still hated admitting it.

"Your Galen sounds like a fool," Noah said.

A pang shot through Danny. "I told you already—he wasn't my anything. Turns out, he was barely my friend."

"Underscoring my point perfectly."

Danny just hummed in reply. The admission had cost him, each word bristling with jagged little spikes that hurt on their way out. He was lighter having said them, though, and especially to Noah whose eyes held no judgment. Despite the walls still standing between them, he *was* someone Danny could count on. Danny knew it in his bones.

Aware of the many eyes watching them, he covered the hand Noah had pressed over Danny's heart with his own. "Are you going to tell Callahan his cover is blown?"

"Probably," Noah said. "I don't think this is the right time, though."

"Why not?"

Noah's smile grew so tender Danny could hardly bear it. "Too many extra ears listening, and I don't think he'd appreciate it."

He looked almost sorry as he drew their joined hands down and exposed the pendant once more. But Danny wasn't sorry. He'd needed the reminder that this wasn't real. He and Noah weren't here alone. There was a van full of cops out there just waiting for a sign this operation would yield more than a night out on the town for a pair of civilians and Detective Bert Callahan.

Who wasn't alone when Danny and Noah located him in a booth set near the back of the room. His aura was *super* tense, too. Probably a given, considering someone was all up in his grill despite the clear 'fuck off and die' in Callahan's glare. Danny knew just from the cop's body language that the someone in question was a vampire. He wouldn't have guessed in a hundred years that he'd know the someone too, and that they'd decimate the good feelings he'd managed to summon simply by turning around and flashing a familiar, impish grin in Danny's direction.

Why was the universe so clearly intent on fucking him over?

"Dan!" Gaiety lit Galen's pretty brown eyes. "Hello, darlin', and how have you been?"

"Hey, G." Danny knew he just sounded tired. "What are you doing here? I thought Tribeca was still your go-to turf."

"It is when I want it to be," Galen said. "But I've heard some truly wild stories in the last several days about blood sacks maybe being stalked around The Last Drop. Hardly surprising after the news outlets mentioned the place by name." He appeared so genuinely baffled, Danny almost smiled. "I *had* to come by and get a look for myself. Nothing seems much out of place, sadly, except maybe you. What are *you* doing here, Dan?"

Danny shrugged. "I'm still a member. It's just been a while since I came in."

"Long enough that you caused a stir. I was out back when you got here but word travels fast when long-lost faces make an appearance. And yours isn't the only one I recognize." Those laughing eyes moved over Noah. "We know each other, yes? From here or another bar in town?"

Danny's stomach twisted. Shit. He'd never considered Noah and Galen might know each other. And that was damned stupid given how small the vampire world could be, even in a city of nearly nine million souls. But surely Noah would have said if he'd recognized Galen's name … right?

"I was just thinking the same," Noah said. His eyes caught some light from the direction of the bar, and the shine in them hit Danny hard. What if Noah enjoyed the act of bloodex even more with his own kind? The newest fledgling vamp would make a better match than any fragile human and Galen was so very appealing. Yet Noah's smile was almost bland. "I'm sure we've passed each other by in this place or another bar, though I couldn't say when."

"Funny then, seeing you here with a bleeder I know well." Galen's expression had turned smug. "Dan and I had a lot of fun before his ridiculous human brain got in the way."

Ugh.

An itch to storm off came over Danny, but he didn't have a chance to react before Noah stepped forward. He set a bottle of black cherry soda down in front of Callahan, then gestured for Danny to sit while Galen watched them slide into the booth.

"What does bring you here tonight, Dan?" he asked. "The last time you and I spoke, you told me you were done with this scene for good." His gaze fell on the scarf around Danny's neck for several beats too long, before shifting to meet Danny's. "I take it something's changed? Or are you here chasing monster stories too?"

Heat climbed Danny's cheeks. He didn't doubt Galen had spotted his black eye too, even in the low light. "Maybe a bit of both. And … well, I can't believe I'm saying this, but I'm glad we ran into you."

He heaved a big breath. The NYPD had a clear idea about how this night should play out. Callahan expected to take the lead once Danny and Noah had introduced him to the right people. He was the only cop among them, after all, and the lead detective on the deaths that had occurred in the West Village parks. He was also going to be well and truly pissed watching Danny flush those carefully crafted plans right down the toilet.

Danny got it; he really did. He didn't feel even a little sorry, though.

"We're looking for someone, G." He kept his eyes trained on Galen's despite Callahan's muttered warning. "A human, we think, with a means to draw blood. They've already picked off four donors who came into this bar. And if anyone's heard something *real* about a person like that, I know it would be you."

CHAPTER 15

"The fuck is he doing?" Cho muttered in Noah's ear.

Hell if I know.

Noah could almost feel Callahan bristling, his glare so hot it was a wonder Danny and the table between them didn't burst into flames. Noah understood. The man had a right to be angry at his operation being hijacked by a civilian with an extremely personal stake in the investigation. He gave Callahan a warning look anyway, sure they had to let this play out. The Danny he knew was methodical and grounded, not at all someone who'd go off script without reason. Particularly with Galen, a blood eater whose relationship with Danny had sounded stormy at best.

Noah *did* know that vampire's expressive face though they'd never spoken before tonight. And it took no effort at all to track the change that came over Galen at Danny's words and see the light in his eyes harden.

"Dan." Galen's tone was polite to the point of being cold. "If I *had* heard of such a creature, do you honestly think they'd still be alive?"

Danny's gaze flicked to Callahan and then back. "Ah. No." He swallowed. "But I know how you feel about humans trespassing into your world. How strict you are about the bloodex and keeping your donors healthy. And that's why I'm asking you this. There's truth in the wild stories you've heard. Someone is out there harvesting blood from donors, then leaving them behind like trash in the street, and it looks like every one of the bleeders was in this bar on the night that they died. We could use your help finding whoever is doing this, G."

For several moments, no one at the table moved or spoke. The air between Danny and Galen changed, pulsing with a new energy that made Noah restless. Whatever had happened between them, it was obvious each still knew which buttons to push to provoke a reaction. And Galen's slow smile only intensified Noah's unease because watching another fanger ogle the human he wanted sucked, no pun intended.

Danny's not yours.

Noah wanted to sneer. He knew that. Danny was a person, not a thing to be owned, and Noah wouldn't allow anyone to even consider anything but. He liked the idea of wiping the grin from Galen's face anyway and would do just that if he didn't come up with something useful in the next sixty seconds.

"Who is *we* exactly?" Galen asked instead. "Because I doubt these friends of yours are baking bread at Nice Buns."

"That's not up to me to say."

"Then I guess we're done talking."

Callahan pinned Galen with a searing look. "And I guess you won't mind being arrested for criminal obstruction, Mr.—"

"Galen will do." He laughed merrily. "You're a cop, huh? That fits, what with the attitude and being so tense you're about to implode. I'm not sure if I should be turned on or angry that you're threatening me."

Danny ran a hand down his face. "Galen, come on."

"Oh, all *right*." Galen rolled his eyes. "I assume this is all off the record?"

"Definitely. Galen's a writer," Danny said to Callahan, who pinched the bridge of his nose. "Do you wanna talk here?"

"Certainly not. Let's take Officer Angry over here somewhere more private."

Cho snickered in Noah's ear. "Danny sure knows how to pick 'em."

Noah bit back a grunt. Sliding out of the booth with the others, he followed Galen toward a back section of the space cloaked in a thick gloom. They approached a series of oversized black-and-white prints, and Galen ran his fingers along the side of the largest then pulled it toward him, revealing a hidden door. He vanished through it without a backward glance, Callahan following just behind while Danny and Noah brought up the rear.

Blackness rose around them as they clustered inside the opening, pierced only by the glow of lights from the distant bar. Those pinpoints were swallowed when Noah pulled the door shut, and the music from the room beyond became muffled. In the next second, a bulb flickered to life overhead, casting its light over them, followed by a second and third and more, the long string of lights illuminating a corridor that stretched out before them lined with doors on each side.

As if he'd already forgotten them, Galen walked off, but Noah took a moment to check on the humans. Danny's steady gaze came as no surprise; he knew what to expect in these back rooms and that nothing would come to pass without his permission. Their burly companion was another story, however, and he literally stank of discomfort.

Sour heat poured off Callahan, edged with a tang of dread and the ever-present tobacco, and the challenge in his eyes as he stared at Noah spoke of a man on the defensive. Understandable, given he'd volunteered to walk into the midst of a species he loathed and was hating every second. Noah toyed with the idea of gloating. The insults he'd endured over the last year made it hard not to revel some in Callahan's struggle, but he knew better than to let his amusement show. Callahan needed his wits about him, or he'd be no good to Danny or the victims who'd died in the West Village parks.

Those men were the reason they'd come here tonight and why Noah didn't hesitate to take Danny's hand as they followed after Galen.

No noise came from the rooms they passed, their footsteps along the stone floor and the distant thump of music from the bar the only sounds among them. The silence became total once they passed through a door Galen had opened and it was closed firmly behind them. Nothing they said would be audible to Cho and the cops in the van parked outside either, thanks to walls as thick as those found in any bunker.

In the meantime, Callahan was eyeing the furniture as if it might bite him.

Galen raised an eyebrow at him. "Are you sure he's really a cop?" he asked Danny. "Because I can tell by the smell that he's freaked."

Danny pursed his lips like he was trying not to laugh. "I'm sure. Detective Callahan is investigating the deaths you heard about. Noah is in forensics."

Real surprise colored Galen's bright eyes as he turned them on Noah. "Vampires can't be cops."

"No, they can't," Noah agreed, "and I'm not one. I'm just a civilian who most of the police force doesn't want anything to do with."

"Until they do, hm? Always the way." Galen tutted. "Well, you're a better blood eater than I am if you're willing to help them anyway. And I have to assume that means the police have decided the killer isn't one of us. They'd be rounding up the Nosferatu otherwise, with you at the top of their list. Am I right, Detective?" His expression turned scornful when he didn't get an answer. "I suppose I should be thankful you're not wasting my time with denials."

With a pointed look for Callahan, Galen seated himself in the chair nearest him. "So. What made you think your cases could ever be connected to the bloodex scene?"

"I haven't been convinced that they're not," Callahan replied. "A body drained dry is something I'd expect more from this scene than anywhere else."

Galen furrowed his brow. "Do you honestly believe that's what goes on here?"

"It doesn't matter what I believe. Each victim had a hole in their jugular and died from shock caused by massive blood loss." Callahan spread his hands. "Regardless of what led up to the killings, someone went out of their way to make it *appear* that a vampire was involved, at least at first glance."

Slowly, Galen nodded. "All right. I take it there's more?"

"There is. Indicators on each victim place them inside this club shortly before they were killed, sometimes within hours. That tells me those men had a connection to someone or something inside these walls, and whatever went on between them was about more than getting their rocks off."

"And that tells *me* you have nothing on the blood eaters, Detective. If you did, my ass would be in a holding pen somewhere right now with a dozen other of my kind." Galen turned his attention on Noah. "What isn't this slab of meat saying?"

Oh, how Noah wished Cho and the cops in the van could hear how wildly off course this adventure had gone.

"Anything bloodex-related to the cases is circumstantial at best," he replied. "No blood at all was found at the scenes or in the days since and the wounds on the victims' necks were made by something mechanical. Save for one, there were no bite marks at all. That said, it does appear that each man visited The Last Drop not long before they died."

"That's why we're here," Danny threw in. He gave Noah a half-smile before gently dropping his hand and walking to a seat near Galen's. "The cops want to understand what the victims were looking for when they came to this bar."

"I'm sure you could have told them yourself, Dan. But why

are you helping them at all?" Galen frowned at Danny. "I want that story before you say anything else."

Callahan ground his teeth so hard they creaked. "Are you serious? You've got enough information, kid—the rest is on a need-to-know basis, and you're not on the list of people who I consider needing to know. I don't have time for this shit."

"I wasn't talking to you, big guy," Galen said mildly. "I was talking to Danilo here, so how about you be a good boy and sit down while he catches me up."

Callahan leveled a glare Noah's way. "You're enjoying this, aren't you?"

Noah absolutely was. But he didn't answer because Danny sat and started talking just as Galen had asked, filling in details about the incident at Bleecker Playground and the deaths that had occurred both before and after his assault. Galen's devil-may-care attitude fled, leaving him grim-faced, but he remained doubtful any member of The Last Drop could be responsible for the murders or stalking Danny.

"The bleeders who come to this bar are harmless. A large percentage rarely see these back rooms or even become donors," Galen told Callahan. "They're curious about the bloodex and about us"—he gestured between Noah and himself—"but that's all it is. Curiosity. They want to gawk and squawk without ever offering themselves up and that's perfectly all right. Not every human is wired to be a donor. And for those who *are*, well. Their focus is on giving blood, not taking it."

Callahan frowned. "Yeah, I get that part, I think. I still say it's shortsighted to presume our killer can't be a donor, too."

"I don't know. I can't see it at all," Danny said, shaking his head slowly. "The more I think about it, the less likely it seems. Unless we're talking about a blood play kink here and that doesn't fit with the donor/vampire scene. So why would a donor even think about spilling blood with another human? There's literally no point in doing it if you're not with a vamp."

"Explain," Callahan urged. "What wouldn't you get if you bloodex with a human?"

Danny's grin was crooked. "I can think of a few things, but the most obvious are that it wouldn't be a true bloodex. That only happens with a vampire."

"Right. Fanger meets human and boom, they suck."

Noah met Galen's harried look with one of his own, but Danny belted a laugh.

"You're being too literal. I'm not talking mechanics even though, yeah, that is a thing. I'm talking *sensation*." His eyes grew brighter. "Connection, too, because both play a big part, at least from my perspective. When it's happening—when a vamp is feeding and you're *there* in the moment, it genuinely feels like a fantastic high. Like the best drugs you've ever had, mixed up with every good feeling you're capable of in body, mind, and soul."

Danny sat forward in his seat. "That kind of high doesn't happen unless a vampire spills the blood, Bert. So if the guys in the parks wanted a true bloodex, how did they *not* end up with a vamp?" He turned to Noah. "You said it yourself—the wounds on the victims' necks are like hole punches. I seriously doubt they were meant to bring pleasure."

Callahan nodded slowly. "That's part of the connection you mentioned."

"It can be, sure. I mean, a bloodex feels good no matter what, but it can be unreal if the vampire and donor are simpatico."

"If they're a couple, you mean?"

Danny shook his head. "Again, too literal. Good chemistry between strangers is enough to make a bloodex feel better than the best sex you've ever had, even if you hardly touch beyond the bloodletting. That's what I mean when I say a bloodex between humans can't truly happen. There's only one way I'm gonna get that high if I want it and that's with a vamp. Drugs can come close and actual sex maybe more so, but they're still pretty pale in comparison."

The intensity in his gaze—the naked longing there—had Noah shifting in his seat, despite his promise to himself to stay focused on the case. Keeping his distance was proving impossible now that he knew how Danny tasted. Had watched him surrender, then beg for more, eyes liquid as he clung to Noah. Like Noah was the only being in the world who mattered.

Noah wanted more of that, case and the cops be damned.

Callahan frowned at Danny. "So, if I let you … spill my blood or whatever, I'd feel different than I would if Green was the one doing it, right?" His grimace cracked the rest of them up.

"Of course you'd feel different," Danny said. "You probably wouldn't feel anything at all if it were me, unless you have a kink for blood play."

"I absolutely do not."

"Hey, no judgement from me." Danny cocked his head at the detective. "Have you ever given blood?"

"Sure, a bunch of times."

"How did you feel when you did it?"

A thoughtful look crossed Callahan's face. "The same as I normally do, I suppose. Annoyed at being poked in the arm but otherwise no different."

"Exactly. Feeling no change during and after minor blood loss is common." Danny smiled at him. "Bloodex is the opposite. No part of being a donor feels like 'meh, no big deal.'"

Galen chuckled. "You should try it from the blood eater's end."

"Hard pass." Callahan wrinkled his nose again, but he seemed less combative now and instead genuinely interested in hearing whatever came next.

Danny glanced around at them. "So, again, if the guys in the parks wanted a bloodex, what were they doing with a human who had to use tools?"

"And who was the blood for?" Callahan mused. "We still have no idea what became of it."

"I think that there's … more." Noah blinked as another part

of the picture became clear. "Evidence tells us the vics came to this bar but, other than Aaron Josephs, almost nothing indicates they were actively involved in the vampire/donor scene. What if they were new to the community? And the night they walked into this bar was also the night they died?"

He looked at Danny. "Josephs is the outlier. We know he was a regular in the scene. He'd have known what to expect when he came here but also what *not* to expect, namely that a bloodex without a blood eater would ever feel the same."

"*Oh.*" Danny's eyes got big. "That's why there were no bite marks on the bodies. If the other guys were newbies, they wouldn't recognize the nuances. They might have gone for what they thought was the next best thing, just on somebody's word."

"Especially if they were paid." Galen's tone was as grave as his words and Callahan immediately shook his head.

"Selling human blood is illegal," he said. "Everyone knows that."

"Everyone knows the vampire underground market is a real thing too," Galen replied, "and that the same illegal human blood is an extremely popular item."

"Fuck." Callahan shook his head at Noah. "If we go with this angle, the vics are unfamiliar with the scene. They come to The Last Drop looking for like-minded people but meet the perp instead who feeds them misinformation and sweetens the pot with money. It's a decent working theory. And you're right, Green. It doesn't explain what happened to Josephs."

"Unless money was a lure for him, too," Noah said. "Most of the bills we found on Josephs' desk were flagged overdue— maybe he started donating for cash in an effort to pay them off."

"I can see that." Danny shrugged when the others looked at him. "This city's expensive and while Nice Buns is in the black now, it's never guaranteed. Running your own business can be one drama after another and there were lots of months I barely made rent or had money to feed myself and forget about health insurance." He scoffed at Callahan's grimace. "What are you acting all scandalized for? There's no way underground market blood is the funkiest thing you've talked about this week."

A rusty chuckle came out of Callahan. "Fair enough. I believe we've come full circle, though," he said with a glower for Galen, "and this time you're gonna answer. Have you heard anything about humans spilling blood the way fangers would or not?"

"I'm not sure we should leave them alone."

Noah followed Danny's line of sight to the cop and vampire in the next booth. Galen and Callahan had been talking for a while, even before the four of them had come back out to the bar, plotting ways for Galen to ask questions around the community without giving too much away. While Callahan was still acting grouchy, he didn't seem entirely put off by Galen's obvious amusement, and Noah was starting to think maybe the guy just liked having someone to bitch at who didn't give a single goddamn what he thought.

"They're not alone. And I think they're okay."

"Yeah? I don't know." Danny frowned. "It's like Callahan's trying to goad Galen into biting him."

"Maybe he is. Could be he really is kinky," Noah said, and smiled at Danny's snicker. He'd never be a fan of Galen's, but watching him toy with Callahan was fun, and the resulting battle to stay calm playing out on the detective's face was particularly gratifying. "But they're in the middle of a crowded bar, Dan, with a literal van-load of cops waiting outside to sweep in if anything goes wrong."

"Heck yeah," Cho said in his ear.

Danny, however, pulled the pendant with the wire over his head then slipped it in a pocket. "Thanks for reminding me. And please, don't call me Dan." He scrunched up his nose. "The only people who call me that are Galen, my mother, and strangers who don't know any better. I really don't like it."

"Apologies. I thought maybe it was a pet name or term of endearment."

"God, no. A term of annoyment is more accurate. 'Dan' just doesn't feel like me, you know? I'd much rather hear my full name if you can't manage 'Danny'."

Noah smiled at him. "I like Danilo."

"Thanks." Danny's answering smile was soft. "I like it, too. And Galen knows it. As does my mother. They just don't give a shit about what I want. Lucky for me, I don't need to be around either of them anymore, and that saves me the energy of getting pissed off."

Ordinarily, Noah might have teased Danny anyway, simply to hear him laugh. But the sadness in the human's eyes spoke of more than simple irritation at being called the wrong name. Something painful that Danny wasn't ready to share.

Noah found himself hoping that would change. Even knowing how foolish he was being when he and Danny had so little time together.

So, he let it go and did the first thing he thought of to lighten the mood by kissing Danny right there in full view of everyone, including Detective Bert Callahan.

CHAPTER 16

The edges of Danny's world grew soft as Noah kissed him deeper, exactly as he wanted. This was the part of the thrall he liked best when he was in the mood. The way it made everything around him—the bar and its patrons, the cops and the vampires, the killer out there waiting for who the fuck knew what—recede so Danny could stop thinking and just breathe.

Kissing was what he needed right now. More lips and tongue and the nip of dangerous teeth, while his bones went as gooey as sweet caramel. Noah's touch on the side of his neck, burning like a brand and the heat rippling under Danny's skin. A groan came out of him when Noah drew back, eyes crinkling at the corners with his grin.

"Sorry. I should have asked if you'd mind."

"Clearly I didn't," Danny said. "Will you take me out of here? Callahan's got what he wants with Galen, and I just want it quiet."

"I'm sorry, but I can't leave just yet," Noah replied. "Not until the operation's over and I've walked you and our detective friend back out the door."

"He's a big boy."

"Yes, and his gun won't be worth shit if Galen decides he's had enough foreplay and gets on with the meal."

Danny laughed so hard his eyes watered. Noah kept an arm around him the whole time, as if to keep him from falling apart. And it could be he was. His hands didn't normally shake like this, and God knew why his heart was galloping like he'd been sprinting hard. Which left him clinging to the only thing that made sense in his world as he let himself go.

Funny how falling apart felt almost good.

"Thanks," Danny said when he was able. "I swear I'm okay."

Noah rubbed his back. "I know you are."

"Even when I'm disgustingly emotional?"

"Maybe especially then."

"Oh, the things you say." Danny wiped his eyes. "I'll be right back. This human needs a bio break and maybe another drink or three. I'm hoping I can count on you if I need to ride piggyback later."

"Of course."

"I like how you didn't even blink at the suggestion."

Noah chuckled. "As you said earlier, we've spoken about far stranger things tonight than me carrying you home."

Home. Danny's gut tumbled at the word. He really didn't have one right now. He couldn't go to Thea's or his dad's. His studio was not only still off limits but fucked all to hell if the pictures he'd glimpsed were accurate. Which left him with Noah's apartment and every assurance that he was welcome to stay for as long as he needed. That was the real problem, right there. Noah's place had started to feel like home to Danny and he couldn't imagine wanting to leave.

He was safe in those rooms. With Noah. Had been from the beginning, despite all the complaining he'd done about needing to be in his own place. Which did him no good at all when the guy using a word like 'home' had already made it clear he didn't get attached to bleeders.

Danny didn't know how to articulate those thoughts. He

could hardly wrap his head around them as it was. So he said nothing and tried not to flinch when Noah eyed him closely.

"Everything all right?"

Oh, sure. I like you more than I should and hate the idea of being anywhere you're not. Otherwise, no big deal beyond some fucker who might want me dead.

"Uh-huh." Danny slid out of the booth but paused to look down at Noah. "I was just thinking that it's been fun being back here with you."

"I thought the same. We could come back here sometime, if you like, when things have calmed down."

Danny swallowed hard. "I'd like that. I shouldn't have stayed away from the scene for so long. I mean, I needed a break after Galen, but I could have had it and still gone to the bars with my friends. Who knows? We might have met way before you walked into Nice Buns pretending you knew anything about bread."

Meeting sooner wouldn't have saved you from falling in so deep you're about to drown.

Danny walked off, only dimly aware of his surroundings and the people in them, several of whom trailed into the restroom behind him. He was at the sinks when a plaintive noise pulled his attention back to earth. Checking the mirror, he saw two pairs of feet under the door of the stall nearest him just as another sigh floated into the air.

"Steven. Please."

The woman beside Danny met his gaze in the mirror, and she grimaced before taking off. Danny bit back a smile. Few rules applied in blood bar restrooms where species and genders mixed freely and the dude in the stall sounded wrecked, words all mumbly despite the quiet shush that followed. Moving to the hand dryer, Danny froze as the stall door rattled, and he quickly grabbed a wad of paper towels from the dispenser. Sexy times in the restroom just weren't his thing, not in a bar like The Last Drop with dozens of nooks a thousand times cleaner and more private. Not that Danny was judging. Or staying either, because the noisy stall guy outright *groaned* and that got Danny moving for the exit and out of it as the stall door rattled again.

He was only steps from the end of the hallway leading back to the bar when someone grabbed hold of him, and a hand clamped over his mouth.

"I've been looking everywhere for you."

Danny stiffened at the low croon. He bucked against the arms wrapped around him but couldn't get loose, and dread stormed through his body as a sharp, cloying odor filled his nose.

Oh, fuck no.

Struggling harder, Danny thrashed in his efforts to break free, shouting against the palm that muzzled him, knowing no one would hear him over the music unless they were close by. Which no one seemed to be. Not with the man holding Danny backing deeper into the shadows, dragging him away from the bar and the crowd.

Digging his heels into the carpet, Danny threw himself backward, triumph racing through him as the back of his skull connected with something hard that made a satisfying *crunch*. The guy holding him staggered but Danny did too, because not once in his years of TV and movie watching had any character mentioned that delivering a headbutt hurt like a motherfucker. His world spun, pinpoints of light swirling before his eyes, and his feet tangled together as he was wrestled through a door. Cold air washed over Danny, and he stumbled again, because that meant this guy had gotten him outside into the alley that ran behind the building and where the hell were Noah and Callahan and every-fucking-body else?

"I thought I was hallucinating when I saw you at the bar," the guy—*that* guy—said, breath damp against Danny's cheek. "I mean … I look for you for days with nothing and tonight you fall into my lap? Shit, if I'd known you were in the scene, I'd have done all of this differently from the start."

Danny choked on a cry as the guy gave him a rib-creaking

squeeze. Despite the stumbling they'd done, he didn't sound winded at all, and his grip was like iron. He was half-carrying Danny now, seeming unbothered by his fighting, and the fresh burst of terror racing through Danny made his heart thump so fast he thought it might burst. He shouted weakly, unable to draw a full breath as a crashing sound came from behind them.

"Dude, what the hell!?"

The man holding Danny let him go suddenly, and Danny caught a glimpse of a figure running toward him before he was shoved from behind. Off-balance, he went down in a heap on the pavement, but the impact hardly registered as he wheezed out the safe word he'd been given.

"Harlem. Out back, in the alley."

Fuck. Danny didn't know if the pendant he'd stuffed in his pocket was still there or even functioning but sure enough, he heard more running steps and voices yelling followed by tires screeching nearby. Lights flashed blue and red, blinding him, and there were warnings echoing around him as feet pounded pavement. Danny cringed when someone reached for him, but he caught a glimpse of Noah sprinting past, his speed far above human while Callahan and a number of uniformed cops chased behind.

"Holy shit, this is *insane.*"

Danny didn't know that voice. But he was too dizzy to do more than hope its owner wouldn't hurt him while he worked on remembering how to breathe.

A long fifteen minutes later, he was seated in the back of the CSU van while Cho fussed over him, and a kid named Baird Noors watched with big, shocked eyes. He'd interrupted Danny's abduction when he'd slammed through the club's fire door in a self-righteous snit, intent on tearing into his hookup for ditching him in the restroom and taking off with a different guy. While Baird had been right about being ditched, he clearly knew now that something very uncool had gone down between his hookup and Danny. He looked freaked out and impossibly young as he eyed the cops swarming the alley, and his voice was small when he spoke.

"Am I under arrest?" His shoulders slumped as Cho shook his head. "Thank fuck."

"We're going to have some questions."

"Yo, I don't know anything—"

"You witnessed a crime and probably saved this man's life," Cho fired back. "The person you met here tonight is dangerous, Mr. Noors—you're lucky you're still breathing."

Danny closed his eyes. Fortune had looked favorably upon them tonight, and maybe especially on Baird Noors. He hadn't known what he was walking into when he'd crashed into the alley, but his outrage had saved both his skin and Danny's, and if it took a while to sink in, Danny understood. He still had trouble wrapping his head around everything and he'd been living in this surreal world for days. He'd just about made up his mind to hug Baird until he squeaked like a chew toy when Noah and the cops jogged back into the alley empty-handed, and Danny found himself fighting tears.

That fucker's still out there.

He kept his eyes on his hands in his lap to keep from losing it while Baird told them what he knew about Steven, the guy he'd met through Poisoned Waters, a hook up app used by the bloodex community.

"I hardly know him," Baird said. "We started messaging a couple of days ago and he said he had a club pass, so when he asked to meet up IRL I figured why not?"

"You've met a lot of vamps this way?" Callahan asked, e-cig already in hand even though he couldn't smoke in the van.

"Sure. Well, I don't know if *a lot* is accurate. I'm in a Master's program at Columbia and, between classes and work, I don't have a ton of free time to party. Steven's not a vamp, though."

Callahan's expression hardened. "You're sure?"

"Yeah, totally. He did a decent job hiding it when we were

just messaging, but I figured it out once he was actually in front of me."

Danny jerked his head up, the hairs on the back of his neck prickling. "He lied about being human?"

Baird gave him a definitive nod. "He talked around the topic of species when I asked him straight out but used all the right language to let me know he was looking for a donor. I'm not sure what he thought was going to happen when we got face-to-face and I saw for myself he was meat."

"What did happen?" Callahan asked. "Clearly, you told him you knew."

"Yeah."

"So, why did you stay? It's not as if this Steven needed a donor."

"I stayed for some cocktails. You would have too if you'd dragged your ass down here from the Bronx and found out the whole night was predicated on a lie," Baird said. "Buying me a couple of drinks was the least that loser could do."

Callahan's lips twitched. "Fine. Steven offered to do more than buy you some drinks, didn't he?"

Baird's answering smirk made it clear the kid's earlier nerves had faded. "You already know how this story ends."

"I do. But I also don't think you've told me everything," Callahan said. "Like that Steven offered to spill your blood anyway. Maybe even pay you for it."

"Selling blood is illegal." Baird was sober now. "Steven talked about the bloodex, sure. Said he was good at it, and he'd had a lot of practice. Said he could make me feel good." He fiddled with the leather cuff on his left wrist. "Maybe he could have. But, like I said, I've been in the scene a while now and no way was I letting some rando who lied about being human spill my blood."

"Smart guy. How'd he take it when you turned him down?"

"I didn't get a chance. He was still talking about his skills when he led me into the bathroom. And man, I'm all for a danger wank but this"—Baird waved at the scene around them —"is fucking ridiculous."

"For real." Danny's laugh sounded dry and weird, and he knew everyone's eyes were on him.

Baird bit his lip. "I didn't realize at first, but I think he followed you in there. Cause we'd barely started messing around before he said he had an idea for a third and bolted." He set his hand on Danny's arm. "I heard him call a name and figured he knew whoever it was. Otherwise, I'd have come looking for him sooner."

Numb again, Danny nodded at the kid. "Not your fault."

There was more talking. Callahan arranged for Baird to be taken to the precinct and meet with a sketch artist, then spoke about some leads Galen had agreed to track down for the team. The consensus was that they might be getting somewhere despite Danny's close call, especially if they could access data from the Poisoned Waters app or the club's membership list to learn more about Steven. Danny found it hard to care. He felt both wired and disjointed, like his skin didn't fit, and was yawning so wide his jaw cracked. The only things he wanted were silence and sleep and Noah, and he couldn't hide his relief when Callahan finally told them to go the hell home.

Noah's door was hardly closed behind them before Danny pushed into his arms, fully expecting Noah to put him off. Insist Danny needed food or sleep or to process his goddamned feelings, all things Danny needed infinitely less than to simply be with his vampire.

But Noah didn't say anything and instead swept Danny off his feet.

Oh, God.

Danny's heart hurt. For the first time in hours, he let his fear go, and sagged into Noah's touch, forehead coming to rest against Noah's as Noah kissed him hard. Danny soaked it up greedily, humming softly into Noah's mouth as he was carried to the bedroom and laid him out on the bed. But Danny couldn't bear to let go of Noah and grabbed him, pulling Noah down until he'd stretched out on the mattress too and they were snuggled close, torsos pressed together tight and their legs in a tangle.

The kisses went on and on, until Danny could barely breathe, and still, he couldn't get enough. He ached with want, balls already throbbing like he was close to coming. And maybe he was. He gasped when Noah eased back enough to mouth at Danny's jaw and heard the desperation in his own shaking voice when he spoke.

"Noah."

"I know." Noah nosed at Danny's throat, grip just short of bruising, and nipped at the tender skin. "I'm sorry I wasn't there."

"Don't. You couldn't have known. None of us could."

"We went there to find him. We should have—"

"*No.* I don't want to talk about it. I just want this. You." The break in Danny's voice made Noah shudder.

"I want you too, Danny. So goddamned much."

The mournful note in his voice hit Danny square in the chest. He settled back against the mattress as Noah stripped them both down, and got lost in the best possible way, reveling in kisses that cycled between fevered and languid. Noah touched him all over, then mouthed the base of Danny's throat, hand closing over the back of his neck while Danny hung on, floating on big swells of bliss.

He peeled his eyes open again when Noah moved away, watching in breathless silence as he pulled a bottle of lube from the nightstand. A tremor started in Danny's belly, and he had to press a hand to his mouth to keep himself from babbling about how much he *loved* this. The fire he felt with Noah. The pleasure that arced between them each time they touched, so true it crushed him flat.

Turning back, Noah trailed wet fingers over Danny's cock, but it was his smile that really took Danny apart. The way Noah seemed to see inside him, past the walls Danny'd put up to safe-guard his heart. Those walls had always been his bedrock. And now they were dust. Thanks to this unhuman man who made Danny feel like he could be truly open with someone for the first time in years.

He spread his thighs wide, skin prickling as Noah slid his fingers behind Danny's balls, and the final remnant of his control went up in smoke.

"Oh, my fuck. Noah. Don't you dare stop."

Noah chuckled lightly "Mmm. I think you love that."

"I do," Danny whispered, shudders tearing through him as Noah pushed a finger inside, the breach releasing another torrent of sensation. Eyes squeezed shut, Danny pleaded without truly knowing what he said, chest clenching when Noah's lips brushed his cheek.

"I've got you, Danny."

And yeah, Noah did. He teased and fingered, slipping a second digit inside Danny, while Danny tried in vain to remember the last time he'd felt so good and came up with noth-ing. His eyes stung as Noah kissed the line of his jaw before moving lower, breath moving like a whisper over Danny's skin.

"I—" He didn't know how to ask for what he wanted, or if he even should. He only knew he wanted this to go on forever and hoped that it would.

Noah crowded in closer then, licking and sucking at Danny's neck with an intensity that sent a frisson of something unnam-able snaking down his spine.

You're prey.

He should have been afraid. Danny knew what Noah was. How deadly he was under that gentleman's front, and that each time they came together, Danny's life could end. But Danny's fear responses were so tangled up with the lust and need that flooded him, he didn't know anymore where one ended and the other began, or even really care.

His toes curled at Noah's low growl, and everything in him

tensed as the hard edge of teeth skimmed the mark on his neck. But then Noah followed the almost-bite with a kiss and the contrast of hard and soft sent Danny reeling, his whole body begging for more as moisture gathered at the corners of his eyes.

He'd never felt so out of control. Or loved it so much.

"Danny. Do you want this?"

More than anything, Danny thought, though he could only nod. And nothing could have been truer. He was already braced for the bite when Noah took hold of his chin, eyes flashing blue fire when Danny met his gaze.

"I need you to say it. To know you want this with me."

"I want this," Danny whispered. "Noah, *please.*"

A shudder shook Noah's frame. He kissed Danny hard, fucking deep with his tongue, and Danny's chest constricted to the point of pain. Reaching down, he took himself in hand, choking on a sob when Noah pulled away at last and sank his teeth into Danny's throat.

"Baby."

The endearment came on Danny's gasp as he lost it, orgasm swamping him in the bare second he had before the bloodex obliterated everything. He tumbled and flew at the same time, ragged breaths hitching, but it all seemed far away. He grew light, floating far above the fear that had dominated his world for days, sure Noah would anchor him if Danny went too far.

Except … Danny wasn't sure he wanted an anchor. Not anymore.

He couldn't move. Could hardly breathe around the rapture crashing through him, not that he wanted to. Because nothing —*nothing*—outside of this room and Noah mattered. Not the slowing of his heart, or the shroud of grey stars unfurling around him. If Danny never got up from this bed again, that sounded just fine. All he had to do was let go and wait until his consciousness flickered and finally went out.

But the moment didn't come. Instead there was pain as Noah wrenched away, followed by a flood of light and noise, someone's hoarse cry in his ears as Danny tumbled back into a body that felt broken and cold.

"Should've kept going," he mumbled, voice scratchy around the rocks in his throat. He tried like hell to peel his eyes open when Noah didn't answer but couldn't manage even one. "Why'd you stop? We could still—"

"Don't," Noah said. "You're not in the right frame of mind for more. Or for talk."

He sounded so sad, Danny's grief rose and grabbed him, and he covered his eyes with one shaking hand so he could hide his tears. But he did as he was asked and stayed quiet as Noah wiped him down. He needed this care. Knew even more how much Noah wanted to give it. How keeping Danny warm and safe from the rest of the world made Noah feel good, too, at least for tonight.

As sleep moved in to take him, Danny couldn't help wondering why. And who Noah Green might have been, once upon a time.

CHAPTER 17

November 15
Monday, 3:00 P.M.

"Where did you find these, Noah?"

Glancing up, Noah looked to where Danny stood on the other side of the room with a plate of food in his hands, his attention on a set of framed black-and-white photographs depicting Times Square at night.

Danny cocked his head. "They remind me of the prints hanging on the back wall at The Last Drop last night. Not that I was really seeing them, I guess, and it was dark. But they were definitely of the city at night with lots of white light. Kind of … old timey."

Noah had to smile. He supposed any image older than Danny's actual age would appear 'old timey' to eyes as young as his. "You have a good eye. I took those photos. The ones at The Last Drop, too."

"Huh. Well, you know I want to hear about that."

Danny stepped closer to the prints, frowning at them. He'd crashed hard after the second bloodex but roused multiple times during the night, sitting up and talking nonsense while his eyes looked inward. He'd allowed Noah to ease him back down each time and had stayed in bed until well after noon, but he didn't appear rested at all and instead frail in a way he never had before.

Noah didn't like it. And that had him weighing his options as he walked to Danny's side. They had more important things to talk about than how and when Noah had taken those photos. The grim messages Callahan had sent during the last several hours. Where Noah and Danny would be after Danny was ultimately allowed to go back to his life. The bond growing between them that was already far deeper than friendship. Danny pushing Noah to take more blood than both of them knew was wise. How, for the first time, Noah had wanted to do it.

Not to kill Danny. But keep him. For as long as the planet they were riding continued to circle the sun.

"Baby."

Noah held his breath at the whispered memory, unsure he was ready to talk about any of it. And that was another thing that troubled him.

He didn't do this. Leave things unsaid with a donor or want more than attraction and blood. He didn't get attached and *couldn't* with Danny, who wouldn't stay young and strong. Not forever. Danny was so terribly vulnerable to threats he'd hardly known existed until this week. He could—would—be gone in the blink of an eye. Nearly had been last night. And even thinking it made Noah ache in ways that frightened him.

So, he made a choice to put off piercing the fragile bubble of peace surrounding them for a little while longer. And tipped his head at a photo of a New York at night Danny had never known.

Glossy, rain-slicked streets reflected the glow of neon signs and storefronts piercing the gloom of the scenes. Humans rushed through them, blurry figures indistinct beneath their umbrellas, like ghosts flickering in and out. A woman stood in the mid-ground, her back to the camera and head bare to the rain, set apart from the others by her stillness.

"This is Joy." Noah reached out and touched a fingertip to the tiny figure. "She and I ran together for many years."

Danny stared for several long moments before he spoke. "And when were these taken?"

"1940 and 1941."

"That explains some stuff." He turned to Noah. "Your speech is formal sometimes, especially for a guy who looks so young. I also don't know many dudes under seventy who keep the same kind of music on their playlists as you. Jazz and big band were my lolo's jam. My grandfather," he clarified, and Noah could practically see dates flashing in his eyes. "Is that when you were turned? In 1940?"

"No. I was turned in 1919, shortly before my twenty-third birthday."

"Damn, son. You're old."

Noah huffed a laugh. Cho had gaped at hearing he was over a hundred years old, so this teasing was a more than welcome change. Perhaps not surprising either, given Danny's experience with vampires.

"How old is Galen?" Noah asked.

"Fifty-five. A child of the Sixties and a whippersnapper compared to you, huh?" Danny winked, then swung his attention around the apartment and the other prints on the walls. "So you took all of these photos? Even the ones of the beach? Cause honestly, 'vampire' and 'beach' aren't words I'd put together."

"I have to go at night, but I enjoy the beach almost as much as I do the city. All that empty sand and water, the stars overhead brighter than you'd ever see here. You've never seen water so dark. It's beautiful. Plus no people around to bump into when I go for a swim." Noah smiled at Danny's chuckling. "Yes, all of the photos are mine. Which probably makes me sound like a narcissist."

"Meh." Danny popped a grape in his mouth. "You're one of the last people I'd expect to show off. Now that you *have* said it though, I'm curious about why you hang them at all."

"They remind me of who I am and where I've been. Places beyond New York. I've lived all over, but I always come back here when the time seems right. This city still feels like home."

"Even after a hundred years?"

"Even then." Noah nudged Danny's shoulder with his and got a small laugh in return. "The photos give me perspective. Of years and people. Living in a world where everything changes while I stay the same is strange. The photos—freezing that second in time—help keep me grounded."

"Huh, I guess that makes sense. It's not exactly the same, but my job does that for me. My dad and his family, Thea and me— we've been fully assimilated. We feel and even look like strangers when we go back to the Philippines and people treat us as such, though it's all very good-natured." Danny sounded wistful. "Nice Buns is a way for us to tie the family's past to the present and remember where we came from, even if we can't ever truly go back. And even though I believe a person's job doesn't have to be who they are, baking is a big part of me. I can't imagine not doing it."

Noah nodded. And knew he couldn't keep Danny in the dark any longer about what had been happening with his case. "I need to tell you something."

"Okay." Danny glanced toward the kitchen and started walking. "You mind if I get some more coffee first? Because you've got the face that says you've been talking to Bert, and I have a feeling I'll need my whole brain to keep up. Is it something bad?"

"Yes."

Danny's movements stuttered a second before they resumed, and he set the plate on the kitchen island before turning to the stove where the coffeepot still sat on a burner. "What is it?"

"The police have been working with the district attorney to trace the man who attacked you through his profile on the Poisoned Waters app, but it's going to take some time and probably more than one subpoena."

"That figures."

"In the meantime, that man was in your building again last night. Your neighbor across the hall from your unit was killed, Danny. Not long after you were nearly abducted from The Last Drop."

Coffee forgotten, Danny covered his mouth and nose with one hand, eyes huge when they met Noah's. His color fled, but it wasn't until his knees wobbled dangerously that Noah understood Danny was holding his breath and he shot forward so he could grab hold of him.

"Whoa," he said in the calmest voice he could manage. "Take it easy and breathe for me, Danny."

A strangled noise came out of Danny and just like that, he sagged to the floor, half in and half out of Noah's hold. "F-fuck," he croaked out, then buried his face in his hands, elbows braced on his knees.

Carefully, Noah settled onto the floor beside Danny and wound an arm around his shoulders. "You're okay," he said more than once as he coached Danny through breaths in and out, just as he had that first night at Bleecker Playground. Slowly, the stiffness in Danny's posture lessened, but he didn't raise his head until the sky visible under the shades on the windows had grown rosy.

"Sorry."

"What for?"

"Losing it again. I just … fuck. Poor Heide." Danny's eyes were red-rimmed but dry and his expression so haunted it hurt just looking at him. "She was really nice," he said. "More than just a neighbor, you know? I don't … God, I don't understand what the fuck is going on, Noah. I can't."

"I know. And I'm sorry." Noah didn't bother stating the obvious. They didn't know yet why the man who called himself Steven was draining men of blood and leaving them to die in West Village parks or why he'd killed Heide Brown. Why he was after Danny or how he could come and go from a building that was under surveillance. Understanding probably wouldn't bring Danny comfort either. So Noah let him lean in and didn't stir until Danny was ready.

"Will you show me the photos of my apartment now?"

"Of course."

Together, they got to their feet and Noah made sure Danny was seated in the desk chair at the workstation before he logged into the police lab's portal. His phone chimed repeatedly with messages, and he knew it was only a matter of time before Callahan or Cho or both would be knocking at the door. Noah didn't care. His energy right now was on keeping his friend sane.

"I've already curated these, so all you need to do is concentrate on your apartment."

Danny's lips thinned. "Instead of on Heide, you mean?"

"Yes. There's no reason for you to see those images unless the police ask."

"I can handle it, you know." Challenge sparked in Danny's eyes. "I'm not as weak as you think."

Squatting, Noah set a hand on Danny's knee. "I don't think you're weak at all and have no doubt you could handle it. But you knew Heide Brown. She wasn't a stranger you read about in the news. She didn't die the way the men in the parks did." He slowly shook his head. The crime scene at Heide Brown's apartment had been vastly different from those in the parks around the West Village. Her throat had been slashed and she'd struggled, only to die sprawled on her back, hair wet with blood and her unseeing eyes open. "I see scenes like the one in her apartment every night and I *know* you don't want to remember her like that."

"Okay." The word came out in a near whisper as Danny dropped his gaze. "I believe you. But I want to do whatever I can to help."

"I know you do. And you will. Are you ready?"

"Eh. Nothing like a bloodex with a panic chaser to keep a body guessing but yeah, I'm ready. Show me."

Noah smiled. He really admired this human. The strength and compassion beneath the pretty exterior, and the steel that ran through Danny's gentle heart.

They went through the police photos slowly, Noah scanning them again for unusual details while Danny simply stared, his features growing even more pinched as the minutes passed. The studio had been tossed from end to end, drawers, cabinets, and shelves emptied of their contents and strewn across the floor. Dirt and ruined plants filled the old fireplace, which Danny had been using to house a tiny indoor garden, and he groaned over the state of his kitchen and the broken jars of condiments and spices that sat in the sink.

"Fucking A, man." He scrubbed his hands over his head. "I don't get it. Why would he do that?"

"Do what exactly?"

"Trash the food! The cops think this guy went through my shit trying to figure out where I'd gone, right? So why go through my refrigerator? It's not like I keep an address book in with the jar of pickled beets—what was the purpose of breaking it and dumping the contents in the sink?"

Noah frowned. Much of the damage in the apartment had been written off as pointless destruction, but Danny made an interesting point. "Is there anything else in the photos that strikes you as off?"

Danny leveled a flat stare at him. "The place looks like a tornado hit it. *Everything* I see here strikes me as off. Like, I guess he didn't find the bed behind the couch since it's still in one piece, even though he pulled everything out of the bookshelf?"

That was another odd little detail. Compared to the mess covering the rest of the apartment, the couch near the windows was neat, cushions still in place. And why?

Noah tapped his fingers on the edge of his keyboard then straightened. He could do more. Document the scene himself and use his heightened senses. Maybe find something—anything —to ease Danny's distress.

"Are you up for another field trip tonight?"

Danny gave him a small but real smile. "I guess? But if you're thinking about The Last Drop, I'm gonna get drunk first. As much as I've always loved the place, last night totally sucked and I need to be fully lubricated if you don't want me losing my shit."

"No, not the bar. I'd like to go over the scene at your apartment. I thought I'd get Callahan to sign off on you coming with me so you can grab some things."

Danny bounced a bit in the chair. "Get the fuck out, really? But what about …?" Bottom lip between his teeth, he flicked a look at the monitors.

"It is still a mess," Noah allowed. "Your building super arranged to have the foodstuffs and broken glass removed from the sink, but nothing else has been touched. Cleanup will be on you once you're able to, ah, go back home."

"Which will be never-fucking-ever at this rate."

Noah ignored the muttered oath. "You need to be ready. It won't be easy seeing it, Danny. So, if it gets to be too much at any point while we're there, just say the word and I'll have the uniforms bring you back here."

"Okay." Danny's nod was jerky. "Thank you for saying that. I appreciate you being straight with me and not holding back but why didn't you tell me when I first came out here?"

Because I was being selfish.

"I wanted to give you some time before you had to deal with another awful thing," Noah said. "Maybe it wasn't my place. But I wanted to be a good friend."

"You were. Even though you don't like getting close to bleeders like me."

Noah sighed at the barely concealed hurt in Danny's eyes. "I don't usually. But nothing about getting to know you has ever been usual. I *shouldn't* hold anything back from you, even when I think it's the right thing, and if we could start over again, I would have told you right away I wasn't human. Hearing that boy last night say he couldn't get a straight answer from Steven—"

"It wasn't the same thing at all." Danny stood too and got right in Noah's face. "Don't compare yourself to that fucking asshole. Baird asked him, straight out, but I never asked you, not even once. And I should have." Stepping back, he turned his gaze to the windows.

"There were enough pieces I should have wondered if maybe you weren't human," Danny said. "But I didn't want to know. Not knowing made it easy to like you without worrying about shit I couldn't control. Like having to decide how I'd feel about getting close with another vamp when I'd already sworn I wouldn't ever again."

For a second, Noah wanted to laugh. Clearly, he wasn't the only one with rules about who he'd let into his life. "What made you swear off my kind?"

"Galen. He made me realize that being with a vampire means putting myself last and I'm done living my life that way."

"I don't understand."

"I know. And that's on me." Danny walked to the windows. "Galen wanted two things from me—research for his writing and blood. While you're nothing like the *other* murderous asshole who's fucking up my life, you do have things in common with Galen, Noah, namely looking at humans as less than yourselves."

Dumbstruck, Noah stared at Danny's back, the silence stretching on for so long Danny finally turned around and pinned Noah with a glare. "I don't think you're less than me, Danny," Noah said. "I never have. And I'm sure I've never said anything even remotely similar to you."

"Haven't you? You don't get involved with bleeders—you just hook up when you want to feed. Same as Galen. As far as he cared, I was a blood bag he could use whenever he felt like it.

He's with someone, you know. A ... blood eater like you. Was the whole time we were together." He winced at Noah's muttered curse.

"Is that why you called it off?"

"No. Galen is a lot of things but he's definitely not a liar. I knew he and his partner were poly. They'd sometimes take a third if they liked them well enough. Only vamps, though. Of *course*." Danny laughed, a bitter sound with jagged edges, then looked away. "You should have seen Galen when I asked him if I could meet his mate, maybe be their third. It was like I'd said something so offensive he didn't know whether to crack up or punch me."

Danny's voice grew distant as he continued, as if he were talking to himself. "The sad thing is that I hung on for a while anyway, even knowing I didn't have a chance in hell. Because I had a plan, see. I was going to change Galen's mind. Make him want me for more than the blood. Make him care about me. I wanted to mean something to him, you know? To matter. And it took way too long for me to understand it was never going to happen." He sighed. "I've spent the last year reminding myself that whatever anyone else thinks, I am *not* worthless."

"No, you're not." Noah took a single step forward but stopped at Danny's full-body flinch. "Danny—"

Spots of color burned high on Danny's otherwise wan cheeks, and he held Noah's gaze for only a second before dropping his eyes. "I know. But it's easy to believe you are if people you love say it enough that they finally break your heart."

He slipped past Noah, murmuring quietly about needing a shower, and Noah let him go. What did he know about love? Or heartbreak or any of the complicated feelings that ruled humans' lives?

He didn't want complications. He'd frozen his own heart against them a lifetime ago and, until his path had crossed Danny's, been fine on his own. Running with other blood eaters over the years had been fun. He'd enjoyed the companionship they'd brought him while they'd explored the world. But there'd been nothing deep there. Just easy affection, adventure, and sex. Which made walking away painless, because when someone got bored, no one's feelings were hurt, and it was simple to exchange a smile and know there was room somewhere in the future to meet up again.

Nothing about Danny was simple. A tender soul lived beneath the street-smart exterior, his spirit more raw than most people would guess. And he needed so much. His emotions ran deep. He needed to know he was wanted, for more than his blood or body. He needed family. A home. Too many things Noah simply didn't have it in him to give. Even though he wanted to.

Staring out at the city beyond the windows, Noah frowned. He could keep Danny safe for now. Ensure he lived until the man who'd been hunting him was no longer a threat. If that took a human lifetime, Noah would deal. A human life lasted almost no time at all. And he liked being Danny's friend, despite the complications. Liked making Danny feel good and wanted because he was.

If Noah were being honest, he couldn't imagine walking away right now, even knowing this thing between them wasn't made to last.

The shower's hiss brought him back to the here and now, and he crossed the apartment to the already steamy bathroom.

"Danny?"

"Be out in a minute."

Danny's tone was brusque, but the salty scent of tears had Noah stripping down without another word. Stepping into the big clawfoot tub, he closed the curtain behind him and stared at Danny, whose skin had flushed red in the heat while soap suds slid down his back. The sight would have been gorgeous but for the misery pouring off him and Noah couldn't step forward fast enough to hold him close.

"I'm sorry," he murmured.

For a moment, Danny stood stiff. But then the rigid set to his shoulders softened and his head dipped, his next words were so low they were nearly lost under the roar of water. "What for?"

"That someone made you feel like you didn't matter." Setting his cheek against Danny's, Noah palmed Danny's belly, supporting him as he pressed his lips against Danny's ear. "I have a feeling it wasn't only Galen who did it to you. If *I've* made you feel that way, I'm sorrier than you can know. You matter, Danny. I'll tell you the same again and again until you believe me."

Danny covered Noah's hand on his belly with his own. "You don't have to. But thanks. I'm happy to hear anything you have to say for as long as I have you."

Turning in Noah's embrace, he slid his arms around Noah's neck and held on as the steam and heat rose around them.

CHAPTER 18

"I can't believe I did that."

"Neither can I." Noah's tone was wry. "I'm trying not to take it personally."

Danny smothered a laugh. They'd climbed into bed after the shower and spent much of the late afternoon and early evening talking. When Danny'd been awake that is, and not dozing off in the middle of a conversation. He'd surfaced just now thanks to Noah's phone chiming on the nightstand, and he felt zero motivation to move. Even the prospect of going back to his apartment to grab a few things didn't appeal when he could have six-foot-plus of vampire stretched out beside him instead looking all rumpled and kind of adorable, as well as a bit drowsy.

Danny ran a hand over Noah's hair and messed it up more. "Do you ever sleep?"

"Yes." Noah gave him a smile. "But I won't while you're here."

"Won't you be tired?"

"I'll manage. I don't usually need much beyond a few hours every three or four days anyway."

"Usually?"

"Now and then a sleep will take hold and it can be days before I'm conscious again."

"Days?" Propping his head up on his fist, Danny gazed down at him. He didn't like the idea of that at all. "What would happen if you just didn't wake up again?"

"I don't think it works that way." A line appeared between Noah's eyebrows. "I suppose I'd be none the wiser if it happened though, and it really wouldn't matter."

Pain flared in Danny's heart. "It would matter to me." He didn't bother hiding his hurt. "I'm pretty sure Cho wouldn't be happy about it, either."

"You're right." Noah's face fell. "I shouldn't have said that. It's just …"

"What? Weird someone gives a shit about you?"

"Maybe." Noah turned his eyes on the windows and the city lights beyond them. "It's been a long time since I've felt close to a human. Made friends with them the way I have Cho and … you. So much of what you might think is weird is my every day, Danny, and I'm not sure I know the difference anymore."

"I understand."

"I'm not sure you can—not really." Noah's kind tone removed most of the sting from the rebuke. "Did Galen ever sleep around you?"

Well, shit. "Uh." Danny frowned. "No. He'd close his eyes sometimes after a bloodex, but I don't think he actually ever slept."

Noah nodded sagely. "Because it wouldn't be safe. For either of you. We dream you know, just like any living thing." He took hold of Danny's hand. "I could forget myself. Strike out before I'm truly awake and hurt someone. You."

"I understand what you're saying. I have a hard time believing you would though."

The furrow between Noah's eyebrows grew deeper. "You can't know that. I don't know it, even after all this time, and I hate admitting it. There are still things I don't fully understand about myself and maybe never will." He wrinkled his nose, then sighed. "Sleeping habits could be a whole chapter in the hand-book I sometimes want to write."

"What, like *Self-Care for Vampires*?" Danny teased, delighting in the way Noah's eyes instantly brightened.

"I was thinking more like *The Vampire's Guide To Staying Alive*."

Danny whooped quietly. "Oh, my God. You should write that. Even if it were ninety-percent bullshit, it'd still make an assload of money."

"Probably. And then the rest of my kind would show up bearing torches and stakes."

"Really? Why?"

"Most vampires aren't big on sharing, especially with humans. Sometimes not even with each other. Some form the kinds of covens you read about in science fiction stories, but most stay solo or run in pairs or threes."

Never with humans. Which Danny already knew.

"Did you run with the vampire who made you?"

"For a while, yes. His name is Morgan and he taught me a great deal about how to live this life. How to get around in my world and yours, and cross between the two when needed."

"Like working with mortals?" Danny asked.

"Yes, exactly. Back then, the species didn't mix day-to-day the way they do now and there was misinformation out there that had been circulating for millennia. Humans didn't know how vampirism worked. That when a bleeder was turned, the virus changed them but they didn't die. We were thought to be literal revenants, called back from the grave by forces unseen. That we slept in coffins and would cower before religious icons. The number of times I've had crosses waved at me or been doused in holy water …" His smile was almost fond.

"I'd never even been truly close to a supernatural myself until the night I met Morgan and had no idea how to handle myself after I was changed. I was lucky he took me under his wing instead of leaving me to my own devices." Noah slowly shook his head. "I have no idea what my life would be like now if he hadn't."

Danny rubbed Noah's hair again but more gently this time, and he was struck by how somber he'd grown.

"After a few years, Morgan wanted to travel and I didn't, and we parted ways. He left me this apartment so I would have a safe place to stay while I was alone."

Danny heard a world of hurt in that word 'alone.' "He didn't come back?"

"No. He said he was done with this city and had a whole world to explore. I ... it was difficult knowing he wanted to leave, but I respected his wishes."

"Couldn't you have gone together? I mean, I'm glad you're here and I know you've said New York has always felt like home, but there wasn't anything ..." The pieces came together in Danny's head before he'd even finished speaking.

"It was your family." He laid a hand on Noah's cheek and frowned when Noah didn't meet his eye. "You stayed instead of leaving them behind."

"Yes. My mother and father, my sister, Ellen—they were still living. My parents lived here in New York. I wanted them to move to Boston and move in with Ellen, but they wouldn't, not for a long time."

"Because of you?"

"I'm not sure."

"I'm sorry, I don't understand."

"None of us did." Noah turned a weary look on Danny. "What happened to me wasn't something they'd ever expected. I told you—we knew nothing about supernaturals except that they weren't like us. When the species mixed, it was rarely peaceful. Families like mine didn't acknowledge vampires and shifters unless they were forced." His laugh was strained. "They pretended every day that millions of souls didn't even exist right under their noses. Until they couldn't anymore because the world changed and the supernaturals decided they didn't want to keep living underground."

Oh, wow. Danny bit his lip. He'd studied history at school. Knew the Great War had brought an army of supernatural beings out of the shadows to keep the nations running while the humans had battled each other. Noah would have been the right age to fight as a soldier in that war if he hadn't already been turned.

"Were you part of the change?"

Noah nodded once. "I was. Nothing was ever going to be the same, even before the fighting had ended. The supernaturals were done hiding. And the humans ... well. Too many thought that we'd all go back to pretending the blood eaters and shifters didn't exist." His laugh was threaded with pain.

"Can you imagine that kind of arrogance? Believing they could just turn their backs and act like nothing had happened when *everything* was different and changing? The only way people like my parents knew how to cope was fighting the change tooth and nail, even though it was already obvious to everyone there wasn't any point."

Noah met Danny's gaze. "I'd never been in a blood bar or gotten closer to a vampire or a shifter beyond rushing past them on the street. I didn't know a goddamned thing about supernaturals that was truly useful or relevant. But I knew there was no going back. We had to change and learn how to live alongside one another. I believed my parents knew it too, even through their denial. I hoped one day they'd get there. But in the end none of it mattered because one night Noah Green disappeared and didn't come back."

"Oh, Noah." Danny sighed. "Is that how you felt? Like you'd disappeared?"

"I did, Danny. The human in me faded the moment I met Morgan and just like that, it was over. No one human cared that I hadn't asked for it. That the only reason I didn't die that night was because Morgan thought my eyes were pretty and decided to keep me around. All I knew was that I couldn't get near my parents without worrying I'd eat them, and they didn't want anything to do with the freak I'd become."

A sick feeling rose in Danny's gut. Hundreds of laws protected each species now, and a bloodex without consent was a serious offense, never mind an actual transformation. But when the supernaturals had first come out of hiding, there'd been nothing to stop vampires from gorging on humans whenever they hungered. From taking people like Noah and forcing them into lives they hadn't asked for or wanted.

"I didn't have the kind of control I do now. Knowing my parents despised what I'd become … that just made it harder. I was so angry with them for turning their backs on me," Noah mused. "For not understanding I needed help. Them. And they could hardly bear seeing me. They were good people and deeply kind and loving, but only toward humans. I'd never truly understood that about them until I stopped being one of them and realized they didn't like that reality at all."

"I'm sorry," Danny said, and was. Immensely so. He'd known the same kind of loss. Suffered the pain of ties being cut over something he couldn't control, and everything in him went out to Noah. "I had no idea."

Noah gave him the barest of smiles. "The irony is that I'd have been a disappointment even if I hadn't been turned. I'd just started to become aware I was attracted to both men and women and had no idea how to tell them."

"Oh, fuck." Danny couldn't help laughing, though he broke a little more for his friend. "Noah!"

"I know. I hardly understood it myself at the time. But it didn't matter. I was turned and my parents never got over it. We stopped speaking after they finally moved to Boston with Ellen and that, as they say, was that."

It hadn't really been the end, though. Danny could tell from the hurt throbbing under Noah's words. "You never saw them again?"

"No. I didn't see the point. I couldn't bridge the gap between our worlds. They didn't want to." Noah frowned. "Letting them go was easier than fighting for something I wasn't sure any of us truly wanted." He gave Danny a sidelong glance. "I must sound very cruel."

Danny shook his head. How he wished he could lie. Assure Noah his parents had loved him, in spite of their fear; they'd just done a shitty job of showing it. He knew better than to wish for a moment of redemption that would never come to Noah or himself. And they both deserved more.

Leaning down, he brushed his lips over Noah's temple. "You did what you could. And I'm sorry they let you down. That they weren't there for you when you needed them."

His own problems seemed suddenly small compared to the pain Noah must have known, hurts that might never heal with his parents and sister long dead and buried. Any remaining descendants would be distant enough Noah had probably lost track of them, maybe even on purpose. Danny thought it made a sad sort of sense, too. What good would it do Noah to get attached to someone who wouldn't be around to live with him into forever?

The thought turned Danny's blood cold. While Noah hadn't used those exact words, he'd been saying as much for days. He didn't do attachments to humans because, odds were, someone would be hurt in the end. Except Danny had never once considered Noah might be talking about himself. Which made his eventual withdrawal from this bubble they were sharing right now seem all the more inevitable.

Pain twisted through Danny. Yet he didn't fight the pull toward Noah. He kissed him instead, slow and languid, like they had nowhere special to be and all the time in the world to get there. He let Noah draw him close and tangle their legs together under the bedding and gave in to the sensations washing over him in a heavy, wonderful wave.

He savored every second. Stopped thinking about the royal

mess of his life. About the man out there who wanted to hurt him. That his neighbor had died. And groaned as a hand came to rest against the bite on his neck, the mere touch shooting sparks under Danny's skin and straight to his balls.

"You want?" he mumbled against Noah's lips, despite knowing better than to ask for what they both wanted. There wasn't time for a bloodex and recovery if he was going to keep his appointment with the cops. His dick still went from interested to hell-the-fuck-yeah at Noah's low growl.

"You know I do." Pulling back, Noah dipped his head and nosed at Danny's throat. He inhaled deeply, breathing Danny in, then pressed his lips over the mark in a kiss that made Danny ache. "But I'm okay just doing this, too, if that's all right."

"Course it's okay," Danny grumbled. "But if you want more—"

"I don't," Noah said, his voice even lower. "We can just be, Danny, without anything else."

Danny didn't answer. Wasn't sure he could over the lump in his throat, and he had no idea what to make of Noah's words. The bloodex was everything the vampires needed from humans. Or so Galen had always said. But Noah was *so* different. He seemed … content just lying there together, wrapped around Danny like he was exactly where he wanted to be.

Maybe it was. Danny sure wasn't going to argue when snuggling up like this made his next words come a hundred times easier.

"My mother disowned me after I came out. I was sixteen. She left us—my dad, sister, and me—and moved to California. I haven't seen her in maybe five years."

Noah rubbed Danny's arm. "But your father stayed here."

"Yeah. And Thea, of course. My mom tried to get her to move out west too, but Thea was already eighteen and she wasn't having it."

"Tenacity being a Kaes family trait."

The gentle tease made Danny smile, despite the hurt that still felt fresh even now. He'd been so young when his mother had left. Watching her walk away had wrecked him. Knowing she didn't want him and despised her own son. His dad and sister had been the only things that'd kept Danny from falling apart completely. He'd forced himself to get up every day and act like he knew how to live his life, just to keep them from worrying. Which they'd done anyway.

Danny closed his eyes as a memory seared through him.

"How can she be so mean?" Thea asked, her voice choked after another phone call with her mother that hadn't gone anywhere. *"Who fucking cares if Danny likes boys?"*

"I don't understand it either. Or where this is coming from." Keoni sounded weary. *"Your mother's had concerns for a while about marriage equality and Pride, and how they conflict with her own faith and morals. But I never thought she'd be—"*

"Intolerant against her own son? Or how about selfish and hateful?"

"Thea."

"She left us, Dad. Because she thinks something is wrong with her child."

"And me," Danny's father said quietly. *"She thinks I failed him somehow."*

"That is the stupidest thing I've ever heard. And Mom has been saying a whole truckload of extremely stupid things."

"I don't think she's wrong about this, though. I did fail Danny."

"Dad, no."

"I should have done a better job at protecting him and you. It's my job as your father, honey. It just never occurred to me I'd have to protect you from your own mom."

"How could you have known?" Thea's voice got muffled, like she was pressing her face into her father's shoulder because he'd swept her into a hug. *"I love you, Dad, and Danny does too. It isn't your fault you married an asshole."*

Danny's dad chuckled. *"I know. It's just that sometimes it feels like it is. I hate that she hurts you and your brother, and that I can't fix it."*

They hadn't known Danny had heard them. He'd come home early from baseball practice and stood frozen just outside the kitchen, listening to their tears and cold comfort. He'd wished harder than he had for anything that he could make it all better. Get his mother to return. Go back in time and squash his own coming out words and work hard at changing himself so she would keep loving them. Keep loving him.

Wishing didn't get Danny anywhere though. He'd slipped back out of the house and stayed gone until his father's increasingly anxious calls had drawn him back to the house where he and his sister had grown up. He'd never been truly at home there again.

Noah propped himself up on one elbow as Danny finished his story. "It wasn't on you to fix things," he said. "You didn't do anything wrong."

"I know." Danny winced at Noah's raised brow. "I do. Mostly, anyway. It's hard not to feel like I didn't fuck up. If I hadn't been … *me*, maybe she would have stayed. But my dad disagrees. He thinks she used my coming out to get what she wanted—away from us. And if it hadn't been me coming out, she would have found a different reason. It got easier dealing with it over time and it's better with Reba on the west coast. For me, anyway."

Noah's expression gentled. "Reba is your mother's name?"

"Uh-huh."

"When did you last see her?"

"Like I said, it's been a while." Danny pursed his mouth. Talking about his mother was never easy, but he found he didn't mind it so much with Noah. "I was still in culinary school. Some classmates and I had been to a casino in Connecticut and we were on our way back to the city. We pulled into a rest stop for snacks and a bio break, and I went with the guy I was seeing at the time to buy coffee for everyone. She was standing at the next register."

Danny ignored the fire in his face, but his heart pounded

when he caught Noah tracking it, gaze growing darker. He ran a fingertip over Danny's cheek and Danny closed his eyes, soaking up the sensation as the whisper-soft caresses continued.

"She stared at me like … like she'd never seen me before," he said. "Like she couldn't believe what she was seeing."

"You were still a boy when she left. Seeing the man you'd become probably came as a surprise."

"Maybe. She didn't say anything. Neither did I. I didn't *want* to talk to her, either, because I knew it'd all be bullshit. So I waited for the coffee order to come up and paid, then walked out of the place with my guy and the tray, and we met up with the rest of my friends."

Noah hummed. "I'm glad you weren't alone."

"Yeah. Me too."

Rolling onto his side, Danny wallowed in how raw just talking about that godawful afternoon left him. The way his mother had watched him, eyes hard and bright, as if she'd expected a scene. The tension in her expression had changed when Danny had looked her up and down in silence. She'd appeared confused. Maybe even disappointed. But Danny hadn't been interested in a fight or hearing her years-old reasons for throwing a family away. He'd only wanted to get as far away from her as possible.

If Noah noticed how hard Danny clasped his hands together now just to keep them from shaking, he didn't say a word.

CHAPTER 19

"You sure you want to do this now?" Noah glanced at Danny, who was staring warily at the yellow Crime Scene tape stretched across his apartment door the way he might a live wire. "We can come back tomorrow, if you'd rather."

"I feel like you forget sometimes that you can't actually be outside during the day," Danny said. "And besides, we're already here. May as well make good use of the time." He heaved a big breath and looked to Cho, the two exchanging a nod before Cho stepped forward.

Noah kept his attention on Danny, who'd been oddly subdued since they'd left Noah's apartment. There were lines around his eyes and mouth Noah knew hadn't been there before, and he seemed genuinely nervous as Cho cut through the tape.

"Are you coming in with me or …?" He met Noah's gaze. "I don't know how this works."

Cho spoke before Noah could. "I need the vampire whammy across the hall at Miss Brown's."

The words were clearly not what Danny had wanted to hear. He blanched and shot a quick glance over his shoulder at his former neighbor's door, which was similarly crisscrossed with garish yellow tape, and his posture tightened as Cho carried on speaking.

"Officer Tate will be stationed outside your door, and she'll grab us quick if something comes up. Here." He passed Danny an armful of protective gear that included a PPE mask along with the usual booties and latex gloves. "We can't do much about the smell, but the mask might make it feel less like you're breathing in swamp once you're inside."

"Uh." Danny stared at the bundle of gear, then stooped so he could set most of it on the floor. "Because of all the smashed food?"

"That's right."

"Okay."

Noah bit back a sigh. Danny had been so strong throughout this ordeal. Fierce—almost defiant—in his determination to get his life back *and* help the police, even when his own fear had nearly overwhelmed him. But now that he was here, standing on the threshold of his own apartment, he appeared almost checked out, his affect so flat it was like looking at a stranger. That worried Noah more than he liked to admit. Danny had limits, just like any living thing. The longer he stayed in this weird limbo between worlds, the harder it got for him to bounce back, and that spelled disaster no matter how you looked at it.

"You're cleared to take clothing and belongings, but please restrict your movements to the closet and dresser as much as you can," Cho said to Danny. "I'd avoid touching anything beyond those areas, not that you'll want to, given the conditions."

Danny pulled the blue shoe covers over his borrowed boots. "That sounds really not awesome. Am I allowed in the bathroom?"

"You are, but I wouldn't if I were you. There is significant broken glass inside and outside the door and I'd hardly call it safe."

"Great." Danny's face twisted as Noah pushed the door open and a sour smell poured out into the hallway. "Oh, *wow,* that is vile. Guess you were right about the mask." He pulled the PPE up over his mouth and nose. "Not sure I'll want my clothes if they're just going to smell like the inside of a garbage can."

"We'll run them through the wash at my place." Noah was sure he sounded flip, but the vegetal stink in Danny's studio was minor compared to scenes he and Cho sometimes worked. "I don't think it'll be a problem."

"I hope not. I'm not exactly in the mood for shopping. Though I guess I'll have to, given ... everything." Pushing past Noah, Danny stepped a few feet inside then stopped and stared around. His voice was thready when he spoke. "*Fuck.*"

A hand on Noah's shoulder kept him from following, and then Cho was speaking in a low voice.

"I'm sorry, man." His eyes shone with sympathy when Noah looked his way. "I know you want to be there for him. But right now, I need you working. Need you to check over the scene across the hall and help me figure out what the fuck I'm missing. Because I *know* there's something here and if I could just place it—"

"Okay." Noah fought an urge to clench his fists. He couldn't be in two places at once and honestly didn't know where he'd do the most good, keeping Danny in one piece or solving the case that was breaking him. "I just ..." He looked Danny's way again and saw he still hadn't moved. "I don't think he should be alone."

"He's not. Tate's not going anywhere and it's not like you and I will be far. Danny can meet us by the back stairwell if he finishes first."

"Stairwell?" Noah frowned at him. "The one leading to the roof? What did you find there?"

"I'm not entirely sure yet."

"And what made you look?"

"You did." Cho's lips twitched. "Callahan said you made a crack about the roof deck at your place not being accessible to the average person. That made me curious about how accessible the roof of *this* building might be—"

"Because if it is, someone could climb the fire escapes and enter through the bulkhead," Noah finished.

"That's right, homeboy. I think there's something behind the walls if you can believe it."

"I'm surprised you haven't found whatever is back there already."

"Eh, I wanted to wait for you."

"In case you needed someone to crawl into a dusty, dangerous place that might damage or kill the average person?" Noah's narrowed eyes made Cho laugh.

"You know how I feel about spiders."

"I know you're ridiculous," Noah muttered. "You really think there are going to be spiders inside the walls?"

"Fuck, yeah, I do." Cho wrinkled his nose. "There's bound to be cobwebs and ten kinds of ooky stuff all over the goddamned place so yes, there are going to be spiders."

"I thought CSIs loved bugs," Danny called out. He'd moved a bit deeper into the apartment and was squatting beside a pile of things on the floor. Though his eyes were bleak over the mask, he chuckled through it when Cho flapped a hand at him.

"That's just on TV! Though I will say we have a guy on staff who's an amateur entomologist and he kicks so much ass. He's amazing at establishing TOD just by analyzing maggots."

Danny's next noise sounded suspiciously like gagging and Noah thought he looked a bit green.

"Are you okay?"

"Living the dream," Danny said. "Smelling the smell too, which is really quite impressive. Ugh. Give me ten and I'll be right out."

Still, Noah lingered. He didn't like leaving Danny in the wreckage of the place he called home, not knowing when he could come back. It felt wrong. And strange. Like a piece didn't quite fit though Noah had no idea what might be out of place in the middle of so much chaos.

"Do you want me to wait with you until Callahan shows?"

"Nah. That'll keep us here even longer. You go on, Noah." Danny waved without glancing back and reached for what looked like a sneaker. "It's not like anybody can get into this place without coming through a wall."

O

Noah and Cho had just started on Heide Brown's apartment when Callahan arrived, his brow knit so deep Noah wondered if maybe it wasn't a permanent condition. Somehow, the detective still managed to scowl deeper as he strode up to Cho.

"What the fuck did I hear about you wanting to knock holes in the roof?"

"Those words never came out of my mouth," Cho replied. "I said I wanted to take a closer look at the stairwell leading to the roof and holes that might already be there, not to make new ones."

"You think there are holes in the walls?"

"I'm not sure. The perp gained access to this building somehow and the bulkhead on the roof seems a likely entry point, what with fire escapes at the front and rear of the building. It wouldn't take much for someone my size to reach the ladder closest to ground level, and it'd be almost no effort at all for a taller guy like you. Once they were in the building, all they'd need to do is find a place to hide."

"About that," Noah said. "There've been cars stationed outside the building since the morning Danny was attacked at Bleecker Playground, right? Did anyone report any movement on the fire escapes?"

"No. But there's only been a car stationed at the front of the building, not the rear," Callahan said, voice grim. "Between

Kaes's bakery, your building, and this one, we were already stretched thin. I just don't have that kind of people power."

"Son of a monkey." Noah glanced at the matching set of narrow windows on the front wall of Heide Brown's unit. There were only so many cops to go around on any given night. Didn't mean any of them liked it or knowing this investigation might be in a different place if only they'd had more sets of eyes. "So, the perp *could* have made use of the rear fire escape. Were there signs of forced entry on the bulkhead door?"

"Nope," Cho said. "We checked after each break-in. We recovered some prints as you know, but they were smudgy, like someone wiped the door down and only did a piss-poor job. I thought I might get lucky with the banisters in the stairwell though, so I spent some quality time in there tonight and found a whole bunch of weird."

Callahan gave a noisy exhale and moved his hand in a *get on with it* motion. "I'm assuming that 'weird' has something to do with the holes you think might be there?"

"Yup. The walls up there are old, as in wood panels aged and expensive enough to have been part of the original construction." Cho shifted his attention from Callahan to Noah. "They also sound hollow if you knock, which tells me there's space of some kind behind them. Could be a crawl space or maybe a maintenance shaft that opens up somewhere else in the building. Remember that story a couple years back about the woman who found a hole behind her bathroom mirror?"

"I do." Callahan said. "It opened up into an abandoned apartment nobody knew was there and it was clear that someone had occupied it at some point." He shuddered. "Straight up horror story stuff, man. Wait. Why haven't you already checked out these supposed holes-in-the-wall?"

"You asked that Noah go over this scene about nine-hundred times, so I figured that took precedent," Cho said, prompting some grumbling from Callahan that sounded a lot like 'fuck my fucking life' before he turned to Noah.

"You get everything you need in here, Green?"

"I believe so, yes."

Noah glanced around, skimming the studio with his gaze once again. Blood spatter had hit the wall at the front of the apartment, indicating Heide Brown had been near the windows when her throat had been slashed. Based on the bloodstains they'd found on the furniture and floor, they knew she'd been mobile for a short time and probably struggling toward the door. She'd made it partway across the room before the injury overcame her and left her to bleed out in a large pool just beyond the disused fireplace. The place was a messy picture of a sudden, violent death. And Cho was right. Something beyond the mayhem didn't quite fit here either, and Noah could almost feel it hovering just out of reach.

He stared harder, looking the place up and down, and paused when he reached the studio's drop-panel ceiling. It was made of the same crappy Styrofoam that had been used in Danny's apartment and didn't fit well at all with the studio's pearl-gray walls and white trim.

"Did you look at the other units in this building?" Noah asked Cho.

"No." Callahan bobbed his head back and forth a few times as he thought about it further. "We interviewed every resident to see if they'd heard anything from this apartment or Danny's but it's not like we dusted for prints. Why?"

"I'm not sure. But Cho said it too. I feel like I'm missing something and can't place what it is."

"Huh." Callahan cleared his throat. "Well, I say we move this party to the stairwell and see whatever Cho thinks is there. Especially since he was too chicken-shit to check it out on his own." He eyeballed Cho, as if daring him to protest, but Cho broke up laughing.

"Yeah, I'm busted."

"Uh-huh. You were right to wait for back up, though."

Callahan shot him a smile as he turned for the door. "Show me your weird."

"I could take that so many ways, Bert."

"And I pray you do not."

The detectives carried on teasing while Noah followed behind, but he slowed as they passed Danny's door. He caught a glimpse of Danny, head down as he pawed through an armful of things, then traded a quick nod with Officer Tate before he kept on walking. Danny'd made it sound like he needed space to manage this stranger-than-strange kind of night, and Noah would give it to him despite everything in him wanting to do the opposite.

The maintenance stairwell at the back of the building was some distance from the residential staircases and elevators used by the building's occupants to traverse its five stories. It was nicer than Noah had expected, and he agreed with Cho that it likely dated back to the building's original construction. However, Cho's assertions that the rich woods of the stairwell would be festooned with 'ooky stuff' fell surprisingly flat once Noah saw them himself and the sense of something being out of place pricked at him harder than ever.

He cocked his head, his disquiet increasing as he regarded the nearly pristine space. They knew from Danny that this building's roof hadn't been converted and was off limits to the tenants. They sometimes accessed the space anyway, primarily for sunning themselves on the 'tar beach' during the summers. Those activities tapered off when the temperatures dropped, however, leaving the staircase unused beyond a sporadic need for air vent maintenance. But if the steps saw little foot traffic for most of the year, why were they so clean? Why was the whole *space* so clean?

"This isn't right." Moving slowly, Noah climbed to the midway point of the staircase and gestured around them. "This place should be dusty. Thick with it, actually, and I'd expect to see shoe prints from when Cho and others used the stairs to get to the roof. Danny told us the building super is a slacker at heart, so it seems unlikely he'd dust a staircase, especially one that's hardly used. But I think someone has, including the walls."

Callahan turned his attention to the wall nearest him, frowning at a flat wooden panel that measured three or so feet on each side. "Why would anyone dust walls ever?"

"To keep them clean, obviously. Or prevent someone from noticing you'd touched them. Someone like a nosy CSI who's been poking around the building." Without touching it himself, Noah moved a hand over one of the panels, then turned and caught Cho's eye. "Who already suspects there might be space behind them."

"Yeah." Cho's gaze was steely. "I say it's time we add back some dust." Descending the steps, he picked up his kit while Callahan glanced between him and Noah, eyebrows rising high as comprehension dawned.

"You're going to fingerprint the walls?"

"I am." Climbing again, Cho squeezed past him and Noah, stopping a few steps from the staircase's top. "Any space back there would need to be below the roofline, or you'd just be out in the open air."

Noah got out of his way, grabbing the camera from the bag so he could capture more images of their surroundings. It wasn't long before a curse caught his ear though, and Callahan whistled long and low.

Ghostly fingerprints littered the paneled wall when Noah looked up, revealed against the dark wood by silver magnetic powder. Clusters stood out along the lower left and upper right edges of one panel in particular and Cho's expression was practically gleeful as he looked down at Noah.

"That's where this fucker's been hiding—inside the goddamned wall. Noah, can you get up here and help me, please?"

They made quick, careful work of lifting the prints with tape, then transferred them to acetate cards for safekeeping. Noah sealed the cards inside evidence envelopes, but he'd hardly finished before Callahan reached for the panel himself.

"I know you'll want to print every inch of this place but making me wait is torture and completely unnecessary." He grinned in the face of Cho's exasperated sigh. "You have all night to do the rest!"

Cho grumped and complained, but Noah had caught their buzzing excitement too, and watched eagerly as Callahan gripped the panel's edges. He doubted any of them breathed when it shifted easily under his touch, then lifted away in a single flat piece. Silence reigned as Callahan handed the panel off to Cho who quickly set it down, and together all three stared into the wide hole that had been revealed.

Motions deliberate, Callahan shone his flashlight into it, exposing what Noah assumed was an attic. The raw space extended several feet forward before opening to the left, and wood planks had been laid over the floor joists to form a rough floor. Much taller and wider than a typical crawlspace, there was ample room for a man over six feet like Noah to move around if he stooped. Someone shorter wouldn't need to stoop at all.

"Holy fuck-sticks," Callahan said, voice genuinely awed. "Assuming that keeps going left, it'll run over every apartment on the floor below on this side of the building." Turning, he looked at Cho first, then at Noah. "Including Heide Brown's."

CHAPTER 20

A fog had descended as Danny'd stepped into his apartment. Talking to Noah and Cho had helped clear it some, but once they'd gone across the hall to Heide's, it'd wrapped around him like wool blankets, heavy and smothering. Distantly, he recognized the fog as a defense mechanism. It dulled his senses enough to blunt the awfulness of the stink and mess around him. And Danny felt pitifully grateful for that.

Moving through the fog took real effort though, and he blinked wearily as he gathered his clothing from the wardrobe sandwiched between the couch and the windows. A sweater, some shirts, two pairs of jeans and his boxers; he'd never owned a ton of clothes and God knew if anything matched. Danny couldn't bring himself to care, not with so much devastation staring him in the face.

Stop being a drama queen.

Ignoring that bitchy voice, he set the clothes on an empty shelf and walked to the studio's door so he could close it. Noah wouldn't want it shut, he knew. Noah was gone, though, off working with Cho and Callahan. Danny'd heard them talking about a stairwell and something that might be in it but hadn't paid much attention as they'd passed by. The cop standing guard by Heide's door glanced at Danny now but said nothing, nodding politely before she cast her gaze back down the long hall.

So maybe it didn't matter if he closed the door. If the cop didn't care, who did? And Danny needed the duffel hanging from the hook on the door's back or he wouldn't be carrying much out of there.

Bag in hand, he returned to the wardrobe, then winced as he caught sight of himself in the mirror hanging inside one of its doors. Carefully, he pulled down the face mask, knowing he looked like utter hell. The bruise under his eye had reached a greenish-yellow stage and did his pale skin no favors. It'd been a day—or more?—since he'd last shaved, and he thought the longer beard stubble on his cheeks and chin looked strange. Much like his clothes, which hung all wrong and made the scarf Danny was still using to hide the bite on his neck even more conspicuous.

Fuck, he was in for so much crap. The second Callahan got a peek at that scarf, he'd know it had nothing to do with the show Danny and Noah had put on at The Last Drop to make people believe they were together. Because they *were* together and nothing about it felt like make-believe. Not after the things they'd shared with each other today. The secrets Noah had spilled and the tenderness he'd shown, and the comfort he'd given so freely when Danny had needed it.

That all had to matter.

The connection between them was real. It wasn't one-sided. And they were already bound to each other by something much stronger than blood lust.

He hoped.

Danny drew an unsteady breath. He needed to believe it with a desperation that scared him. He couldn't go back to being just friends, only seeing Noah at the bakery and flirting over the bread he couldn't eat, while Cho waited out in the van. Danny needed more. If Noah didn't … well. Danny wasn't sure how he'd handle it.

A flash of color half-hidden under the edge of the couch caught his eye then and, kneeling, he pulled at it, understanding only as it started to come loose that the flat piece was a photo that had come loose from its frame. The snapshot of Thea and their parents in fact, battered and scratched now, and Danny's eyes pricked with sudden tears as he stared at it.

God, his life was an unholy mess. His neighbor had died, for fuck's sake, and though everyone had been careful to say Heide Brown's murder was in no way Danny's fault, he knew better. The killer had been in this building repeatedly and if Danny had been home instead of hiding out at Noah's, the guy wouldn't have gone after anyone else.

That would have been better for everyone.

Danny slipped the snapshot into his pocket, then eased himself down onto the floor. He hadn't felt this beat down in a very long time, like every nerve in his body was frayed. He couldn't help wondering if maybe the voice in his head wasn't right, too. If life wouldn't be a hell of a lot easier for everyone without him around.

With that, he relaxed into his misery. Hugged his knees and closed his eyes, head hung low as sorrow and grief rose up past the fog, swirling together in his chest. Danny breathed past it, aware his cheeks were wet and his nose clogged but losing it right now was okay.

Crying was better than numb.

The storm finally passed, leaving him emptied out in a good way, and he sat for a while blinking until his vision was clear. Wiping his face with his hands, he shifted his weight, one knee falling to the side as he prepared to stand, then paused as a squeaky scraping noise drew his attention upward.

Eyes widening, Danny watched a panel in the ceiling above him disappear, leaving a square of black nothing. A lean figure filled it, then lowered itself through, hanging suspended for only a second before it dropped onto the couch cushions with hardly a sound.

Danny could only stare, jaw slack as a man clad in dark clothes stepped off the couch and loomed over him.

"About time you got home."

That voice froze Danny's blood. In a flash, he was hauled to his feet and crowded against the wardrobe, and arms came around him in that iron-like hold. Danny stared into the mirror's reflection at a face he'd never seen in its entirety with green eyes so pale they were nearly yellow and narrow, unremarkable features. The man he knew as Steven was about his own age and smiled as he pressed something cold against Danny's throat.

"I'll cut you if you scream."

Danny swore his balls shrank up into his body. "I won't." He barely had breath to speak as it was, and his knees shook when Steven pressed the blade into his skin a bit more. "Promise."

"Good boy. This place smells bad enough without adding a whole lot of blood to the mess just yet."

"Y-your fault it stinks in here."

Steven gave a low laugh. "True. It's a necessary evil. Rancid odors usually get people out of a space real quick. Except for the Crime Scene guys, of course. I'm sure they smell worse on the job every day. But they've been too busy looking around at everything else to notice someone hiding in your ceiling."

"How the fuck did you get up there?"

"There are lots of hidey holes in old buildings, if you know where to look, especially off basements and roofs." Steven raised his eyes to the ceiling, then glanced left to right. "There's a whole attic up there everyone else forgot. I guessed as soon as I saw that cheap-ass excuse for a ceiling."

Danny's vision wavered, going gray and fuzzy for a second before it swam back into focus. "That's how you got in. H-how you got to Heide."

"Yep. Well, I used your keys the first time, but I knew the cops were going to make it hard to come back the same way. So,

I went to the roof, figured I could hang out until nightfall, then use the fire escapes to get in and out. But I found the holes in the stairwell walls and that just made everything so much easier." Steven grinned at him. "You and your neighbors really need to be better about bolting the bulkhead door."

"I'll, uh, mention it at the next tenants meeting." Danny let out a shaky noise that might have passed for a laugh. He had to swallow twice before he could ask the question that burned him every time he thought it. "Why did you kill them? And her? Heide never did anything to you. Sh-she couldn't even give the cops a description."

The man holding Danny appeared almost thoughtful. "I killed her because I felt like it. That's why I killed them all. And why I'm going to kill you, too." The emptiness in his eyes made Danny's skin crawl. "You were dead the minute you bumped into me in the park, Danilo Kaes. You just didn't know it."

"But I didn't see your face that night or at The Last Drop. Never even knew what you looked like until tonight." Cold sweat gathered at the base of Danny's spine. "I couldn't have ID'd you even if they'd brought you in for a lineup."

"Well, damn." Chuckling, Steven leaned in even closer. "I almost wish I'd known. Especially now that I know what you are."

Lifting the knife just slightly, he used it to slice apart the scarf around Danny's neck until it dropped away, leaving the bite mark exposed. The room went swirly and gray again and Danny had to fight harder this time to find his way back. Steven's voice seemed to come from a long distance.

"Like I said at the bar, if I'd known you were part of the scene, I'd have done things different. Maybe we'd have met sooner and this whole mess could have been avoided. Well. You'd still be dead, of course. But it would have been so much less of a pain in the ass for both of us."

Steven tutted with his tongue, the sound almost teasing. "I guess that means you were born under the unluckiest star in the universe, friend. Because there's no way in hell you're walking out of here alive now."

"The cops—"

"Will never know how I got in or out. By the time they find you, I'll be back up through the hole and headed for the roof." Steven dropped his gaze to the knife against Danny's throat and he stared as if fascinated by the mere sight. "It really is a shame more blood needs to be wasted, though. Since it's the only thing a fucking meat sack like you is good for."

"I'm not—"

Steven clamped a hand over Danny's mouth, eyes blazing hot. "You are. You're enslaved, friend. Do you understand that? A whore to creatures that aren't even human. You let yourself die a little every time they feed and like it because it makes you feel good. Then you go back again and again for more. You're damned, Danilo." His lips curled in a sneer. "You deserve to be put out of your misery."

He pressed the blade into Danny's throat. The wound stung, burning in a way Danny found terribly familiar, and he clenched his eyes closed rather than watch himself bleed. He couldn't help bucking hard against the arms holding him, and he shouted against Steven's fingers. And wasn't that funny? That the need to fight was so strong now when he'd felt almost too tired to go on only minutes ago.

The knife dug deeper as he struggled, its bite sharp and so clean. Danny cried out again, voice breaking when this time the muffled noise was met with a sudden, tremendous racket. Noises he recognized as the studio door crashing open and multiple voices shouting, ordering the man behind Danny to step back and drop his weapon, to put his hands on his head.

Just for a second, Danny wondered if maybe things would turn out all right.

Peeling his eyes open, he met the killer's gaze in the mirror's reflection again. The flurry of noise and motion faded under the intensity of those weird green-yellow eyes and time stretched, grinding to a halt until it was just Danny, Steven, and the knife. They stared each other down, neither acknowledging the shouts or urgency in them, until Danny heard Noah call his name, the panic so clear in his voice Danny swore his hair stood on end.

Steven narrowed his eyes, mouth twisting cruelly as his hold on Danny tightened and he drew the knife across Danny's throat. The wet warmth on Danny's neck didn't seem real.

He closed his eyes again, knowing he'd been a fool to hope this night wouldn't end in death.

A snarl rent the air. And the last thing Danny saw before blackness ate him whole were shining blue eyes.

"Is his name really Steven?"

"Yes." Detective Callahan stood at the foot of the bed, teeny pad of notes in hand. "Steven Eustace, born and raised in Queens, used to work for the family business putting up plaster and drywall all over the city. That's how he knew to look for the attic space in your building."

Danny nodded. "Makes sense, I guess. He said … something about holes in old buildings. Places to hide." He stole a glance at Noah, who sat silent by the bed, his shirt and coat cuffs stained with blood.

Noah had been there when Danny had come back to himself in the Emergency Department at Lenox Health, bandaged and sutured and still scared out of his mind. He'd held Danny's hand and made sure he had blankets and a full cup of ice chips while the doctor spoke with them, explaining how lucky Danny had been. Another centimeter to the right and the knife would have cut into his trachea. Eustace had also missed the major veins and arteries as he'd sliced, probably thanks to Danny's struggling, which had made it possible for Noah and Cho to slow the bleeding while they waited for the ambulance.

Noah hadn't said much to the doctor. He'd stayed quiet

during Danny's transfer to a room on a different floor of the hospital too, and a week ago his silence probably wouldn't have phased Danny much. Noah wasn't exactly a chatterbox and his vibe on any typical night was politely reserved. He didn't let people in and very few souls knew the vampire behind the CSU cameras. Danny did know this vampire though, well enough he could feel something was wrong. Noah was *too* quiet. His gaze kept sliding out of focus too, and it left him looking … lost, almost, and so dazed that Danny found himself wondering if it was possible for a vampire to suffer from shock.

A lump rose in his throat. He swallowed carefully, mindful of his injury, but even that small motion instantly caught Noah's attention. Mouth a grim line, he pressed the cup of ice chips back into Danny's hand, unaware or uncaring that Callahan was watching them closely.

"We're still unravelling Eustace's story and putting the pieces together," Callahan said.

"His motive, you mean?" Danny asked.

"Yes, but I also meant his connection to the bloodex scene and the other victims." Callahan exhaled noisily through his nose. "A lead we got from your friend Galen panned out and pointed us in the direction of The Sanguine. Have you heard of them?"

"They're a syndicate. They deal in items wanted on the vampire underground market."

"Right. And at the top of the list of items wanted is whole human blood, donor not included."

That was no surprise. Not every vamp liked blood bars or dealing with humans, and Danny was well aware some would pay a small fortune for blood that came without strings.

"Eustace hooked up with them about a year ago," Callahan said, "acting as a liaison for donors looking to make a quick buck."

"So he went to the bars," Danny guessed. Donors flocked to them night after night; anyone in the market to buy human blood was sure to hit gold provided they knew who and how to ask. If the promised payment was high enough, anyone—newbie or not—might find it tempting. A queasy feeling rolled over Danny then. "Is that how he met Aaron Josephs? The first guy who died?"

"The first victim we named, yes. Josephs wanted to pay off his debts and selling his blood to The Sanguine through Eustace gave him an easy way to get there." Callahan sighed. "Unfortunately, Eustace developed a habit of pushing the donors too far and after a couple ended up in the hospital, the syndicate cut him loose."

"So he started working freelance."

"Yes. He had a … converted shed in back of his building where he did his business and kept the equipment for collections and storage." He tapped his own jugular. "All he had to do was find the donors, then keep the blood cold and under wraps while he trolled for a buyer. It never took long to sell. It seems things went smoothly for a while but without the syndicate's oversight, Eustace started pushing the donors further and further, and we all know how that turned out in the end."

Danny ate more ice chips and tried not to gag. "I don't think it was ever about harvesting blood," he said, words coming slowly. "At least not by the end. Eustace told me he killed Heide and the others because he wanted to. And that I deserved to die." He felt more than saw Noah's gaze on him. "He said I was enslaved to the vamps.

A whore. Told me I'm damned."

Callahan grunted softly. "That fits with what we've been hearing. The guy hasn't stopped talking since the docs patched him up and I can't tell if he hates Nosferatu or idolizes them. Maybe he doesn't know either. He for sure hates the donors. And at the rate he's confessing to crimes, I'm going to be buried in reports for weeks."

He paused then, his attitude gentling. "Danny, you should know the press are calling him the West Village Nightstalker. We found a collection of wallets in the shed where he did his work, and each has a driver's license or ID card. The ME's getting busy matching them to bodies and the FBI's offered to lend a hand."

Danny set the cup of ice chips down and wiped angrily at his eyes. "Fucker. How many did he—?"

"I'd rather not say." Callahan shook his head when Danny tried to protest. "We don't truly know yet because he may have had more than one residence. But long story short, Eustace is going to spend the rest of his natural life in prison, and you and Green helped make that a reality."

Noah shifted in his seat, gaze piercing when Danny looked his way. "How do you feel about that?"

"Not terrible?" Danny frowned. "Selling blood is illegal but I don't care if that's how people make a living. Eustace wasn't doing that, not for a long time. Maybe he started out like anyone else in the underground market, just connecting buyers with sellers, but he wanted to hurt people. Liked it. I heard it in his voice in the park and when he grabbed me at The Last Drop, and I *saw* it in his eyes tonight. He was enjoying himself. Hurting me, talking about killing."

Danny couldn't help his full-body shiver and was never more grateful for the hand Noah slipped into his. His voice sounded shredded when he spoke again. "The guy belongs behind bars. If I have to testify to put him there, sign me the fuck up."

Callahan smiled. "Good man. It may not come to that. Eustace has already confessed to killing Heide Brown and injuring you, as well as draining the guys he left in the parks."

"I'm surprised he can talk at all, considering you shot him," Danny said.

"With a *taser*. And only because he wouldn't quit even after Green had disarmed him." Callahan lifted his eyes to the heavens. "The guy hardly needed treatment!"

"Unlike you." Noah's voice was low and tense in a way that made Danny hurt. "If Cho hadn't been there—"

"I know." Danny rubbed his free hand over his head.

"Believe me, I know. Can we just never speak of this night again?"

"For the time being, sure," Callahan said. "I'll come back in the morning and see how you're doing, and we can finish up then. The doc who stitched you up said you'll probably be ready to go home by then and I don't mind driving you up to your sister's. I told her not to bother coming down here at this hour, but she got the guest bedroom ready in the meantime."

Danny stared at Noah. "You called Thea?"

"Detective Callahan did, yes." Noah let go of Danny's hand and looked away. "She needed to know. And you need someplace to stay until after your apartment's been cleaned."

In the silence that followed, Callahan tucked his pad of paper away and stepped forward.

"You should expect to hear from the DA's office, Danny," he said. "They've started building the case against Eustace, but we haven't finished questioning the guy yet and I know they'll want more information from you about … well, everything." He extended a hand to Danny and though he didn't quite smile, his expression was kind. "I'm glad you're okay. And thank you. Don't hesitate to call me if you have any questions."

Danny shook the detective's hand and listened as he and Noah exchanged polite goodbyes, but the bulk of his attention stayed on the vampire seated in the chair beside the bed. He waited until they were alone before he spoke again.

"Am I going to see you after tonight?"

Noah still didn't look at him. "I think it'd be better if you didn't."

Danny breathed for a beat just to be sure he still could. "Why?" he got out. "Because Steven Eustace tried to kill me?"

"Because I'm as dangerous to you as he is. Maybe more so." Noah raked a hand through his hair. "You were hurt, bleeding badly enough you could have died. And I was afraid to even get near you because I knew if I did, I'd lose control."

"Except you didn't." Danny ignored the pain in his throat.

"I'm still alive because you heard Eustace talking to me through the ceiling. You pulled him off me!"

"*After* he cut you." Noah's voice broke and the sound battered Danny's heart. "I wasn't fast enough to keep you from being hurt. And we both know that it could so easily be me that hurts you someday. Kills you. Without even meaning to because I'm—" He sighed. "I don't want that. I won't."

"You think you're not hurting me right now? Because you are." Eyes burning, Danny slapped his hand against the sheets. "And fuck you for thinking I don't get a say in how this plays out."

"But—"

"*No.* This isn't only about you. I'm in this too, Noah. And I'm asking you, please. Don't do this. Don't walk away just because you're scared."

"I'm not scared, Danny." Noah clasped his hands together so hard, several knuckles popped. "But I won't watch you die."

"I didn't!"

"You will."

Someday. And I can't stop it from happening.

Danny swallowed against the unspoken words. "This is bull-shit," he started, voice wobbling, but Noah was already shaking his head, jaw squared and steel in his eyes. The walls coming up around him were almost palpable.

"It's not bullshit," he said quietly. "We can't need each other, Danny. I have to stick with my own kind. Humans aren't right for me outside—"

"Of the bloodex, yeah."

You're enslaved.

Danny couldn't help flinching. With Noah, he was more than a donor. Noah was more than a vamp, and this thing they had was so much bigger than getting off through blood and sex. He *felt* it and thought Noah did too. But if Danny was the only one ready to acknowledge that—the only one ready to gamble everything—they weren't going to make it. That had his hands shaking almost as much as his voice.

"You're wrong." He clenched his eyes shut, hating the pain he could hear in his voice. Hating how much this hurt and that he'd known it was coming all along. Noah had been candid from the beginning about not wanting attachments with humans. And Danny hated him for that too. "You're wrong, Noah. About vampires and humans, and me and you. We both know there's more between us than blood. The problem is, you're not ready to be honest about that. And I don't know how to be anything but."

Danny turned onto his side and pressed his face into the pillows, soothing the fire in his cheeks against the cool fabric. He didn't want the guy who'd kicked him to the curb to see him fall apart. And there was no way in hell he was going to watch Noah walk away.

CHAPTER 21

December 11
Saturday, 2:00 P.M.

"I need paramedics at 12 Grove Street, now."
"Don't you die on me, Danny. Please don't—"
"Noah, more pressure on the wound. Press harder."
"But I don't want to hurt him."
"You don't want him dead, right? So do it, damnit, or we're going to lose him!"

Noah put his face in his hands. He hated thinking about this. And that he couldn't seem to stop.

Peeling Eustace off Danny. Struggling to subdue him. Wanting to kill him.

Danny on the floor. Body limp under Noah's hands.

Blood pulsing hot from the wound in his neck. Cooling on Noah's skin.

Cho's frantic efforts to keep Danny alive.

Callahan barking into his radio, eyes wild.

Ping.

Dropping his hands, Noah pulled his phone from his pocket.

He'd lost track of how many times it had chimed, and he groaned at the number of missed calls and messages. It vibrated again in his hand then and a new message from Cho popped onto the screen.

Knuckles hurt from knocking. Should I use my key?

Noah stared for a second, then slowly tapped out a reply. *I'm on the roof.* He wasn't surprised that the phone rang or to hear Cho already talking when the call connected.

"—sure I even want to know what the heck that's about, Noah. Are you okay? I'm guessing yes since you can still answer the phone?"

Noah glanced at the skyline he'd been staring at all day, voice rusty when he replied. "I'm fine. Why are you here?"

"I was in the neighborhood and thought I'd stop by, make sure you were good."

"Why wouldn't I be?"

"Oh, I don't know … because I told you to take time off and now you're sitting outside during daylight hours when we both know that could end you?"

"I'm sitting under the shelter."

"Which will be zero help if the skies clear and light gets under the edge."

Point to Cho. The overcast day had made it possible for Noah to stay out as long as he had, but he had no guarantee the sun would stay hidden. His skin felt parched as it was, and the thirst itching at the back of his throat tingled all through him, like tiny sparks of fire that lit his cells from within. Still, the discomfort hadn't been enough to drive him inside. These days, the small set of rooms he'd always regarded as a refuge was too quiet, and he couldn't find space inside them where he could truly settle.

"Look, I know you're pissed with me, but I'm coming in now," Cho said in his ear. "Your neighbor has been out here twice giving me the stink-eye and I don't think she believed me when I said I was a cop. I probably look too Asian." He snorted.

"I want to be inside the door before she calls 9-1-1 and I have to explain myself."

Noah thought about protesting. He wasn't happy with Cho or the mandated time off, and he wasn't in the mood for company. He didn't feel like explaining why he'd stayed outside past the time it would be safe. But he said nothing as keys jingled and deadbolts clacked, and frowned when he heard a softer sound, almost like Cho was cooing. "Who are you talking to?"

"The child on my back."

At first, Cho's smug tone and words didn't make sense, but Noah sat up straighter in his seat when they did.

"You brought Kage here?"

"I did. Her grandma has the day off so where I go, Kage goes." Cho's sing-song voice was met with a squeal. "Besides, it's been a long time since you guys hung out and I figured it was time for a visit with Vampy Uncle Noah."

"Vam-pee! Un-ca! No-ah!" a little voice called out and Noah put a hand over his eyes.

"Oh, my God. What have you done?"

"All of the ridiculous things. Do you need me to come up there with an umbrella or can you get back down on your own? I'd bring Kage but it's not exactly beach weather for humans. Plus, I'm afraid you're more terrifying than usual right now."

Dropping the hand again, Noah sighed. He'd spent time with Kage before but *never* when he was hungry. Or strung out and so damned tired he almost didn't know his own name. "I'll come down," he said, "but I need to feed. Please take the child and yourself into the bedroom."

"Of course. We're going there now, aren't we, Kage girl?" A gleeful sound like 'Heck, yeah!' came over the line, followed by a door slamming closed. "We'll just lock ourselves in," Cho said, "and go through Noah's stuff for extortion material until he stops wanting to eat us!"

Noah snorted before he could stop himself. He felt like hell.

Had no idea why Cho would come to his home, with his daughter for God's sake, which might mean there would be all sorts of strange human refuse in Noah's trash before long. But he also felt less alone than he had only minutes ago, and that mattered somehow.

He went back to scowling after he spotted a bakery box on the kitchen island though, resentment bubbling up in him at the reminder of things he couldn't have. Specifically Danny, of course, who Noah hadn't seen or spoken to since Steven Eustace's arrest. But cutting off contact hadn't stopped him thinking and wanting, or from feeling like utter shit at having walked out on someone who'd just nearly died.

Luckily, Cho had stepped in without Noah asking and taken his place. Sort of. He'd visited Danny regularly, both during his recovery and after, and seen for himself how life had indeed gone on for the Kaes family. And though Cho rarely spoke directly about them or the bakery to Noah, he found small ways to communicate that Nice Buns and its owners were flourishing.

Noah set the blood bottle he'd drained in the sink. He'd been grateful to Cho for being both kind and subtle about it, and that he'd always hidden the bakery boxes from sight, even knowing Noah could smell the goods tucked inside them. There'd been no hiding of boxes today though, which painted Cho as the biggest pain in the ass Noah had met in the hundred-plus years he'd been around, something he didn't hesitate saying when Cho walked out of the bedroom with Kage in his arms.

Cho blew off the insult without blinking. "Still hangry, huh? What were you doing outside during daylight hours?"

Noah just shrugged. He knew better than to lie to Cho, who'd worked with Noah long enough to have formed an under-standing of how well the vampire body instinctively recognized unsafe conditions. Admitting he hadn't cared enough to head back inside would leave Noah raw and way too exposed though, and he took pains to avoid meeting Cho's eyes.

He waved at Kage instead, who grinned and wriggled in her

father's arms until he set her down. And that's when Noah became hyper-aware of pointy things all over his apartment, including his teeth.

"This place isn't child-proofed, Cho."

Cho made his eyes big. "You don't say! Jeez, Noah, I had no idea." He chuckled when Kage took off running in Noah's direction and waved a hand at them both. "She'll be okay. Just keep an eye on her for a minute while I get her food, and I promise I'll take over."

"All right."

"Hi, Noah!" Kage shrieked, and Noah knelt so he could catch her when she launched herself at him.

"Hello!" He set her down immediately, but she just rushed him again, and he sent a look across the room to Cho who appeared terribly amused.

"Your face. It's like you don't know whether to laugh or scream in terror."

"That's about how I feel." Noah gulped as Kage practically climbed his torso. "I'm not fit to be around children."

"You're doing fine!" Cho rounded the island. "Just keep her from wrecking the place and herself for the next five minutes, and then we can talk about why you've been a sulky emo fanger for weeks."

Noah fought off another scowl. Peeling Kage off his body, he set her down and held out his hand, which she grabbed without hesitation.

"Let's go!" she urged, tugging at Noah with surprising strength toward the workstation in the corner.

Noah gave her a smile before he called back to Cho. "I haven't been sulky or emo."

"You're right. It's more like you've been in mourning."

The sudden change in his tone took Noah off guard, as did the tightness on his features. Cho looked worried as he transferred bread from the box to a plate, and Noah made his tone gentler when he spoke again.

"Mourning isn't right either."

"You sure?" Cho's frown grew even deeper. "Because you've never been much of a clown, Noah, but it's like I've had a new photographer with me for the last month and he's been about as much fun as a prostate exam."

"Okay, wow."

"Shit, I'm sorry. Oh, no."

"Shit, I'm sorry, oh no!" Kage echoed cheerily, and Cho met Noah's grimace with one of his own. He was snickering helplessly though, and Noah liked the sound.

"You're right," he allowed as he got Kage settled in his desk chair. "I have been moody."

"Yeah, you have. But I don't want an apology," Cho said. "I want the guy I like working with back. And not see you so down on yourself that it's like you forgot how to interact with humans."

Noah wasn't sure he remembered how to behave around his own kind at this point, never mind the bleeders. Life had become gray and dull in the weeks since he'd last seen Danny. And while little outside of work held Noah's attention these days, it sounded like Cho thought he was failing at that, too.

"I'll do better, Cho. Especially when we're on scene. I know I had to do some re-shoots last night at the house on Sugar Hill but that really wasn't my fault."

"Agreed. It's not like anyone expects a raccoon to run off with a crime scene marker." Cho smiled at him. "You know your work was good regardless. But I assumed it was also distracting being in that neighborhood and knowing that Danny's sister and dad live there too."

Another point to Cho. Noah'd been on edge as they'd walked the scene in Harlem and excruciatingly aware of the crowd of curious onlookers. The real problem was that Noah felt off at *every* scene they were called to these days, no matter where in the five boroughs they were sent, and that made him want to laugh and curse all at the same time.

He'd documented crime scenes in every neighborhood of New York during his time with the NYPD and never been rattled, not even when they'd been called to the building his parents had once called their home. Now, he was tense on every call, particularly until he got a look at the victim and could confirm he didn't know them. The closer the crimes occurred to places Danny might have been, the more distracted Noah became, because it seemed even simple proximity messed with his conviction that Danny was truly out of harm's way.

He didn't bother hiding his sigh. "Why are you here?" he asked again.

"Rude." Cho walked back around the island and set a plate on its top, then made grabby-hands motions to his daughter. "Snack time! Come and get some buns, girl."

"Yay!" Kage slipped out of the chair and took off running toward her dad.

"Seriously," Noah said as he followed behind her. "Is everything okay? Because I know you weren't just in the neighborhood."

"Technically, we were by the time we made it to the bakery." Cho hauled his daughter up and settled himself on one of the island's chairs with Kage in his lap. "And yes, everything is fine. I meant what I said. I wanted to check on you. I know you're not happy about taking time off, but we both know you need it. You're not okay."

Noah sat in the other chair and watched Kage happily tuck into her plate. "No, I don't suppose I am. But I don't think taking time off will help."

"I knew you were going to say that. The thing is, you need to get your stuff together, homeboy. All this pining isn't healthy, even for a non-human. You should talk to Danny," he said, then sighed at Noah's headshake. "It's obvious you're both hurting and there's absolutely no reason for it."

Of course, a human would think that. And Cho *was* only human. He couldn't truly know how time worked on human hearts and minds or how incredibly short their memories really were. Danny's heartache wouldn't last. He'd heal. No doubt already was. Someday in the not distant future, he'd find someone human who suited him better and his memories of the time he'd spent with Noah would fade to nothing.

Noah wished he could say the same of himself. He'd never connected with anyone the way he had Danny. Had never become so attached to anyone, not even the blood eaters he'd run with in the past. Their moments together had been fun and exciting, like fireworks, all flash and bang without much underneath. Nothing profound or real. Like the kinds of feelings Noah'd had for Danny after just a few days.

You never fell for any of the others.

Noah rubbed his temples with his fingers. What the hell was wrong with him? Outside of those three very intense days, he hardly knew Danny Kaes. They'd just been getting to know each other before the attack in Bleecker Playground and subsequent killings had forced Danny to shelter within these apartment walls and rely on strangers for protection. Being trapped had fueled the spark between them, feeding Danny's anger and helplessness until he'd piled his feelings for past partners—Galen in particular—onto Noah, a woefully poor choice for any human.

He'd been right to walk away that night at the hospital, even as it left him gutted. He'd hated the sick expression that had crossed Danny's face as the understanding of what Noah was about to do had clicked. The way he'd turned his back. The smell of his sorrow had shamed Noah through every step he'd taken in the opposite direction. Walking away had been the only thing *to* do to save them both though, and God knew, Noah would take hurting over watching Danny die. Which was exactly what he'd have to do someday if he'd followed his foolish heart and stayed.

Noah couldn't bear the thought.

What if you didn't have to?

Noah gave himself a hard, internal shake. God, no. He wasn't going there. Even *thinking* that way was madness. He wouldn't wish this strange existence on another person, especially Danny. He deserved more. Deserved *life*, after fighting so hard to hang on to his own. A family and a future, all the things Noah had lost many years ago in a single stroke of bad luck. Noah wouldn't do that to anyone he cared about the way he did Danny.

"I'll be fine," he said to Cho, who appeared wholly unconvinced. "I just need some time."

"Yeah, Danny said the same. I'm not buying it, though, from him or you."

"You've said something like that twice now." Noah frowned. "What do you mean? Is he …?"

"Overwhelmed and angry that his friend let him down? Yeah. He does a good job of keeping up pretenses, but I can see it on his face sometimes, like when he thinks no one's watching. He lost his whole life for a while, Noah, and hasn't gotten some of the pieces back even now. His friend died and he could have too, and you walked away and left him to sort things out on his own."

Noah's chest squeezed so hard he could hardly get out the words. "I didn't—*don't*—want to hurt him."

"Then do yourself a favor and stop."

"Sthop!" Kage echoed around a mouthful of food. Face bunched up adorably, she waved a finger at Noah, the motion throwing crumbs every which way. "You sthop, Noah."

"Okay, I will." Noah managed a smile for her. "I don't know how to do this though," he said, more to himself than Cho. "Or how being with him won't end badly."

"I hate to break it to you, but it kind of already ended and none of it was pretty."

"Not helpful."

Cho shrugged. "Danny told me that the worst part is knowing you think you're doing the right thing. Because that means you're choosing to be a shitty friend. But the cool thing is that this is real life. Not a movie or a book with only one path. You can change the ending if you want to."

"That doesn't make it right, Cho. There's a reason you don't see a lot of relationships between vampires and humans."

Cho rolled his eyes. "And no reason one between you and Danny *couldn't* work if you tried. They're not entirely unheard of, you know. Provided you want it and Danny will even speak to you now, which I'm not one-hundred percent sure will happen."

"Way to kick a guy when he's down."

"Believe it or not, I'm hoping I can help," Cho said, but his next words sent Noah's heart through the floor. "That's why I'm giving you the heads-up that Danny's not in Harlem anymore. I know." He held up a hand. "I should have told you before last night, but I didn't even think of it."

Noah waved him off. "Doesn't matter. Why did Danny leave his sister's? I thought he was staying there until the repairs at the studio were finished."

"He was. Until he went back to work and got fed up riding the trains back and forth every night."

The room emptied of air. Noah knew Danny rode the subway; public transportation was a way of life in New York if you wanted to get around. He'd never considered that boarding an underground train during off hours could be considered risky, however. Or how easily that same simple act could put Danny side-by-side with a man like Steven Eustace at *any* hour in the day.

"Danny crashed at Merlin's for a couple of weeks." Cho said from somewhere a long way off. "But the repairs on his place are finished, and he was back home as of yesterday morning. Noah? Hey. Take a breath, big guy."

"Okay." Closing his eyes, Noah inhaled through his nose, abruptly aware the room was swirling around him. He swayed in his seat, but then Cho had a hold of his shoulder and was gently guiding him forward so he could rest his forearms on the countertop.

"Damn. You're an even bigger mess than I thought. When did you last sleep?"

"It's been a while." Noah didn't know what to feel. He was absolutely a mess. So tired he couldn't muster the energy to be embarrassed by his loss of control. He didn't need sleep as urgently as humans, but he did require *some* and it'd been weeks since he'd been able to do more than doze. He buried his face in the crook of one elbow, aware of Cho's hand on his shoulder and a much smaller hand patting his hair. "Thanks, guys."

"You're welcome," Kage replied.

"Does this happen a lot?" Cho wanted to know.

"No. Honest," Noah said. "I know I haven't been at my best, but this is over the top even for me."

"I'm not sure if that's good news or bad. I hope I'd notice if you were about to keel over on the job but, like I said, you've been quiet the last couple of weeks, so it's possible I'd miss the signs."

Carefully, Noah levered himself upright. "Signs? Signs of what?"

"That you're struggling. With depression, I think, and maybe anxiety."

"Not … no. Vampires don't get depressed."

"Who says?" Cho's voice was droll. "I thought depressed was a vampire default."

Noah sighed. "You know what I mean, nerd."

"I do. But seriously, who says you can't be depressed?" Cho settled a drowsy-looking Kage against his shoulder as he spoke. "Thinking it doesn't make it so. We've already established that you're not okay."

"Okay." Noah set his arms on the counter again. "I don't know if I'm depressed exactly but … I didn't think I'd miss him like this."

"You were friends before everything changed, so I can see

that. He misses you too. He acts like it's no big deal, but I think it got under his skin when you ghosted him."

Great.

Noah stared at the counter. Cho was more right than he knew. Danny'd been left behind before by people he'd cared about. Which only made Noah walking away when he knew his friend had needed him that much worse.

"I hate that I let him down."

"You should tell him." Cho gave him a small smile. "You know, for a guy who doesn't like getting close to humans, you're *really* terrible at following through."

Laughing made Noah ache but he found he didn't mind, and he made his voice quiet so as not to rouse a now dozy Kage. "I didn't used to be. I was an expert at keeping your species at arm's length. You and your kid wore me down. And Danny. Maybe Callahan too, in a very weird way."

Cho let out a snort. "I just imagined the face he'd make at hearing that and oh, it was epic. I'm glad you mentioned Bert though, because I asked him to meet us here."

"Ugh. Why?"

"He's worried about you. Not that he'll admit it, but he said he'd come over and help me yell some sense into you. Because you need to straighten this shit show out. This," he said, with a wave in Noah's direction, "isn't working at all, for you or me."

"As long as you're happy, of course," Noah muttered. He could hardly remember a time when he'd felt this … drained. Back in the beginning perhaps, right after his change. When every attempt he'd made to see his parents had imploded and left him feeling battered from the inside out.

Maybe Cho was onto something with this vampire depression thing. Noah'd shut himself down over the last several weeks. Worked at being numb. Made it there most days. Today had cracked him wide open again, and he hurt so much it scared him. He'd take it, though. Because, oddly, the ache was better than nothing at all.

Cho stood and lifted Kage with him. "I'm going to put her in the bedroom, if you don't mind."

"Sure." Shifting, Noah moved his head enough he could see his friend's eyes. "Cho? What if I can't fix things with Danny?"

"I'm not saying you can." Cho ran a hand over Kage's back, his smile lessening the sting of his words. "But I think you owe it to yourself and Danny to try. And I know you'll regret it if you don't."

CHAPTER 22

"Hey, kid."

Danny turned from his coffee to see Detective Callahan weaving his imposing figure through the morning commuters crowding the bakery. The guy was smiling at Danny, and he hoped his own smile looked just as natural.

"Good morning, Bert." He liked this big cop. Would always be grateful for the work he'd done to catch Steven Eustace and put him in jail. But just seeing him brought up a lot of ... *stuff* that had Danny's leg bouncing under the table.

Maybe because it was just past seven in the morning, and he'd been looking forward to heading home for some after-work chilling. Or maybe because Callahan walking through the bakery's doors made Danny think about who *hadn't* walked through them in over a month or called or texted or communicated by carrier pigeon. And that didn't make any kind of sense, either. Danny saw Cho every few nights and never felt nearly as nervous as he did right now.

"Please, join us." Danny gestured at an empty seat on his left, then across the table to his father, who'd been watching the exchange with Callahan. "This is my dad, Keoni. He's here to taste-test some new recipes and give the Kaes family stamp of approval. Dad, this is Bert Callahan, the homicide detective who worked on my case." Genuine happiness went through him when his dad's brown eyes lit up and he stuck out a hand for Callahan to shake.

"Are you here for my son or his goods?" Keoni asked as Callahan settled into the vacant chair. "Danilo was about to head out, but I'm sure we could convince him to stay if you have time to join me for what promises to be an excellent breakfast."

Callahan's grin grew wider. "Thank you, sir, I appreciate that but I'm just passing through. I have a meeting with the DA's office about your son's case later this morning and, honestly, this is the first time I've worked a day shift in a while—I need about a gallon of coffee." He raised a hand to Thea, who had come out of the kitchen just then with trays of fresh rolls. "Figured I'd pick up some food to fortify myself and check in on Danny in the meantime. See if he and Noah Green were done competing for gold in the Dumbass Olympics."

Danny choked on a mouthful of coffee, but his father *laughed*, a knowing glint in his eye.

"No medals yet," Keoni said to Callahan.

"Because men can be idiots, regardless of species." This from Thea, who'd walked out from behind the counter and now stood beside Callahan's seat, a hand on the man's shoulder and a smile on her face. "Hey, Bert."

"Traitors," Danny muttered without heat. Teasing aside, his family had been rock-solid in supporting him in the wake of the murders. Not that Danny had been truly surprised. Tenacity was a Kaes family trait, just as Noah had said, and Thea and Keoni had been far more focused on Danny being alive than giving him grief for hanging out with vamps.

He'd told them about his connections to the scene and Galen, and how he'd come to know and lose Noah. They'd listened and hugged him and there had been no ultimatums or demands he rethink his life, and not a single suggestion he have his head examined and body exorcised. They still had questions, of course. His dad in particular worried about safety and, perhaps, even the state of Danny's soul. Danny did his best to assure them that, yes, he knew what he was doing when it came to the scene. As far as knowing what to do where Noah Green was concerned … well. Danny didn't want to talk about him with anyone.

"I'd disagree if I didn't know better," Callahan said to Thea. "Yeah, we're a hardheaded bunch. But I like to cut our species more slack."

"That's nothing new," Danny muttered. "You're not exactly subtle about hating supernaturals, Bert, especially vampires. Or maybe you just save it all up for the one you have to work with."

Thea furrowed her brow. "Danny."

Callahan gently shook his head at her. "No, your brother's right—I don't have a lot of tolerance for other species. But I've been working on my attitude, and it wasn't even an order from the brass." He met Danny's smirk with one of his own. "Green hasn't been around much to see it, but I'm sure he'd be insufferable about the whole thing."

Wait. Noah hadn't been around? Why the hell not?

Danny hated himself a little for wondering. He didn't want to care about how Noah lived his life. For thinking he was doing Danny a big fucking favor by staying away and doing it so well it was like he'd ceased to exist at all. Danny was going to his grave pissed as hell about that.

Still, he couldn't help remembering how shellshocked Noah had appeared the last time they'd seen each other. Withdrawn, with eyes almost haunted, and Danny knew he'd been hurting though Noah'd refused to say so. The idea Noah might still be in pain … damn. Yeah, Danny wanted to know more. Needed to, really, and it was like torture waiting for Callahan to finish placing an order with Thea so Danny could circle back to the topic of his erstwhile friend.

"What did you mean by Noah not being around?"

"Just what it sounds like," Callahan said. "Green's taking time off. I have no idea what that means, though." He wrinkled his brow. "What does a vampire *do* on their time off? It's not like they can go to the beach and chill in the sun."

Except Noah did chill at the beach. By moonlight of course, but he enjoyed exploring the dunes and long, empty stretches of sand, and swimming under the stars. He'd told Danny as much during one of the nights—or days—they'd spent together, and the lonesome feeling that rose up in Danny squashed his anger and nearly stole his breath. He missed those talks. Missed hearing Noah's voice, whether he was sharing little details about his own life or cracking up over one of Danny's goofy jokes.

"Why don't you ask him?" Danny made his voice light. "I'm sure he'd tell you if he isn't already gone."

"I guess I could. Not sure he's going anywhere, though, which is sort of the problem." Callahan no longer appeared amused. "Cho thinks Green is burnt out. He ordered the guy to use some vacation time and come back rested."

Danny leaned forward in his seat. "Say what now?"

Callahan held up a hand. "You didn't hear any of this from Cho or me. Green wants you to get on with your life, blah-blah-blah, and we're not supposed to talk about him to you."

"You're doing a really good job with that." Danny said and heard his dad chuckle.

"I do a really good job with everything," Callahan replied.

"Uh-huh. And you won't mind if I pump you for more intel?"

"Not at all." The detective pulled his wallet from his pocket and tipped his head toward the counter where his bread and a huge to-go cup of coffee waited. "Give me a second to pay for my food and we can walk out together."

Danny nodded, though the motion was absent. His thoughts were several blocks west, with the guy he'd been doing his best to forget. Knowing Cho worried about Noah's state of mind concerned him, especially with Callahan wanting to talk about it too. In spite of his bitching, Danny thought the detective *liked* Noah. He was obviously willing to share his thoughts with Danny, something not even Cho had done.

"I don't get it," Danny said. They'd said goodbye to Keoni and Thea and were headed for the shop's door. "Cho was in here yesterday—why didn't he tell me Noah's been struggling?."

"You told us not to mention Noah's name, remember? Cho wanted to be respectful of your wishes whereas I don't give a shit." Callahan gave him a shit-eating grin and heat spread over Danny's face.

"I shouldn't have done that." He held the door open, then followed Callahan outside. "Making decisions about what people can or can't say isn't fair to anyone."

"Yeah, well. That includes you, Danny." Pausing on the passenger side of his car, Callahan regarded him steadily. "You talk all you want about how you're not interested in Green anymore, but it's clear to just about everyone that you are."

"I know." Danny jammed his hands in his pockets. "I don't want to be, but I can't turn it off. Believe me, I've tried."

"I'm sure you have." Callahan tipped his head at the door. "Climb in and I'll drive you to your place."

"You're, uh, not gonna smoke are you? I know it's your car and all but—"

"I'm not going to smoke." Callahan rounded the front end of the car and popped the locks on the doors. "I quit a couple of weeks ago. And for the record, I'm still grumpy as fuck about it so you can just keep the congratulations to yourself."

It was a few minutes before they were headed down Bleecker Street, but Callahan picked up where they'd left off as if no time had passed at all.

"For what it's worth, Green did the right thing by walking away when he did."

Danny frowned. "Of course, you'd say that. And you may not believe it, but Noah tries hard to be a good person. I think that might be his jam, actually, because he's noble and a big idiot, just like my sister said." He tried not to pout at Callahan's quiet chuckling. "Please shut the hell up. I'm allowed to recognize Noah wanting to do the right thing without being happy about it."

"I know. But you do get it, Danny. Get Green, really, in ways I never will. I think that's what makes you perfect for each other."

Danny knew he sounded sad when he answered. "You may be the only one who thinks so, then. Noah doesn't even think we can be friends."

"Yeah, well, Green has been known to be wrong."

Danny wasn't sure what to make of that, so they rode in silence until Callahan finally turned onto Grove Street. He eased into the first open spot they encountered, and Danny was pleased to see they were a mere half block from his front door.

"Seriously, thank you. I know it's only a three-minute ride, but my feet appreciate the lift."

"No problem." Callahan picked up the coffee he'd placed in the cup holder and quickly cracked it open.

"You wanna come up?" Danny jerked his thumb at the car door. "I haven't eaten a real meal yet and while I don't have a new table yet, I'm happy to share my kitchen counter with you." He'd be happy to get more info on whatever the hell was going on with Noah too, since the opportunity was right there in front of him.

Callahan graced him with a smile. "Thanks, that's a nice offer. I'm happy where I am, though, and I have plenty to share." Reaching back, he brought the Nice Buns box onto the front seat and gestured toward it. "Help yourself."

"Uh, thanks." Feeling strangely off balance, Danny opened the box and withdrew a maple-iced *pandesal* while Callahan picked out *kahilim* stuffed with cranberry pudding.

"Fucking A, this is good," he muttered around a big bite. "You're really good at your job, kid. How'd your apartment turn out? Cho told me it took longer than you wanted but I figured it was a sign your building super was doing a good job."

"He did okay." Danny knew he sounded less than enthused. A month ago, talking about his apartment's renovation would have been exciting, and the results were quite nice. But he felt more deflated than anything when he thought about the studio these days, just like he did about a lot of his life. He gave himself an internal shake as he tore the roll of bread in half. "The place looks great. Fresh paint and new floors, and the Styrofoam ceiling is gone, baby, gone."

"I know you don't miss that."

"You'd think right? It was gross but ... Heide and I—" He paused. Danny could talk about his former neighbor now without his voice breaking but saying her name still made his heart throb. "We'd have friends over for fancy drinks parties and, afterward, we'd stick the cocktail trinkets into the panels over her bed. Like pins in a cushion, you know? Plastic flamingos and sharks and those little paper umbrellas. Whatever tchotchkes we happened to have on hand."

"Are you sure that was you?" Callahan cocked an eyebrow at him. "Because that all sounds both whimsical and fun and like nothing you'd do."

"Hey, I can do whimsy. I'm a fun guy, damnit, or used to be."

"If you say so. You sleeping okay?"

Callahan knew about the bad dreams that had plagued Danny after the last awful night with Eustace, and how hard it became for him to turn off his brain enough to slide into sleep. Having fought his own battles against sleeplessness, he'd given Danny a lot of good advice, as well as the names of some therapists who worked with the NYPD helping cops and civilians who'd been scathed by trauma on the job.

"Yes and no." Danny bit into his bread. "I sleep a couple of hours a night now and it's getting better. I count that as a win and my therapist does, too."

"Good." Callahan took a long sip of his coffee, then swallowed. "Do you ever talk to her about Green?"

The hairs on the back of Danny's neck prickled at his oh-so-light tone. "What's going on? Is Noah in some kind of trouble?" He swallowed as a terrible thought slammed into his brain. "Because of me? And what happened with Eustace? Is that why he's having to take time off? Because that is *crap*, Bert, and you know it. Noah saved my life."

Callahan made a quelling motion with one hand. "Chill. Green is not in trouble, over Eustace or you or anything else. Just the opposite, in fact. The brass are so impressed with his work they're changing the rules about the kinds of work supernaturals can do for the department. He could be certified to work as a CSI despite not being a detective."

"Well, shit. That's huge." Danny bit his lip against a smile. "He must be so stoked."

"I'd hope so. I'll always have mixed feelings about working this job with supernaturals but, for what it's worth, I think Green would be good at it. If he wants to."

"Why wouldn't he? He told me he really likes working with the CSU."

"Well, like I said, Count Sucks-a-Lot hasn't been himself lately." Callahan frowned. "Cho's been talking with him but isn't sure he's getting through. You might, though."

Danny blinked at him. "Noah doesn't want anything to do with me."

"Untrue," Callahan said. "He just made you think that so it'd be easy for you to walk away."

"I didn't walk away. Noah did. And yeah, maybe I didn't fight him on it, but I won't make someone stay if they don't want to. I respect myself too much for that."

Danny swallowed hard. The funny part was that Noah would probably approve of his decision. Cheer Danny on, too, because that was what friends did, even after claiming they didn't want to be friends anymore.

Callahan, in the meantime, had started looking cranky. "You know what? Good for you and I mean that sincerely. But I don't think you're really hearing me about Green, and maybe it's because you don't remember everything that went down the night Eustace made his last move. How much blood had spilled by the time we found you with him."

"Yet you still tased him."

"What was I supposed to do? The guy wasn't giving up, Danny. He came at Cho and me, and if Green hadn't already pulled him off you, I'd have been forced to use a bullet. Maybe shot you or Green in the process. And yeah, Green probably would've been okay but I didn't actually *want* to shoot him."

Danny forced himself to hold the detective's stare.

"He saved more than your life that night," Callahan said, "but you were the only one bleeding. And Green never broke. I gave him so much shit when he brought you back to his place that first night, after the scene at the playground. Said you couldn't be safe around him. Didn't believe him when he insisted he wouldn't hurt you. Still didn't after you'd been there for days and had marks on your throat, and the two of you were making cow eyes at each other like none of us would notice."

Danny tried and failed to keep a straight face. "Knock it off."

"You know I'm right." Callahan smirked. "But that night with Eustace, Green didn't even blink at the blood. He peeled the guy off you and disarmed him like it was nothing, and we both know he could have ripped the guy's throat out. Was probably dying to and no one there would have stopped him."

Memories flickered to life in Danny's brain. Fear. Pain. An awful snarling that should have terrified him but didn't. Hands on him, strong but still gentle, and urgent voices, pleading. Demanding Danny hang on. Anchoring him, despite the ice in his veins. Danny shivered now as his whole body strained to recall more images hovering just out of reach.

"The second he'd pulled Eustace off you, it was like Green forgot about the rest of the world," Callahan said. "He kept pressure on the wound in your neck while Cho checked you out, and there was blood all over their hands. Green rode with you in the ambulance and the medics said the *only* thing that fang-faced motherfucker was concerned about was making sure you were okay. Honestly, I think you scared him."

Nodding, Danny thought back to Noah running out onto his roof in full daylight, simply because he'd thought Danny had been in danger.

"Noah's strong," he murmured. "So much stronger than any of us realizes. Maybe even himself."

"You would know, man, like I said. You're probably the one person in the world who actually knows him at all. And, sappy as it sounds, I think the guy needs you."

Blinking, Danny dragged his forearm over his eyes, drying the tears that had gathered in them. "Fine. But I don't know what to think. Noah was adamant the last time I saw him that we stay away from each other. He doesn't *want* to talk to me."

"Yeah, he does. I know this because he's waiting for you upstairs."

"He's …" Danny stared at Callahan and nope, the words still didn't make sense. "What?"

"I did him a favor and got him into your building. Left him in the hall outside your apartment maybe two hours ago. Your super offered to open the door to your unit but, of course, Green said it wouldn't be right to enter your apartment unless you were there."

Danny brought his eyebrows together. "I'm surprised you didn't just go to the roof. Pretty sure it's been established the bulkhead door isn't exactly secure."

"And I'm pretty sure what you're describing is called *breaking and entering*, an activity I like to avoid." Callahan sounded disgusted but there was no real ire in his tone. "But now that you mention it, Green was definitely eyeballing the fire escape."

"You're both out of your minds." Danny gave a shaky laugh. "I don't understand. Why come to me now? And why here?"

"You're asking the wrong person." Peering through the car's windshield, Callahan nodded in the direction of Danny's building. "So, go. Talk, do whatever, and sort through your shit. Green can't exactly leave while it's still light, so if you need to kick his ass out, call me and I'll come back for him." He paused. "Unless you want him gone now?"

Danny shook his head. "I guess I don't. I'll talk to him."

Funny how calm he sounded, even to himself, when his whole body was thrumming at the idea of seeing Noah after weeks of radio silence. Danny wanted to run—no, sprint—upstairs so he could do what? Crush Noah in a hug? Tell him how much he'd been missed? Ask him what the fuck he was thinking by not jumping at the chance for a job as a CSI?

Or maybe why he'd dented Danny's heart and ghosted?

That had Danny feeling grim as he climbed out of Callahan's car. A bit like smacking Noah upside the head too, or maybe shaking him for being a total dumbass. He'd get some ranting in while he was at it, and let Noah know exactly how much he hated having decisions made for him by people who didn't talk them through first.

Fire built in his belly as he walked inside and boarded the elevator, and his anger had flooded back by the time he reached his floor and stepped off. However, everything faded as Danny laid eyes on his wayward friend, replaced with a heady rush of gentler emotions, relief and affection chief among them, followed by longing so intense he found it hard to breathe.

God, he'd missed his vampire.

Noah's not yours.

Yeah, Danny hadn't forgotten that. But right or wrong, everything in him was still drawn to Noah and whether it was down to the blood exchange or a more complicated kind of chemistry moving between his brain and his heart, Danny didn't know. Or care. Not with Noah having broken the stalemate and taken a chance Danny would listen instead of throwing him out of the building.

Danny strode forward, gaze locked on the figure before him. Noah was seated outside Danny's door, his back against the wall and long legs stretched out on the floor before him. He made a peaceful picture with his eyes closed and head tipped back, but even from a distance, Danny saw he was paler than usual and drawn, features sharper than only a few weeks ago. As if he'd lost weight. An impossible thing since vampires didn't truly eat.

They could stop feeding, though, Danny reminded himself. Vampires could starve. And just like humans, they could walk away from a trauma and be broken up inside.

CHAPTER 23

Sitting out in the open with his eyes closed was probably a stupid idea. Possibly even trespassing. Granted, Noah'd been running on empty long enough he wasn't sure he'd recognize a bad notion from a good one and didn't yet know where coming to see Danny Kaes fell on the good idea/bad idea scale.

The same uncertainty had carried him into the 10th Precinct at two o'clock that morning where he'd asked for Bert Callahan who, wonder of wonders, was seated at his desk and not in his car. The detective's eyes had gone wide when he'd seen Noah in the waiting area, but he'd wasted no time bringing him back through the bullpen and into a small conference room. He'd listened as Noah'd asked for his help, then folded his hands together on top of the table, as if needing that time to gather his thoughts. And throughout that tense silence, Noah's doubts had towered ever higher.

Why had he come to this human for help? They'd worked well together recently and might in the future, and Callahan had seemed sympathetic the other day when he'd joined Cho in coaxing Noah to reach out to Danny. Noah still suspected Callahan did so only grudgingly. The man had been candid about not wanting him around and his opinions on supernaturals being dangerous. Callahan would no doubt say something along those exact lines when he finally opened his mouth.

But that hadn't happened. Callahan had not only agreed to help Noah get into Danny's building, he'd offered him a lift to Grove Street.

Proof again Noah had zero idea what he was doing and maybe never had.

"Are you sure you don't want to call Danny first instead of dropping by unannounced?" Callahan had asked. "I know you were trying to do the right thing by staying away, but there's always a chance he'll tell you to stick your apology straight up your ass."

Noah'd laughed wearily. "Setting up a formal meeting won't change that. But going over there feels like the right thing to do for Danny, so that's what I want to happen."

Once in the building, Callahan had stuck around for a while, exchanging pleasantries with several of the residents on the floor as they'd emerged from their units to begin their day. They'd remembered Callahan from the police investigation which made it easy for two tall men to loiter outside Danny's studio door without raising alarms.

The overall noise in the building had decreased as the humans had exited the building, and a lazy warmth fell over Noah, increasing tenfold after Callahan had said his goodbyes too. He'd settled himself on the floor and basked in the quiet, aware that, for the first time in weeks, he felt almost relaxed. His thoughts had grown wispy, and he'd been edging into a fuzzy gray space that felt something like rest when a ding at the end of the hall signaled the elevator's arrival and, seconds later, a familiar scent slammed into him.

Salt and yeast and something uniquely Danny Kaes punched every nerve in Noah's body into full alert. He jerked bodily, eyes flying open, and scrambled to his feet to find Danny standing a short distance away, face wary.

"Hey, Noah."

"Hello." Noah tried to sound easy, but he couldn't help looking Danny up and down, cataloging each limb and muscle with his gaze, and finding each as perfect as he'd remembered. Danny's cheeks were ruddy, from the cold outside or maybe emotion, but he appeared whole and strong and fully recovered, as if he'd never been injured at all.

Thank God.

Relief poured through him, so fast his head spun, and mixed with a yearning to touch the human in front of him intense enough he made fists of his hands to keep from reaching out.

"I hope this is all right," he said quickly. "I know I should have called first, but—"

"No, it's fine. Callahan told me you'd be here."

Noah blinked. "He did?"

"Uh-huh." A wry smile curled Danny's lip. "I guess he thought it'd be better if I had a heads-up, seeing as I haven't heard from you in almost a month."

"I see." Noah dropped his eyes to the floor. "I'm sorry about that."

"Okay. I'm sorry, too."

"What? Why?" Troubled, Noah looked up again, then swallowed hard when he noticed Danny had come several steps closer. "What are you apologizing for?"

"I don't think I ever thanked you properly for saving my life." Danny's expression was softer now, more open as he stared into Noah's eyes. "You get that, right? And that you did a lot for me even before Steven Eustace pulled out his knife?"

"I didn't—"

"Yes, you did. You let me stay with you after I was mugged and helped the cops solve my case. Kept me from falling apart. And when Eustace tried to kill me, you stopped him in a way nobody else could."

Noah balled his fists. "Not before he hurt you. Or before he dragged you out of The Last Drop. Or even the first night, when I should have met you for breakfast."

"It was dinner," Danny said. "But you could say the same about any of the cops in my building or The Last Drop. Callahan and Cho, the others—none of them got to me in time. An officer stood right over there, Noah, and had no idea what was going on behind that door. If you hadn't shown up at exactly the right moment, I'd be—"

"Please don't say the word 'dead.'"

"Okay. Then I'll say the words 'thank you' again." Danny spread his hands. "Because, like I said, I didn't when I had the chance and that just isn't right."

"I don't need a thank you, Danny." Noah's scowl was met with one just as deep.

"Too fucking bad because you're gonna get one."

They stared each other down, Noah's heart flipping madly at the mix of amusement and defiance he read in Danny's eyes. Oh, how Noah had missed this stubborn, infuriating human, who teased and bickered and cared for the people who were important to him. Who brought his whole self to the world and faltered sometimes, just like every living thing, but kept coming back stronger.

This person made Noah feel alive. And Danny needed to know that before they both ran out of time.

The cruelty of that truth must have shown in Noah's face, because Danny stepped closer again. He didn't touch Noah or even reach out, but his gentle voice was like a caress all its own.

"You okay?"

"I don't know," Noah almost croaked. "About anything. But I want to apologize for being a bad friend, both by staying away and coming back. I want what's best for you, Danny, and I'll be damned if I know what that is."

"Call me selfish but staying *in* my life would be a good start." Danny answered Noah's sigh with one of his own. "You think we're a bad fit and I'm in danger when I'm around you. Maybe some days there's a little truth in each of those notions. But I think—no, I know—we've proven that we *can* make this work. We just have to want it. I'm sure you don't want to hurt me, Noah. Won't. Fuck, even Callahan thinks you've got the vampire whammy under control and that's saying something."

Noah groaned. "It's also specific to you, I think. I don't know how I'd do around another human, but you're right—I won't hurt you. I'd hurt myself first."

"I can see that." Danny bit his lip.

"I'm not sure 'control' is the word I'd use either, because I tried so goddamned hard to not think about you and failed every day." Noah leaned back against the wall. "This has never happened to me before."

"What do you mean?"

"I don't have trouble letting go. I move on when it's time. I don't look back or hope for things I know I can't have." Noah ran a hand over his head, as much to keep himself from reaching for Danny as to keep his voice steady. "Wishing is a thing only children should do, and I learned that a long time ago. Back when …"

"You said goodbye to your family." There was no question in Danny's voice and, out of nowhere, Noah really wanted to sit on the floor again. He closed his eyes instead and hauled in a long breath.

"When I said goodbye to my humanity. The kindest thing—for everyone—was to leave it all behind so they could get on with living while I did the same. Without longing for things no one could change. The blood eater in me and the passage of time … they're immutable and pretending otherwise is a fool's errand. Meeting you made me question everything and I can't get you out of my head."

"Maybe you should stop trying." Danny had his arms crossed when Noah opened his eyes, and mirrored Noah's stance with one shoulder pressed against the door of his apartment. "Try listening to what your heart has to say instead of your head and see if your life gets easier."

"Oh. I'm not sure what's left of my heart. So much of the human in me was destroyed after I was changed." Noah suspected he appeared as sad as he felt. He didn't see the point in pretending to be otherwise, though. Not when he'd promised to be truthful with Danny, no matter how hard the words were to hear.

"I hate knowing you feel that way," Danny said. "But you *didn't* lose everything, Noah. You didn't disappear. You're still you. One of the best people I know. And maybe that means there's still human left in you or our species aren't so different. Or maybe you're unique. Human or vampire, you're still someone I like *so much*. You think I'd talk to just any guy who ditched me while I was in the fucking hospital, then acted like I didn't exist?"

"God, I'm sorry. You have no idea how much."

"You're right, I don't. Just like I'm still not sure what you're doing here or what you expect is going to happen."

"I want to talk." Noah hoped Danny could see how much he wanted that, though neither moved a muscle. "Only if *you* want, of course. About the things we said to each other at the hospital that night and why I've been acting like the world's biggest ass." He forgot himself, reaching for Danny without thinking, then hurriedly shoved his hands in his pockets, movements careless enough that one of them tore. "More than anything else, I wanted to know you were all right."

Danny cocked a brow. "Hasn't Cho been reporting on my general state of being?"

"Only when I've asked. And only to say you were healthy and doing well. He didn't ... Cho doesn't tell me what the two of you talk about." Noah shrugged. "I wouldn't expect him to, either, because he's a good friend to you, just like he is to me."

A solid minute passed before Danny stood straight and pulled his keys from his coat pocket. "Would you like to come in?" he asked, his grin small but so genuine Noah had to smile back.

"I would, yes."

He waited on the threshold as Danny stepped inside first and pulled the blackout curtains on the windows down. His cheeks were red when he came back for Noah, and he glanced around the mostly empty space as if seeing it through new eyes.

"I haven't had time to put up any holiday lights or shop for more stuff. You probably remember Eustace wrecked anything that wasn't nailed down. Even my books and photos, the fucker."

Noah remembered all right. Images from that night were imprinted on his memory with the clarity of a high contrast negative. He knew where blood had been spilled and broken furniture had lain. The physical wreckage was gone now, and though the tiny space was rather barren, Noah liked seeing the freshly plastered ceiling and repainted walls. Almost as much as he liked seeing Danny back in one piece.

"Pretty much the only thing he didn't break was the bed," Danny said, "and I'm not embarrassed to admit I haven't folded it back into storage since coming back. Yes, I've been dining in it. I try to take meals standing at the kitchen counter but man, sometimes I gotta sit and picnic-style on the floor is only fun when you haven't worked a ten-hour shift on your feet.

"Anyway." He had his hands on his hips when Noah turned around and was smiling warmly. "What do you think? Probably not a surprise that the new ceiling is my favorite part."

Noah wanted to agree. Tell Danny he could use his bed for anything he wanted including every meal, whether he had other furniture to sit on or not. But just then Noah could hardly breathe, let alone speak. Because Danny had removed his coat and scarf and revealed the livid pink line on his neck running from under his left ear almost as far as his Adam's Apple.

"Jesus, Danny." All right, apparently Noah hadn't lost his power of speech. But he was still messing up spectacularly, his words sending pain streaking across Danny's face, a thing Noah had hoped never to do again. "Oh, fu— I'm sorry. I shouldn't have said that."

Cheeks paling, Danny turned slightly away. "It's fine. I forgot you hadn't seen it and I know it's, uh, a lot at first glance. I should have warned you before I"—he waved a hand at his throat—"before you had to see it."

Noah frowned at the way Danny's gaze skittered past him to the far end of the room. He had to act fast before Danny walked out thinking God only knew what. "Don't do that."

Danny went still. "Do what?"

"Make excuses for the way I've behaved. Your scar caught me off guard, yes. I hate that Eustace hurt you. Even more that I couldn't stop him before he got to you. But that's on me, not you. If I'd been with you while you were healing—"

"I'd still have a scar." Pulling off his knit cap and the bandana underneath, Danny scrubbed his fingers over his head, mussing his dark hair into soft, spiky tufts. "I'd still bleed and age and have needs you never have to think about." His quiet voice made Noah ache. "I can't change being human, Noah, any more than you can change being a blood eater."

"I don't want you to change anything."

"Since when?" Danny glowered at him. "You've said the only thing you need from humans is blood and, once upon a time, I'd have been fine with that. The problem is, I want more than the bloodex with you. And the really, *really* shitty part is not knowing how to talk to you about any of this without feeling like you'll disappear if I say the wrong thing."

Noah willed himself to be calm. "Nothing you say will be wrong. Even if it were, I'm not going anywhere."

"Yeah, because you'd turn into a walking, talking man-shaped torch the second you stepped outside."

For a second, Noah held Danny's stare. And then they were laughing, the sound winding around Noah and holding him steady as it painted new color on Danny's cheeks.

"That was out of line," Danny said after he'd recovered, "even though we both know it's true."

"Physically, yes, it is." Noah stopped smiling. "I *will* leave if you'd prefer to be alone. But I won't disappear. I'd like to be a part of your life if you want me in it."

Danny nodded slowly. "Sounds nice. I wouldn't mind working on being friends again and see how that goes."

Disappointment pricked at Noah, but he shook it off. He hadn't expected instant forgiveness, not after the way he'd behaved. He was happy to follow Danny's lead. If the route to whatever they were going to be to each other wasn't straight, he had as much time as Danny would give him to travel it together to its end.

"I'd like that," he said. "We could start with the late-late dinner we never had a chance to meet up for. Though, I guess at this hour you'd want breakfast."

Danny flashed him a grin. "Food is food, yo. I had a snack just now, but I could eat again. We just need to figure out something for you. Let me wash the bakery off first so I can think, and I'll be right out," he said, already heading for the bathroom. "Go on and make yourself comfortable."

Noah smiled as the door clicked shut behind Danny. There were no guarantees things would turn out all right. He had hard work ahead of him to re-establish some trust. But the connection to Danny was still strong. Just being close—hearing his voice and breathing him in, knowing he was whole and safe —was so good. And Noah felt more at ease than he had in a long while.

Removing his wool coat, he laid it over the foot of the bed then sat down beside it to wait Danny out. He listened to the shower's distant hiss, eyelids dropping shut, and the next thing he knew, a warm hand had settled on his shoulder.

"Noah."

"Mmm?" Warm, moist cedar filled his senses, and it was all Noah could do not to sigh. He peeled his eyes open and peered up at Danny, who'd changed into a t-shirt and joggers, hair and skin still damp from the shower. Beautiful. "Sorry. I was just—"

"Sleeping sitting up from what I just saw," Danny finished for him. "Is that a vamp thing or a you thing?"

"I have no idea." Noah sat straighter. "But I don't think I was truly asleep."

"Yeah, I disagree. Are you feeling all right?"

"Yes, of course."

"How come I don't believe you?" Danny cocked his head. "Look, I appreciate that you've wanted the attention on me. I mean, I'm the one who got knifed and ended up in the hospital."

"I haven't forgotten."

"Okay, but maybe you're rusty about how to be friends with humans. Or me, at any rate. Because if we're going to do that, we have to take care of each other and right now it feels like you need the care a lot more than me. You look exhausted, and I say this as a friend. I don't think you're all right, either."

Noah glanced down at his hands, his insides trembling. "I'm not. It's been a while since I felt like myself."

"I think I see that." Danny settled onto the mattress at Noah's side, and even that nearness rocked him. "When did you feed last?"

"Two days ago."

After Cho literally talked me down off the roof.

Noah couldn't say that out loud. Not with his thoughts sliding around so much they weren't making sense. Or with Danny watching him so closely.

"I haven't wanted to feed," he admitted instead. "And I haven't slept." He licked his lips at Danny's low curse but didn't look up. "It's like my body forgot how to do it at all until now."

"Christ, you are impossible."

Noah blinked as Danny practically shot up off the bed then stooped over him, hands on Noah's shirt buttons. He worked them open without a word, his expression intense and almost angry. He wasn't throwing Noah out though, and suddenly it seemed very important to Noah that Danny know how much that meant to him.

"I missed you," he said without meaning to, then blinked as Danny went still, hands still on the buttons.

Fuck, he'd messed up. Likely squandered the only chance he would get to fix things. Danny's eyes said as much. But then again … maybe Noah fixing things was secondary to making sure Danny knew the truth about how he felt. And, really, Noah had already exposed so much of himself to this human; what difference did it make to show him a bit more?

"I missed you so much, Danny. Every day I stayed away. And I lied. When you were in the hospital, I told you I wasn't walking away because I was scared, but the truth is, I was terrified." He nearly gasped when Danny nodded, then peeled the shirt off Noah's shoulders.

"I believe you," Danny said. "And I want to talk about it. Once you're more awake."

"I'm …" Noah frowned as Danny gently guided him down onto the mattress. then turned his attention to Noah's boots and socks. "You don't have to do this."

"I know." Tapping Noah's knees, Danny waited for him to lift his legs onto the mattress, then drew the bedding up over him, jeans and undershirt and all. "This is probably a moot question, but do you think you can sleep now? I remember you saying you don't like to do that around humans."

"There are humans and then there's you." Noah turned onto his side. "But I came here to talk."

"And we will. Later. About a lot of things, Noah, just so you know. Because I am still really fucking mad at you."

"All right."

Noah breathed in, battling to keep his wits about him, but it was no use; his eyelids were simply too heavy. The mattress beside him dipped then, and there was a wonderful warmth from having Danny close. He hummed without shame and burrowed a little deeper into the bedding.

Danny chuckled softly. "Jerk. Is this one of those times when you don't wake up for days?"

"Feels like it. Sorry."

"It's all right. I'll figure it out as I go." A light touch skimmed along Noah's cheek, the pad of a thumb like velvet. "I meant it. I'm still angry with you. But I'll be here when you wake up."

Noah sighed. Speaking took real effort now. "Be careful. Might not be … Don't forget what I am."

"I won't."

"Promise."

"You're awfully bossy for a guy who showed up uninvited, y'know," Danny grumbled. But then he stroked Noah's cheek again. "I promise I'll be careful."

CHAPTER 24

Lying beside a slumbering vampire was very fucking strange. Sure, Danny'd shared beds with boyfriends and lovers before but this ... yeah, totally different. He couldn't drag his eyes from the sight either, staring at Noah long past the time he should have been sleeping himself, mind whirling with the question he couldn't stop asking.

Why was he here?

Noah had apologized and said all the right things. In typical Noah fashion, he'd appeared more concerned with being heard than finding forgiveness, too. But so what? And why now? He'd had weeks to find Danny and talk about how he'd fucked up, and yet he'd continued to cut Danny out. Until now.

Clearly, something had changed. Including Noah. Who wasn't himself at all.

He'd blinked out like a bulb once horizontal, conscious and talking one second and out cold the next. The shallow rise and fall of his ribs with each breath had been his only movements for over an hour now and Danny had never seen anyone lie so eerily still. Outside of the man he'd found in Bleecker Playground, anyway, but that guy had been dead.

Way to be morbid, dude.

A mix of horror and shame heated Danny's face, but then Noah did move, fingers twitching slightly before he balled his hands into soft fists. They opened again, almost like he was grasping for something, and he gave a little sigh. Something about the whole thing caught Danny's heart.

He inched closer on the mattress, watching Noah's eyes move slowly back and forth beneath his closed lids, tracking images only he could see. Danny remembered that vampires could dream, a thing he'd never have known had Noah not told him. But Danny didn't know a lot of things about this confounding creature who, at least until he'd passed out, had seemed determined to stay in Danny's life and wanted him exactly as he was.

Vulnerable. Flawed. Human.

Danny closed his eyes. Noah was all those things too, to varying degrees, even the last, no matter how much he denied it; he'd simply been better at hiding. And that right there was exactly the reminder Danny needed to guard his stupid heart. Because the one thing he did know now was how badly Noah could hurt him, and he'd be damned if he'd let it happen again.

Internal pep-talks about being strong and cool-headed went out the window once forty-eight hours had passed and Noah was still out. While not exactly scared, Danny felt pretty freaking unsettled. Waking up beside a silent, unmoving figure got *weird* when said silent, unmoving figure stayed that way despite the rest of the world carrying on and, instead of a *Vampire's Guide For Staying Alive*, all Danny had was cryptic instructions for assembling the bookcase he'd bought.

He sipped his coffee and sighed. Noah'd told Danny he always woke up from the longer-than-typical sleeps. However, he'd also admitted he didn't know why they occurred in the first place, so what if he didn't wake up this time? Or wasn't …

himself when he did? What if Noah looked at Danny the same way he would a steak and ate him without meaning to?

"Vampires don't eat steak, dumbass," Danny muttered to himself, then snorted softly into his cup and nearly drowned himself in the process.

This extended temporal pause was messing with his head. Concerned about leaving Noah alone, he'd asked Merlin to fill in for him during their last shift, then spent the evening dreaming up recipes and ordering enough flat-pack furniture to replace everything Eustace had broken. His brain had shifted into overdrive and proved impossible to corral when the methods Danny typically employed when he wanted to feel in control—running, hanging with the fam, and baking until the counters were overflowing—were simply not options.

Though, now that he thought about it, he probably could have filled the whole apartment with buns and Noah would have kept right on sleeping.

Danny smiled. Control was a myth, no matter what he told himself, and he'd ceded every trace of it when he'd befriended Noah Green. Noah had done the same, in his own way. Opened up as much as a supernatural could after having been around for over a hundred years and watching the humans around him live and die.

Was it any wonder Noah stuck with his own kind? Danny didn't think so. He just didn't know where that left them now.

The air changed subtly then, shifting just so, and Danny glanced up without truly knowing why, right into Noah's gaze. Danny held his breath. There was no recognition in those eyes. Nothing warm. No reason or logic. Only absolute attention as the hunter always lurking beneath the gentleman's veneer stepped forward.

Be careful.

Noah's warning in mind, Danny set his coffee cup down without breaking eye contact. There was a blood supply in the fridge. He'd ordered it yesterday after waking up, sure Noah would feel differently about feeding once he was rested. Danny just needed to make Noah understand that before either of them did anything they might regret later.

A low growl reached his ears as Danny put a hand out toward the fridge.

Oh, God.

Grasping the handle, he popped the door open, his insides shriveling even as a terrible longing surged inside him to cross the room to the bed. To Noah, who was waiting, body coiled under the bedding. Preparing to spring and take down his prey. Take Danny, who closed his eyes to stop himself from moving.

"There's blood in there," he said, his voice small, but the words were barely out before the space around him shifted, buzzing with a tension that made Danny press his lips together over a gasp.

Noah was close. But he didn't make a sound. Danny's hackles rose in the smothering quiet, and he didn't dare move. A sound caught his ear, like a hushed inhalation, then another only inches away. He was being scented, sweat and musk and fear breathed in and savored, and he knew he must smell really fucking good if the low rumble that followed was anything to go by. Knees wobbling, Danny gripped the edge of the counter, eyes squished shut even tighter as he fought not to scream.

He wasn't sure he'd ever been this frightened. Not even when Steven Eustace had looked at him with absolute murder in his eyes. But fear was only part of it and a wave of need hit Danny hard, so big he almost lost his footing. Oh, how he wanted to give in. Step forward and offer himself up. He only had to move.

Don't forget what I am.

Danny clung to those words through his horror. He knew what he was dealing with. It was a minor miracle he was still breathing instead of pinned under the thirsty vampire in his kitchen who was very much not in his right head. But then again, the blood eater was Noah, who'd sooner hurt himself than Danny. Knowing that helped Danny fight off the terrible urge to surrender and, eyes still screwed shut, push the refrigerator door open wider.

The shaking started as Noah fed with what sounded like terrifying speed, the cap of one bottle hitting the hardwood floor, followed seconds later by a second then a third. His skin crawling, Danny's eyes popped open all on their own when Noah growled again, the sound so raw it sent heat licking up Danny's groin. He stared at Noah, taking in the slack jaw and half-lidded eyes. Then Noah tilted his head back and groaned, every muscle in his body tensed as he flew high on the rush.

God, he was beautiful.

Noah's chest heaved as he sucked in great draughts of air, no doubt still scenting Danny. According to Galen, humans smelled best when they were frightened or sexually aroused, and the combination of both was a heady mix few vampires could ignore. Danny suspected that was the cause of Noah's next lusty groan. He still didn't make a move, however. Not even when the empty bottle in his hand cracked in his grip.

"Shit." Motions just the tiny bit tipsy, Noah set the bottle on top of the refrigerator alongside the others. He flashed a sheepish look in Danny's direction and though his eyes were still glazed, it was clear he was coming back to himself. The chaotic energy crashing through Danny mellowed at once, the dread fading in the rush of feelings that should have been so much more frightening.

Danny had *missed* this. Missed Noah, all tall and hot as fuck, and the small, closed-lipped smile he didn't hand out to just anyone. Talking with him and learning who each other was. The way his hair got messy when he put his head on a pillow. The freckles. Hearing him laugh, and watching it light up his eyes. Touching and kissing him and sharing too much pleasure to catalog.

Yes, Noah was a vampire and potentially dangerous for the

average person to be around. Danny wasn't an average person, however, just as Noah was not an average vampire.

Danny had to stop himself from grabbing him.

"I missed you, too." He gulped at Noah's wide eyes. "I should have said it before you went to sleep, but I couldn't. Seeing you here after all those weeks of radio silence took me off guard.

"Don't get me wrong," he rushed on when Noah's lips tightened, "I was really happy to see you and I'm ... fuck, I'm so glad you're here. It was just out of nowhere, even after Callahan gave me the heads-up. I think I'm still taking it all in."

"I understand. It's all right if you don't feel ready to tell me things yet." Noah was so earnest. "I know I have work to do before you're going to trust me."

"That's not ... okay, I see your point. But I do trust you, Noah, or want to. I'm just honestly confused. Because you went from ghosting me to sitting outside my door, literally overnight." Danny knew he sounded petulant and hated it. He just couldn't help it when the memory of how utterly shitty he'd felt following Noah's disappearance was still so fresh. "I thought about it a lot while you were asleep, but I still don't have a clue. What made you come here?"

"I knew I had to come to you if I expected you to take me seriously. People you care about have walked out on you before."

"Including you. Kind of a dick move considering the things I told you about myself."

Noah blew out a long breath. "So I've been told. In some of those exact words. I haven't been a good friend to you and I'm truly sorry."

Danny swallowed past the rocks in his throat. The shame on Noah's face tempered his anger, but he was still raw. He'd felt betrayed by someone he'd trusted when Noah had walked away, and it had hurt more than a breakup.

"Why did you do it?" His voice was smaller than he liked.

But Noah sounded just as insecure when he answered, and Danny saw how much the words cost him.

"I couldn't see how staying with you would end well for either of us. Being together put both of us in danger—your body, my heart. The idea of losing you is …" Noah shook his head slowly.

Danny didn't reply until he was sure he could do so without losing it.

"Okay. You're the most logic-driven supernatural I've ever met. Normally I admire a pragmatic person, but it makes you more of a pain in the ass than anything else. And confusing as fuck because I'm still human and you're still really, really not." He waved at the empty bottles sitting atop the refrigerator. "If we can't change that, why bother trying for some kind of happy ending you don't think is in the cards?"

"Maybe it is in the cards. Because *I* changed in here." Noah set a hand on his chest. "I told you already that I never had trouble letting someone go in the past. When it was time, I didn't fight it. Until I had to let go of you and understood I didn't want to at all. And couldn't."

"Couldn't? But you did."

"On the surface, maybe. Something in me was still reaching out. I started looking for you at crime scenes. Dreading seeing the victims' faces until I could be sure they weren't you."

Danny's heart tumbled right through the floor.

Oh, Noah.

"The closer we got to a place where you might have been, the worse I felt because you *weren't* there and even though I was relieved that you hadn't been hurt it was actually painful facing that," Noah said. "It didn't matter where I went when all I wanted was to be near you. I care about what happens to you, Danny, truly. How you are and whether you're happy or feel good. Whether you're safe. And that's new. I'm still wired like killer up here." He tapped a finger to his temple. "But it's not all instinct and drive. I have feelings for you that aren't about blood or sex, and they don't go away when I can't see you."

"Fuck." Danny's hand trembled as he ran it through his hair. "Talk about burying a lede. You don't fool around once you've made up your mind, huh?"

Noah made a soft noise. "I'm not sure I know how. That could be a vampire thing or just me—I don't know. But I'm certain I've never felt this way about anyone. I want more of that and you, for as long as I can have it."

Danny reached out, pulling Noah into his arms, and every doubt still plaguing him fell quiet for a few vital moments. He needed this. They both did. Just touching Noah soothed Danny's rough edges and centered him unlike anything else. Noah held on tighter as Danny's shivering increased.

"Danny—"

"If you try to take even one word of that back, I'm going to kick your ass so hard," Danny muttered against his shoulder.

"I don't want to take it back. Any of it."

"Okay. Good. You hurt me, you know."

"I do. I want to make it better."

"Well, you're here. And you came knowing I might not want to hear anything you had to say. It means a lot to me that you'd try."

"I want to do more than try." Noah's voice was quiet. "You woke me up, Danny. Made me understand I've been shut down for such a long time. Since I was brought into this life, I think. Maybe I needed to be that way—closed off—just to survive. But it means I've been walking around for over a century without truly *seeing* what's in front of me. Without feeling anything deeply and that changed when I started falling for you."

Tears pricked at Danny's eyelids. Pulling back, he brought his hands to Noah's face and stared at him, still trying to understand how this could be happening when he'd been so sure Noah had moved on. And though Danny didn't voice his thoughts, they must have shown in his eyes because Noah's expression grew wistful.

"What is it?" He traced the scar on Danny's throat with gentle fingers, then moved the hand to clasp the back of Danny's neck, holding on just as Danny liked but looser, as if trying to give him room to move away. "Did I say the wrong thing?"

"No, you didn't," Danny whispered. "And that's just it. I'm still trying to get my head around you being here, Noah. That you came back after the way we ended things at the hospital."

"I've been coming back to you from the beginning. Certainly since the first time I saw you but maybe even before."

"What do you mean?"

"I didn't plan to meet anyone when I stopped outside of your bakery on the first night. I can't even tell you what made me stop in the first place." Noah gave him one of those tiny smiles. "I didn't know you were there, but something pulled at me anyway. Made me want to know ... more, I suppose, though I had no idea why. Maybe it was the music and laughter coming from the kitchen. Your voice or scent, or some other tiny detail I picked up on without even knowing it." His brow furrowed. "When I finally laid eyes on you, it was like you were the only thing I *could* see. You grinned at me through the bakery window, and it was maybe three seconds before someone stepped between us, but that was enough. I wanted to do more than stand outside and look in at you."

Danny remembered too. Spotting a tall, rangy someone in front of Nice Buns, their hands in their pockets. Eyes shining in the lights from the shop and a small, pleased smile. "You didn't come in that night."

"No. I needed a strategy for acting as if I belonged. It took almost a week before I hit on buying food for the guys at the lab. That made it easy to keep going back." He looked almost shy. "Until I felt like I shouldn't."

He kissed Danny, slow and sweet, and it was like they were saying 'I'm sorry' and 'I missed you' all over again. Danny crowded closer, winding his arms around Noah's neck and going deeper until they were both breathing hard and his whole body was melty. When Danny finally broke away, Noah kept his eyes shut, gripping Danny's waist and his mouth a thin line.

As if he were trying not to speak.

Danny sighed. "If we're going to do this, you have to talk to me, Noah. Especially about the hard stuff. Like why you're still thinking this thing is doomed, even now."

"I don't want to think that. You have no idea how badly." Noah opened his eyes. "But there are things I can't give you, just because of what I am. Family, legacy, a future. Things humans want."

What the hell?

Danny stared at him, trying to wrap his brain around what had to be the weirdest conversation he'd ever had with a supernatural. "You think about things like that?"

"No. And that's exactly my point. I don't think about them because they're not possible. For me. For *you* on the other hand—"

"They could be, yes, if I wanted them. But I already have all the family I need. My dad and sister, my friends and the crew at work. Cho." Danny shrugged. "There are people out there I haven't even met yet who might come to matter to me. Having 'a future' means different things to different people, Noah, and not every human wants children or a legacy or any of that cr—oh."

He blinked and took a breath, aware he'd been winding up to rant against heteronormative bullshit with a *vampire* who'd been turned the year before an amendment was passed that allowed women to vote.

So, Noah's concept of 'family' might need some updating. In the grand scheme of things, that wasn't exactly terrible.

"Sorry." Danny rubbed Noah's arm. "I appreciate what you're saying here. But some families are chosen and that's how I've always pictured my future."

"What if you change your mind?" The haunted look was

back on Noah's face and his gaze flicked to the scar on Danny's throat. "You have so little time on this planet."

While I'll have forever. Without you.

The unspoken words hung over them as Danny took Noah's hand in his own. He could imagine the pictures in Noah's head right now. Danny on the floor, bleeding out from the wound on his neck. Working with Cho to try and slow it while Callahan barked orders into his radio.

How were they going to get past this?

Danny was only human. He *wouldn't* be around forever for Noah.

Unless ...

Quickly, he licked his lips. Maybe it was best not to think too far ahead, considering he and Noah still had a ton of work to do just getting their friendship back online.

"C'mere." He tipped his head toward the bed. "Let's hang out and talk. I can't say I'll *never* change my mind about things I might want today, but neither can anyone else. Not even you. You changed your mind about being with a bleeder, right?"

"About being with *you*, not just any bleeder." Noah sat on the mattress and pulled Danny down bedside him. "And if I'm honest, I'm not sure I changed my mind so much as opened it to the possibility."

Danny nodded. "That's what I'm talking about. Today and tomorrow are loaded with possibilities we haven't uncovered yet. Like how the police department all of a sudden wants to make a certain supernatural photographer a full CSI."

Surprise streaked across Noah's face. "You heard about that? Wait. How did this get to be about me?" he said with a laugh.

"It's not *all* about you—don't be conceited," Danny teased and took Noah's hand. "My point, though, is that things change every day. The future isn't set in stone. And neither are we, Noah. So, I say we do whatever we can to shape the future into what we want it to be."

CHAPTER 25

Noah liked the sound of that. He wanted to believe they could do it. Shape this impossible thing he and Danny were building and make it work for both of them. Know Danny would choose him over an average and much more human life.

He already has.

Noah swallowed past the ache in his heart. "I want that with you. A future we make as we go. But I can't stress enough that I don't know what I'm doing or how this is going to work."

"Well ... I don't have any idea either." Danny leaned over and kissed him gently. "Which means we *have* to make it up as we go."

That made Noah smile. "You don't have a plan?"

"What, for life? Sadly, no. But I'm choosing to be okay with that." Danny set his chin on Noah's shoulder. "This is going to sound lame, but I've been trying to live more in the moment since the whole thing with Eustace. Be present in the here and now and more appreciative of what I have."

"Not lame at all."

Losing Danny—watching him nearly die—had been a wakeup call for Noah, too. Losing this human would break him, possibly for good, and there was nothing he could do but wait for it to happen.

Unless he didn't.

Noah shook the thought off. He couldn't let himself go there. Yet. Not when he had so much work to do getting Danny's trust back. He needed to live in the moment too and appreciate what he had in the right here, right now.

Just be.

He and Danny had skipped past all that during their first time around, after the incident in Bleecker Playground had turned their nascent friendship into something far more complicated and intense than either of them had been ready for. Now, without cops in the hallway or strict orders not to stray out of doors, time with Danny could become ordinary in the most lovely, comforting sense of the word.

Noah was surprised by how much he wanted that ordinary time and he made the most of it in the week that followed. Together, they assembled the last of the furniture Danny had bought and strung pink and white fairy lights over the ceiling and windows. Noah let Danny kiss him, uncaring of where they were or who might see, and stretched alongside him out on the couch/bed in the studio, no real goal in mind but to make each other feel good.

"I'll miss these pre-dawn walks with you," Danny said as they headed back to Grove Street one morning. Noah liked to meet him after his shifts at the bakery, and though sometimes it was a race to get back to the studio before the sun made its first appearance, they still made it fun. "That's okay to say, right?" He frowned. "Because I'm also totally happy that you feel good enough to do your CSU thing again."

"Very okay." Noah agreed. "I'll miss the walks too but I'm ready to go back to the lab after New Year's. I went in and spoke with Cho and the unit deputy inspector last night, just to get everything squared away."

"Deputy inspector, huh? Look at you." Danny squeezed

Noah's arm. "And when do you start the classes to get certified? I know you're excited about it, even though you have the vampire serenity thing going on." His happy expression turned thoughtful. "Are you going to carry a badge? And a gun?"

"Ah, no. I'll have a special ID and some of the gear I wear will be different when I'm out in the field, but it'll still be boring navy tac wear. I won't be a cop, even after I'm a CSI, so no badge and no firearms."

"I'm okay with that. Arming a vampire kind of sounds like overkill anyway. And I'm glad I won't have to worry about where I put my hands when I want to grab your ass."

Noah laughed at his smirking. He loved the simplicity of just being with this person. *His* person, who offered unwavering support as Noah did a lot of painstaking work putting himself back together. Coped with his trauma. Talked candidly about his guilt at being front and center during the West Village Night-stalker case but unable to solve it sooner. Owned the anxiety and depression that dogged him sometimes and might for the next hundred years. Or forever.

These days, Noah was doing a whole lot of coping and talking and owning, often with Cho and even Callahan, and definitely with the NYPD's mental health team. He talked with Danny the most though, opening up about his job when he could but also whatever else came to mind. Memories he'd never shared with anyone about the blood eaters he'd known and the city he'd watched change, and the family he no longer missed but hadn't forgotten. Danny always listened, so much trust in his eyes Noah felt humbled to his core, every time.

Noah glanced at the graying sky now. "Can you get a night off this weekend? I know it's short notice, but I was thinking Sunday. If you think Merlin won't have a meltdown."

"He'll be fine," Danny replied. "Sunday is the day after Christmas, you know, so I'm sure the holiday spirit will be high. What did you have in mind?"

"A night outside of the bubble. I feel as though I've been

keeping us holed up in your apartment a lot and that hardly seems fair."

"I never thought about it like that. But I certainly haven't minded." Danny's words came slowly, and there was caution in his tone that caught Noah's attention. "I think I've been a little ... greedy about spending time with you, too. Getting as much as I can before you go back on duty and start spending all of your free time with Cho."

"Danny—"

"You know I'm joking. Work time and free time are not the same things. And you make a good point. Going out would be nice. We could hit up The Last Drop!"

"Yes. I don't want you to ever feel like you're stuck in one place. You had enough of that when Eustace was still out there and you couldn't go home."

"Hey." Danny stopped walking. "Being a homebody is a completely different thing to hiding out. You know that, right?"

His eyes were soft as he looked up at Noah. And that was one of Noah's favorite things about the time they'd spent together. Being able to see for himself that the hunted expression he'd glimpsed in Danny's face so many times before Eustace's capture was gone.

Noah smiled. "Yes."

"Good. Because I don't care where we spend our time."

"Neither do I. As long as you're in it."

"You're a big vampire cheeseball. Which is making me think about bread recipes now and, damn it, I wanna mack on you instead."

"So, do it," Noah said, and laughed when Danny grabbed his hand and almost sprinted the rest of the block.

Once inside the building, Danny hit the call button for the elevator, then crowded Noah against the wall, his eyes alight with mischief. He kissed Noah deep, his body heat delicious, and they only pulled away from each other at the elevator's chime. Noah hauled Danny up off his feet as the heavy doors rumbled open and carried him aboard, Danny's cackling joyous. His dick was already hard against Noah's hip, and when Danny kissed him some more, Noah didn't bother swallowing his growl, loving the shiver that rolled through Danny's frame.

The doors opened and Danny shot past them, his hand wrapped tightly around Noah's. "Fuck, that was hot," he muttered. "Might have been fun if we'd gotten stuck between floors."

They jogged down the hall to the door and Noah tried for patience as Danny dug in his bag for his keys. But he soon gave up, too entranced by the nape of Danny's neck peeking past the edge of his scarf. Stepping up behind him, Noah set his hands on Danny's hips and nosed at that delicate skin, breathing in yeast and salt and Danny. "Mmm."

"God." Danny's voice shook. "Noah, I—"

"Me, too."

A bone-deep demand to feel and taste took hold of Noah. He needed more than kisses and sweet touches this morning, and the rest of the world receded under a singular desire to bring his human pleasure.

Danny got the door open at last, his bag and coat landing in a heap on the floor before he was on Noah again, mouth hot as he worked Noah's coat off his shoulders. There was a mad scramble as they moved across the tiny room to the couch, cushions sailing in all directions while they somehow wrestled it open and fell down together, the sounds of their mirth bouncing off the walls.

"I should shower," Danny muttered as Noah slid the bandana from his hair. "Don't want to stop touching you though, and I think the stall is too small for us both."

"We can try it out later," Noah promised, "but right now I need you here."

Something unspoken passed between them then, their movements becoming less frenzied as they stripped each other down. Danny rolled onto his back and spread his thighs, making room for Noah, who settled between them with a grateful sigh. He kissed Danny deeply, and Danny's eyes were glazed when Noah pulled back at last.

He dropped his gaze to Danny's torso, admiring the miles of skin beneath him as Noah skimmed his shoulders and chest with his fingertips. Cream touched with gold and so wonderfully soft. "Beautiful."

He traced the healed bite near Danny's collarbone next, then the fresher scar left by Eustace's knife and everything in him felt squeezed with too many emotions to name. Both wounds had spilled Danny's blood. Each could have killed him. But Danny had wanted Noah's teeth on him and still did.

No. He wanted *Noah*, whether he fed tonight or never again. Just like Noah wanted him.

This is about more than blood.

"Yeah, it is." Danny's whisper let Noah know he'd said the words out loud. He was smiling when Noah looked at him, cheeks gone a tantalizing pink. He spread his hands over Noah's back, his hold strong, and his expression was adoring, as if Noah were the best thing he'd ever laid eyes on. "You just have to believe it."

"I think I'm getting there."

"I think you are too." Danny bit his lip, voice suddenly gruff. "I can't tell you what it means to me that you've been willing to try. For me. Us." Pulling Noah down, he kissed him, speaking quietly between each press of lips. "I missed being with you like this. The way you make me feel. Everything."

New desire rolled through Noah, mixing with the good, happy feelings and buoying him up. "I missed it too, so much. I had no idea."

He hadn't expected having to write this chapter in the vampire handbook. He knew Danny would help him write it and any others that came along though. They were in this together and they'd figure things out, if and when they got weird. Which they would, he was sure.

Danny moaned as Noah licked the spot he'd normally bite and tipped his head back to give Noah more room. But Noah shoved down the rising urge to feed, surer than he'd been in a long time of what he wanted for himself and his donor. More than spilled blood. More than the high. He wanted to make Danny fly in a different way right now and fly along with him. And that had him pulling back enough to meet wide, startled eyes.

"What is it?"

"I don't want that right now," Noah got out. "I just want you. If you do, I mean. It's fine if you want me to feed instead, but—"

Danny stopped his babbling with a kiss. "Like you really have to ask," he teased. "I know you're a gentleman and all, but I am a sure thing."

"You are not. I don't take anything about you for granted." He growled when Danny squeezed his ass.

"Fuck, I feel like I'm gonna blow, and we haven't even done anything," Danny groaned. "There's lube in the nightstand, and I'm happy to report it hasn't been opened."

Mine.

Noah stifled his grumbling. This was not the time to think about who else might have been in this bed. Not when he had plans to take Danny apart. Lacing their fingers together, he pinned Danny's hands on the pillow above his head, then kissed and licked at his throat until Danny was whining, hips moving slowly against Noah's in a wordless plea for more. Only then did Noah turn him loose.

But Danny pounced the second Noah let up and dragged him into a kiss so scorching it was a while before Noah even thought about untangling himself. He was panting by the time he did, and his hands were unsteady when he reached for the nightstand.

Turning back, he found Danny on his belly with his arms wrapped around his pillow, watching Noah with a look that could only be described as smug. Danny arched his back, popping his ass in the air and shaking it playfully while Noah wet his fingers, and he smiled at the way Noah took his bottom lip between his teeth. His eyelids fell to half-mast the second Noah reached over and stroked his ass and thighs though, and he let out a soft little hum.

"Mmm, Noah."

A tremor started deep in Noah's belly. He coaxed Danny up onto his hands and knees and bent over him, dropping kisses along his shoulders just to hear him sigh. He loved the way this human responded to even the slightest touch.

Trailing his fingers past the small of Danny's back, Noah slid them between his ass cheeks, then teased his rim, reveling in Danny's small shudders. He pushed a finger slowly inside, and groaned along with Danny, whose body had tensed in a way that told Noah to go slow. Nuzzling Danny's shoulders, he soothed him with quiet words until the tension in his frame faded.

"S'been a long time," Danny murmured.

Without speaking, Noah leaned in closer, and Danny turned his head so their temples met.

"Haven't been with anyone like this for a while." His voice sounded dreamy. "Almost forgot how it could feel."

"I want to make you feel good." Noah smiled as Danny rocked back onto Noah's fingers then forward again, a gasp on his lips.

"You do," Danny said as another shudder shook his body. "Really, *really* good."

Noah teased him some more, still careful as he eased a second finger inside. Danny whined but the sound was eager, and his body stayed pliant as he continued rocking forward and back in slow, sinuous movements. Noah was so hard himself he almost hurt, each drag of his dick against Danny's thighs a torture he never wanted to end.

"Need more than fingers," Danny ground out. Panting, he dropped his head forward, flushed skin already shining with sweat. "Oh-h-h, God, please." His voice broke. "Need … I, oh, fuck."

Noah withdrew his fingers and held him for a beat, sensing Danny's need to center himself. He shifted his weight back when Danny seemed calmer, but it was all he could do not to growl as he admired the body before him, so strong and beautiful and—

Mine.

Swallowing down the word, Noah spread Danny's ass with his hands, then traced his rim with the head of his dick. He pushed forward slowly, eyes slipping closed at Danny's moans, quiet and constant as Noah sank deep. Noah almost stopped, worried his hold on Danny's hips was growing too tight, but Danny seemed not to notice. He arched his back with another plaintive sound, body trembling as he pushed back, and a wonderful ache spread through Noah like fire.

He moved his hand to the base of Danny's neck as he bottomed out and pressed the flesh with his fingers the way he knew Danny liked. The motion seemed to melt Danny completely and he lowered his chest to the mattress, head pillowed on his folded arms.

Noah couldn't remember a time when he'd felt like this. So vital and alive. Maybe even human, though he wasn't truly sure he remembered what that was like anymore. And it didn't matter anyway.

A soft noise like his name caught Noah's ear and he leaned over Danny immediately, caging him with his arms as he eased them both down so he could cover Danny's body with his own.

"Danny." He nuzzled Danny's cheek and kissed his slack lips, and the quiet reverence in his own voice was echoed in Danny's murmur.

"Baby."

How Noah loved hearing Danny call him that.

He fucked into him, going deep so Danny gasped and arched his ass higher to meet the rough thrusts. He cried out when

Noah nipped at his jaw, then angled his head on the pillow to expose his throat further. Offering himself if Noah wanted blood.

A part of Noah did, of course. He was a bit thirsty, and it had been too long since he'd tasted Danny's blood. Even the memory made Noah's mouth water and the darkest part of his vampire side want to drink and never stop. But even now, Danny trusted Noah not to go too far. And knowing that—seeing and feeling it here in this bed, after everything they'd been through—made Noah trust himself too. And just like that, he was teetering on the edge of falling apart in a whole different way.

He growled deep, almost snarling, and loved the way Danny gasped and thrashed as his body's natural fear response kicked in. The movements sent spikes of sensation through Noah, and he got lost in his need to crawl inside the human beneath him and stay there.

So close.

Danny writhed and cried out in Noah's arms, but when Noah reached beneath their joined bodies, he lost it almost with being touched. His face and neck flushed dark red as he came in Noah's hand, and though Noah kissed him through it, he was too far gone to truly kiss back. Danny tried anyway, his motions sweet and clumsy, and at last brought a hand up to card his fingers through Noah's hair.

"That's it," he murmured. "Wanna feel you, Noah. Know that you're mine."

I am.

Without warning, fire flashed through Noah's being in a devastating wave that flung him as high as any blood exchange he'd ever known. And Noah let go. Face pressed into Danny's neck, he drifted, sure that when he was ready to float back down to earth, the steady thump of the strongest heart he knew would get him there.

CHAPTER 26

Six months later, June 1
2:30 A.M.

How about a late-late-dinner?

A string of emoji followed the message on Danny's phone's screen, including a steak, an egg in a frying pan, and enough mugs of beer that he was laughing as he answered.

Does someone have plans to get me drunk?

They do now, came the reply. *Meet at the diner around 4 if you can.*

Chuckling, Danny tucked the phone in his back pocket. Playful texts from Noah were a good omen any night but Danny was particularly happy to see some now. Noah and Cho had been out of town for almost a week working a case in Philly, and while Danny'd tried to keep his whining on the down-low, he'd missed his vampire an embarrassing amount.

"Was that your tall boy?" Merlin smirked at him from the other side of the display case. "I'm guessing yes because you're all moony and love-struck."

Busted.

Danny simply shrugged. He wouldn't deny being either since he'd been grinning like an idiot over tiny food-shaped icons on his goddamned phone. He could pretend his face wasn't flaming though. "Yeah, that was Noah. He got back yesterday around noon while I was still mostly unconscious."

"Wanky."

"Zip it."

"Why didn't you take a day off and screw each other silly?"

"Because neither of us had enough notice for a day off." He glanced around to ensure no one on the crew was listening. Everyone at the bakery knew he and Merlin were friends beyond the workplace, but this conversation was definitely on the fringes of appropriate. "We're both off for the next three nights, so that'll give us more time to catch up. I'm meeting him at the diner on Grove so he can feed me before ...."

"Yeah. Roger that, loud and clear." Merlin cackled. "Isn't Charon's out of the way from your new place?"

"A bit. I still haven't found a place I like as much that's closer to home. But I figured I'd move the last of my stuff out of the studio while I wait for Noah to get around whatever gory shit he's been working on tonight."

"Barf. But I don't mind keeping your boxes company until you can move them," Merlin said. Danny had moved out of the apartment on Grove Street very gradually and a last load of belongings still remained even now that Merlin had taken up residence. "It's just one little stack. Although, this is probably a good time to tell you I used a box labeled 'random orphaned stuff' as a makeshift table yesterday when I had some friends over, so please ignore any strange marks that may or not have been made by curry."

Danny set the box of leftovers from the night's sales on the rolling rack at his side. "I'll keep that in mind. Also, ew. You know I left some TV trays in the back of the closet, right?"

"Oh yeah—they were also full at the time. It was an ... extensive curry party. Two of my friends are shifters and they can really put food away." Merlin laughed. "*Another* buddy who happens to be a carpenter got a look around the place while she was over. Says she wants to design a table that somehow fits into the bookshelf beside the fireplace. Could be fun, even if I don't understand the physics. Do you miss the tiny house life?"

"Can't say I do, but I always liked that apartment," Danny replied. "That corner of the neighborhood, too. Like, the diner alone makes it worth living there." He wheeled the rack through the door Merlin held open, then pushed it into the short hall that connected the store to the kitchen.

"Totally! I've only been there a month and I never want to leave."

"Because you had two roommates at your last place, Merle. A studio all to yourself must feel like heaven."

"Dude, so much. It's so fucking quiet to be almost eerie. I literally woke up the first few nights I was there like, 'shit, some-thing's not right.'" Merlin rolled his eyes at himself, but he was smiling as they parked the rack by the sink and started unloading the trays. "Thanks again for helping me get into the place. I'm sure arranging a sub-lease for me probably derailed your plans to shack up with Noah, and I feel kind of bad about that."

"Yeah, don't. I stopped sleeping in the studio right after New Year's and only went back for clothes and mail and things I couldn't live without. Arranging the sublease just finalized everything." Danny bumped the fist Merlin held up. "I should probably be thanking you."

"No need, no need." Merlin winked. "Love looks good on you, my man, and I'm not just saying that because you sign my paychecks."

That easy comment about love struck a chord with Danny that resonated through him for the rest of his shift.

He liked having it in his life. Knowing it showed on his face, as it did on Noah's when he caught Danny's eye across the length of a room. Things were *good* between them and so much less complicated than anyone might have guessed. Sure, they were still working out the details of how to combine a human's life with a vampire's, but Danny's faith didn't falter. He loved and was loved in return, and that knowledge bolstered him through the complicated moments. Like the time Danny ended up in the ED with an epically awful bout of food poisoning and Noah was *sure* he was dying.

Conversations about mortality were complicated enough without puking your guts up the whole time. Danny and Noah had those conversations like clockwork though—*sans* puke of course—and while some people might have found the whole idea morbidly weird, it worked for them. Especially Noah, who was really coming into his own.

He'd continued to work on his mental health, speaking with the NYPD's mental health team by choice rather than under orders from Cho or any other superior. He'd gone back to work too, buzzing with new energy that had carried over into his CSI training and enabled him to become certified in half the time it normally took a human. Noah, of course, had shrugged off the accomplishment as not a big deal given he didn't have the same sleep requirements as his fellow human recruits.

Noah'd been the one to first voice the idea of combining the Green and Kaes households, a purely academic move since Danny and Noah were already spending most of their time off together. While the studio on Grove Street had been their original haunt, they'd migrated to Noah's place over time, and that had felt right, too. Danny was as comfortable in Noah's home as any place in his life, and it didn't hurt that the apartment was both bigger and three blocks closer to Nice Buns. Besides boasting a killer roof deck and views, the supernatural concierge staff also afforded the building with security that helped chill Noah's instinctive drive to keep his human safe, and that was another clear win in Danny's eyes.

Ensuring your vampire had adequate time off was another chapter he planned to add to the *Vampire's Guide For Staying*

Alive they'd not-very-secretly been writing. And he smiled to himself now, knowing he had the next three days to make sure Noah not only got some time off but enjoyed it.

O

"Hi." Noah slid into the booth beside Danny a couple of hours later, his eyes warm. "Have you been waiting long?"

Danny shook his head. "Uh-uh. Got here about ten minutes ago. How's the city's hottest CSI?"

"Cho is fine. But *I* am ready for some time off."

Danny laughed. "I'm sure you are. And where is Cho? Still searching for parking?"

"Actually no—we found a spot on the next block. He told me to come on ahead while he made a call though and I don't think he's talking to his mom. So ..." Noah waggled his eyebrows up and down a few times. "I suspect he's talking to the mysterious person he's been seeing."

"Oh, r-e-e-eally?"

Danny eyed the big windows at the front of the diner. Noah didn't gossip much, so this was a rare treat and Cho did appear intent as he stood on the sidewalk outside, phone pressed against his ear. He'd admitted to going on some dates in the last couple of weeks but, so far, kept all additional details close to the vest.

"What makes you think it's whomever?" Danny asked. "Or have you been listening in on the conversation? Because I would *totally* support the use of supernatural abilities in this instance."

Noah laughed. "No, I haven't been eavesdropping. I just have a feeling, is all. Nothing to do with the vampire whammy."

"Mmm, that's a pity." Danny sipped his beer and set it down, then shifted his whole focus onto Noah. "You know how much I like the whammy."

"Yes, I do."

Leaning in, Noah stared at him hard, hitting Danny with a

full-on thrall that made his bones jellify. The hum that started in Danny's center made his sigh shaky.

"Damn you," he muttered, fighting to keep his eyes fully open. "You know better than to do that to me in front of other people."

"I'm sorry."

"I don't believe you." Danny delighted in his vampire's smirk. "You might be in a second though, because starting with me in a public place like this was a big mistake."

With effort, he slid a bit closer then tipped his head back, purposely showing off the skin on his throat. The response in Noah was immediate, his eyes flaring hot. However, his motions held only grace as he raised a hand to Danny's neck, where he set his palm over the bite wound Danny did little to hide. Noah kissed him, slow and easy, and though the meeting of their lips was really quite chaste, Danny's blood thrummed with the heat arcing between them.

"Mmm." He moved his eyelids in a slow blink. "Need it tonight. You."

"I need it too. And you were right. I'm very sorry I started this because now I have to wait to finish." Noah kissed Danny again before sitting back. "If I promise not to do it again, am I forgiven?"

"Maybe." Danny chuckled. "Ask me in a while."

After the meal was over and they'd said good night to Cho, a giddy feeling came over him. The buzz hadn't come from the two beers Danny'd drunk during dinner though, but from Noah, who kissed him on the sidewalk outside of the diner and made his head spin.

Even after six months, he couldn't get enough. Shivers ran through him as they made the trek to West 12th, and the blocks between the diner and the apartment seemed to stretch on forever. But then they were home, Noah pulling Danny into the bedroom where he kissed him some more, and the promise of teeth beneath those plush lips made each movement addictive.

"Want you." Danny rose onto his toes so he could link his arms around Noah's neck, and the move sent his head tipping back in a wordless invitation. Noah nosed at the throat offered him without hesitating, the coarse scrape of his beard stubble delicious. "Yes. That."

Surrender swept over Danny is a welcome wave as they stripped each other down, each reveling in the other's touch. He burned with it as he guided Noah onto the bed where they knelt in the middle of the mattress, and his throat constricted, though he couldn't have said why.

"I missed you," Noah said quietly as he ran a hand over Danny's ribs. "Could hardly wait to get back."

"I was the same." Danny kissed the line of Noah's jaw. "I expected you to wake me up when you got home yesterday afternoon, by the way."

"I thought you *were* awake for a bit, but then you told me you had hot dogs for feet, and I knew your brain was still out there in dreamland."

Startled, Danny sat back on his heels. "I said *what?*" He watched Noah's slow grin, then tipped his head back and cackled. "I never said any such thing!"

"You did." Noah chuckled. "Apparently, they made it hard to buy shoes, so you planned to make some from bread. Seemed reasonable given your expertise in the field."

Danny laughed until his sides ached. His sleep-talking occurrences were fewer these days, but his rest had been poor during Noah's week away, leaving him punchy and his brain primed to serve up a special kind of random weirdness when he did sleep. The warmth of their shared enjoyment made Danny feel good regardless and Noah's touch was loving as they lay down together. Still giggling, he covered his eyes with one hand.

"I'm sorry. Hot dogs for feet! I have no idea where that came from, but please tell me I didn't say anything else so totally off-the-wall?"

"You were calmer after the frankfurter discussion." Noah set his hand on Danny's belly. "Then you told me you loved me and some other mushy stuff."

"Aw. I know you live for the mushy stuff."

"I do."

Ducking his head, Noah pressed his lips against Danny's wrist and the simple sweetness of the gesture made Danny's heart throb. He relaxed into the kisses that followed, coasting on a heady mixture of affection and hunger. It was a long time before they broke apart and Noah's glazed, almost drunken expression sent power surging through Danny.

He loved doing that. Practically leveling this powerful creature with kisses alone.

"Mmm." Noah set his fingers just above Danny's right collarbone, gaze fixed on the mark on the skin. He licked his lips slowly, so they shone in the lamplight, then parted them just enough to show a hint of teeth.

Danny bit back a groan. Lust charged the air, winding itself around them with near palpable force. Yet Noah still had the presence of mind to take Danny's hand and look him in the eye.

"Do you want this?" he asked, voice so reverent it poked Danny right in the feels.

Rocks clogged his throat. He fell a little deeper in love every time they did this. Because Noah always asked permission to feed, even knowing Danny would never refuse him.

"Yes. I do."

Sweat sheened Danny's skin as Noah turned to the nightstand. He closed his eyes, humming as wet fingers wrapped around him, and turned into Noah's kisses. Each one zapped his strength a bit more until Danny's limbs were so heavy, he could hardly stir. He forced himself to move anyway, the need for touch too intense to ignore. He palmed Noah's ass with clumsy motions and reveled in his snarl.

The flame that had been building inside Danny since they'd met at the diner licked through him. He hissed quietly as Noah lowered his mouth to Danny's neck, bathing the bite wound with his tongue before he sucked gently without teeth. Already floating, Danny held on to Noah's hair, using the soft, short locks to ground himself. He bit his lip as slick fingers pushed inside him and everything else melted under the feedback loop of being filled while a tongue slid over the pulse in his throat. Danny bore down mindlessly, his moans coming non-stop as Noah pumped in and out of him in a slow rhythm that drove Danny wild. A cry tore out of him as Noah curled his fingers.

"That's it." Noah's lips moved against Danny's damp skin.

"Need you inside me," Danny whispered, then shuddered hard as Noah gently withdrew his hand. "Oh, *God.*"

"I know." Noah tried to soothe him with a kiss, but it went from loving to scorching in the span of a heartbeat and they were both breathing hard by the time he shifted his weight backward onto his heels.

Pushing Danny's knees toward his chest, Noah rose over him, face intent as he lined up their bodies. He pressed forward slowly, splitting Danny open with a single, long stroke that filled him and quieted some of his craving.

Finally.

Danny swallowed a sob. Reaching up, he grabbed Noah's shoulders, drawing Noah's gaze from where their bodies were joined, and the world around them slowed. The burn in Danny's body changed, becoming a sweet, all-consuming need that he welcomed like an old friend. He pressed his knees into Noah's ribs and watched his face change, loving expression going feral as he leaned in and set his lips against Danny's throat. He brushed the softest of kisses there before baring his teeth against Danny's skin, and Danny's body tensed, craving more and more and more in the tortuous seconds that passed before the bite they both wanted came.

Yes.

The world exploded around Danny before melting away, and he rode the edge for what seemed an endless time, finally breaking apart into bright waves of bliss. Lost in the pleasure,

Danny could still hear Noah's voice against his ear, and though the words were too far away to truly understand, he knew he was safe.

Noah had him and wouldn't let go.

O

"Mmph." Rolling up onto his elbow, Danny propped his head in his hand. He had no idea how long he'd been out, but he was clean and dry, which meant Noah had wiped them both down while he'd been too blitzed to notice. "I didn't mean to pass out on you. Again."

Noah gave him a smile, looking for all the world like a big sleepy cat curled up beside him. "You needed it. Besides, it's only been an hour or so and I was dozing myself."

"I suppose that's all right then. I was feeling a bit selfish."

"Why? You give me so much. More than anyone ever has." Noah leaned a little closer. "I hardly know how to—"

"You'd better not be thanking me for sex, Noah Green, because that is, like, the opposite of romantic." Danny bit his lip against a fond smile. "Honestly. You don't ever have to thank me for this."

"I know. And I love you."

Noah's small, shy smile crushed Danny's heart so flat it was a wonder it could keep beating. No one else got that smile. It was only for him, the one being in the world who truly knew Noah.

He carded the fingers of his free hand through Noah's gloriously messy hair. "I love you too."

They were still learning. Still mapping their adventure. How and even when they could ensure that Danny was around into forever. And Danny felt surprisingly okay with not knowing exactly how it was all going to play out. Neither of them knew what to expect beyond today. But not knowing didn't scare him the way it might have in the past. He'd figured out who and what he needed in this here and now, and that was something many beings out there—whatever their species—were never so lucky to know. So Danny hung on to the good feelings that came from being loved and sent them back out into the universe as much as he could.

The End

AUTHOR'S NOTE

Thank you for reading! I hope you enjoyed Noah and Danny's story as much as I enjoyed writing it. If you'd like to see more of the MonsterBoard world, be sure to let me know. I'd also be grateful if you'd consider adding a short review on Amazon, BookBub, or Goodreads.

I've always been a big fan of vampires. I grew up reading about them in novels and watching them in movies, and I find the enduring mythology around these rather dashing figures endlessly intriguing.

I'm also a *huge* fan of pandesal. Like Danny, I'm part Filipino and some of my fondest memories of visits to the Philippines center around the breakfasts I shared with my grandparents and aunts: fresh pandesal bought that morning, cheese, and tsokolate (hot chocolate). If you've never had the opportunity to try Filipino cuisine, I hope you get that chance soon!

ACKNOWLEDGMENTS

Wanky is a catchphrase of the one and only Santana Lopez of *Glee*, portrayed by the unforgettable Naya Rivera.

ScanStation: Leica Camera

SoleMate: Foster & Freeman, USA

Glee: Ryan Murphy, Brad Falchuk, Ian Brennan

INKED IN BLOOD

If you enjoyed *Overexposed*, check out *Inked In Blood*, an urban fantasy/paranormal romance short story by K. Evan Coles and Brigham Vaughn.

O

Inked In Blood

Jeff Holloway is a twenty-five-year-old skater with a killer smile and lots of free time on his hands. He's also a vampire who prowls the dark corners of San Francisco looking for entertainment and his next meal. Lately, he's been spending lots of time watching a tattoo parlor in the Mission District, where someone tall, artistic, and handsome has caught his eye.

Santiago Alvarez, the forty-three-year-old owner of Iron & Ink has a huge secret. He lives a quiet life, finding joy in his career and his friends, but it's caused him to shut himself off from dating and getting close to anyone romantically. When he bumps into Jeff on the sidewalk near his shop, he's intrigued but hesitant to let anyone get close.

An unexpected event one night will change everything for both men, and neither of their futures will ever be the same.

CHAPTER 1
JEFF

"No doubt, I've told you before, but that board is gorgeous."

Jeff glanced up at Suzie, the hot little brunette headed his way. He smiled at the admiration in her gaze, but he was used to being the object of people's attention. Such things came with the territory when you stood six foot one and rode a forty-two inch longboard as beautiful as the one under Jeff's foot. And Suzie's focus was definitely on the board.

"Thanks," he said, "and yes, you've said so before." He pulled his sunglasses off and sat up straight in the café chair where he'd parked himself. "If I recall correctly, those were your very first words to me ever."

Suzie chuckled and swept her long hair over her shoulder. "To be fair, I actually meant to compliment you on your face that day. But I got a good look at your board and bam"—she smacked her hands together—"it was love at first sight."

Jeff smirked. "Girl, you've got a one track mind."

"And you're just not that into me, so where's the harm?" Suzie's hazel eyes sparkled. She tipped her head in the direction of the buildings clustered behind them. "I'm meeting Tim for a bite to eat and spotted you—thought I'd see if you wanna join."

"Not hungry yet." Jeff eyed the red-hued October sky over

their heads. At 6:40, sunset was still at least ten minutes off. Plenty of time for Jeff to ride downtown. He'd be ready to eat by then, but even if it took some time to find the right thing to whet his appetite, he'd have the rest of the night to prowl around the city. "Maybe see you later?"

Suzie nodded. "Tim mentioned a band playing at Backlit tonight if you're interested."

"Cool." Jeff knew the beer hall well and liked its energy. "I'll be around there anyway."

"Of course you will. You're in the Mission every night after dark, Jeff."

Jeff scoffed. "Untrue. Just because it's usually the place we run into each other doesn't mean I'm there every night."

"Pics or it didn't happen." Suzie stepped onto her board and pushed off. "I'll text you!" she called back over her shoulder.

Jeff waved. The first whispers of hunger trailed across his gut as he watched the girl depart, and he slid his sunglasses back onto his face.

Time to scare up a little dinner.

He rode his board south along Battery Street, Suzie's words in his head. Sure, he spent a lot of time in the Mission District, but lots of people from Suzie's and his circle of friends did too. Jeff was almost guaranteed to run into someone he knew among the crowds—no matter what day—and there was rarely a shortage both strange and familiar, kept Jeff from misbehaving, and that was a plus.

Maybe he needed to mix it up a bit, though, just to keep things from getting stale. Jeff turned right onto Market Street. He might head up to North Beach or over to the Castro or the Haight. Union Square could be fun, and, again, lots of people around who'd remind Jeff to watch his manners. Surely, there were pretty things and people all over this city that could capture his attention, at least for a little while.

None of them so well as the sight of a tattoo needle against flesh, drawing blood from soft skin and leaving bright splashes of pigment behind.

Tendrils of lust slid through Jeff's groin. He recalled the buzz of the tattoo iron and long fingers that wielded it, and his hunger immediately increased. Funny how his various appetites worked.

The sun had slipped under the horizon by the time Jeff merged onto Turk Street. The sky shaded indigo. Jeff slowed his board with each block, then stepped off between Taylor and Jones Streets, the smell of beer and cigarettes strong in the air. He sensed eyes on him and a number of bodies in motion just out of sight. Jeff popped the board's tail into the ground with one foot and flicked it up into his hand, then moved off the street into a shadowed alley.

"It's Mace," a deep voice said, so low anyone else would have missed it. "Spotted a mark on Turk. I'll be late."

Jeff drew lots of attention anytime he stopped in the Tenderloin. His whole being screamed young, fresh, and rich, and the people on these streets didn't view him as a threat. He wore Levi's and hoodies, black Vans on his feet, and a sweep of his dark blond hair flopped onto his cheek. Jeff had freckles for God's sake, which automatically marked him as a piece of meat in their eyes. The irony of that idea always made Jeff smile, and he did so now, his eyes on a hulking figure who appeared at the head of the alley.

This had to be Mace, a guy Jeff thought might be in his late twenties. His sharp eyes moved over Jeff's preppy clothes and hair, then lingered on the board in Jeff's grip for a few seconds longer. Mace's arms remained by his sides, but he held his hands loose, however. He stepped forward, moving with the confidence of a man who'd faced dangerous situations before. Jeff knew as much from the way Mace came at him, head cocked and expression light, as if he were amused.

Of course, Mace had never faced someone like Jeff.

Jeff didn't bother toying with him. He didn't even let the guy get a word in edgewise but dropped the board forward onto its wheels and hauled Mace in the moment he drew close. Mace inhaled sharply, and the tangy scent of adrenaline flooded from his pores. Jeff's cock hardened.

"Oh, man," he murmured a second before he closed his eyes.

Jeff pressed his lips against a warm, soft throat, and Mace uttered a single whimper that trailed off into a sigh the moment Jeff bit down. His body grew rigid in Jeff's arms. Jeff groaned low in his chest, his thirst exploding as his brain registered the heat and salt of the blood in his mouth. Then Mace's limbs relaxed and his torso seemed to mold itself to Jeff's. He made a soft sound that was audible over the frantic pounding of his heart, and he slid his arms around Jeff and snuggled in a little closer.

ABOUT K. EVAN COLES

K. Evan Coles is a mother and tech pirate by day and a writer by night. She is a dreamer who, with a little hard work and a lot of good coffee, coaxes words out of her head and onto paper.

K. lives in the northeast United States, where she complains bitterly about the winters, but truly loves the region and its diverse, tenacious, and deceptively compassionate people. You'll usually find K. nerding out over books, movies and television with friends and family. She's especially proud to be raising her son as part of a new generation of unabashed geeks.

K.'s books explore LGBTQ+ romance in a variety of settings.

Website
Newsletter

ALSO BY K. EVAN COLES

Wicked Fingers Press

Stealing Hearts

Thief of Hearts (Novella)

Healing Hearts (Novella)

Open Hearts (Novel)

Stealing Hearts #4 (2022)

Hooked On You (Novel)

Overexposed (Novel)

(Short story version included in the Working Stiffs COVID-19 Charity Anthology)

A Hometown Holiday (Novella)

Moonlight (Short Story)

Pride Publishing (Totally Entwined Group)

Boston Seasons (Novels)

Third Time's the Charm

Easy For You To Say (TBD)

Tidal Duology w/ Brigham Vaughn (Novels)

Wake

Calm

The Speakeasy w/ Brigham Vaughn (Novels)

With a Twist

Extra Dirty

Behind the Stick

Straight Up

Off Topic Press (Self-Published)

Inked in Blood w/ Brigham Vaughn (Short Story)

Made in the USA
Monee, IL
26 February 2022

91881972R00177